"I beg you to please allow me to take you to the Promenade tomorrow, Miss Fredericks.

"And not for any wager," Perry continued. "You are fairly isolated here, I know, and I would correct that."

"You would, would you?" Amelia answered, running her gaze up and down his body in a way that would make a lesser man fear for his motives. Impressive young woman, Perry decided; handsome in her way, and quite intelligent. Very pretty eyes, that just might see too much. "Will you also be truthful with me?"

Perry sat down, spreading his coattails neatly, and crossed one long leg over the other. "I am nothing if not truthful, lies being so fatiguing to recall when necessary."

"All right, then. Why are you here?"

"The wager, Miss Fredericks, remember?"

Amelia frowned, and Perry felt his first pangs of guilt. It took him moments to recognize this response, as he had so seldom experienced that particular emotion.

"Michaels has done it again…playfully perfect."
        —*Publishers Weekly* on *The Butler Did It*

Kasey Michaels is a *New York Times* bestselling author of both historical and contemporary novels. She is also the winner of a number of prestigious awards.

Already available from
Kasey Michaels

THE BUTLER DID IT

IN HIS LORDSHIP'S BED
(short story in *The Wedding Chase*)

SHALL WE DANCE?

Kasey Michaels

MILLS & BOON®

*First published in Great Britain 2005
by Harlequin Mills & Boon Limited,
Eton House, 18-24 Paradise Road, Richmond, Surrey TW9 1SR*

© Kathryn Seidick 2005

ISBN 0 263 84520 6

153-0905

*Printed and bound in Spain
by Litografia Rosés S.A., Barcelona*

To Tracy Farrell,
with many thanks.

Lavender's blue, dilly, dilly,
lavender's green;
When I am king, dilly dilly,
you shall be queen.
                        —Anonymous

A Brief Primer

Georgie Porgie, pudding and pie,
Kissed the girls and made them cry...
—Anonymous

In 1795, OVERBURDENED with debt, not at all in good odour with his family, Parliament, the populace—or his tailor—His Royal Highness, George, Prince of Wales, known also as Florizel, Prinney and "that extravagant jackanapes," at last succumbed to pressure from all of the above and agreed to a marriage with his first cousin, Princess Caroline Amelia of Brunswick-Wolfenbuttel.

That the prince had earlier entered into a morganatic marriage with Maria Fitzherbert, both a commoner and a Catholic, definitely two huge no-no's for the prince, was deemed irrelevant.

That the princess Caroline was, at twenty-six, already rather long in the tooth for a bride, loud, over-blown, often filthy—both in her language and in her personal hygiene—was overlooked by the Parliament that would settle the prince's debts if only he would marry the woman, settle down and for goodness sake provide an heir.

Ah, the sacrifices one must make for one's country. And yet, ta-ta Maria, hello princess (and at least temporary solvency). Men can be so fickle.

On the occasion of their first meeting, and already set to marry in three days, the prince took one look at his blowsy betrothed and said to an aide, "Harris, I am not well. Pray fetch me a glass of brandy." And then he retired from the room, leaving the princess to comment to that same aide, "I find him very stout and by no means as handsome as his portrait." In another age Harris would have written a very profitable book about the whole thing....

Meanwhile, back with the prince and his bride, it would be a vast overstatement to suggest that the marriage that followed proved to have been Fashioned In Heaven.

Love match or not, the pair managed to produce an heir, Princess Charlotte, and then they toddled off in disparate directions, the prince back to his normal pursuits (back to his middle-aged Maria and to spending money), the princess all but banished from the palace and her child (to become the darling of the citizenry and to spend lots of money).

In short, they both went about making total fools of themselves, living outrageously, spending prodigiously and openly disparaging each other in print and in deed. Since the prince had turned, politically, to the Tories, the princess, naturally, gravitated to the Whigs. Their only connection at all, their daughter, Charlotte, died in childbirth while Caroline was out of the country being as naughty as she could be, although never quite naughty enough for the prince to gain the divorce he so desperately desired.

But in 1820, George III, long ill, died, and suddenly Florizel was the king. His first thought, after rejoicing that his allowance would be raised, had to be that, if he was now the king, then—E-gods!—the hated Caroline was now his queen consort.

This was not to be borne!

The first thing the prince did was to delay his formal coronation for a year, launching a kingly demand that a way be found to discredit the new queen for her personal behavior, paving the way for that longed-for divorce.

The first thing Caroline did was to have a launch of her own—setting sail from Italy to England, to claim her rights as queen, dilly-dilly.

History reports what happened next, but imagination conjures its own scenarios....

Choosing Up Sides

Birds of a feather, flock together,
And so will pigs and swine.
Rats and mice, will have their choice,
And so will I have mine.

—Anonymous

PERRY SHEPHERD, Earl of Brentwood, was bored with being bored, which was the only way possible for him to reconcile himself to the fact that he had knocked on the door of his uncle, Sir Willard Humphrey, Minister of the Admiralty, Retired.

The earl had been rather adroitly avoiding his uncle for quite nearly three weeks. And he would have continued to ignore the man's pleas to meet with him if not for the fact that it was already July, the London Season was over and everyone was still very much in superficial mourning for the late king, so that Town was dreadfully dull.

Still, if he left for the country without seeing his uncle, Perry knew the man would follow him. The only thing worse than being trapped in a room with Uncle Willie was being trapped on an estate with Uncle Willie, with no bolt-hole available.

So here he was, in his uncle's black-and-white tiled foyer, stripping off his gloves, handing over his cane and removing the curly brimmed beaver from his blond head, relaxing the square jaw that was the only thing (save the scar on his cheek, which was, by and large, more attractive than detracting) keeping this green-eyed, near god of a man from being too pretty.

He adjusted his cuffs, quickly surveyed his reflection in the gold-veined mirror on the wall and knew that his new jacket suited his tall, lean, broad-shouldered figure admirably.

Goodness, but he was a sight, not that his uncle would notice.

"Ready, Hawkins. Shoulders back, loins girded, belly only faintly queasy. We may proceed. Take me to mine uncle."

"Ah, My Lord, Sir Willard will be that pleased, if I may say so, begging your indulgence at my frank speech, sir," Hawkins, butler to the great man, probably since before The Flood, said as he ushered Perry down the long hallway that led to his employer's private study.

"Pining for me, is he, Hawkins? I suppose I should be flattered," Perry said, adjusting the black armband that was his bow to the Royal Mourning, and quite understandable, considering the fact that George III had been locked up in his apartments, mad as a hatter, for over a decade, so that his passing did not exactly blast a large hole in everyday life. "Tell me, do you have any idea what flea Uncle Willie has got in his breeches this time?"

"None, My Lord. He's been tight as a clam about the—that is, I'm sure I shouldn't know, sir."

"Not to worry, Hawkins. I'm sure I shouldn't, either. But, alas, it would appear I'm about to find out. Announce me, my good fellow, then prepare to abandon the field before you are witness to Uncle Willie embarrassing us all as he throws himself on my neck, tears of joy racing down his cheeks."

"Oh, I think he might be beyond that, My Lord," Hawkins said, then knocked on the study door, opened it, announced Perry, turned to smile at His Lordship—rather piteously—and then took to his heels.

Perry, one eyebrow lifted, watched him go, so that he staggered under the unexpected blow as a large, beefy hand slapped him once on the back, then grabbed hold of his wonderfully tailored jacket collar and all but hauled him into the study.

"At last! Damn your eyes, Perry, anyone would have thought you were dead."

Adjusting his jacket, now that his uncle had released it, Perry smiled at Sir Willard Humphrey. "I had considered putting about precisely that rumor, but I at once realized what a definite crimp it would put in my social life. Good morning, Uncle."

"Don't you good morning me, Nevvie. Where in thunder have you been hiding yourself? I've been sending notes round every day. Twice, yesterday."

"Really? I had no idea. Well, that's it, then, I shall have my butler sacked the moment I return to Portman Square." He frowned. "Damn shame, that. I have rather a fondness for Fairweather, have known him since I was in short coats."

"Cheeky. Always were cheeky." Sir Willard deposited his considerable bulk into the chair behind his desk, his whalebone stays creaking as he bent himself almost in two. "Reminds how much you give me the headache, boy. You've been avoiding me. But I've heard about you. Going here, going there, racketing about like a useless twit without a care in the world—or for it, for that matter."

"Guilty as charged, especially that last little bit," Perry said, lifting the stopper from a decanter on the drinks table and holding up the decanter to his uncle. "No? Very well, although I feel the sot, drinking alone."

"It's eleven in the morning, for God's sake. You shouldn't be drinking at all. Tea, that's the ticket. You can't dunk a buttered scone in Burgundy, boy."

"Nor would I want to," Perry said, sitting himself down on the deep green leather couch completely across the room—ignoring the pair of uncomfortable chairs facing the desk. His left leg neatly crossed over his right, the stem of his glass resting on his bent knee, he smiled again at his uncle. "So? Are you going to tell me, or am I going to be forced to guess?"

"Do you have to perch yourself all the way over there? I'll have to shout to—oh, hang it," Sir Willard said, pushing himself out of his chair, forced out of his seat of authority by his insufferable nephew, who only batted his eyelids as he gave a wide, closemouthed and definitely not-innocent grin.

"I sit here as a favor. You need the exercise, dear Uncle," Perry said, then arranged his handsome features in a frown of concentration and attention. "But to continue?"

"Continue? When in blue blazes did I start? You're

a confounding piece of work, Perry, always were, always told everyone you were. If I were to tell England the truth about you no one would believe me."

"They'd probably lock you up with your own strait waistcoat," Perry agreed, then sipped at his burgundy. "Wait, come to think of it, you're close to that now. Don't you know our new good king has left off his stays? The explosion could be heard for miles."

"You're a fool, Nevvie."

"True. Everyone knows I'm a fool. An amicable, titled, sinfully wealthy, well-dressed and exquisitely turned-out fool, but a fool nonetheless. Oh, and heartbreakingly handsome." Perry sighed theatrically. "I've so many gifts."

"And that's why you're here."

Perry's left eyebrow shot heavenward. "Because I'm pretty? Gad, if I'd known it would call me to your attention, Uncle, I would have dropped a sack over my head."

"Would you stop? It's not just that face of yours. I need you because of what the world thinks of you, in total." Sir Willard turned round one of the chairs and wedged his bulk into it. "Let me begin at the beginning."

"Oh, please, Uncle, I beg you, don't do that. Adam and Eve, the apple—it's all so tedious. Start at the middle, why don't you? Most things start there."

Sir Willard's neck was becoming rather red. "The war's been over for years, Perry. *Others* have come forward to take credit for their service to His Majesty in the more…covert activities of the thing. You could have medals. You could be lauded. You could—"

"Toot my own horn, while many of those who crept about in secrecy like me now lie dead in foreign soil, if they weren't carted back here in vats of pickle juice and then stuffed into the family mausoleum? No, thank you, Uncle. I'm happy as I am."

Sir Willard rubbed at his red, bulbous nose. "All right, all right, I won't force the issue, not when I consider how well your ridiculous modesty suits the mission."

Perry paused in the action of sipping on the Burgundy. "The mission? You may be right, Uncle, perhaps I should forswear spirits before noon, although that leaves only water, which, as we both know, can be even more dangerous to my health. But no, I couldn't possibly have heard you correctly."

"You heard me correctly, Nephew," Sir Willard said, reaching behind him for the folded scrap of broadsheet that lay on his desk, then tossing it at Perry. "You've seen this?"

Perry unfolded the rumpled square featuring a rather detailed woodcut. "A poorly executed rendering of Her Royal Highness, Princess Caroline, disembarking in Dover, surrounded by, if we can believe this, both her extensive entourage and a wildly cheering crowd. Oh, and a dog. Yes, what of it?"

"What of it? She's come back, that's what of it. Come back to claim her share of the throne."

"It is hers to claim, isn't it?"

Sir Willard looked ready to tear at his hair—which would have been difficult, as he'd parted with the last of it a good two decades earlier, leaving nothing but huge bushy white eyebrows and a bald pate above them. (Sir Willard was possibly the only man in England to still be wishing back powdered wigs.)

"We in government can't have it, Perry. She's totally unsuited to the role of queen. My God, man, she's been running about the world with a paramour, and a foreigner at that. In plain sight. Thumbing her nose at all of us. Putting a crown on that head would be sacrilege."

"I think England has put the crown on quite a few heads that might not have been precisely up to the honor," Perry said, tossing the rendering onto the couch. "May I dare a bit of treason and suggest that our recently elevated king could be numbered among them? Last I heard, you know, he was crowing to everyone that he was present at Waterloo. If he had been, which we all know he was not, there wouldn't have been a camp stool large enough for him to hide his shivering bulk beneath when the battle began."

"I like you better as a fool than when you're being supercilious," Sir Willard said. "But all right, all right, I'll take the gloves off, shall I?"

"Do whatever pleases you, dear Uncle, it makes no nevermind to me," Perry said, wondering if his favorite club would be serving spiced ham today. He was quite fond of spiced ham. "Anything so that I might kiss both your rosy-red cheeks in farewell and toddle off on my aimless, pointless pursuit of pleasure once more."

He was lying, of course. Perry was very interested in whatever his uncle would soon say. It was always interesting to learn how the minds of aged men in power worked, as they so very often worked in ways that had a lot to do with the benefit of aged men in power, and the devil with the rest of the world.

Sir Willard leaned forward in the armchair. Well, he attempted to lean forward. But his bulk had rather stuck between the arms, so instead he rested his elbows on them, clasped his hands together, and pushed his melon-with-eyebrows head toward his nephew.

"Shall I summon Hawkins, Uncle?" Perry asked, doing his best to keep his expression sober. "And perhaps a winch?"

"If you weren't so damn rich I could threaten to cut you out of my will, no matter that you're my only surviving kin. Now, listen to me. Princess Caroline cannot be crowned queen next year when Prinney—His Royal Majesty—has his coronation. She simply cannot."

Perry scratched at his forehead. "You want me to kill her? Isn't that sliding a tad far over the edge, Uncle, even for such a staunch Tory as yourself?"

"God's teeth! No, I don't want you to kill her. We… that is, I want you to spy on her."

Perry dropped his chin onto his chest and looked at his uncle from beneath his remarkable winged eyebrows. "Oh, most definitely my hearing is gone. Your hair, my ears. What a terrible legacy of physical failings in our family, Uncle. You want me to what?"

"You heard me. I said spy on her. You're a spy, ain't you? And a damned good one. That's the part of you I want, not that other part—I prefer not to remember what else you were ordered to do during the war."

"A sentiment I share, Uncle," Perry said tightly, then took a sip from his wineglass. And the man wondered why he didn't go about, crowing of his exploits?

"Yes, yes. Rather sordid, bloodthirsty bits, some of that, eh, although necessary to our pursuit of victory. So we won't talk about that. The king has put it to us to find a way to discredit the princess, gain him a divorce. His Cabinet, Parliament—we've been ordered to find a way."

"And I'm that way?" Perry sat back, lightly rubbed at his chin. "Oh, hardly, Uncle."

Sir Willard shook his head. "Not just you. There's plenty of dirt already been dug, enough for the House of Lords to introduce a Bill of Pains and Penalties."

Perry got to his feet, returned the wineglass to the drinks table. "I've never heard of such a thing."

"Truthfully, neither had I, but we've been assured it's legal, if an ancient process, rather outside our more commonly known legal system. Liverpool found it, and you know what a stickler he is. If she beats down a vote on the thing by Parliament, she's queen. If we prove our case, the king gets his divorce. The procedure will be announced by the end of the week, possibly as soon as tomorrow. Think of it, Perry. If this works, he could marry again, provide another heir now that Princess Charlotte is lost to us."

"Now there's a vision that I would not want burned into my mind—Prinney riding atop some poor sweet princess sacrificed for her fertile womb. And again, not oddly, the request for a winch would probably not be unwarranted."

"You're lucky you're speaking only to me," Sir Willard warned him.

"And you're lucky, Uncle, I don't run hotfoot to Henry Brougham and the Whigs and tell them what's afoot. Digging up dirt to divorce the queen? It's unconscionable, even for you whacking-great bunch of rabid Tories."

"So is watching the aging royal dukes running about, deserting morganatic wives and dozens of their bastard royals in order to wed any princess they can find and put an heir on her. We look like an island of rutting idiots. The world is laughing at us. Think on it, Perry. All that stands between England and anarchy at this moment is young Princess Victoria. We saw what happened with Princess Charlotte. This cannot be allowed."

"So Prinney has to be shed of the queen, marry again, somehow produce an heir, possibly two or three. That's the crux of this? You know, Uncle, I'd like to believe you, but I don't. Our new king just doesn't want his wife anymore, does he? Not only does he detest her, she's more popular than he ever was. Or have you been so stuck—forgive me a small jest—here in your study that you are unaware of the spoiled vegetables and fruit that are tossed at our sire whenever he dares poke his nose outside the palace?"

With no small effort of will, Sir Willard disengaged his impressive girth from the chair and retrieved the rendering, furiously waving it in front of Perry's nose. "See the girl? The one behind the Princess Caroline, just stepping onto the pier, holding on to that dog? Goes everywhere with the woman. She's your entrée into the princess's enclave."

Perry snatched the paper before his uncle began beating him with it. "The queen's enclave, Uncle. If Prinney is king, Caroline is queen consort."

"Don't bother me with trifles, not with the kingdom in such a damnable mess. Meet this girl, pay court to her, do whatever you must do, but get yourself accepted into Caroline's circle. That's where your pretty face comes in. Caroline likes pretty faces. Watch, observe, poke into closets, read any papers you may find locked up, and fetch me something the Lords can use to bring the dratted woman down. For England, Perry. And there's not much time. The Lords convene this Pains and Penalties business in a few weeks."

Perry squinted at the page. "Who is she? The artist wasn't precisely inspired—all the faces look rather alike."

"She's Amelia Fredericks, one of the waifs Her Royal Highness has brought into her motley entourage, all but adopted. Remember how Caroline set up that supposed orphanage in Kent? No, of course you don't, that was years ago. To hide the bastard son she formally adopted at one point, we all say, but can never prove."

"Hiding her own son with a bevy of orphans. I'd call that inspired. This girl? She's also one of those orphans?"

"Yes. The daughter of one of the princess's maidservants, I understand, who perished in childbirth. Whatever, she's been with the princess all of her life, a close companion and probably confidante. Meet her, romance her—I wager there will be orgies, knowing Caroline—and you will be in a perfect position to report on all that lascivious behavior, anything the Lords might use to discredit her. You're a fool, Perry, a dilettante. Not threatening at all. You're perfect for the job. No one would ever suspect you."

"I believe I have, in this past minute, been insulted in more ways than I care to count," Perry said, idly stroking the thin white scar on his left cheek with his thumb. "But tell me. If I say no, then what happens?"

"Then we'll send someone else, who might not have your pure heart and chivalrous ways. Why, he might feel that the only way to infiltrate the princess's enclave would be to seduce this Miss Fredericks. Ruin her. Not that you'd care a fig, eh? You don't care a fig for anyone."

"How very naughty of you, Uncle, to pink me straight in my pesky honor as a gentleman." Perry held up the broadsheet yet again. "I read here that Her Royal Highness is quartered with Alderman Wood. My, my, he was Lord Mayor of London once or twice, wasn't he? What happened? Was she turned away at the palace, or didn't she chance a rebuff?"

"Wood offered, and it avoided a circus, with the populace there to witness it. But she's already found other quarters in Hammersmith. Right on the water. I do believe our impudent queen enjoys the notion that her many admirers—and, yes, I admit she does have them— can choose to travel across the water to make their bows to her. The woman has a love of theatrics that is most embarrassing."

"Unlike our new king, who is staid and retired and quite above showing himself off. Why, the Pavilion at

Brighton is no more ornate than a monk's cell, I swear it, if said monk had a fondness for silk, gilt and minarets. But, yes, I understand. Who did you have in mind?"

"What?"

"Whom did you have in mind to seduce Miss Fredericks? You must have all but given up on me by now. So? His name, Uncle."

"Jarrett Rolin."

Perry controlled his expression with some effort. "Rolin? I thought he left town with his tail tucked between his legs after that debacle at Westham's a month ago."

"Yes, I'd heard about that. The Marquis of Westham is your good friend, isn't he? Odd, that, considering he's the one who sliced that scar into your cheek."

Perry spared a moment to think of his good, once hotheaded friend (hence the dueling scar on Perry's cheek) and their very recent coup of routing Jarrett Rolin after the rotter had attempted to kidnap Westham's beloved.

"Never mind that. Rolin is a bastard. A pretty bastard, but a bastard all the same. The man lives to seduce innocents. You can't think to use him."

"Can't we? He's perfect, Nevvie. An outcast from Society for the nonce, hiding out on his estate in Surrey. The princess adores outcasts, feels an affinity for them, I believe. But, as I said, he would be our second choice."

"You know, Uncle, if I have a failing in life it has always been in underestimating you."

"Only that, Nevvie? If you applied to me, I could provide you with a detailed list of your shortcomings. Now hurry along, dear boy. Miss Fredericks awaits. Oh, one thing more. Report here tomorrow and I'll explain."

"I could be on the continent by tomorrow," Perry suggested, his hand on the door latch.

"True, but you won't be. I do so enjoy honorable gentlemen. And you are that, Perry, for all that you're also an idiot. Tomorrow at two, agreed?"

Perry inclined his head slightly, then departed, carrying off the broadsheet he'd grabbed up, hoping the artist had at least gotten the slim female figure right.

"I COULD BE SKINNY and bony like you, you know, instead of more fashionably plump," Her Royal Majesty said as Amelia Fredericks entered the small salon overlooking the Thames. "If I so wished."

"Yes, ma'am," Amelia said, smiling at the queen as she placed a fresh dish of boiled sweets on the table beside the woman, then retook her seat in front of the window. "A lovely day, isn't it, although the sun doesn't seem quite as bright here as it did in Jerusalem."

"Nothing seems quite as bright here," the queen said, her scowl warning Amelia that another fit of hysteria was knocking on the door of the woman's consciousness, eager for admittance. She had, just minutes earlier, climbed up into the boughs of the queen's injured pride and dragged her down with the promise of the boiled sweets. "Rainy, dreary, damp. And that pile they call a palace? Blow your skirts up over your head, just walking down the hallways on a windy day. I hate it. I hate it all. I hate them all. And I'm old, and I'm ugly, and I'm fat. I hate me!"

The dish of boiled sweets landed on the fireplace grate and smashed into several pieces, the candies skittering everywhere.

Amelia suppressed a sigh. "I'll ring for someone."

"No! Leave it." The queen blinked rapidly, her kohl-darkened eyes already tearing. "I must stop this. I must collect myself. That sniveling selfish bastard will not do this to me. I am queen!"

"Yes, ma'am, that you are," Amelia said, her gaze shifting toward the thick pages of vellum sitting on the table in front of the queen, all stiff and important and covered in official seals. "This means nothing, ma'am, less than nothing. His Royal Majesty is desperate, and desperate men make mistakes. Mr. Brougham said as much before he left us."

"Henry Brougham, Amelia, wants what he has always wanted, to use me to further his own ends. It has been this way for years. I could have settled for a sizable allowance and exile, you know, but Brougham talked me out of it, talked me into coming back here. He's still talking, damn his eyes. You think he cares a fig for me? Tories, Whigs. They fight each other, using me as their battlefield, their cannon fodder."

Amelia nodded. That was her role, to agree, to silently nod, and she knew her place. Chafed at it, but knew it.

"I should never have come back here. Even the old king tried to use me, damn his soul. Sick? That's what they said, that he was sick, off his head. And I still say that the old madman tossed me down on a couch soon as he came back from opening Parliament—when was that? Oh, I remember. Back in '02, while George and I were still pretending. Threw me down, Amelia, and would have had his way with me, were it not that the couch had no back and I was able to kick him off, roll free of him. I never moved so fast, before or since. Filthy Hanovers, the worst of our family. Users. And they all did their best to use me. Me, and my poor Charlotte, lost and gone these two terrible years. They kept her from me, you know, even when she cried for me, begged for me. And now she's gone. My own child…"

Amelia's soft heart was touched. Her Royal Highness could be crude, could be cantankerous, could be ridiculously generous one moment and horribly selfish the next; dangerously free with her affections and her words. Mercurial. But, at the bottom of it, at the heart of it, the woman hadn't had the best of lives, and Amelia loved her dearly.

And, loving her dearly, she said the first thing that sprang to her tongue, "We can leave again, ma'am. The world awaits, all of it eager to please you."

The queen, her coal-black hair fresh from another visit with the dye pots, nodded fiercely, the childish curls bouncing around her rouged cheeks. "Yes, yes. We could go. Pergami would fly to me, I know it, if I were to abandon this damn, damp island. Byron left, you know. Ungrateful England all but tossed him out." She blinked back tears. "He was such a pretty boy, even with that twisted foot. I could have had him, you know, if I'd but crooked a finger in his direction. Chose Spencer Perceval instead. He was helpful, but not pretty. Sir Sydney Smith? Ah, he was almost pretty, and reportedly hung like a—"

"Yes, ma'am," Amelia said placidly.

"But you know, Amelia, I only really committed adultery the once—three or six times, in truth. But that was with the husband of Maria Fitzherbert."

Amelia couldn't help but smile at Her Majesty's reference to the king's morganatic bride. The queen's outrageous statements, as well as her rather erratic behavior, had lost the power to embarrass her years ago. Still, she had to steer the woman back on point, even as she'd stupidly let it slip that she wished to put England behind them once and for all. "So, dear ma'am, shall I give the order? We can set sail by week's end. Paris. Rome. Anywhere your heart desires."

The queen snorted. "I doubt we could make Dover on what's left of my allowance. That hangs in the balance, you know. The king—I spit on calling him thusly—holds the purse strings now. That's another part of this Pains-and-Penalties business. My pain, the penalties he'd order. I have to win, Amelia, or else he'll control every aspect, every penny in my purse, every bite that goes into my mouth. He'd like nothing more than for me to live in penury."

"Then we stay," Amelia said, continuing to guide her queen back toward the correct, the only, path, without letting the woman see the leash. Amelia had been against their return, but also knew they had no choice but to stay and fight now that they were here. But it had to be the queen's decision, at the end of it.

The queen's sigh ended in a curse that had a lot to do with hungry mice finding a home in her estranged husband's bowels. "Yes, we stay. We stay and we fight. Oh, Amelia." She moaned piteously, holding out her hands so that Amelia left her seat and took those hands in her own. "I do it for you, my dearest girl. Not for me, for I am old, and ravaged, and have no future save pain until death. For you, for my dear William, for all of you. And for England! England needs me! England loves me!"

With the queen's many rings painfully biting into her skin, Amelia smiled and dropped into a deep curtsy. "And England thanks you, my queen."

"Yes, yes, of course, there's all that drivel, too," the queen said curtly, releasing Amelia's abused fingers as the pendulum of her mood swung once more. "Look at that mess. For God's sake, girl, get someone in here to clean it. Am I to live in filth as well as penury?"

"Yes, ma'am," Amelia said, hiding a smile as she gave the bell rope a tug, then returned to gather up the official notice of the Pains and Penalties that had made for an exceedingly hysterical morning. "With Your Majesty's permission, I shall retire to the kitchens to personally order strawberry tarts for tea. Your favorite, ma'am."

The queen was suddenly girlish, her cheeks coloring even beneath the spots of rouge, her smile shy. "I really shouldn't indulge, not when I must prepare to meet my subjects. I needs must look my best."

"You are always at your best, ma'am, and dear in the hearts of everyone," Amelia said, knowing the words sounded old and worn but unable to think of new ones, and the queen waved her away, toward the kitchens.

BERNARD NESTOR sat at the rude table in his ruder kitchen, devoid now of even the single servant he'd had to turn off, and studied the copy of the Bill of Pains and Penalties he'd stuffed into his coat just after Henry Brougham had given him his congé and told him never to darken his door again.

Gratitude. There was none in this cruel and unenlightened world. He'd been a loyal Whig, a loyal employee of Henry Brougham's, a diligent worker.

And what had he gotten for this devotion?

He'd gotten the sack, that's what he'd gotten.

Too rabid. Too rigid. Too intense. Too much of a danger when clear heads, not hotheads, are needed. That's what Henry Brougham had said.

Five years. He'd worked, slaved, and with little financial remuneration, for five long years, monitoring Princess Caroline's movements, warning Henry Brougham in time to head off at least a half-dozen disasters as the woman made a fool of herself across the continent.

And now, now when the queen really needed him, he'd been cast aside as too fervent, too volatile, too dangerous.

England needed their new queen. England needed the Whigs back in power. England would become another France, with its own bloody revolution, if the king and those damn Tories were left to their own devices.

The world was black or white to Bernard, right or wrong, innocent or guilty and with no shades of gray. The world was reasonable this way for Bernard, and it was so much easier to tell the Good from the Bad without having to invest in any heavy thinking.

He stared at the rather dirty tumbler of inferior wine that was all the penny-pinched younger son could afford before his hand shot out, sweeping the thick glass off the table, only to have the thing *thunk* against the floor-boards; not even giving him the solace of smashing into a thousand pieces.

Fools! They were all fools! Didn't they know how much danger the queen was in, the Whigs were in, now that this damned Pains-and-Penalties nonsense was fact?

He grabbed at the pages, glaring at the crabbed, hurried writing, as he'd had to take Henry Brougham's copy into a dark closet with only one candle to aid him as he'd copied it, word for damning word.

He found what he was looking for and read the words aloud:

"…to deprive Her Majesty, Caroline Amelia Elizabeth, of the Title, Prerogatives, Rights, Privileges and Exemptions of Queen Consort of this Realm; and to dissolve the Marriage between His Majesty and said Caroline Amelia Elizabeth."

Bernard picked up the wine bottle by the neck and drank deeply. "Treason. Blasphemy." He frowned, then decided he was right. Yes. Even blasphemy, if he sort of tipped his head and squinted as he looked at the thing. "But how to stop it? God knows the wretched woman is guilty of every charge against her, and more."

And Bernard knew, because it had been Bernard's job to know.

Pergami. Bartolomeo Bergami, now Pergami; now even—courtesy of the then Princess Caroline—Knight of Malta, Baron de la Francine. *There* was one for the books: the upstart Italian paramour, elevated to such a station by reason of what could only be assumed was his talented cock. For the privilege of servicing a loud, overblown, ridiculous creature, he had been given money, titles, position…and a deep gravy boat for all his relatives to swim in as part of Caroline's entourage.

The Tories would destroy her, through Pergami. The pains would be clear, the penalties clearer.

And England, under the Tories, would go down in the annals of history as one very large failure.

Unless…unless he, Bernard Nestor, was right, and he was always right. For, in *The World as Seen by Bernard Nestor,* he was forever cast in the leading role, that of hero, savior. Why, when he thought of himself that way, he even thought of himself as being taller, wider. With a chin.

He pushed himself away from the table and staggered, rather drunkenly, to the locked desk in his small sitting room. He shook his head to clear it (a fruitless effort, alas, for the fanatic in Bernard had evicted clear thinking years earlier), then unlocked the drawer that held everything he knew about one William Austin…and the other one.

He turned pages in the slim portfolio, reading yet again that Caroline had been all but physically ejected from the royal household in 1797, all but barred from her own child.

He read again that William Austin was believed born in the first month of 1801, and later adopted by the princess. Unlike the Tories, Bernard had done his best this past year and more to locate proof of William Austin's legitimacy, that he had *not* been a bastard birth. Wouldn't that turn everything on its head! It was brilliant, absolutely brilliant, a coup that would give Bernard everything he had always wanted.

But he had found nothing that hadn't already been discovered.

About William Austin.

He had, however, as he'd investigated, one by one, all the orphans Caroline had collected, been drawn to one Amelia Elizabeth Fredericks.

Her mother supposedly perishing in childbirth, Amelia Fredericks had been brought up among the coterie of assorted waifs Caroline had accumulated, although she'd formally adopted only William Austin.

Where better, Bernard had concluded, to hide but among a crowd? And how better to hide what must remain hidden than by allowing everyone, even steering everyone, toward another target altogether?

The girl's name was not at all significant. Everyone

seemed to name their children after royalty, and Caroline had probably had the liberty to do the same for the supposed orphaned child. This, in itself, was not remarkable.

Bernard turned a few more pages, until he came to the pen-and-ink reproductions he'd bought, one from a hawker here in London, one he'd paid a pretty penny for, on his own, from a contact he'd made in Italy.

On his left, Charlotte Sophia of Mecklesburg-Strelitz, mother of the new king and for whom his only daughter had been named, both Charlottes dead and gone these past two years. A handsome woman, not beautiful, but definitely striking. Regal.

On his right the orphan, Amelia Elizabeth Fredericks.

And then he located the third, a rude reproduction of George Augustus Frederick, now George IV, in his flamboyant youth.

Squinting, Bernard Nestor looked for physical resemblances and, in his mind, found them.

AMELIA STOOD in front of the mirror in her bed chamber in the residence overlooking the Thames, her head tilted slightly to the left as she looked into the assessing eyes reflected there.

She felt silly, the dreamer once again conjuring hopeful dreams.

The queen had been correct in what she'd said. They looked quite unalike in their form, their figure.

But the eyes were the same soft brown, a common enough color. The hair was the same auburn...although the queen's had gone silver years ago, and now went blond, black and even red, depending on the woman's whim and her choice of dye pot or wig.

Her nose was not quite so long as the queen's, but bore the same rather aristocratic line; her top lip more full, her cheeks and chin not quite so rounded.

And yet, at times, during the bad times, when the queen cried into her cups, she still would cling to Amelia and call her "sweet daughter," so that the very first thing Amelia had done upon their return to England was to send a maid off to procure a copy of *Memoirs of Her Late Royal Highness Princess Charlotte Augusta.*

She'd devoured every word of the thick tome, inspected every illustration; even compared the sampling of the princess's handwriting with her own…and she'd wept for Princess Caroline, the banished mother, now the unwanted Queen of England.

She wasn't at all like Charlotte, Amelia had decided, was no more or less than the grateful orphan who had been taken in, made to feel a part of the household, the way William had been, the way the others had been. But, like the others, she'd dreamed. What if the rumors were true? What if William really was the bastard son? And if not William…why not one of the others? Why not she herself?

Amelia had been both ignored by the queen and doted upon by the queen, had been taken into the queen's confidence on many occasions. She acted now as companion to the queen, she mothered the queen, as it were. How marvelous it would be if there was more than this lifelong connection of proximity. How marvelous if she were not an orphan, if the woman she so worried for and yet admired was her own mother.

Stupid. Stupid, stupid, wishful dream…

William had seen Princess Charlotte, been in her company, until her father the then Prince Regent had found out and begun the horrible campaign to completely keep the queen from her only child, removed her from her mother's household forever by the time she was eight years old.

Although only slightly younger than William, Amelia had never been allowed to be in the same room as Princess Charlotte. She'd only catch glimpses of her, confined to the housekeeper's quarters until the royal heir had been denied further visits to the household. Amelia had been moved Abovestairs then, and into near-constant association with the then Princess Caroline, even as William was given shorter and shorter shrift.

And thus the childish hopes, the childish dreams…

The only painting Amelia had seen of Princess Charlotte had been one of Caroline, then Princess of Wales, and her infant daughter, that had traveled everywhere with them; from England, to the Continent, to Italy, to Jericho.

And the dream had remained…

Until the book. Until the illustrations. Any childish hope, any lingering silly, romantic dream she had still harbored that the queen could be her own mother had been dashed when she'd seen the illustrations of a grown Princess Charlotte. They were nothing alike. Not really. And William, wherever he had taken himself off to this time, was no more alike to Princess Charlotte than chalk was to cheese. William had let his dream die; and so should she.

Ah, childish dreams. Childish hopes. Silly yearnings.

They had no part in her life, and had to be vanquished, set aside, for she was a woman grown now, and beyond childish things.

And she had a Responsibility to the queen, that poor, frightened, persecuted creature who had not given Amelia life, but had, in her way, watched over that life.

Her thoughts returned to the book she had read, read again and then hidden away at the very bottom of her traveling trunk, beneath a cloak she'd long ago ceased to wear.

What a sad story, what a heartwrenching commentary. The prince who married without love, the princess who had been exiled almost the moment she had expelled the heir from her womb. The determined campaign to show the princess in the worst of all lights, to besmirch her name, brand her a harlot, keep her from her daughter, exclude her from Society.

Only the king, poor mad George III, had dared to champion her, but poor mad George had forgotten her, as he had forgotten the world, and now he was gone. Caroline's sole protector from her husband's determined campaign to destroy her no longer stood in the way of that destruction.

If the princess—now the queen—had decided to remove herself overseas and at last live up to her terrible reputation, to enjoy life after her near imprisonment by her husband…? Well, what of it? Her only child was dead, her grandson dying with her. Why shouldn't she seek some happiness for herself?

And they had been happy, hadn't they? The traveling, the adventures, all the glorious people they had met. Even Pergami; laughing, teasing, lighthearted Pergami. They'd frolicked on the shore of Lake Como; the princess had danced the nights away, laughed the days away, hidden her sorrows, her demons. They'd ridden into Jerusalem on donkeys, visited all the Holy Places, gone by water to Syracuse. The princess had been happy, or at least as happy as she could be.

But then she became the queen.

"And now this," Amelia said aloud, turning away from the mirror, to glare at the official document that had so disrupted their small household. "The lengths to which he will travel to humiliate and debase his own wife. How can anyone hate so much? Why the horrible man doesn't simply find a way to have her beheaded and be done with it is beyond me."

Amelia, startled at her own words, turned back to the mirror, to confront her reflection. "My God. Would he? Would he dare…?"

"SHE BELIEVES THIS? Stap me, Mama, next she'll be telling us she sees multicolored elephants copulating on the ceilings."

"Nathaniel, don't be crude," his mother said. "And be quiet, for goodness sake, or your father will overhear us. You know how he always manages to be around just when I want him elsewhere."

"Yes," Sir Nathaniel Rankin, baronet, said as he split his stylish coattails and sat down beside his mother in a small anteroom located in Lady Hertford's town mansion. "I imagine he'd order coaches to Bedlam for the pair of you. Blister it, Mama, Aunt Rowena's a nice enough old tabby, but—"

"My sister is not a nice old tabby," his mother interrupted.

"Grandfather should have insisted she marry, Papa says. A husband and a gaggle of children may have settled her."

"I know, I know," his mother said, sighing. "And Edmund was such a nice man, even with the squint. But Rowena would have none of him. She has always been much more enamored of her dogs."

Nate closed his startlingly blue eyes, pinched at the bridge of his nose. "I'm little more than an infant, Mama. Should I be hearing this?"

His mother's ivory-sticked fan smacked against his forearm even as the woman giggled. "You're so naughty, Nate. Shame on you. Now, to be serious."

"Do we have to be?"

"We do, yes. I told you Rowena's fears, but I didn't tell you their foundation."

"Now that's a thought I've never had. Aunt Rowena needs a reason?"

"She can be silly, I know. But this time? This time she may be right."

"Someone wants the new queen dead. She read it in

her tea cup, or Tarot cards, or maybe saw it in some clouds. I remember. You only said it the once, but I remember. Did her tea leaves also line up to spell out a list of suspected assassins? Only seems fair."

"No, they—I mean, she did not, but the answer should be obvious," his mother said, then leaned closer, to whisper into his ear. "The new king, of course. He loathes the poor thing."

"Also not exactly mind-boggling news. He's loathed her for decades. And done squat about it, may I remind you?"

"But she hasn't been queen for decades, Nate. Think on it. He detests her, we all know that. The crowd jeers him, cheers her. Not to mention having to share the coronation with her, place the crown on her head? Why else do you think he has postponed the ceremony for a full year?"

"In hopes she'll go away? Yes, I can see that. She'd get bored, cooling her heels here, hie herself off somewhere to see the muffin man, and miss the whole thing."

"You're not nearly so amusing as you think you are, you know," his mother said, snapping open the fan and waving it beneath her chin. "He plans to divorce her, strip her of any right to the crown."

"But Aunt Rowena believes he's going to have her assassinated, not just divorce her. But why would he do that, if he can get Parliament to do his dirty work for him?"

"Because it might not work, that's why. At least that's what your father says. He's embarrassed to be a part of it." She leaned closer once more. "He has heard that they'll be examining evidence that is most distasteful. Stained bits of clothing snatched from hampers, dried residue from chamber pots, all sort of tawdry evidence."

"Well, that's fairly disgusting."

"I should say so! Then your father foolishly said the king would be better served to just arrange some fatal accident for the queen and be done with it."

"And Aunt Rowena heard him? What a dust-up that must have caused."

"Exactly. Your father is a brilliant man, but can still be extremely obtuse, just like the rest of your sex. And now Rowena's taken it into her silly head that the queen is in mortal danger. So you see, you have to do it."

"No."

"Nate."

"No."

"Nathaniel, Rowena is your godmother."

"Damn."

As the law of averages (and Aunt Rowena) would have it, for every Perry Shepherd there is, also roped into the thing against his will and better judgment, a Sir Nathaniel Rankin.

And for every Bernard Nestor, alas, there is also an Esther Pidgeon. As dedicated as he, as rabid as he, but with her motives and loyalties in direct opposition to his, Esther believed the only way for the king to reign easily was to have that totally unsuitable Caroline removed, permanently.

To Esther the supposed queen is a slut, a whore, a

flighty, unwashed animal, and her name must not be spoken in the liturgy each Sunday when the Crown's loyal subjects were asked to pray for their king (pulling out and holding up religion like a sword was always such a marvelous rallying point for people like Esther).

Sister of the publisher of one of the lesser newspapers in the city, she'd already been made privy to this magnificent Bill of Pains and Penalties, and had spent half the evening rejoicing at the news.

This was her time. At last. She had been good, she had been patient, and now her time had come!

It is amazing how a woman like Esther Pidgeon can take one evening's casual tumble into bed at a house party a quarter of a century earlier and mold that night, twist it about, until the Grand Florizel has become the Love of One's Life, sadly pining for his dearest Esther but kept from her side by his royal duties. Why, he has even spent those sad, lonely years trying to find substitutes for her…all his women aging, fat, motherly. Just like Esther. Really. Especially the "fat" part.

But that was Esther, a woman who had dedicated her sad life to worshipping this oblivious man from afar.

And so the Bill of Pains and Penalties filled Esther with joy. For a while.

Now, as midnight neared, she paced the floor of her small chamber tucked into the second floor rear of her brother, Lewis's, house and worried, then worried some more.

What if it didn't work? What if Caroline slipped free

of justice, as she had done the first time? Men, left to their own devices and shortcomings, often bungled things, badly.

Esther stood in front of the mantelpiece in her night rail, gazing up adoringly at the colored print of her dearest Florizel, a print she had surrounded with sprigs of rosemary and pretty pink bows, the whole of it lit by candles she placed on the mantel reverently, every night.

And then she would pull over the small embroidered stool, stand on it, stretch herself up, up, until she could place a kiss on Florizel's hand—or whatever part of the man's anatomy seemed appropriate for her mood, but it's best not to dwell on that—before retiring to her lonely bed with two glasses of wine. One for herself, one for Florizel.

As Esther abhorred waste, she eventually would drink her absent lover's wine as well and, over the years, the two glasses had somehow grown to two bottles, so that if Esther wasn't always deep in her cups, she continued to make a valiant effort to become so.

But tonight? Tonight she was angry. Enough! She had suffered enough! Waited long enough!

Was she destined to live always in the shadows, waiting for Florizel to feel free to come to her? Or would she at last step up, stand up, and fight for what was hers? Yes! Yes, she could do that.

Caroline must die, Esther decided halfway into that night's second bottle; there was nothing else for it. And anyone—anyone at all—who might dare to stand in the way of Esther's...um, the king's happiness, must die along with her.

All that was needed was a way, some way for Esther to insinuate herself into Caroline's household.

THE SOON-TO-BE rather crowded household of the new queen woke hours earlier than the mistress of the place, to tend to their duties, to crowd around the butler, Carstairs, and listen to what the king had been up to now, then to tiptoe about the house, knowing it was going to be a difficult day. A difficult month. A difficult life…

Amelia, awake and dressed before dawn, had already penned a new menu for the day—one that consisted of Her Royal Majesty's particular favorites—and she finally ran down the housekeeper-cum-companion, Mrs. Maryann Fitzhugh (and if that had been Fitzherbert, the woman would have been turned away in an instant!).

Mrs. Fitzhugh had come to the door, highly recommended and greeted with relieved resignation; for a housekeeper familiar with English ways was definitely needed, as was a paid companion, if Amelia was to go out and about at all during their time here in the house by the water.

Amelia felt certain she should have checked the woman's thick sheaf of references, but time had been of the essence and still was, as the household was far from complete.

In the few days they had been in residence, Amelia had already learned that Mrs. Fitzhugh was…somewhat odd.

She chewed peppermints constantly, which was not all that terrible, except that the smell was at times overpowering (at least Amelia knew when the woman was approaching). She talked to herself, for another, and was doing so now, as Amelia entered the woman's small quarters down a hallway from the kitchens.

"Should we be here, Mrs. Fitzhugh, in this den of iniquity, no matter that it's just what we thought we wanted? Are we that selfish?"

And then she did that other thing that made Amelia uncomfortable. Mrs. Fitzhugh answered herself.

"Now, now, Maryann, she's the queen, after all. One can't climb much higher than to be housekeeper to a queen. Could have been a scullery maid, but he did better than that. And you know that's not the whole of it, not by a long chalk. I vow, Maryann, you can be such a ninny."

"Mrs. Fitzhugh! That was cruel!"

Amelia rubbed at her forehead, wondering if she should interrupt the two halves of the strange whole of Mrs. Maryann Fitzhugh, and then decided that if she continued to think of the woman as two persons, *she* might soon begin talking to herself.

"Mrs. Fitzhugh? Yoo-hoo," Amelia said, rapping her knuckles on the doorjamb. "How are we—you—this morning?"

Mrs. Fitzhugh, her back to Amelia, lifted her hands to smooth her neat brown hair tied up in its usual severe bun, then turned to face her employer's whomever (Mrs. Fitzhugh was still sorting that one out).

"Oh, good morrow, Mistress Fredericks," she said, stretching her mouth into a tight smile. "I would have attended you if you had but rung for me."

"Yes, I know," Amelia said, entering the room, which was so neat and clean she was surprised it didn't squeak. Everything here in England was so stiff and clean, and rigid. So unlike the easy atmosphere of Italy, for instance. "But I have penned some modifications to today's menu and I thought you would prefer to present them to Cook?"

Mrs. Fitzhugh took the piece of paper, squinted at it as she silently mouthed the words, then frowned. "Partridges, mistress? I don't know, mistress. The markets have already been open for two hours or more, and Cook would have to take herself there, to fetch good ones."

"Oh, no, I can do that, if you'll accompany me."

Obviously Amelia's response wasn't the one Mrs. Fitzhugh had wished to hear. "You want to go pawing over raw birds? Can you do that?"

"Alas, Mrs. Fitzhugh, my folly knows no bounds. Yes, I believe I am up to the task. But you're correct. Everything will have already been picked over, won't it? Perhaps tomorrow? In the meantime, please ask Cook to do the best she can with the remainder of the list?"

Mrs. Fitzhugh nodded, and Amelia turned away, only to turn back when the woman said, "Carstairs took himself off, you know, mistress."

"What? But he— What will we do without a butler? I don't understand."

"He read us all from the newspaper, mistress, and then said he would not stay in a den of iniquity. Those were his very words, mistress. 'Den of iniquity.' Two of the footmen and one housemaid hied off with him."

"I see," Amelia said, lifting her chin. So that's where the den of iniquity remark had come from. She'd wondered. "Very well. Thank you, Mrs. Fitzhugh. Carry, um, carry on?"

The woman dropped into a very shallow curtsy. "I shall do that, mistress. And shall I put up a post for a new butler, two footmen, one housemaid…and I would very much like a helper of sorts. Can't be traipsing about with you, mistress, and riding herd on the staff at the same time."

The headache that had been knocking on the back of Amelia's eyes finally gained admittance. "No, thank you, Mrs. Fitzhugh. I believe I can manage to have an advertisement posted…somewhere."

Amelia then headed to the breakfast room and the refolded newspaper that had been placed beside her plate.

She refused to look at it, acknowledge the thing's presence. It was bad enough to know the truth of what was being planned, without adding supposition and titillation to the thing.

When one of the footmen still remaining—one that had traveled with them from Italy—entered the room with a fresh pitcher of water, she held up the newspaper and said, "Gerado, if you would burn this, please?"

The footman went through a complicated choreography of tilted head, shrugged shoulders and broadly waved hands. "These Englishers," he said sadly. "Our poor queen. They try…they…*fare polpette di qualcuno.*"

Amelia quietly translated, and then smiled, for Gerado had said that the English were trying to make meatballs out of the queen. "In England, Gerado, that would be mincemeat, but I agree with you. Still, we are here, and we have no real choice but to stay the course."

"*Scusi?*"

Amelia also shrugged, though never so eloquently as the footman. "*Quando si è in ballo, bisogna ballare,* Gerado."

"Ah!" Gerado said, then made another complicated and, Amelia was certain, disparaging movement of his hands meant to encompass all of London, all of England, before he smiled. "For our queen," he said, and then saluted.

"Yes, Gerado. For our queen. And, for our queen, since Carstairs has fled, I would ask you to attend the door, if we have visitors. Thank you. You may go."

The footman bowed and retreated, muttering under his breath.

Amelia just sat there, her elbow on the table, her chin cupped in her palm, her words to Gerado playing again in her head. *Quando si è in ballo, bisogna ballare.*

When at a dance, one must dance. It was her favorite Italian saying, as it described, she believed, her own life. She was here, for good or ill, as the housemaid's orphan turned companion to a reviled queen; the buffer, the guardian, the protector. Whatever. She was here, whatever her role, and she would dance.

"And hopefully without our toes being stepped on too much," she said, then looked out over the Thames, wishing she were looking at Lake Como instead, and saw the boats. So many boats, of every shape and size, all of them passing back and forth slowly in front of the building, while those in the boats stood and pointed and stared. Ruder contraptions bobbed on the water, filled with hawkers holding up meat pies and parasols and spy glasses, the better to see the queen.

The queen would see them, too. There was no escape from what had been set in motion, not with the king's death, but from the very first time Caroline of Brunswick had first set food on English soil.

Amelia stood, crossed to the window and determinedly drew the draperies shut, wondering if she could make the queen believe that those in the boats had all come to salute her…not just to gape at a new oddity in their midst.

PERRY SHEPHERD had not so much as lifted his hand to the knocker before the door to his uncle's household was opened by a liveried footman and he was ushered through to the great man's private study by an entirely too-amused Hawkins.

"You're late, Nevvie," Sir Willard barked from the couch, where he sprawled against the protesting leather, his left leg raised onto the seat and wrapped in at least ten yards of white cotton cloth.

"Gout again, Uncle? My sympathies," Perry said as he ignored the uncomfortable chairs in front of the desk and deliberately seated himself behind the desk, in Sir Willard's chair.

"Get out of there, you insolent puppy," his uncle ordered, but Perry stayed put. "Oh, very well, stay there. But don't touch anything."

"Like this?" Perry asked, fingering a letter opener with the head of some fantastical animal carved onto the hilt. "Or perhaps this?" he asked, picking up the top sheet from a pile of papers stacked on the blotter. "'My dear man,'" he quoted, "'how good to hear that you have corralled your nephew for the mission, although I reserve final approval of your judgment until we have word of his success. He is not averse to poking in laundry hampers, I should hope?'" Perry put down the page. "Not signed. Who the devil wrote this? Liverpool himself? My, my, am I supposed to be impressed? Or insulted? Let's see, what else is here?"

"Put that down! Put it all down! You're to spy on Princess Caroline, not me."

"Queen Caroline, Her Royal Majesty, et cetera, et cetera," Perry said. "You really should try to get that right, Uncle Willie."

"Don't call me Uncle Willie. And shut up." Sir Willard struggled to sit up, holding on to one beefy thigh with both hands as he aimed his aching foot toward a small footstool. "Show some respect for your elders, will you?"

"Of course, Uncle. Forgive me. I suppose it has something to do with that whacking great lump at the bottom of your leg. Perhaps if you were to shift your mourning band to it? Give the thing a touch of dash? Just a suggestion, you understand. I'm not really amusing myself. Truly."

His uncle glared at him. "You've decided not to take any of this at all seriously, haven't you? You're here, but you're letting me know that you are here under duress, and you're going to make the entire exercise as difficult on me as you can. Correct?"

"Mostly," Perry said, stroking his cravat. "You forgot that I'm also going to make broad, rather vulgar jokes at any opportunity. I won't be able to help myself."

"Yes, I know, which is why I brought you back here today." Sir Willard reached for the cane propped against the couch and banged it hard against the wall, twice.

Perry was just about to give in and ask what the devil his uncle was up to when the door opened yet again and in walked...well, what was it, precisely?

"I harkened yer signal, guv'nor," the man (definitely a man, or else one horribly shortchanged woman) said, pulling at his forelock before hooking a thumb in Perry's direction. "This be him?"

"This be Perry Shepherd, Earl of Brentwood, in point of fact," Perry said, bowing slightly even as he remained seated. "And who, pray tell, my good man, be you?"

"Don't be facetious," Sir Willard ordered crisply. "This is Clive Rambert. He's a Bow Street Runner I've hired to accompany you at all times."

Perry smiled, then chuckled, deep in his throat. "Oh, I don't think so, Uncle. I really, really don't think so."

"Strange. I don't remember asking your approval of the arrangement. Rambert here is the best, or so I'm told. Sniffer like a hound. He'll keep you to the straight and narrow, and watch your back while he's at it. Won't you, Rambert?"

"Right yer are, guv'nor," Clive said, winking at Perry. "Pretty bloke, ain't yer?"

Perry closed his eyes, pulled at his nose. "I watch my own back, Uncle, thank you," he said quietly, reining in his temper.

"Not this time, my boy," Sir Willard told him. "You watch the queen, Rambert here watches you and reports to me. You seem to have this failing, Nevvie. From time to time you conveniently forget I'm alive."

"Reading my mind again, Uncle?" Perry said, easing himself to his feet. "And now, if you'll excuse me, I'll be on my way. Alone."

Sir Willard struggled to sit up further. "Listen to me, Perry. Rambert here is an eyesore, I grant you—"

"Aw, guv'nor, that hurt, that did," Clive said, not looking in the least insulted.

"Don't interrupt your betters," Sir Willard barked, and Clive subsided into a subservient pose that carried with it more than a hint of suppressed insolence that said better than words that here was a fellow who'd lived by his wits for a long, long time. A man who, to Perry's mind, was a born sergeant. He'd always had a certain fondness for sergeants, as they did what they were told by their commanding officers, unless they could find a way to do it as it pleased them—meaning, without getting everyone in his charge bloody killed.

"As I was saying—"

"Never mind, Uncle," Perry said, holding up one hand. "I'll take him."

"You'll…?"

"I said, I'll take him. I even think I might like him."
Perry turned to Clive. "You like me, Rambert?"

"I'm gettin' used to yer," the Runner answered cheekily. "Ain't half so thick as the guv'nor here thinks, are yer?"

"Not even a quarter so thick, Sergeant," Perry assured
him. "Where did you serve?"

Clive sprang to attention, snapping his ankles together, which were the only place the man's bandy legs
touched each other. "The Peninsula, sir."

"Ouch. Those were some bad times."

"And some pretty señoritas, sir, if yer take m'meanin'."

Sir Willard subsided against the arm of the couch.
"God, what have I done. Two minutes, Nevvie, less than
two minutes. And you've corrupted the man."

"Oh, Uncle, someone got there long before me. I'll
just reap the benefits. Come along, Clive. There's someone I'd like you to meet."

"Where are you taking him? Who is he going to meet?"

"A tailor, Uncle. Or did you really think Clive here
would fool anyone in that red-robin waistcoat?"

Sir Willard blew out his cheeks. "I've stopped thinking when it comes to you, Nevvie. It does me no good,
anyway. Just don't bollix it up, hear me?"

"GEORGIANA? Georgiana, don't you hear me? Answer
me, girl!"

Georgiana Penrose blinked twice and lifted her gaze
from the morning newspaper that had at last been dis-
carded in his study by her stepfather, Mr. Bateman. Mr.
Bateman wasn't the sort of gentleman who believed

women couldn't read; he simply was of the opinion they should confine their reading to fashion and sermons, and the occasional housekeeping guide. "Yes, Mama? I'm so sorry. I was just reading—"

"I am not at all interested in what you were doing, child," Mrs. Bateman said, speaking what Georgiana knew to be exactly the truth, but she'd known it long enough that her mother's lack of affection no longer had the power to sting.

"Of course not, Mama. The affairs of our country are not at all of interest."

"We leave that to the gentlemen, yes." The woman brushed past Georgiana on her way to the couch. "What interests me is this. Whatever possessed you to order round my carriage?"

"Oh. Is it out there already?" Georgiana lowered her blond head and poked her spectacles back up on the bridge of her nose. She'd hoped to be long gone before her mother left her bedchamber, something the woman rarely did before noon. "I, um, that is, I didn't think—"

Mrs. Bateman rolled her eyes heavenward. "Is this your answer? That you didn't think? My word, Georgiana, have I left you in the country so long that you've turned imbecilic? Answer the question posed."

"Yes, Mama," Georgiana said quietly, still averting her gaze. What could she say? *No, Mama. You left me in the country so long, I grew a brain and learned how to survive on my own.* But that would only begin an argument she had no hope of winning, and had no great desire to win, now that she thought of the thing. "I had hoped to pay a visit to my friend, Miss Fredericks, this afternoon."

"Fredericks? I don't know the name. You have a friend here in London?"

Georgiana chose her words carefully. "Yes, Mama. Amelia Fredericks. We were at Miss Haverham's together for a term. You remember? You had sent me there when you and Mr. Bateman were courting? Amelia and I have kept up a correspondence of sorts, but I hadn't known she'd returned to England after a considerable time spent abroad. I should very much like to see her again."

"Without my permission? Honestly, Georgiana, you have all the common good sense of a turnip. I need to know much more about this Amelia Fredericks before I'll give my permission for anything remotely resembling a giggling, schoolgirl reunion between the two of you."

"Well, yes, Mama, I understand that," Georgiana said, pleating the skirt of her morning gown between her fingers. This was going to be fun; rather like tossing a fox into the middle of one of her mama's hen parties. "Amelia is, um, she's companion to Her Royal Majesty, the queen."

"Queen Charlotte? But she's dead. I distinctly remember that."

"No, Mama, not that one. Queen Caroline," Georgiana said, silently berating herself for believing, if even for an instant, that her mama ever got the straight of anything, at least not on the first go.

Still, in the end, her mama did not disappoint.

"Queen Caroline! You know an attendant to the new queen?" Mrs. Bateman collapsed against the back of the couch, fanning herself with her handkerchief. "My God, girl, this is magnificent!"

Ah. And now to play the silly little girl who doesn't understand anything, the simpleheaded, country-raised twit with no notion of how Society worked, how her mother's brain worked. Georgiana did her best to frown, look stupid. "It…it is? But isn't Mr. Bateman a Tory, Mama? I don't think they like her."

Mrs. Bateman, obviously recovered from her near swoon, sat up once more, an almost predatory gleam in her narrow blue eyes. "Tory, Whig, they're all just stupid men who like nothing more than to strut about pretending they've the consequence of a flea. But you? You have entry to the queen's residence. My dear little Georgiana."

Georgiana, who didn't remember ever being her mama's dear little anything, quickly got to her feet, mission accomplished, and eager to be on her way. "Then I'm to be allowed the carriage?"

"Yes, yes, of course. But not that dreadful gown. Don't you have anything better?"

Georgiana looked down at her sprigged muslin, the gown her mother had, days earlier, decreed more than suitable, even if it was a good five years old. "No, Mama."

Mrs. Bateman got to her feet. "We shall have to remedy that, won't we? You'll be running tame with your little friend in Hammersmith. That's where she is, you know. Hammersmith. There will be social gatherings.

Subdued, of course, what with the old king dead, rest-hissoul, but I don't see such a trifle interfering with the queen's love of gaiety. Yes, yes, new gowns, at least three. And I'll need at least three myself, if I'm to accompany you at these gatherings."

Oh, no. No, no, no. This was not a part of Georgiana's plans. "You, Mama? You'd go to Hammersmith? Mr. Bateman might not bother to object to my visiting Amelia, but would he want his wife socializing with the woman about to go on trial?"

"Damn," Mrs. Bateman said under her breath, so that Georgiana pretended not to hear.

"I'm sure I can locate a suitable companion to accompany me on my visits, Mama," Georgiana said quickly, knowing she knew no one. No one. And where would she find a suitable companion?

"Miss Penrose?"

Georgiana turned, to see the butler standing in the doorway. "Yes, Simmons?"

"The carriage is outside, miss, and the horses become fretful if left standing."

"Oh, of course," Georgiana said, gathering up her bonnet, pelisse and reticule from the couch where she'd laid them, then turned to curtsy to her mother. "I shan't be above a few hours. But I sent round a note, and Amelia is expecting me."

Mrs. Bateman waved a hand distractedly. "No, no. No hurry. I wonder if Mr. Bateman would be agreeable to just one trip to Hammersmith? He knows I can be quite grateful…"

Georgiana escaped the room as her mother plotted her next move, eager to be on her way.

SIR NATHANIEL RANKIN took the land route to Hammersmith, unwilling to maneuver his way through all the assorted boats moving back and forth in front of the queen's residence like bees buzzing around a hive.

He still could not quite believe he was on a mission commissioned by, of all people, his dotty aunt Rowena. But here he was, sitting in his curricle, looking at the entrance to the queen's residence, cudgeling his brain for a reason to knock on the door, ask admittance.

"Hallo. I'm here to offer my services to the queen. What service? Bodyguard. You know, in case Prinney comes tiptoeing around with a hooded man toting an ax?"

"Sir Nathaniel Rankin, baronet, to see Her Royal Majesty. Announce me, man!"

"Sir Nathaniel Rankin to see the queen on a matter of some urgency."

"Hallo there, beautiful day, isn't it? Would you care to buy some apples?"

Nate dropped his chin onto his chest. He'd gone mad, that was it. Stark, staring mad. He had no way of gaining admittance to the queen's presence. And even less idea of what he'd say if he somehow managed to get within earshot of the woman.

An elderly town coach bearing yellow wheels but no crest moved past him and into the circular drive, just to have the off wheels all but tipping the thing into a ditch alongside the drive.

"Cow-handed idiot," Nate mumbled, mildly interested as the driver set the brake—an unnecessary precaution, as the coach would go nowhere until it was lifted out of the ditch—and opened the door, extending a hand to his passenger.

Nate saw an arm emerge, a hand taking the coachman's hand, to be followed by the remainder of a female who then paused half in and half out of the coach, desperately trying to keep her skirts at a modest level, her spectacles on her nose and her frankly unbecoming bonnet on her head, all while looking a long way down to the ground.

The coachman struggled one-handed, to put down the steps.

"Putting down the steps won't help, you twit. She'd have to go uphill to go downhill," Nate said to himself, tossing the reins to his snickering tiger and heading off across the road, to the rescue.

Actually, the young woman could be said to be rescuing him from having to return to Aunt Rowena and admitting he'd failed in his mission.

"No, no," he heard the young woman pleading as he neared the coach. "Stop pulling, please. I'll manage myself somehow."

Nate snapped his fingers and the coachman, still holding on to the woman's wrist—cowhanded with more than the reins, obviously—turned to look at him. "There you go, my good man, you've got your orders. Unclench your paw and step back. I'll assist the lady."

Whether he recognized Nate, or just his finely cut

clothes, or if he was simply relieved to hand over responsibility for the young lady, the coachman stepped back sharply.

"Hallo?" Nate called out, keeping his distance even as he leaned forward to smile into the coach, for the young woman had disappeared again—falling back inside once the coachman had let go of her. "I say, may I be of assistance?"

"Good God, yes," said a muffled voice from the dimness inside the coach, and Nate suppressed a chuckle as one slippered foot appeared, followed by two gloved hands that grasped at either side of the doorway. "If it weren't for these dratted skirts and this dratted bonnet, I could—who is that?"

"Sir Nathaniel Rankin, miss, delighted to be at your service. Now, if you could just, um, *boost* yourself toward the door? The coach is listing rather dangerously over the ditch, and I'd hate to see it entirely tip over before I can yank you, er, assist you out of there."

"I most thoroughly agree!" said the young woman, and more of her appeared in the doorway, minus the now-crushed straw bonnet he'd glimpsed earlier, revealing more of her face. "Hallo."

Nate smiled. "You know, miss, there really is no entirely polite way to do this. So, if you don't mind?" Before she could answer, he took her slim waist in both hands and lifted her out and up and then down, once her feet had cleared the bottom of the door.

Her hands were on his shoulders, his still on her waist, as she looked up into his face, her spectacles hanging only on a single ear, so that one rather lovely eye was uncovered and seen to be rather unfocused. "Oh," she said, but she didn't let go.

She was slim and rather tall, and with a mass of honey-blond hair that probably fell to her waist when it wasn't locked inside that thick coil at the back of her neck. Her eyes were blue, like his, but much larger; appealingly large and innocent. She had lovely lips on a rather wide mouth, a tip-tilted nose, and she smelled like violets. He thought it was violets.

"Sir Nathaniel was it?" she prompted in a very pleasant voice. "You…you can release me now."

"Hmm? Oh, right. Yes, of course," Nate said, then grinned. "You first?"

Twin flags of color appeared in her cheeks at once, and she dropped her arms to her sides, as if his shoulders had just caught fire. "How…how rude of me, Sir Nathaniel. I should by rights introduce myself."

"I would like that above all things," Nate said, surprised to realize he not only sounded sincere, he was sincere. "Let me fetch that dratted bonnet, shall I?"

"You heard me," she said, adjusting her spectacles.

"I'm afraid so, Miss—?"

"Penrose. Georgiana Penrose." She took the bonnet, scowled at it, punched it back into some semblance of shape and jammed it back onto her head, tying the pink ribbons beneath a rather determined chin. "Are you on your way to see the queen, Sir Nathaniel?"

Opportunity rarely knocked to such advantage. "Yes, I am, as it happens, Miss Penrose. May I suggest I have my tiger bring my curricle over here and we might travel the remainder of the drive together?"

Georgiana looked to the curricle sitting across the roadway. "The entrance is only a hop and a skip—but arriving on foot wouldn't look quite the thing, would it? That would be nice, Sir Nathaniel, thank you."

Nate made short work of summoning the curricle, putting his tiger to assisting the coachman right the coach, handing Miss Penrose up onto the seat, and then a few moments later depositing her on the ground once more—again by the simple expedient of picking her up at her tiny waist, as she didn't seem to mind.

Offering his arm, they climbed the front steps, and Nate lifted the knocker, twice, then waited for someone to answer the summons.

That took some time, during which Nate tried for something else to say to Miss Penrose and could think of nothing. How unusual.

The door opened, and a liveried footman eyed them curiously. "The queen, she is not receiving today," he said with a thick Italian accent, and attempted to shut the door once more.

"Oh, no, wait!" Miss Penrose said, actually putting out her arm to press her palm against the door, an action that classified her, in Nate's mind, as a real Trojan. "I am Georgiana Penrose, here to see Miss Amelia Fredericks. At her invitation. Please, tell her I'm here?"

The footman looked at Georgiana, looked at her hand, pressed against the door, looked at Nate. "Also to see Miss Fredericks?"

"Naturally," Nate said as he handed the footman his card, still allowing fate to guide his moves. After all, anything was better than "Would you like to buy some apples."

"Miss Fredericks, she's in the bath. Always in the bath, Miss Fredericks. You'll have to be waiting."

"We can do that," Nate said, looking around the marble-lined foyer, wondering how this indiscreet fellow had been set loose to attend to visitors. "Where is the major domo?"

"Scusi?"

"The butler, man. Your superior?"

"Cane grosso!" The footman made several gestures with his hands, none of them flattering. "He has put the tail between the legs and run off."

"I see," Nate said, his Italian rusty, but not beyond knowing the footman had called the absent butler a big dog, which he imagined was some sort of insult. "But enough chitchat, my good man, riveting as it has been. Lead on."

The footman twisted his face into an expression half confused, half amused, and motioned for them to follow him.

Nate once again offered Miss Penrose his arm.

"I thought you said you'd come to have an audience with Her Royal Majesty."

"I did? Well, curse me for silly. You must have misunderstood," Nate said smoothly, avoiding her gaze.

"I don't think so, but it would be likewise silly to argue, wouldn't it? How do you know Amelia?" Georgiana asked as they followed the footman to a small reception room just to the right of the foyer.

"I don't," Nate said, waiting until Georgiana had seated herself before taking up a position of power—he hoped—in front of the cold fireplace; it had always seemed to work for his father. "Would you care for the truth?"

Georgiana looked at him curiously. "You were going to lie? Oh, don't tell me you're some nasty journalist, or one of those horrid men determined to destroy the queen's reputation."

Nate looked down at himself, then frowned at Georgiana. "I look like a nasty journalist? In this coat? Well, that's lowering, isn't it?"

"I'm sorry," she said, then that determined chin rose once more. "No, I'm not. Why are you here? Amelia is my good friend, and I would be devastated if I've somehow aided you in entering an establishment you have no business entering."

"I'm no bogeyman, Miss Penrose," Nate said, and gave up telling her anything but the embarrassing truth. "I'm here because my aunt Rowena, a considerable admirer of the queen and missing more than a few slates off her roof, if you must know, believes that the king may be out to murder her. The queen, that is, not Aunt Rowena, although, with my aunt, you can never really be sure. I couldn't turn down my aunt's request that I come save the queen from a dire fate—disky heart, you see—and was sitting across the road, cudgeling my brain on how to get myself past the butler when you came along. So, when you get down to the bottom of it, I suppose I'm here to save the queen from the king's axman, which you have to admit is dashed brave of me."

Georgiana slowly took off her spectacles, then just as deliberately replaced them. "I see. You're a madman, Sir Nathaniel, and a very bad liar. Would you mind terribly if I screamed for help now?"

"Oh, must you? Don't be so chickenhearted, Miss Penrose. I'd really much rather you allowed Miss Fredericks to believe that I am your very persistent suitor, welcomely so, which would give me a jolly solid reason for accompanying you here today, and every day you visit with Miss Fredericks. You do plan to come here often, I most sincerely hope? Aunt Rowena would be over the moon if you do."

Then he grinned again, knowing that grin to be one of his more appealing attributes (his mother always said so). "Besides, although I've only just come up with the idea, it's rather good, isn't it? If we don't look at the thing too closely."

"You…you want to pretend to be my suitor? Are you mad? We don't even know each other."

"True," Nate agreed, trotting out his smile for another airing. "But that can always be remedied. Please, Miss Penrose, have pity on this desperate man. We'll visit with your friend, then drive back to town to make a call on my aunt. Five minutes in her presence, Miss Penrose, and I promise you, you will understand everything. Oh, and pity me greatly into the bargain."

He kept smiling, attempting to look harmless, as she

stared at him, seemed to be measuring him up against something or other. "What was that saying about looking a gift horse in the—" She closed her mouth firmly, then began again. "Very well, Sir Nathaniel, I agree. But only for this one time, unless your aunt can convince me to the contrary. Otherwise, my mother will accompany me on future visits here. And you'll behave yourself? You won't make a fool of me?"

He sat down beside her, lifted her hand to his lips. "Georgie, my sweet—I can hardly call you Miss Penrose, now can I, and you can call me Nate—Miss Fredericks is going to believe you are the happiest, most adored woman in the world."

"That's enough sloppiness for now," Georgiana said, pulling her hand free. "Our meeting has probably been inevitable. We're both quite insane, you know. *Nate.*"

"True enough, Georgie, but no one will notice if you do something about that hair," he said, pleased with himself. "Fetching color, but it's sort of falling apart thanks to that dratted bonnet."

Georgiana hopped up and went to the mirror hanging above a small table. "Yes, I can see that. My brains are leaking out. You wouldn't happen to have a comb, Nate, would you?"

AMELIA STOOD looking out one of the windows in her bedchamber, rhythmically pulling a silver-backed brush that had been a present from King Joachim himself through her still-slightly-damp hair while she watched the parade of boats. If anything, there were more of them this afternoon.

Queen Caroline had decided to take to her bed for the day, clutching a locket with a lock of Princess Charlotte's hair inside it, twined with a lock of her stillborn grandson's hair. The new king had such a keepsake, and Caroline had bribed at least a half-dozen individuals and threatened several more with revealing their past indiscretions, and had at last been delivered of a similar locket only three months earlier. Whether or not the hair truly had come from the princess and the young prince Amelia didn't know, and didn't inquire.

Still, rather than cheering her, comforting her, the locket had reduced the queen first to tears, then to anger at the world (and her husband and his family in particular), and then had settled into a deep melancholy that worried Amelia no little bit.

Do broken hearts really kill? If they did, her dear queen would be dead within the year.

Another young woman would worry for her own future, what would happen to her once the queen was gone, but this had never occurred to Amelia. She had been forced long ago to live in the present…except for those times that she lived in her dreams. Dreams that appeared more difficult to come by, as she had left her childhood behind and was now faced with more reality than it might be possible for one determined, yet virtually powerless young woman to deal with, no matter how she might wish it.

No prince would come to rescue her, mount her on his large, white charger and take her off to his castle in the clouds. No secret papers covered in seals would show her birth to have been more than it was. No aging, mourning queen would gather her to her bosom and tell her that she was, indeed, her own child, born of a great love between Caroline and some near-mystical hero out of a penny press novel she'd encountered after her banishment from her husband's side.

Amelia had dreamed the dreams of any orphan.

But she also knew none of that was real. These boats were real. The writ of Pains and Penalties was real. That sad, rapidly deteriorating woman lying in a darkened chamber, clutching a locket to her bosom and surrounded by her powerful enemies and her zealous supporters who cared more for themselves than they did that poor, frightened woman. All that was real.

Amelia sighed, turned away from the window, and allowed her majesty's maid to sweep her hair into a simple, upswept style, as the housemaid who had left with Carstairs had been hers. "How is your brother doing, Rosetta? Is he enjoying his new position of footman, do you think?"

"*Non, Signorina.* Gerado, he gets himself all about with each new thing. Too much for his brain, *si? O bere o affogare.*"

Amelia nodded. To Rosetta, Gerado was in over his head, and did not know whether to drink or drown. Poor fellow. It was time she broached the subject of sending their Italian servants back to Italy. Already their complaints about "this damp island," and "this strange tasteless food" had become a daily litany.

Besides, Baron Pergami was necessarily absent. No

need to have all these reminders left behind, many of them his poor relations, now was there? The queen had enough on her plate.

And when Her Royal Highness found out, as she had to do, that some of their former servants were being brought from overseas just to bring testimony against her, accepting money to do so? Mr. Brougham had taken Amelia aside and told her as much, and the information could not remain hidden much longer.

Yes, the Italians would have to go, much as Amelia would miss them. Because some of them, like Gerado, like Rosetta, had perhaps seen too much.

"I believe fussing will bring no improvement, Rosetta, thank you. Please return to the queen, who may need you, and I'll finish dressing myself," Amelia said as she got to her feet. After all, it wasn't as if she had anything more pressing to do, isolated as they were here at Hammersmith.

"CLIVE, FAR BE IT from me to spoil your fun, as nobody admires a spoilsport, I'm told. But I do believe you're courting trouble there. In other words, it might be best if you stopped flapping your arms like some flightless bird and sat down. This miserable boat rocks enough as it is, without your enthusiastic assistance."

"Love the sea, I do, M'Lord," Clive Rambert said, chancing a look over his shoulder at the Earl of Brentwood, the man he considered to be his real new employer. "Went by ship ta the Peninsula, and back again. Always on the lookout for one of those mermaids.

My mate, Sergeant Raymond, he see'd one the onc't. Masses of purty blond hair, and nary a stitch on her, neither."

"And you believe this," Perry Shepherd said, yawning into his hand. "How very droll. However, I had thought better of you than that, my friend."

Clive sat down abruptly in the front end of the small boat Perry had rented for the trip across the Thames. "He lied ta me, sir?"

"I'm only hazarding a guess, Clive, but yes, I think Sergeant Raymond might have been tugging on your ankle with that one."

"Well, blast me for a Johnny Raw. Spent weeks peekin' over the side of the ship, looking for one of them mermaids." Then he brightened slightly. "Are you sure, M'Lord? Maybe they all left the ocean, and swum themselves up here more? Lovely place, the Thames. Could be dozens of them out there, not just the one I was hopin' for. I'd swim here, iffen I could swim."

Perry stuck a cheroot between his teeth and put a light to it. "Then I doubly implore you to remain seated. Because, if you harbor any niggling thought that I might leap into the water after you to effect a rescue, you'd be quite disappointed as you sank to the bottom. Now, straighten your jacket, man. We'll be there soon enough, once we're through this press of boats."

Clive looked down at his new jacket. He was proud of it, he really was, but he wasn't certain if the earl thought it looked well on him, or was simply amusing himself at Clive's expense.

The jacket was blue, very dark blue, and with two rows of brass buttons lining the front. There were pretty golden braids on the shoulders, some of the fringe actually hanging over the ends of those shoulders, to drip down his arms.

And the hat. The hat was something very special, that was for sure. One of those high-domed contraptions with wings on each side, and more gold braid. Almost exactly what the captain wore on the ship that had brought him back from the Peninsula.

"Are yer sure, M'Lord, that I can be wearin' this? I look like a bloody admiral."

"Please, Clive, let's not insult officers of the Royal Navy with such comparisons. It's as I told you—the newest thing, all the crack. Why, I saw three very important hostesses in the Park yesterday, in much the same outfit. Long skirts, mind you, and not Wellington trousers, but still, much of the same style."

Clive's beady eyes all but bugged out of his ferret face. "Wimmen? I looks like wimmen? Here, now, that's not nice. Sir Willard warned me about yer, that yer're always on the look-see for a lark, but that's just not nice, to be usin' me for a giggle, M'Lord."

"You've never wished to captain a ship, Sergeant? I most distinctly remember, back in that most amusing shop we found, you telling me that perhaps you'd made a mistake, not going to sea, as you greatly admired the uniforms."

"Yeah…that's right enough. But wimmen? I'll not be wearin' this again, M'Lord."

"Dear me, man, of course you won't. One should never repeat oneself, once one has made one's first impression."

"Who's one? You talkin' about me again, M'Lord?"

"Never mind, Clive," Perry said, taking another puff on his cheroot. "Go back to playing captain of the seas, if it pleases you. We'll be docking shortly, and I'll be damned glad to be off this leaky tub."

As the leaky tub was actually a wide, flat-bottomed contraption boasting not only four heavily muscled oarsmen but a white silk canopy (fringed) that provided shade for His Lordship, who had been sipping wine from a real crystal goblet and munching on grapes from a large basket of assorted fruit, Clive only rolled his eyes and muttered, "Officers. Bloody soft, all of them. Took umbrellas into battle with them, they did. Twits."

"What was that, Clive?" Perry asked, barely able to stifle a chuckle.

"Nothing, M'Lord. Just thinkin' about this lady what yer're goin' ta see. Goin' ta impress her all hollow with this here boat."

"Yes, the boat. Heaven knows she won't be in the least taken with me. How you cheer me, Clive."

The runner hid a grin. "About time," he told himself, and snuck another look over the side, because Sergeant Raymond still could have been speaking the truth.

"IF WE'RE STILL SPEAKING with the gloves off…Nate…I think I should—"

"That's it, Georgie. *Nate.* Use it until my name spills

right off your tongue. We wouldn't wish to stumble at the first gate, now would we?"

"If you'd stop interrupting? I was making a confession here," Georgiana said, pushing her spectacles back up onto the bridge of her nose.

"Good grief. I'm courting a sharp-tongued miss, aren't I?"

Georgiana bit on the inside of her cheek for a moment as she stared at him, then asked, "Finished?"

"Done for, I think would be the proper term," Nathaniel said, bowing to her.

"Good. Now, what I told the footman? That I'd sent round a note and Amelia knows I'm coming here today? That, um, that wasn't quite truthful. I said it first to my mother, and it seemed like a good thing to say to a mother to placate her, but when Amelia sees me you'll know I was, um, as I said, stretching the truth a little."

"Stretching the truth? I think that would be more in the way of a lie. And a whacking great one, at that. Tell me, is she going to toss us both out on our ears?"

"No, no, of course not. We're the best of good friends, even if we haven't seen each other in years."

Nate tipped his head and looked at her with blatantly teasing scrutiny. "Anything else, Georgie?"

"Yes. Don't call me Georgie. I hate it."

"Well, that puts me in my place. So sorry, Georgiana."

"That's much better, thank you." Georgiana struggled for something else to say, wondering what was keeping

Amelia. They'd been waiting a good quarter hour now, and no one had so much as brought in a tea tray.

"And you'll allow me to send your carriage home while you accompany me to meet my aunt Rowena?"

"I said I would, didn't I?" Georgiana snapped, then immediately apologized. "I'm...I'm not very good at all of this, you know. They only just opened my cage and set me free from the country a month ago."

"Keep you locked up, do they? Somehow that doesn't boggle my mind as much as it probably ought."

"Oh, shut up," Georgiana said, very much at home with this strange man, which probably only proved that she was not fit for Polite Society. The man had a title, for goodness sake! "No, don't do that. Tell me again how very respected your family is, and how my stepfather will be throwing himself at your shoetops in gratitude that you've deigned to look my way."

"Pleases you, that part, doesn't it? I'd noticed that. In fact, if it weren't for knowing that this whole sham was my idea, I'd think it was yours."

Georgiana smiled. "Could we just call it serendipity?"

"Among other things, yes," Nate said, abandoning his position at the fireplace, to sit beside her on the couch. "Georgie—Georgiana," he said, taking her hand in both of his, "I think we're going to be very good friends."

Georgiana pulled her hand free, and sniffed at him— yes, sniffed—for she was above all things a practical young woman. "Careful, Nate, or else Mr. Bateman will be posting the banns. You have a mission, remember? To save the queen?"

"Wrong. To save my own skin. The queen's in no real danger. Even our king isn't that harebrained. You'll understand more when we leave here and travel to my family home."

"I thought you said we were going to visit your aunt Rowena."

"Yes, I did. She lives with her sister—my mother—and my poor, beleaguered father. He's the one who is going to be kissing your shoetops when he learns that you are to be my entry to this establishment. Anything to placate my aunt and, most important, silence her."

"Then we'll return to Mr. Bateman's house, and you'll meet my mother and Mr. Bateman? You did promise, remember?"

"Lies upon lies. I remember. I'm not precisely sure why I'm feeling so jolly about all these lies, but I am. Do you need those spectacles, Georgiana?"

The question surprised her. "No, of course not. I only wear them when I want to look bookish, and a horrid bluestocking into the bargain. And when I want to see what I'm looking at," she told him, leaning back slightly against the cushions on the suddenly small sofa. "Why? Mama says I'm lucky to get a third or fourth son, because of the spectacles. And the very slight dowry my late father arranged for me. Are they that awful?"

"Not as terrible as leaving them on your dressing table for vanity's sake, then finding yourself talking up a potted palm at some party, no," Nate said. "But I do believe we could seek out something not half so horrible. That is, more becoming to your face. Spectacles that at least fit."

"They're just heavy." Georgiana slammed the offending spectacles back up on her nose. "Don't all spectacles slip like this?"

"No. They don't. I'm surprised you don't knock yourself senseless at least a dozen times a day, poking at them like that. And the lenses aren't all as big around as moons. I am no expert, but I believe you're wearing gentlemen's spectacles."

"They were my father's, yes, and my mother said they were more than good enough," Georgiana admitted. "But different lenses were fitted for them."

"And in fifty years, you might just grow into them. In the meantime, we can search out better ones tomorrow, before I take you driving in the Park at five for the Promenade, all right?"

Georgiana chewed on this for a moment, mentally cataloging her woefully inadequate wardrobe. "The Park? In public? I thought this was only for Amelia. And Aunt Rowena. And my mother and Mr. Bateman, so they'll let me out of the house and you can play at saving the queen. But I thought that was all."

"Really. The question that immediately springs to mind, Georgiana, is who are you ashamed of? Yourself. Or, more reasonably, of me? My mama, for one, would understand that."

She stood up so quickly she banged a knee against the table and had to bite back a rather unladylike word. Country life and little supervision had done considerable damage to what were supposed to be her fragile female ways. "Now you're making fun of me, and I must warn you, sir, that I am more than capable of giving back as good as I get."

He also got to his feet. "Yes, I'd already noticed that. Dare I say you fair fascinate me?"

Georgiana looked at him, at his slightly unruly black hair, his laughing blue eyes, his altogether handsome face and figure. "Of course I do. I daresay I fascinate men every day," she said dryly, believing not a single word that came out of his mouth, then looked toward the doorway. "What on earth could be keeping Amelia? Do you think anyone told her I'm here? I vow, this is the strangest household."

BERNARD NESTOR made his way to the servants' entrance of the establishment in Hammersmith and knocked loudly on the door.

He'd been up and about very early, and had been hidden behind some shrubbery since seven, in ample time to watch the departure of what he was convinced were the butler, two footmen, and one hatchet-faced woman, all of them carrying their belongings in various portmanteaus and tied-up sheets. The woman most definitely had at least one tall candlestick shoved up under her apron.

The one he'd decided had to be an upper servant, if not the butler, secured himself a hack within a half mile. So he'd followed the others on foot, all the way to the nearest pub, and sat himself down behind them to listen to their conversation.

Good, thoroughly stupid English citizens, the trio of them, all of them appalled by the charges brought against their queen. And all of them finding her guilty because it suited their judgmental spleens, with no need to hear a single fact when supposition was so juicy, and unwilling to spend another night beneath the roof of such a disgraceful woman.

And he'd been right. The fourth person had been the butler, who had already promised to assist them in gaining new employment in a more Christian, God-fearing household.

So the queen needed a new butler, did she? Well, it had been about time Bernard Nestor's luck had changed for the better! And it wasn't as if he wouldn't know how to go on. He had lived in his father's house, hadn't he? He'd survived in that small office behind Brougham's butler's suite of rooms—*rooms* for a butler, with only a single, near-hole-in-the-wall for his most devoted assistant. Yes, he knew how to go on, and that knowledge, plus that niggling problem with the workings of his brain box, gave him untold courage, if not a chin.

Now he knocked again when no one answered, imperiously this time, and when the door finally opened, he stepped inside, declaring, "This is unpardonable. Never before have I been kept waiting! Who are you, woman? A name! Give me a name! Mrs. Fitzhugh? Housekeeper, I'll assume, for your sins. I tell you, now that I am butler here anyone who doesn't know how to behave will be shown the door, do you understand me?

Even you, Mrs. Fitzhugh. Already the queen has been left unattended too long, which is highly upsetting to Miss Fredericks, you know. Well? Cat got your tongue? Show me to my quarters, search out the attics for suitable clothing I'm sure is kept there for upper staff, as my baggage has been stolen by a pair of ruffians on the dock. Oh, and you may call me Mr. Nestor."

THE HOUSEKEEPER headed toward the main drawing room, wringing her still-trembling hands and talking to herself. "I tell you, Mrs. Fitzhugh, I don't remember Mistress Fredericks saying a word about someone to replace Mr. Carstairs. It hasn't been above a few hours since he left. She's a quick one, I'll say that for her."

"Now, now, Maryann," she answered herself, "just because you took the man in dislike doesn't mean there's anything wrong. Best to keep mum. Could get you the sack, seeing as how your background couldn't exactly stand up straight to much of a look-see, even if he said he'd made things all right and proper and—"

"All right, all right. But I can't like the man. He's got no chin. Our uncle Olivér had no chin, remember? Those same shifty eyes. And he never missed a chance to pinch our bottom. I'll not be turning my back on the likes of Mr. Nestor. Shh, footsteps."

Both of Maryann Fitzhugh peeked around a corner of the hallway to see Gerado pacing with his head down, muttering to himself in that suspicious foreigner tongue.

"Here, here. You're not to leave your post. Po-st. Po-sition." She raised one fist, pantomimed a rapping motion. "Door. Knock-knock."

Gerado rolled his eyes. "Visitors for Miss Fredericks. Tea and cakes, *si?* And to tell Miss Fredericks? And, *si*, the knock-knock." He raised both hands, palm up, and shrugged. "Where to go first, *capire?*"

"Yes, yes, I understand," Mrs. Fitzhugh crowed, thrilled at this breakthrough. Why, she was almost talking Italian herself! She pointed to Gerardo's chest. "You…go knock-knock Miss Fredericks. After, you go back to door knock-knock." She placed both hands on her bosom. "I…go kitchen for cakes and tea."

"Idiota," Gerado said, nodding his head as he turned and walked away.

Feeling quite generous, now that she'd managed to settle a domestic crisis Mr. No-Chin Nestor should have by rights dealt with, Mrs. Fitzhugh returned to the kitchens, just in time to answer yet another knock on the service door. Busy place, a queen's residence. How was she ever supposed to do what she came to do?

"Yes?" she asked imperiously, more prepared than she'd been when Mr. Nestor all but barged into the kitchens.

The woman on the doorstep was much of Mrs. Fitzhugh's own age, fairly round—well cushioned—and marginally attractive in a faded sort of way.

She didn't quite look the housekeeper in the eye as she dropped into an abbreviated curtsy. "My name, ma'am, is Esther Pidgeon, and I once served as maid in

the queen's household, when she was Princess Caroline.
I know I am being horribly bold, and I have no current
references, as I left service several years ago to marry.
But now that Mr. Pidgeon is gone, and once I saw that
the queen, that *dear, sweet* woman, has returned to our
shores, I had hoped, foolishly, I'm sure, that I could possibly once more be of service?"

Mrs. Fitzhugh took in every word. "So, you're not
here because Miss Fredericks called you here somehow?"

"Miss Fredericks? No, I'm sorry. I can't say as I can
place the name. We worked under a succession of
housekeepers, but that name is not familiar to me."

A silent conversation ensued:

Maryann: She seems decent enough. But no references? He had to have them for me, so they must be important things to have.

Mrs. Fitzhugh: Oh, cut line, Maryann. You don't
have the foggiest notion how a housekeeper goes on. If
this weren't a household of crazy foreigners, that
strange girl and one batty old woman, you'd never have
gotten a toe in the door, no matter what he wrote. As it
was, best thing could have happened was for that fool
Carstairs to take a flit. He was looking entirely too hard
at you.

Maryann: It would be lovely to have some say in who
is hired, wouldn't it?

Mrs. Fitzhugh: There you go. You want that odd Nestor fellow saying who stays and who goes? Call her your
assistant, why don't you? The girl wanted someone else
anyway. Partridges and all that.

"Very well. You're hired," Mrs. Fitzhugh said, and then bullied one young housemaid who most obligingly burst into tears. All while Esther Pidgeon looked on approvingly.

NATE WATCHED, standing back to keep himself safe from the exuberant hugging and rather hysterical female screeching as Miss Fredericks and his Georgie greeted each other. His Georgie? What was he thinking?

"I didn't know you were in London," Amelia Fredericks said, holding tightly on to Georgiana's hands as the two of them sank onto the couch. "I've already sent you a note, hoping you could come visit, but to your mother's country house."

"No, no, they brought me here, to marry me off to any poor fool who would have me," Georgiana said, then quickly looked up at Nate, panic in her eyes. "That is, um, Amelia? I should like to introduce to you my...my, um..."

"Sir Nathaniel Rankin, Miss Fredericks, although you may feel free to think of me as a prospective poor fool," Nate said quickly, executing what he knew to be an impeccable leg. "A delight, I'm sure. Georgiana has told me that you and she are great friends. How affecting it is to see such joy in Georgiana's eyes."

"Sir Nathaniel," Amelia said, allowing him to bow over her hand. "I cannot thank you enough for bringing Georgiana to me."

"Yes," Georgiana said, glaring up at him. "And now he's going to take himself outside to check on a coach that we passed on the roadway, stuck in a ditch, and offer his assistance in righting it. Aren't you, Nate?"

"I am? Oh, yes, of course, I am, I am. You two ladies just sit here and natter and I'll be out of your way."

A maid entered the room, carrying a heavy tea tray, and Nate grabbed up a freshly baked cherry tart on his way out the door, gratefully leaving Georgiana and Amelia alone to talk about whatever it is females talk about that men don't really care to know.

A half hour later, having enjoyed himself to the top of his bent in putting his back to pushing the Bateman coach out of the ditch, Nate wiped one muddy hand across his cheek as Georgiana appeared behind him, her hands on her hips and a smile on her face.

"You're filthy," she said. "And you look embarrassingly happy about it."

"It was tricky," he told her as he pulled out his handkerchief, which Georgiana took, then held up to his mouth so that he could spit on it. "Oh, I say, Georgiana, don't play mother with me—oh, all right." He closed his eyes, spit on the linen. "The wheel was fairly stuck, but m'tiger and I figured out how to shift it."

She scrubbed at his cheek. "Yes, I know. Amelia and I watched through the window. She thinks you're a very nice gentleman. I think you're an idiot, but a very nice idiot. Now, shall we go meet your aunt?"

"LAND HO, SIR, or ahoy, or whatever it is." Clive scrambled to his feet once more in the boat, putting one foot up on the low bow to steady himself as he pointed toward the shore. "And there be a lady on the boards, M'Lord, watchin' us come. See her?"

Perry narrowed his eyes and followed Clive's pointing finger with his gaze. "It could be, my friend, that we've struck gold on our first shovelful. Seems the artist was more talented than I'd supposed. Not beautiful, but still rather striking."

"She's the one Sir Willard talked about? Miss Fredericks?"

"I think so, yes. But now brace yourself, Clive, or else you'll—ah, too late," he said as the Bow Street Runner, decked out in all his naval finery, toppled head-first into the water. "How very inventive of you, Clive. But, then, I knew you'd come in handy. What a splendid entrée into the queen's residence, although first, alas, I'll probably be forced to save you. You there—yes, you. Mind scooping up my friend with your oar before he sinks again? Don't worry about the hat, it's no great loss. There's a good fellow."

Then he looked to the small pier, where the young woman he most ardently hoped would indeed turn out to be Miss Amelia Fredericks was calling out orders to have Clive rescued, then brought up the hill to the queen's residence.

Life, as Perry Shepherd had often found, was good.

THE QUEEN'S hastily put-together residence at Hammersmith.

Quite a crowded place.

The queen, of course, caught between her broken dreams and an attacking husband bent on destroying her.

Amelia Fredericks, practical, yet still harboring secret dreams, and utterly devoted to her queen.

Perry Shepherd, Earl of Brentwood, sent against his will and better judgment to seek out scandal by his uncle, Sir Willard, a staunch Tory and thus aligned against the queen.

And his faithful (and, at the moment, rather soggy) dogsbody, Clive Rambert.

Georgiana Penrose, Amelia's childhood friend, unaware of any intrigue, but happy to tell most any fib if it puts her in her friend's company and, frankly, keeps her mother and Mr. Bateman away from her as much as possible.

Sir Nathaniel Rankin, baronet, a young man who has reluctantly taken on one chore, protecting the queen on orders from his dotty aunt Rowena, only to find a second, much more enjoyable way of occupying his time.

Mrs. Maryann Fitzhugh, a most unlikely housekeeper, both of her.

Bernard Nestor, out to make any mischief, find any proof that would further his ambition…er, the queen's case.

And Esther Pidgeon, still pining for her Florizel, a woman for whom dreams have become an obsession, and willing to go to any lengths to destroy the upstart queen. Any lengths. Any.

Let The Games Begin

Pussycat, pussycat, where have you been?
I've been to London to visit the Queen.

—Anonymous

AMELIA HAD SPENT a lovely half hour with her good friend Georgiana before an urgent summons from the queen's maid had cut their visit short. With promises to see each other again as soon as possible, Amelia had hastened off to the queen's chamber, expecting to find Her Majesty still abed, still playing at tragedy queen (not that she didn't have good reason).

Instead, she'd found Her Majesty at her dressing table, her eyes half-shut while a fussing maid applied rouge to her cheeks.

As there was no sign that the bathtub had been employed, or even the pitcher and ewer on a dressing table to one side of the room, Amelia knew that the queen was in some sort of rush—and when the queen was in a rush, personal hygiene took a distant back seat to wherever the woman was in a rush to.

"Your Majesty," Amelia said, curtsying to the queen.

The rouge pot and brush went flying when the maid, clearly unprepared for Her Royal Majesty's abrupt about-face in her chair, turned on Amelia to ask in some excitement, "Did you see? Did you see?"

"See, ma'am? I'm sorry—"

The queen fluttered her ringed fingers toward the bank of long windows. "Oh, just go look—look! My people. My subjects! They come to bow to their queen, Amelia, in her hour of greatest need. I will win! You'll see, you'll see. For once in my life, I will best him. I will win!"

Amelia had gone to the windows, knowing what she would see below her, in the water. Boats. Boats and more boats, of every shape and size. And then she leaned closer to the glass. "There are banners," she said. "Signs."

"Yes, yes," the queen said, returning her attention to her toilette. "I had someone fetch me a spyglass. See it? Pick it up, my dear, and read to me from the banners."

Amelia located the spyglass on a table and did as she was bid. "Long Live Our Queen," she read, peering through the glass. "Hip, Hip, Hooray." She saw two more: Kick His Arse, Caroline, and Show Us Some Bottom, Dearie, but those she did not repeat to Her Majesty.

"You have so many admirers, ma'am," Amelia said, sliding the spyglass shut and replacing it on the table. "In England, indeed, in the world. It is so very gratifying."

"Ha! It's tweaking that miserable husband of mine, that's what it's doing. I can see him now, being told of what's happening. Stomping his feet, weeping copious tears into the bosom of his latest fat, aged mistress, calling for his leeches so that he can be bled of his ill humors. My heart has not been so light for years! Oh, enough, enough. When I wave from the balcony all they'll see will be their queen, not her wrinkles," she said, batting away the maid's hand. "Amelia, we must keep them coming here, hold on to their loyalty. Feed it."

Which was how Amelia had ended up donning a light wrap and picking her way down the flights of wooden stairs that eventually led to the small pier where she now stood with three footmen carrying heavy baskets of cakes and fruit, watching a pathetic man being pulled out of the water by the seat of his pants.

"Gently, my good man, gently. We shouldn't wish to crease him."

That voice, laden with amusement. Who'd said that? Who would say such a thing?

Amelia tore her frightened gaze away from the unfortunate fellow just now coughing and gasping on the pier, and looked at the gentleman gracefully picking his way to the front of the lightly rocking boat, then onto that same pier. He planted his cane on the dock, pressed both hands on the knob and leaned forward slightly, to look down at the nearly drowned man.

"Gad, Clive, all that spluttering. I warned you to be careful. Or did you think you'd spied out a mermaid?"

The nearly drowned man choked on yet another cough and raised his face to the man. "I coulda drownded."

"Nonsense, my good man. If you had but stood up, I imagine you could have kept your chin above water. Hmm…perhaps your eyebrows. A pity. If only his legs were straight, he might not have drowned. Correction, drown-ded. How's that for a sorry epitaph? Good thing I saved you."

"You did no such thing, sir," Amelia declared, motioning for the footmen to put down their baskets and help the wet man to his feet. "If anything, I would say you've seen this poor unfortunate's nearly fatal accident as…as some sort of joke."

The man—he was a man, surely; just a man; not some fairy-tale prince—immediately stepped in front of the wet man, removed his curly brimmed beaver and executed a most flamboyant leg in Amelia's direction, his startlingly clear green eyes raking her from top to toe even as he straightened up once more, smiled a smile that all but took her breath away.

"A thousand apologies, miss. A hundred thousand apologies. I am a cad, a heartless cad. But I did warn him." His cool, green gaze still on Amelia, he asked, "Didn't I warn you, Clive?"

"Not near soon enough," Clive admitted as he got to his feet on the slippery dock, then turned in a full circle. "My hat! Where's m'hat? Here, now, somebody fetch up my hat. Three quid that thing cost. Feed me for a month or more, three quid."

"Control yourself, Clive, if you please," the gentleman said, still looking at Amelia, who felt a sudden need to cross her arms over her bosom, for she felt stripped naked by that amazingly intense green gaze. "If I might introduce myself?"

Amelia waved her right hand slightly, as though talking might very well be beyond her at the moment. Never had she seen anyone so…so nearly perfect. Like a dashing hero out of her dreams.

"Thank you, dear lady. I, for my sins, am Perry Shepherd, Earl of Brentwood, delirious to be in your presence, as I had been racking my sorry brain for some paltry excuse to wrangle an introduction. You are Miss Amelia Fredericks, correct?"

"I, um, excuse me?"

"Yes, yes, use the oar, man. Snag it up with the oar. Oh, come on, now, lads, put some back inta it, the thing's floatin' away. Wait, never mind, it's comin' back this way. I can do it m'self. I'll just…lean…out…and…reach for—"

Splash.

"'Once more into the breach, dear friends, once more,'" the Earl of Brentwood said on a sigh, quoting The Bard as he turned about to incline his head to the oarsmen.

Amelia bit back a giggle (horrible of her to be amused, but there was no helping it) as the man named Clive was once more hauled onto the dock, this time with his hat upside down, brim clenched firmly between his teeth.

"God-id," Clive said, then spit out the brim. "Got it."

"Yes, my felicitations, I'm sure," the earl said even as he winked at Amelia as if they'd just shared a private joke. "The only wonder is that you haven't also landed a fish. Shake out the hat, Clive, why don't you, and we'll see if you have indeed been so lucky."

"Not me, M'Lord. Now yerself?" Clive said, trying

to brush bits of water weed off the hat. "Yer woulda come up with a turbot, already skinned and cooked, with a lemon stuck in its mouth."

"Most probably, yes." The earl bowed to Amelia once more. "You will excuse him, Miss Fredericks, as Clive here feels our friendship knows no bounds."

Years of maintaining control of her emotions when presented with the oddest of sights came to Amelia's aid, and she said evenly, "You address me by name, sir. How is that, as I am quite sure we have not been introduced."

Behind His Lordship, Clive shook himself like a puppy, spraying water everywhere, including on His Lordship.

Brushing at his sleeves, the earl said, "I believe Miss Fredericks has suggested you be escorted to the queen's residence, Clive, an invitation I strongly suggest you accept while I remain here and stammer out the reason for this quixotic arrival of mine."

"Wot?"

The earl turned back to Amelia. "Dear Miss Fredericks, much as I abhor such a public confession, I shall answer your question. I could deny you nothing, you see. I…well, this is embarrassing, isn't it? I chanced to see a broadsheet heralding the glorious and most welcome return of Queen Caroline to our shores, and a female figure was captured in the etching…engraving…whatever those things are called."

Behind him, Clive coughed into his fist.

"To continue," the earl said, turning slightly away from Clive. "So…so taken was I by the face the engraver had captured that I knew, simply knew, I had to find a way to meet that face. That face that is so much more than any artist, no matter how talented, could ever hope to capture completely. I begged everyone for a name, until I learned it, then rented that sorry boat on the desperate chance that I might catch a glimpse of you. I did, praise the gods, and demanded I be rowed to shore so I could approach you, hat in hand—"

"Literally," Amelia said, looking at the curly brimmed beaver he held. She had to say something. It was either that, or she'd burst into hysterical laughter. Did the man think she'd cut her wisdoms yesterday? He was lying, and laying it on much too thick and rare for even a hope of being believed.

"Yes, of course. Literally. In hopes I could somehow wrangle an introduction. If not an introduction, then perhaps as I've already said, just a glimpse, a single sight. Forgive me."

Clive stepped close to His Lordship and whispered out of one side of his mouth. "Pitiful, pitiful. Thought yer could come up with better than that, M'Lord. Crikey."

Amelia, like the earl, pretended not to hear.

"Clive? I thought you were on your way up the hill, hopefully to be stripped and wrapped in a blanket. Far be it from me to complain, but you're beginning to smell very much like a wet sheep."

"I suggest we all adjourn to the residence, My Lord," Amelia said. "I should like to hear more of how taken you were with the drawing of my most ordinary face. Perhaps you've written an ode to my chin?"

"She's onta yer, sir. I don't think I can stay here and watch, that's a fact," Clive said, then waved for the footmen to lead the way. "Hop-to, you buggers. You heard the lady. Drop those baskets and move yer dew-beaters. *March.*"

"A military man, you understand. Very colorful language, those soldiers, or so I'm told," the earl explained as the footmen all but ran into each other in their haste to obey Clive. "It's that air of command. Impressed me all hollow, I must say."

"Oh, wait, please. How could I have forgotten? Her Majesty has commissioned me to offer fruit and cakes to her…her admirers. She's up there now, on the balcony of her rooms, waving to—oh, she's gone. Still, I should have everything distributed."

"Orders from the queen, miss? It's on it, I am. *Halt.* Turn about, lads. When I give the word, start tossin' the goodies!"

"Clive, I don't think that's quite the method of distribution Miss Fredericks…" His Lordship began, but the footmen were already folding back the cloths over the baskets and hefting apples in their hands. "Yes, well, never mind. I'm convinced you know what you're doing. Carry on."

Amelia bit her bottom lip, watching as oars churned the water frantically, people flocking in their boats like ducks being offered bread crumbs, as apples, pears, bananas, small blueberry muffins—all were launched into the air.

"Compliments of Her Royal Majesty, you buggers!"

Clive called out, winging a bunch of grapes out over the water.

"Come along, Miss Fredericks," the earl said, holding out his arm to her. "Londoners being who they are, some of them doubtless will begin tossing things back."

Giggling, for the scene was really rather funny, Amelia slipped her arm through his and, together, they all but ran up the winding steps, to the terrace outside the queen's residence.

Amelia stopped, slid her arm free and held up one hand. "No farther, My Lord, until you tell the truth. Or did you really think I swallowed that horribly transparent lie?"

His Lordship stepped back a pace, raised one marvelously expressive eyebrow. "Some would."

"Some, My Lord, would believe the king has no motive save the succession in this latest of many attempts to destroy his own wife. I, however, am not quite so gullible. So, My Lord. Why are you here? Really."

"I couldn't have had my tender heart touched by the sweet image of your face?"

"I don't think so, no. But I will admit that it seems a reasonable ploy, if you were hoping some half-witted female attendant to the queen would be able to wrangle an audience for you. Did Lord Liverpool send you?"

"Liverpool? Please, Miss Fredericks, do not insult me so, even if you continue to insult yourself, which I find most endearing for some unfathomable reason. Although I must ask—why would Liverpool send anyone to the queen?"

"To peek under beds and listen at doors, to gather up any information that, in his mind and the king's, might assist in their persecution of Her Royal Majesty, of course. You wouldn't be the first, you know. I once had to have one of you removed from the Villa d'Este, while we were at Lake Como. I had him tossed in the lake. He landed on his consequence, then floated away."

The earl grinned, ear to ear. "Anyone I know?"

Amelia shrugged. "I doubt he presented us with his true name. Now, please answer my question, My Lord. Why are you here?"

The earl looked at the ground for a moment, then at Amelia once more. "This is most embarrassing. It…it was a wager, dear lady. I was drinking in one of my clubs and rather in my altitudes, I'll admit it, and I wagered with a friend that I, not he, could have tea with the queen. My friend already attempted to find his way in, but he was turned off at the first gate, leaving the field open for me to win. The prize is a monkey."

"I beg your pardon? A monkey? Whatever would you do with a monkey?"

"Yes, as I already have Clive, that would seem superfluous, wouldn't it? But a monkey, Miss Fredericks, is actually five hundred pounds."

Amelia felt her eyelids widen. "You wagered five hundred pounds that you could find a way to have an audience with the queen? Are you out of your mind?"

"If one lends any credence to rumor, yes, I suppose I am, as I do already carry the title of a useless fribble,"

His Lordship said, smiling. "So, am I to be tossed out on my ear, madam, to float away?"

"You should be," Amelia said, folding her arms beneath her breasts. "I don't appreciate being made a May game of, you know."

"That was crass of me, I agree. Cruel. And yet so very close to the truth. Or have you traveled only among the blind, Miss Fredericks? For only a blind man could fail to appreciate your unique beauty. Indeed, once I'd seen your likeness in the newspaper, no other ploy save nearly the complete truth could possibly have occurred to me."

"You're doing it again, you know, attempting to flatter me. I do have access to mirrors," Amelia said, part of her wanting this silly, grinning, lying man gone; another, more romantic side of her believing that there could not possibly be any harm in a light flirtation with this remarkably handsome man. She'd flirted before; one could not be in the company of the queen and her varied coterie of admirers without being the object of some flirtation.

The earl's smile widened. "Do I do it well? The flattering, that is?"

"Exceedingly well, yes," Amelia admitted. "Oh, why not? We're needfully informal at the moment. It's only a cup of tea, and the queen enjoys the company of silly gentlemen. And your man—Clive, is it? He really should have some tea or hot soup before he catches his death. It's chilly here, on the water."

"Even more so in the water, I would imagine."

"Of course. I think the queen will find you amusing. We haven't had a court jester since Italy."

"I live only to serve Her Royal Highness," the earl said as he extended his arm once more.

Amelia took it, and, together, they entered the queen's residence.

CLIVE ENTERED the kitchens behind the footmen, blinked against the dimness after the bright sunlight, looked around and dropped his jaw to half-mast (which was fitting, him being a nautical man and all, at least in his clothing).

"Maryann?"

Maryann Fitzhugh, who had been gathering up cups from the scarred wooden table, turned all at once, the cups dropping to shatter against the stone floor. "Clive? My stars—Clive Rambert!"

"Maryann," Clive repeated, his soft tone so unlike him that any of the men who'd served with him would have wondered if the man was sickening for something. "How long, Maryann?"

"Years, Clive. Years and years."

"Yer were going ta wait, Maryann."

"I did, Clive. I waited."

"Mrs. Fitzhugh?" Esther Pidgeon said, entering the room. "I've settled my things in my room. Rather small, but it shall do nicely. Mrs. Fitzhugh?"

"Mrs. Fitzhugh, Maryann? Is that how yer waited?"

"It's not what you think." Maryann's face paled. "I had no choice, Clive. You got away. You left."

"I went ta war, Maryann," Clive said, slapping his wet hat against his thigh.

"Excuse me," Esther said. "Is something wrong, Mrs. Fitzhugh?"

Maryann shook her head. "No, no, Esther. Nothing's wrong. Clive? You're all wet."

"Noticed that, did yer? I coulda been all dead."

"But that's the whole thing. For so long I thought you were."

"Oh, so you two are acquainted? Isn't that nice. Shall I order…that is…fetch tea?"

"YOU'RE QUITE SURE you don't want me to ring for tea?" Amelia asked as she sat on one couch and Perry sat on its twin, which faced it across a low table. "There is, of course, no possibility that you will see the queen today. She is not receiving."

"My loss, I am sure," Perry said, casting his gaze about the drawing room. "Do you suppose there is some way for me to prove that I've at least been here?"

Amelia blinked at him. "You want to take something of the queen's?"

"In point of fact, yes. I should like to take you, Miss Fredericks, for a drive in the Park. Tomorrow at five, in time for the Promenade?"

"At which time you'd have your fellow bettor hidden behind a tree, to see us drive by, therefore proving that you have won your monkey?"

"And so many say they dislike intelligent women," Perry drawled, making his way to the drinks table he'd

located tucked in below a bank of tall windows. This
was going well; this was going better than well. And he
only felt a little bit guilty. "Sherry, Miss Fredericks?"
he asked, holding up a crystal decanter.

"Yes, thank you," Amelia said, then cocked her head
to one side, as if inspecting him. "So. You're a fribble,
is that the term you used? Perhaps even a ne'er-do-well?"

"A totally useless lump, yes, but not a ne'er-do-well.
Perhaps more of a ne'er-do-anything," Perry said, handing her a glass. "Wealthy, titled, incurious about the
world and how it works, bored into near insensibility by
politics, but utterly fascinated by the cut of my waistcoat, the speed of my horses, the precise mix of my
sort—snuff, that is—the quality of my dinners. Do I
look ashamed, Miss Fredericks? Mine uncle vows I
should."

"Your uncle is sadly disappointed, I'm sure, My
Lord, as you look quite—quite satisfied, with who and
what you are." She shrugged. "But I do believe the
world needs butterflies, as well as worker bees."

"And worker bees need their queen," Perry slid in with
what he thought was near brilliance on his part. "Evidence
of that truth can be found in those who have made their
way here today, to honor her, to welcome her, to place
their hope in her. At least," he ended, frowning, "that's
what Clive tells me. He, you understand, is a worker bee.
I thank you again for your concern for the man."

"He was all wet, My Lord," Amelia said, putting
down her still-half-full glass. "I could do no less."

"And I can do no less than to beg you to please allow

me to take you to the Promenade tomorrow, Miss Fredericks. And not for any wager. You are fairly isolated here, I know, and I would correct that."

"You would, would you?" Amelia answered, running her gaze up and down his body in a way that would make a lesser man fear for his motives. Impressive young woman, Perry decided; handsome in her way, and quite intelligent. Very pretty eyes, that just might see too much. "Will you also be truthful with me?"

Perry sat down, spreading his coattails neatly, and crossed one long leg over the other. "I am nothing if not truthful, lies being so fatiguing to recall when necessary."

"All right, then. Why are you here?"

"The wager, Miss Fredericks, remember?"

Amelia frowned, and Perry felt his first pangs of guilt. It took him some moments to recognize this response, as he had so seldom experienced that particular emotion.

"You really are as silly as you say?"

"Oh, more so, Miss Fredericks, more so. I vow to you, we have yet to scrape the first layer off my shallow self. Fortunately, there are only two of them. The silly layer and the feckless one, I believe it could be termed. Indeed, I am quite a worthless fellow."

"So you say, again and again."

"Yes, this compulsion to confess my lapses to you amazes even me. Perhaps I should set aside an hour this evening, to think upon this phenomenon. But no, I can't. I'm already promised at the theater. Ah, well, perhaps another time?"

"Amelia? I have not been informed that we have a visitor."

Perry immediately leaped to his feet and bowed deeply to Queen Caroline, scarcely able to believe his luck (although he'd always been lucky; otherwise, he would not still be aboveground). "Perry Shepherd, Earl of Brentwood, gloriously honored, at your feet, and at your command, Your Royal Majesty."

He watched as the queen entered completely into the room, her rather garish dress and ridiculous and rather soiled blond wig vying for attention with her rouged cheeks and kohl-darkened eyes. "Amelia? Why was I not informed that the earl has come to see me? Are you keeping secrets from your queen? Am I to trust no one?"

"Your Majesty," Amelia said, dropping into yet another curtsy as she answered the questions. "His Lordship has just now arrived, by boat, ma'am, and I sought to offer him refreshments and ask the purpose of his visit."

"Vetting him for me, were you? Very well, Amelia. Oh, sit down, Brentwood. God knows I'm going to. Amelia? You've dispensed the boons?"

"The fruit and cakes, ma'am? Yes, I have seen to it. The people were delighted."

"I know, I watched through my spyglass, from behind the windows. I watched, Amelia, as you allowed Brentwood here to escort you into my house without my permission." She turned to wink at Perry. "I am much smarter than my husband knows, Brentwood. Are you smart enough to know he's a fool?"

"I fear, ma'am, that I pay little attention to weighty matters. But," he added, smiling, "I would have had to have been locked in a box in a cellar not to know that our king is not in good odour with many of his subjects."

"In good odour? Ha! They loathe him, Brentwood. He is guilty of every crime, every evil, every failing—and yet he comes attacking me? I tell you, Brentwood, I tell you, I cannot bear this, simply cannot—"

"Ma'am?" Amelia interrupted, offering the queen her nearly untouched glass of sherry. "Perhaps it was unwise to leave your chambers? You did say you were unwell."

Queen Caroline snatched the glass from Amelia's hand and downed its contents in one long gulp, while Perry did his best to pretend an interest in the rather depressing hunt painting hung over the fireplace.

The next thing he knew he was on his feet again, as the queen had risen, looking about distractedly as Amelia took her arm, urged her toward the hallway.

"My Queen," Perry said, bowing yet again (dear, dear, but there was a lot of bowing and such to deal with when in an audience with one's queen).

"Not just yours. *England's* queen, Brentwood," the queen countered, flecks of sherry-colored spittle gathering in the corners of her mouth. "I am England's queen, and he tells them I am England's whore."

"Oh, look, ma'am, here's Rosetta, come to tend to you. Would you like me to attend you, as well?"

"A splendid idea, Miss Fredericks," Perry said quietly, realizing that the queen was all he'd heard and more. "I am sure someone will direct me as to where to locate Clive, and then we will be gone. Until tomorrow, for the Promenade?"

"Yes, yes, fine," Amelia said as the queen leaned heavily against her and the two women departed the room, leaving Perry very much alone.

His uncle would probably tell him to take advantage of such an unexpected stroke of luck, and go investigating in cabinets, in corners, in drawers.

But Perry had never planned to do any such thing. He'd accomplished what he'd wished to accomplish— he'd gained entry into the queen's domicile. He never intended to do more, no matter how adamantly his uncle requested more of him. It was only important to keep his uncle from summoning the thoroughly unscrupulous Jarrett Rolin to take his place.

Besides, he already had seen enough, more than enough. The queen was more than candid, more than indiscreet. She was on the verge of losing her mind, if she had not already crossed one bridge too many in her hatred for the king.

Henry Brougham had to know, as he had access to the woman. Many of the most powerful of the Whigs had to know. Yet they would fight this Bill of Pains and Penalties. They would stand behind their queen, in the hopes that her success would mean their return to power.

It was sad, that's what it was, and Perry felt very much in need of a bath, not because of his Tory uncle who would only be delighted if Perry brought him evidence of the queen's supposed adultery, but because of how all of England had their own plans to use, and then most likely discard, this poor, ruined queen.

Perry picked up his hat, cane and gloves and walked into the hallway, to look up the winding staircase. In the middle of all of this intrigue and selfishness and, yes, madness, Amelia Fredericks shone like a beacon of true devotion to her queen, with no notion of personal gain.

He admired that; he admired loyalty. He admired the fact that she seemed to ask for no reward, and not expect one, either.

Spying for England, working to defeat Napoleon, had been what Perry had sought to do, and the thought of recognition, of reward, had been repugnant to him.

He recognized Amelia as a kindred spirit in that regard.

But he was not so simple as to believe that one slim girl could protect the queen from those who would destroy her, or from those who would "save" her for their own benefit. His uncle was a very powerful man, with powerful friends. Liverpool could be formidable.

Brougham? The man had ideals, which made him vulnerable. He did not have the instincts of a shark detecting the scent of fresh blood in the water. But, ideals or not, Brougham, too, seemed more than ready to use Caroline for his own ends, or else he would have urged her to accept the allowance and exile that had been offered her, rather than convinced her to return to claim her crown.

In truth, Miss Amelia Fredericks stood alone in her defense of her queen, if someone did not offer to stand beside her.

"*Tch*, *tch*. You may have made quite a dangerous mistake in sending me here, Uncle Willie," Perry said quietly as he swung his cane up and onto his shoulder and went off, unimpeded by any servants, in search of Clive Rambert.

"YER'RE NOT Mrs. Fitzhugh?" Clive asked, leaning closer to Maryann, glorying in the heady smell of peppermint, gently backing her up against the stones of the far side of the wall just outside the kitchens.

"Never think it, Clivey! I'm still your Maryann Filbert, but who would hire a housekeeper who is not a missus, I ask you? No one, Clivey, as I soon found out."

"There's no Mr. Fitzhugh? Never was no Mr. Fitzhugh?" Clive asked, the sort of man who needed to feel that his questions, answered twice, were necessary to ferret out any lingering lies or truth.

"No, Clivey, no Mr. Fitzhugh," Maryann said, blushing. "I'm pure as you left me."

Clive preened a little, smiled. "That weren't none too pure, Maryann, as I recall the thing."

"Oh, stop it, Clivey," Maryann said, batting the back of one hand against his chest. "You were leaving in the morning to follow the drum. What else could I do?"

Clive sighed, lost in memory. "Yer da woulda flayed me alive…"

"Da's dead and gone, Clivey, these past dozen years or more. I had to leave, as there was nothing there for me once he cocked up his toes. I couldn't stay, not if I couldn't work for the duke, and he was so purse-pinched he wouldn't take me into the house."

"So yer came ta London," Clive said, stepping closer. "Ah, Dovey, it's been too long...."

"Oh, Clivey, if you only knew...."

"Oh, dear God, I've stumbled upon a scene of billing and cooing," the Earl of Brentwood drawled, leaning on his cane. "Clive, my felicitations. I had no idea you were such a terror with the ladies."

"Sir!" Clive said, nearly tipping off balance as he sprang to attention. "It's not...it ain't...I'd never—"

"Ah, you're laboring under the mistaken impression that I desire an explanation, my good fellow? Far be that from the case. However, as I'm leaving now, perhaps you'd wish to join me? After your fond farewells, of course."

"Yes, sir," Clive said, exhaling. He watched until His Lordship had turned a corner in the path, heading for the steps to the dock, then looked at Maryann. "He's a good'un, Maryann. Only a little daft."

"Will I see you again, Clivey? I so hoped to see you again," Maryann asked, touching her fingers to his cheek. To Clive's eyes she was still his Maryann; with no gray in her hair, no lines in her face. And he was still her Clivey.

"Tomorrow, Clive, tell her tomorrow," came his answer, called out to him by the earl. "Miss Fredericks needs a chaperone when we go driving in the Promenade."

"Thank you, sir!" Clive called back, not overly surprised that the earl had lingered out of sight to eavesdrop.

The man probably wanted to know if he was going to give the game away, tell Maryann why they were here.

Clive would have been insulted, if he was easily insulted. Instead, he was reassured that Sir Willard had not stuck him with a beetlehead.

"I've always wanted to drive in the Park, Clivey. You're so important now, aren't you?" Maryann asked him.

Clive drew himself up to his full height, which put the top of his head only two inches below that of Maryann's. "I've been places, Dovey, seen things that would burn your eyeballs straight outta your head."

BERNARD NESTOR, clad in his ill-fitting black rescued from the attics, and smelling badly of camphor, rubbed his eyes a second time, still unable to believe what he could see through the window of his new quarters.

"The Earl of Brentwood," he said aloud, then shook his head. "Sir Willard's heir, everyone knows that. Leaving by the back door? Sneaking about like a thief? Why?"

He nearly jumped out of his too-large shoes when the knock came at his door. What to do, what to do? He was the butler, correct? What could someone want from the butler? He was in charge; he gave the orders.

And solved the problems.

Oh, dear…

"Come, er, come in?"

"Mr. Nestor, sir?" Maryann Fitzhugh said, holding on to the door latch as if it were her only anchor in this world. "I thought you should know…that is, I think Mr. Carstairs would have wanted to know…I'll be accompanying Mistress Fredericks to the Park tomorrow afternoon. But, but Esther will be here. That would be Mrs. Esther Pidgeon? She's, um, my assistant?"

Bernard fought down his nervousness. "Esther Pidgeon, you say?"

"Yes, oh yes, sir, Mr. Nestor. Good woman. I depend on her mightily, sir."

"Very well. If she's, um, familiar with household routine, I cannot see a problem. Is there anything else, Mrs. Fitzhugh?"

"I could take a stitch or two to those drawers of yours? I sew a fine seam. Truly love the needle, I do. Oh! Begging pardon, Mr. Nestor. I never should have said…"

"Yes, yes, you're forgiven, Mrs. Fitzhugh. Now, perhaps you'll apprise me of daily routine under Mr. Carstairs? I…I believe in tailoring my…my butlering to each individual household, each individual need. It would not do to discommode Her Majesty in any way, now would it?"

"DID YOU SEE Her Majesty, Natey? Did you, did you? Oh, sit down, sit down, tell me you saw her, tell me you warned her about what I saw in my—" Aunt Rowena cut herself off before she could say just where she had looked to "see" the queen's demise, and peered suspiciously at Georgiana. "Who're you? I don't know you. I distinctly remember who I know, and I know I don't know you."

"Now, now, Aunt Rowena, we should remember our manners, even in times of great trial," Nate soothed, leading Georgiana into the drawing room of his parents' Mayfair mansion. "Aunt Rowena, please allow me to introduce to you Miss Georgiana Penrose, a most extraordinary young woman and good friend of the queen's companion, Miss Amelia Fredericks. Miss Penrose has agreed to help us save the queen. Haven't you, Miss Penrose?"

"I did no such—oh, yes, of course, of course," Georgiana amended hastily, for she'd now had enough time to see that Aunt Rowena, bless her, was definitely a sweet old tabby who, as Nate had said, just happened to have misplaced several slates from her mental roof. "I am delighted to be of assistance, madam."

"Yes, yes, good. You may call me Aunt Rowena. Definitely Aunt Rowena, as Natey brought you. Sit down, sit down. Tell me what happened. Everything. Every word. Oh, you're such a good boy, Natey."

Georgina bit her lips together to keep from giggling as she visually inspected Aunt Rowena. She had rather suspected the older woman would dress in flowing clothes, lovely pinks and light blues. That she'd have girlish curls on her head, flutter her heavily ringed hands about nervously.

In fact, Aunt Rowena wore unremitting black that buttoned to halfway up her scrawny throat. Her hair was unfashionably short, and white as snow. Her thin hands were gnarled and blue veined. She looked rigid, austere. Until she opened her mouth, at which time she let out the rather appealing cuckoo bird inside the rather forbidding, blackbird exterior.

Above all else, she looked frail. Unhealthily frail, as if she could snap in two under any sort of anxiety. No wonder Nate had agreed to find a way to calm the woman's worries.

Aunt Rowena took a deep breath, sighed. "You know, Caroline and I—she was the Princess of Wales then—we were very good friends. Oh, not very good friends, I'm fibbing here, aren't I? Fibbing, yes. How can royalty be very good friends with a lowly commoner like myself? But we spoke, on several occasions, and she was quite kind each time. Sad but kind." Her hands twisted together on her lap, she leaned forward, toward Georgiana. "He's going to kill her, you know. Kill her dead. Unless Natey here can save her."

"Now, Aunt Rowena, you can't really know that," Nate said kindly, only a hint of exasperation in his voice.

"I can't? I saw it, Natey. I saw it happen. Saw it."

"In your tea leaves," Nate said as he looked at Georgiana as if to add, "I warned you."

"No, not my tea leaves. Never in my tea leaves, Natey. Tea leaves are for small things, little problems, tiny solutions. I saw this in my dream, Natey. And my dreams are never wrong."

"I stand corrected," Nate said, rising to fetch himself a glass of wine, even as a maid delivered the tea service in front of Georgiana, who knew it would be her job to do the honors, pour, as Aunt Rowena looked strong enough to lift a teacup, but nothing heavier.

"Sugar and milk, Aunt Rowena?" Georgiana asked,

then prepared the tea. "Tell me, what did you see in your dream? A knife? A pistol? Poison?"

Obviously delighted to have an interested audience, Aunt Rowena put down her teacup, patted her rather blue lips with a linen serviette and leaned forward. "Well," she said, tossing Nate a smug look, "I saw this bird. Bad bird. Huge, yellow-eyed, orange-beaked monster of a bird. And then a crown, a golden crown, covered in glittering jewels. Pretty jewels. The bird saw it, swooped down and snatched it away. Snatched it, lifted it from the velvet pillow it rested on and carried it off. Flew off! To a graveyard. A dark, dreary, damp and cold graveyard. Dropped it to the ground and flew away. Dropped it into a bottomless grave."

"I…I see," Georgiana said, feeling new sympathy for Nate and his family. "And from that you deduced that the queen is in danger? Excuse me, but could it not have been the king, as well?"

Aunt Rowena blinked. "I did it again, didn't I? I did, yes, I did. I forgot to tell it all. The bird, the crown, the graveyard. All of it, all of it. And the laughing lion."

Nate sat down once more, beside Georgiana. "Oh, well then, the laughing lion. Goodness, Miss Penrose. I don't know about you, but that last bit convinces me."

"Stop it," Georgiana said, almost jabbing him in the ribs with her elbow but stopping herself in time. "There is a lion on the royal crest, is there not, Aunt Rowena?"

The older woman openly preened. "Lions. Lions everywhere. Male lions. All that hair around their heads, you know. Manes? Watching it all, and laughing. Laughing. Your own father said it, Natey. It would make the king very happy to have her dead. That's when my dream made sense. Makes sense. Yes?"

"My father was just speaking idly, Aunt Rowena. I doubt he really—but no matter. You're not to worry anymore, or pest my parents with those worries, promise? Mostly, you are not to worry. You know it isn't good for you to fret. Miss Penrose and I are…we're on the case. Aren't we Miss Penrose?"

"Oh, yes, of course," Georgiana said, her sympathies with the dotty old lady, and with the entire Rankin family, most especially Nate. He was a good man. Sweet. And so very handsome. She wouldn't lie to herself and say she was not attracted to the man.

Then again, when was the last time a man had even come into her orbit? A gentleman, that is, and not the silly boys she'd played with all those years she was left free to run wild in the country while her mother and her new husband forgot her existence.

"Oh!" she said, looking at the clock on the mantel. "I've been gone for hours! I…we really must be getting back to Half-Moon Street."

"Yes, of course. Aunt Rowena? If you'll excuse us?"

Georgiana allowed Nate to help her to her feet, then gave in to impulse and went round the table to place a kiss on Aunt Rowena's papery cheek before they headed for the curricle once more, the old lady calling after them not to forget the bird, the bird of death.

"You were very kind to her," Nate said as he tooled the ribbons through the growing traffic of a Mayfair afternoon.

"You expected me to be otherwise?"

Nate grinned at her. "You never say what I expect you to say. Plain speech, no maidenly simpering. I like that."

"Thank you, I suppose," Georgiana said, and fell into silence.

"And here we are, home again, home again, jiggity-jig," Nate said as they turned onto Half-Moon Street. "Tell me, how dazzling do you want me to be? I want to keep up my end of the bargain, you know. Shall I sing your praises or just stare at you soulfully?"

Georgiana scrambled to collect her thoughts. "I… um…oh, for goodness sake, Nate, you know better than I. Enough to keep my mother from pushing any more linen merchants' sons on me, and not enough that she's ordering the bridal linens, I would suppose."

Nate threw back his head and laughed. "I may have to rethink that drive in the Park tomorrow. I may end up beating away my friend with sticks, if I'm to have any time with you at all."

"YOU'RE TO GO DRIVING in the Park? *You?* While I stay here and molder? I won't have it! How can you even dare to come into my presence, you selfish girl!"

Amelia tried not to wince as a vase she particularly favored went spinning across the room, to shatter against the wall. She'd avoided the queen's chambers for as long as possible after the woman's nap, and now she understood why.

"I don't have to go, ma'am," she told the queen, who had punctuated her outburst and vase flinging by stamping her feet and pouting like a child denied a treat. "You had just but to say so earlier. I'll see to it that a note is sent round to the earl."

Queen Caroline pressed her palms to her cheeks. "No! Go, go! Leave me! Desert me! Everyone else has. William. Pergami. All of them! Oh, I wish I were dead, dead like my poor Charlotte. At least then I might find some peace."

Rosetta rolled her eyes as she walked past Amelia, on her way to the dressing room, to mix some laudanum with water in Her Royal Majesty's tooth glass. *"Non perdere i capelli."*

Don't lose your hair. Rosetta was warning Amelia to hold on to her temper. Which was a good thing, Amelia realized as she unclenched her hands, which she had drawn up into impotent fists. Dealing with the queen was never easy, but sometimes balancing her compassion for the woman against the frequent absurdities and these increasingly high flights of hysteria was exceedingly difficult. And most exasperating.

"Ma'am," she said as the queen threw herself onto a chaise, lifting her forearm to shield her eyes as she moaned. "Ma'am, please, you'll do yourself…injury."

Her anger cooling as rapidly as it had heated, Caroline lifted her arm to peer piteously at Amelia. "He goes everywhere. His father dead in his grave, and he goes everywhere, is welcomed everywhere. But Brougham says I must remain here, be circumspect in all things. I cannot bear it, Amelia. I crave life. I need life. I wither and die without it."

Amelia's tender heart was touched, as it always was, by the sadness of this woman. "We had such parties, didn't we, ma'am? Away from here."

"Oh, we did, we did. And such adventures, Amelia! I have given you the world, and now I take it away again. England takes it away. Beware England, Amelia. England takes everything."

"Perhaps," Amelia said, daring to sit on the edge of the chaise, and take the queen's hand in her own, "perhaps if we cannot be out and about, ma'am, we can entertain here?"

"Brougham would forbid a party, a ball. The old king, remember? My husband can pretend to be in mourning, but I must truly be in mourning. Everything I do is watched, commented upon, condemned. I am without friends. Everyone has deserted me. He may as well have banished me to a nunnery."

Amelia spoke quickly, before Her Royal Highness could take her hysteria out for another flight into the treetops. "Even a small party, ma'am? A very small party?"

"Here?" The queen sat up, all attention. "Not Brougham or his whiny brother. They depress me. Who could we have?"

Amelia kept her gaze steady. "Well, the Earl of Brentwood seems an amusing enough sort, ma'am. And there is my friend, Georgiana Penrose, and an extremely nice young gentleman who accompanied her here today, to visit with me. Sir Nathaniel Rankin, ma'am."

"Your friend? A young woman, then. How I love

young people around me. So full of life. Yes, we could surely do that. A simple dinner party. Perhaps some music later—you could play, Amelia. And cards? Tame stakes, I promise you, but the gentlemen will want to play cards, surely. Yes, yes, we can do this. I can do this. And once it is known that I am entertaining, the invitations will come. You'll see! Tomorrow, Amelia, plan it for tomorrow. No! I will plan. Send me that housekeeper and Carstairs. That's his name, isn't it? Carstairs?"

And here things had been going so well....

"I'm sorry, ma'am, but Carstairs is no longer with us."

Caroline took the glass Rosetta offered her and drank down its contents before her kohl-darkened eyelids opened. "He died?"

Amelia waited until a sniggering Rosetta had retired from the room once more. "No, ma'am. He…he was called away, quite suddenly. A family problem, I believe."

The queen was many things, several of them less than commendable. But she was not stupid, especially in how the world worked when those workings affected her. "He left, didn't he, Amelia. He learned of my latest disgrace, and he ran away. Coward! Hypocrite English! Casting stones when they have boulders enough of their own."

"We are better off without him, ma'am."

"Who else? Who else have we lost to my wretched, lying, vindictive husband?"

"A few others, ma'am, none of them important, there are dozens left. Mrs. Fitzhugh and I are already finding replacements. But I would like to discuss something else, if you feel up to it, ma'am?"

"Does it matter? Bad news does not wait upon my strength."

"Yes, ma'am. I've been thinking, and perhaps it might be best for Rosetta and her cousin Gerado to return to Italy. Where Lord Liverpool can't find them, ma'am."

"My Rosetta? But she has been with us for so long. Even on the *polacca* on our way to Syracuse, Pergami and I. She has been invaluable to me. I could not possibly—" the queen's complexion paled beneath her rouge "—I…I will miss her."

"Indeed, ma'am, we will miss them both. I'll make arrangements for their departure?"

"With all due speed," Caroline said, then closed her eyes, as the laudanum had begun its work.

"It's GONE NINE, boy. I've been waiting all day," Sir Willard said from his place on the couch, his wrapped foot resting on a folded blanket. "What did you do, Nevvie? Crawl here?"

"And a pleasant good evening to you, too, Uncle," Perry said, pouring himself a glass of wine. "Waiting with the proverbial bated breath, were you? While dozens would swear you didn't care if I disappeared from the face of the earth."

"Never mind that. Did you succeed? Did you get in? Did you see the gel?"

"Done, done and done. Anything else, or may I be excused now? I really do have other invitations to occupy my evening, and I took an unconscionable amount of time in my bath, I'm afraid. Something about removing the stench of your nefarious plan to destroy a weak, terrified and most probably powerless woman. Tell me, do you Tories toast each other every time you pound another nail in her coffin?"

"Spare me these melodramatic transports, Nevvie. I do what must be done to preserve England."

"To preserve yourself and your gaggle of cronies, as well as a sad cartoon of a king concerned only with emptying the country's coffers with his insane building projects, now that he can no longer fornicate."

From the doorway, where he had been lingering nervously, Clive Rambert snorted.

"Ah, good," Sir Willard said, spying Clive. "At last, some sanity enters the room. Speak up, man. Report!"

"Sir!" Clive said, coming to attention, although Perry was pleased to see the man stop short of a salute. "We approached the destination by water, sir, able ta make landfall with no resistance."

"And yet, alas, it was not a perfect landing," Perry added, saluting Clive with his wineglass.

Clive took a deep breath. "The earl here, he talked his way inta the queen's residence, sir, and I m'self am happy ta report that I have gained entry ta the kitchens." He relaxed slightly. "Have the run of the place if I wants it, sir."

"He's halfway to seducing the housekeeper, in point of fact. All in all, Uncle, I'd say Clive here made quite a splash," Perry said, at last beginning to enjoy himself.

"Really," Sir Willard said (having a quite literal mind,

and very little humor), looking at Clive. "And you, Nev-vie? Who did you seduce? Is the gel hot for you?"

Perry's expression closed. "Strange. I had never be-fore considered you to be overtly crass, Uncle. Must be the company you keep."

"He was talkin' up Miss Fredericks a treat, sir," Clive said quickly, "just like yer told him ta. They're going drivin' in the Park tomorrow. He did good, sir."

Sir Willard glared at his nephew. "Now, why couldn't you have told me that? Why make me drag it out of you? Tell me the rest. Did you see the princess—the queen?"

Perry didn't hesitate to lie. "I'm afraid not, Uncle. She was otherwise engaged during my visit, I'm afraid. At her prayers."

Sir Willard sniffed. "Praying? Chasing the knife boy around the pantry with her bodice down to her waist is more like it. What's wrong with you, boy?"

"He's goin' soft of Miss Fredericks, sir, if I may say so. Flatterin' her all hollow, but not all in fun, if you take m'meanin'? But he'll do what yer sent him ta do. He's a good 'un, at the bottom of it."

"Thank you, Clive. Perceive me as all but unmanned by your loyalty."

"Yer're that welcome, sir, whatever it is yer said." Clive then turned once more to Sir Willard. "He's takin' me and Mrs. Fitzhugh up tomorrow with him and Miss Fredericks. We're ta be in the way of chaperons. In the Park, sir. Paradin' around with the rest of the toffs."

Perry put down his wineglass. "Yes, it's true. Clive? You'll wear the dark green, please. And come to me at three, so that I might manage your neck cloth. You will be with me, remember, and I do have a certain standard to maintain."

"Yes, sir," Clive said, clearly delighted. "A good 'un, Sir Willard. He's a good 'un."

Sir Willard moaned into his own cravat. "Are either of you going to remember your mission?"

"To dig up scandal to destroy the Queen of England? How could we possibly forget such a lofty, laudatory mission, Uncle? Why, I cannot wait until the delicious moment I might slip free in the residence, to delve into locked cabinets and chamber pots."

"Do you think it would be at all possible of you to stop mentioning chamber pots, Nevvie? We're up to our necks in chamber pots."

"Oh, Uncle, don't say such things," Perry said, pretending to plead with the man. "If this is true, I'll have no choice but to cut you a wide berth when we meet in Society. Upwind, as it were."

Clive shoved two fingers into his mouth and sucked on them, to keep himself from laughing.

"I'm ignoring you, Perry," Sir Willard said, although the top of his bald head had turned rather red. "We've enough chamber pots, we've got testimony to hear from her servants. What we're looking for, Nevvie, are letters. From the queen, to the queen. Love poems from that Pergami fellow, that sort of thing. We understand the queen takes a certain large tin case with her wherever she travels. To date, we have not been able to have a look inside. That's your precise mission. Bring me a letter from Pergami, recounting how he longs to again make love to the dratted woman—any such incriminating drivel—and we may be able to stop this damn nonsense before it reaches the House of Lords. She'll take any allowance we might give her and consent to exile, if we can give her solid proof that we know she is not fit to be queen consort. Find whatever papers are inside and bring them directly to me."

"Most like they keeps it in a box room, M'Lord, right?" Clive suggested, looking at Perry. "Shouldn't be so hard to find the thing with Dov—er, Mrs. Fitzhugh helpin'." He turned to Sir Willard. "How big you say this case is, guv'nor?"

Sir Willard rolled his eyes. "How should I know such a thing? It's a large tin case, man. Find it, Nevvie, pick the lock—that is one of your many dubious talents, isn't it?—and bring me what I need. And do it quickly, Nevvie, or soon all of London will be nothing more than a tawdry circus."

"And it's not now, Uncle?" Perry said, and took his leave, Clive on his heels.

"In a bit of a snit, the guv'nor," Clive remarked as they climbed back into Perry's town carriage.

"Really? I can't in truth say I noticed," Perry said, settling against the velvet squabs as his coachman prodded the horses forward. "Now, Clive, think of me as your tutor, please, as I explain to you the niceties of driving through the Park for the Promenade."

"I'll be hangin' on yer every word, M'Lord," Clive said, leaning forward in his seat that faced the earl's.

"Do we wave ta everyone? That would suit Dovey for a treat."

"Dovey?"

Clive nodded furiously. "Mrs. Maryann Fitzhugh, M'Lord. But she never bracketed herself to no Mr. Fitzhugh. That's just a hum ta get her hired by you gentry coves. She was Dovey back when I knew her, afore I went ta the army. We had us a time, we did. She'd do anythin' for me, M'Lord, feelin' bad the way she is about not waitin' for me, thinkin' me toes cocked up somewheres. I'll bet she could tell us all about that there tin case the guv'nor is so hot about."

"Yes, thank you, Clive," Perry said, wishing away the subject of tin cases, of spying on the queen. He would also be gratified if unsettling thoughts of how Miss Amelia Fredericks would hate him once he'd betrayed her trust would stop crowding his suddenly weary mind.

AMELIA LOOKED ABOUT the crowded Park with a curious, if not delighted gaze. In her travels with the queen, she had seen many sights, in many lands, and this rather sedate parading of exquisites seemed…well, slightly silly.

There were cabriolets, gigs, drags, high-perch phaetons, town coaches, vis-à-vis, and barouches very much like the one she rode in now, although none of them quite so fine or riding behind a better, more sound quartet of horseflesh. There were many gentlemen riding on horseback (as the earl had already informed her that ladies were, for the most part, confined to riding in the mornings), there were couples strolling arm in arm.

And all of them, everywhere, were obviously there to see, to be seen, and to show off their latest finery, like peacocks on the strut.

"So this is the Promenade? I can't imagine why the queen would envy me this excursion," she said to Perry after the barouche had moved forward only a few feet in ten minutes, as every other conveyance seemed to halt each inch or so, to greet friends. "One immense jumble of traffic for an hour, and then everyone goes home again?"

Perry smiled at her. He had a lovely smile, and she really should avoid it if she hoped to be able to concentrate on anything but him, his handsome face and the fact that she was sitting rather close to him, and that his long-fingered hand rested on his thigh, only a few inches from her own. "My congratulations, Miss Fredericks. You have just pointed out one of Society's greatest failings—a complete lack of understanding as to what makes us look like pleasure-seeking, fairly worthless fools."

"I'm having fun," Maryann Fitzhugh whispered to Clive, the pair of them on the facing seat. "You're having fun, ain't you, Clivey?"

Amelia lowered her chin, hoping the brim of her bonnet concealed her smile. "Oh, dear," she said, only loudly enough for the earl to hear her. "I'm being ungrateful, aren't I?"

"Immensely so, most definitely," Perry told her, reaching over to squeeze her gloved hand, only for an instant. "And you've missed the greatest delight so far of this daily exercise, although I'm sure there will be more."

"And that is?" Amelia asked, daring to lift her head once more.

Perry leaned close, whispered in her ear. "The opportunity to laugh at our fellow paraders, of course. Or had you not noticed the spindly shanked exquisite who pranced past us in his red heels not a moment ago, bits of sawdust spilling out of the hem of his breeches."

"Sawdust?"

"To give himself a leg, if I may be so bold, and I am often bold. Buckram padding at the shoulders, sawdust molded to resemble muscular calves. The poor man seems to have sprung a leak. We're a sorry lot, we gentlemen."

"You employ buckram padding, My Lord?" Amelia asked, already knowing the answer. She'd more than once seen gentlemen stripped to the waist to indulge in fisticuffs for the amusement of Queen Caroline, and she felt certain that His Lordship's muscles owed nothing to artifice.

"Oh, now you wound me, Miss Fredericks, and my tailor, as well, I should imagine. Excuse me a moment, if you please. Clive? My good fellow, loath as I am to spoil your fun, I have it on the highest authority that it is never polite to point."

"Er, sorry, M'Lord," Clive said, dropping his hand to his lap and redirecting his gaze to the floor of the barouche. Speaking out of the corner of his mouth, he said, "That was Harriette Wilson and one of her sisters just now on the other side of the path, M'Lord, I'd bet my new waistcoat on it. Didn't know the har—that is, the impures rode in the Promenade."

"They always have, Clive. Some of them, most often those without titles, actually deign to earn their living at it."

"Now I know you shouldn't have said that in my hearing, My Lord," Amelia scolded, blushing. "Is society really so...so loose?"

"Society, Miss Fredericks, left off its stays a long time ago. They just do not, for the most part, publicly advertise that fact."

"As does Queen Caroline," Amelia said, sighing. "I accompany her, My Lord, but I am not in charge of her. Indeed, it wasn't until a few English ladies took me aside, while visiting at Lake Como, and told me, that I realized my queen's behavior was not...was not just what was expected of her. I had no idea we were such an outrage here in England. Everyone seemed to be enjoying themselves, you understand."

"So I've heard and read, yes," Perry told her as the barouche moved forward yet again. "And you were a guest at these...affairs?"

"I was present at our entertainments, yes. Lovely balls, fetes, and Her Majesty herself often would perform in amusing harlequinades in the small theater in the Villa d'Este. Her Majesty enjoys laughter and fun and has a lively interest in people, places. Do you know that we rode into Jerusalem on donkeys? I would not give up a moment of my life with the queen, My Lord."

"Nor should you, Miss Fredericks," Perry said, and his tone was sincere, she was positive of that, and her admiration for him grew.

"I know now that we were at times outrageous, My Lord. Which is one reason this horrible Bill of Pains and Penalties has been brought. But it's not the real reason. It's that the king hates…" She looked over at Clive and Mrs. Fitzhugh and bit her lips between her teeth.

"I say, Clive, I do believe Miss Fredericks and I have decided to climb down and have ourselves a stroll. You won't mind remaining here? You have my permission to wave to whomever you wish, although I would ask that you refrain from whistling at any of the passersby."

Amelia waited as Perry opened the low door and then held out a hand to help her to the ground. "Where are we going, My Lord?"

"We're on the run from the once-pleasant smell of peppermints. Or would I be forever damning myself if I were to say that I am aware of a place in the Park, a lovely wooded area, where those who wish to be alone cannot be observed by all and sundry?"

"Probably," Amelia said, and then smiled as she slipped her arm through his crooked elbow. "Shall we?"

Amelia could not help but notice that, although the earl smiled and waved to seemingly everyone, he did not pause, stop to talk, introduce her to anyone.

It wasn't until they had seemingly without purpose "wandered" into a leafy stand of trees and decorative shrubs that she asked, "Are you ashamed to introduce me, My Lord? The taint of being of the queen's household?"

She looked up at him, to see that his jaw had gone hard, and he guided her deeper into the shade before at last stopping, turning to take her hands in his. "Miss

Fredericks, you know as well as I that you would only be considered a part of the sensation that is swirling around the queen's head. Is that what you wish? To be pointed at—as Clive pointed—and, believe me, the elite of Mayfair are more than capable of behaving much more badly than Clive could even imagine."

She was quiet for some moments, then said, "Amelia. Please. I should like it very much if you were to call me Amelia…Perry."

His expression, which had been close to frightening, softened. "Amelia. Then we've cried friends, if I may use such a mundane expression?"

"I hope we have, yes," Amelia said, her gaze open and steady, because she had never been taught or, indeed, had observed much in the way of artifice. "The queen and I seem to have a sad lack of friends. Or didn't you know that, other than Henry Brougham and his brother, you are the first to visit us since our arrival? Many have sent notes of support, but only a paltry few have visited."

Perry, still holding her hands in his, took a small step backward. "But surely…"

"But surely not, Perry. I am not at all political, but I do believe the Tories would rather be stripped to the buff and paraded through this Park than to be seen tooling carriages or rowing boats to visit Her Majesty. And the Whigs? They wish to be sure she'll win before they'll openly back her. Or am I wrong? As I said, I'm not in the least political."

"If you say so, then I, as a gentleman, have no recourse but to agree with your description of your unpolitical self. However, you have said it exactly right. Society is made up of hungry jackals and shivering gazelles. Both are watching Her Majesty, watching how this will all play out. All of them hoping they will live to see another day."

"No, that's not quite right. The watching has already passed. Her Majesty is already being savaged by the jackals, Perry. The gazelles are hiding. The gazelles can't protect her. And I think the queen knows that, even as she hopes otherwise."

Perry let go of her hands and slid an arm around her waist, leading her deeper into the trees. "And where are you in all of this, Amelia?" he asked.

"With Her Majesty. I know no other home." She wished, yet again, that his eyes were not so all seeing, and that all she could think was how lovely it would be to rest her head against his strong, broad shoulder and give up all her troubles as she placed herself in his care.

"I won't say that I'm not worried about you, Amelia," Perry said, gently maneuvering her so that her back was against a slim tree trunk as he stood before her, his eyes now shaded by the brim of his hat, the sun filtering through the leaves dappling both of them in light and shadow.

"I'm not entirely helpless," she said, and heard her own voice quaver.

"Aren't you?"

She shifted her gaze away from him. "Powerless, yes. But not helpless. I can at least give comfort to Her Majesty in this time of trial."

"So you won't leave her?"

Amelia's head shot up. "No! I could never leave her."

Perry lightly touched a knuckle underneath her chin and lifted her face closer to his. "And you wouldn't, even if you had the opportunity. Would you? You're loyal, even in the face of sure defeat."

Amelia moved her head away. "Don't make fun of me. And don't look at me as if I'm some silly, romantic martyr. I know Her Majesty has flaws."

"And there are so many out there who would pay, handsomely, to learn what you know."

She looked at him again. Had she made a horrible mistake? Had she been so hungry for someone to talk to that she had put the queen in danger? Had she so longed for a friend, a shelter, someone to trust, that she had trusted the first person to be kind to her? Seen nothing but this beautiful man with the winning ways, let her mind believe him some ridiculous prince, some knight in shining armor? "Are you suggesting…?"

He put his hands on her shoulders. "Surely you've thought of it, Amelia."

She bit her lips between her teeth, shook her head. "No, I haven't. And I won't. So if you've brought me here to ask me if I would, then you can just take me back to Hammersmith. I will never betray her."

"I know," he said, and his tone was so soft, so intimate, that she dared to look at him once more. "I've seen you with her, remember? You have a great affection for that sad, unfortunate woman."

She began to relax. "And you don't think I'm being

silly? Shortsighted? After all, if the king succeeds in discrediting her, I cannot see a future in which Her Majesty will continue to exist. His victory will kill her. Literally. Oh, I'm sorry," she ended, blinking back sudden tears. "It's…it's just that I'm so alone. I have no one to talk to about my fears. No one who doesn't have their selfish reasons to support her. No one to trust."

"You have me now, Amelia, if you want me," he said quietly, and then lowered his head to hers.

His lips were warm and firm, and although she'd been kissed before, her reaction to this kiss was completely new to her. She melted against him, her arms sliding around his narrow waist.

He deepened the kiss, and she let him, opening her lips to him, welcoming his tongue as he stepped closer to her, insinuated one leg between her thighs as she was pressed against the tree trunk.

Guilio had stolen a kiss at Lake Como. Silly boy. She'd kissed Jergun in Germany, because he'd asked so nicely. There was that moment in Rome, when she almost believed her heart might be involved, but when Sebastiano had dared to put a hand to her breast she had slapped him, and run away.

She was not unexperienced, surely.

And yet this kiss? This man? She barely knew him, yet felt no hesitation. No warning bells clanged in her brain, no reluctance to allow him even more intimacy tugged at her conscience.

Just his kiss, his hard body taking control of her without force, yet so completely, with such confidence.

And now his hands…lightly skimming down her arms, sliding onto her waist…sliding, oh, so slowly upward…cupping her, molding her.

"Perry…" she breathed his name against his mouth, her eyes tightly closed, because if she looked at him, at this beautiful man, he might just disappear.

He broke the kiss with seeming reluctance, trailing his lips across her cheek, into her hair, his breath teasing her ear. "I'm a very bad man, Amelia, but I would not take back these few moments for my hope of heaven."

As he spoke, he rubbed the pads of his thumbs over her nipples, and they stiffened beneath the soft muslin of her gown before he removed his hands to her waist once more. Clearly, telling him that she felt his an importune assault on her person would be as silly as attempting to make him believe the sky was polka-dotted.

"Her Majesty would tell me that it is wrong to deny what you want simply because the world frowns on anything that makes you happy."

His chuckle was light, infectious. "I like Her Majesty more and more. May I steal another kiss, or have I dared too much?"

Amelia pressed her cheek against his chest. "I think we both have dared too much, here, in this place. I must be shameless."

He rubbed the palm of one of his large, strong hands against her back. "Or very vulnerable in your distress," Perry said, "which would make me a scoundrel of the first water. To prove I am at least marginally respectable,

I'll forgo that kiss, if you will promise me that our first was not our last."

Amelia smiled against the fabric of his jacket. "Now you're teasing me, Perry, so that I am put in the position of having to ask for your kiss. Shame on you."

He put her from him, holding on to her arms so that she looked up into his smiling face. "My folly, you will learn, knows no bounds. And now I have been more than naughty enough for one afternoon, and Clive will surely begin to fret."

He smiled as he straightened her bonnet, then flicked a finger against the side of her nose. "You are bad for me, puss. You make me honest. I'm unfamiliar with the concept. Shall we see if my equipage has progressed more than fifty yards in our absence?"

"Do you know, Nate, I believe these new spectacles have improved my sight? I'm more used to seeing the areas closest to me, with everything else melting into a rather lovely smudge of colors in the background. And, I must say, although I have been in this Park a few mornings, with my mother, I never realized the place was quite so crowded."

"It's not, not in the mornings," Nate told her, smiling at the way she was most enthusiastically looking about her as they strolled across the grass, arm in arm. "Tell me, Georgiana, do you think, if we were to join hands and run toward those trees, we could outdistance your maid?"

Georgiana turned to look back at Imogene, who was

actually her mother's maid, and a woman not best pleased to have been dragged out of the house for a healthful constitutional when her pressing irons awaited her in the dressing room. "She'd tattle," Georgiana said. "Otherwise…"

"I knew it. You're a hellion, aren't you?" Nate asked, unable to restrain himself. "You look like a bread-and-butter miss, all sprigged muslin and pink-cheeked, all blond and soft. But, at the heart of it, you'd rather be traipsing about the countryside, your skirts lifted above your ankles, on the lookout for a grassy hill to roll down. Admit it, Georgiana, this place, Mayfair, that is, is not where you wish to be, is it?"

"Am I a country bumpkin at heart? That's what you're asking, isn't it? Very well. You're right. London is a lovely city, when it's not dirty and crowded and smelly, but it isn't a patch on Sussex. I could not imagine living here more than a few weeks a year."

"All those boring parties and routs and alfresco picnics. The theater, the museums, the shops. Too boring for words?"

"No, that's not it. They're very nice, I suppose. They have their place. But to be like my mother? To exist for London? I'm showing myself to be a sad lump, I'm sure, but I'd much rather be in the country with the birds and the trees…and the rest of the bumpkins."

"My estate is in Surrey, you know," Nate told her as he tipped his hat to two ladies who were looking toward Georgiana in some interest. "I first left it with relief, not realizing how much I'd miss it. Now I come to London for the Season and hie myself back to Surrey as quickly as I can. My mother insisted we stay in town this year to be supporting props to my father. He's known about the queen's return for some time now, you understand, and was warned to keep himself accessible. Just think, I would have already been gone, Georgiana, and never have met you. That would have been a bleeding shame, wouldn't it?"

Georgiana didn't know how to respond, for she felt more than fairly certain Nate was flirting with her even as he worked so hard at playing the gentleman, and was entirely uncertain whether he was merely teasing her or being serious. She had no notion if this was the sort of conversation all London gentlemen indulged in when on the flirt—and she was entirely too honest to lie. So she said nothing.

"Georgiana? Am I frightening you?"

She shook her head and, wonder of wonders, her new spectacles did not fly off her nose. "I think you are a very nice gentleman, Nate. Mr. Bateman was in fact over the moon to hear your name, and my mother has canceled a small dinner party she had planned, with Mr. Harold Goodbody as our honored guest. He's a rather successful draper, I understand, widowed, with four small children in need of a mother."

"E-gods," Nate said. "Is your mother insane? No, don't answer that, as I should never have asked. But, really, has she really brought you here to London to marry you off to a draper?"

"I'm sure Mr. Goodbody is an honorable man, working in an honorable profession," Georgiana said, and then grinned. "And he probably wouldn't mind being shackled to a woman of good lineage and little dowry, and who wears spectacles, and who has been known to ride astride when she hoped no one would see her and report such a serious crime to her mother and stepfather."

"In short, your mother considers you a sad trial and wants you popped off and gone?"

"Oh, most definitely, especially as I seem to insist on growing older even as she strives to tell everyone she is growing younger," Georgiana said, then stopped, suddenly realizing that Nate had led her into a stand of trees. "I had no idea this little pocket existed. Why, it's as if London has melted away, isn't it?"

"Is it?" Nate asked, looking about as if only now realizing where they were...how far they had walked, leaving the paths and walkways and all the people behind (including, quite fortuitously, Imogene). "Well, stap me, will you look where we are? Miss Penrose, have you steered me here with designs on my person? May I say that I am shocked—shocked—to think you believed you could presume on our very short, if mutually advantageous, association and deliberately lead me off to have your wicked—"

"Oh, shut up," Georgiana said, lightly punching him in the stomach.

"Thank God," he said, grinning at her. "I was getting myself in rather deep there, wasn't I?"

"As you are the one who led me here, yes, I would say you were. Do...do you really want to kiss me? Why?"

Nate looked at her. Then he smiled at her. And then he threw back his head and laughed out loud. "Oh, Georgie, you have no idea, do you?"

"So now I'm stupid, as well as a graceless bumpkin. Thank you very much!"

"No, no—you're far from stupid. You're refreshing. You're honest. You are kind, as many would have run, screaming, from me, and from poor Aunt Rowena. You care as little as I do for Society, and don't care a snap who knows it. Good God, woman, you ride astride! And one thing more, Georgie. You have the most beautiful eyes I've ever seen behind those, I say in all candor, most bewitching spectacles. Almost as appealing as those lovely lips, parted now as you no doubt ready yourself to tear another verbal strip off my hide."

He couldn't be further from the truth. "Don't call me Georgie!" she said, just before she launched herself forward into his arms, planting those bewitching lips—no, they were "lovely" lips…she'd heard him most distinctly—against his before either of them had a chance to think.

"I imagine I should be stepping in here, challenging this importuning cad to a duel for attacking a fair lady…except that I do believe it's the other way round. What say you, Amelia?"

Georgiana's eyelids popped open wide at the sound of the drawling, clearly amused masculine voice, and she hopped back from Nate, her arms quickly falling to her sides. Imogene, if they hadn't happily misplaced her at some point, would undoubtedly have cried "Oh, lawks!"

at this moment, and Georgiana would be a liar indeed if she didn't long to make a very similar exclamation.

"Georgiana? Is that you?"

Georgiana kept her back to the intruders on what had been, in fact, the first truly marvelous event of her heretofore humdrum life. "Amelia? Oh, God…"

"Why, Miss Fredericks," Nate said, taking Georgiana's hand firmly in his and turning her about. "How delightful to make your acquaintance again today. And, damme if that isn't the Earl of Brentwood with you. Brentwood, your servant, sir," he ended, bowing.

"I'm missing something here, aren't I?" the earl asked Amelia, and the world in general. "Explain, Sir Nathaniel, if you please? What are you doing, pawing Miss Fredericks's friend this way?"

"I should perhaps ask where you and Miss Fredericks have been, My Lord, as it would appear that you are leaving the wood, not entering it. Not that entering this lovely, concealing stand of trees is anything more than two entirely innocent people seeking the shade on a warm day."

"Oh, stubble it, Sir Nathaniel. We caught you, you caught us. Now, do we swear mutual secrecy as the four of us stroll negligently into the sun once more, innocence brightly shining on all our faces, or do we point accusing fingers at one another?"

"You know Sir Nathaniel, Perry?" Amelia asked, and Georgiana finally took a good look at her friend. Amelia looked rather flustered and quite happy. Reflecting, as it were, how Georgiana herself felt.

Amelia quickly made the introductions, then slipped her arm through Georgiana's so that the two of them could stroll ahead, leaving the gentlemen behind them, to find their own way back into the sunlight.

"Ah, Sir Nathaniel, that's not good. They'll talk about us incessantly, you know," Georgiana heard the earl say. "I don't know about you, but, for the first time in my seemingly useless life, I believe I fear for any recital of my reputation."

Amelia paused for a moment, looked behind her and giggled, then urged Georgiana on once more.

"I didn't know you knew anyone in London, Amelia," Georgiana said as she caught sight of Imogene in the distance, looking ready to burst into either frustrated tears or shouts of recrimination for having been so summarily deserted.

"Oh, I didn't, I don't," Amelia said. "Just you and your beau, and the earl, of course. He'd hoped to win a wager by gaining an audience with the queen, and got me instead. Have you ever seen anyone so handsome, Georgiana? Just like the golden-haired princes we read about in those novels we hid in our room at school."

"He is pretty," Georgiana said, blushing slightly as she added, "although I can't say I'm partial to blond hair on a man. I much prefer—oh, never mind. And stop laughing!"

"Can you believe it, Georgiana? It's just as we talked about, so long ago. You and I, traipsing through London Society with two very well-set-up gentlemen. I'd ask you to pinch me, except then I might awaken, and I don't want to be awake if my dream is so wonderful."

Georgiana gave her friend a quick hug, then sobered. "Amelia? Are we idiots?"

"I am, most assuredly," Amelia said, sighing. "I've only just met Perry…the earl. Just yesterday. And yet… and yet I know I can trust him, that he's sincere. But you? You and Sir Nathaniel have been courting for some time, isn't that what he said yesterday?"

"I, um, that is, yes. Yes. For some time," Georgiana said, not wishing to have Nate be discovered as a liar. Besides, the entire thing was much too complicated, and rather self-serving on her own part. Better to leave things as they stood, and not upset Amelia with thoughts that Aunt Rowena just might be right. Amelia worried about the queen enough as it was.

"Ah, and here is my barouche, still housing Clive and his beloved, who seem to be enjoying themselves mightily," Perry said as the two gentlemen rejoined them. "Sir Nathaniel? It would be a squeeze, but we could take you up and deposit you where you wish to go?"

"My tiger is minding my curricle, thank you, Brentwood," Nate said, bowing. "Perhaps we shall meet again?"

"You may depend upon it, good sir," Perry said, returning the bow.

Georgiana and Amelia kissed goodbye, and Perry extended his arm. "Oh, wait!" Amelia said. "I completely forgot. Her Majesty has decided you three shall be her guests at a small, informal dinner party. If the weather holds, I understand she would like us to dine alfresco, tomorrow at seven? Is that all right with everyone? I know it is very short notice, but Her Majesty is rather used to having her every wish obeyed, and—"

"Our queen commands, and we can do nothing but obey," Perry said, looking, Georgiana noticed, straight at Nate. "An honor, surely, for us all."

"Dashed flattering," Nate agreed, and at last they parted ways, Georgiana having to step quickly to keep up with Nate's long strides.

"What's wrong? You don't care for the earl?"

"I don't know him, Georgiana. Not personally. I was nearly shocked spitless that he knew my name."

"But you do know him by reputation?"

Nate smiled, but it was the sort of weak, half smile of someone who really wished she hadn't guessed correctly. "He's…he may have done something during the war with Napoleon."

"But that would be a good thing, an honorable thing."

"If he truly served. All I really know is that he wasn't in England. So he had to be somewhere, I suppose, doing something."

"Meaning?"

"In a moment, Georgie, in a moment. First, let me push your duenna off on her way. I can't think worth a bent penny with her standing over there, glowering at us. Stay here, while I put her in a hack. She can't say no to me, as I am a gentleman of the *ton*. Comes in handy, now and then, this baronet business. Besides, I don't believe I wish to ride three-up on my curricle again, especially as we've much to talk about."

In mere moments he was back; Imogene, looking huffy but impotent, on her way home.

"Now," Nate said, brushing his hands together as if wiping off the grime of a job well done, "where were we?"

"We were discussing, as you well know, what the earl did during the war, and I've been thinking about what you said while you were getting us rid of Imogene." Georgiana wet her suddenly dry lips. "A spy? You think he was a spy?"

"Or hiding on some warm island until he felt it safe to return. Oh, I don't know, Georgiana. Certainly, as the last of his line, he would be excused from racing around battlefields, exposing himself to danger. I only served here, in the Admiralty, because my parents pointed out I'm the last in our line. But at the same time, if Brentwood did serve, why would he avoid all questions about that service?"

"Modesty? A self-effacing constitution?" Georgiana suggested, then winced. The earl was dressed at the top stare of fashion, carried himself with confidence if not even arrogance and was neither shy nor retiring of nature. "No, I suppose not."

"Look, Georgiana, I'm not saying he should go running about, tooting on a yard of tin, announcing to all and sundry that he did fight for England. I shouldn't care for him if he did—if anyone did, and a few do. There are things that happen in war that are best forgotten, or at least buried, to be brought out only over a few bottles with others who have served. But Brentwood? He doesn't exactly run in my circle, being a good eight years my senior and probably thinking me a green-as-grass looby or whatever, but what I do know is that he loves society, loves cutting a dash. Rides neck or nothing, is more than a tolerable whip. You've seen how he dresses—everything about him is top o' the trees."

"But…?"

"But he's useless, Georgiana. There has to be more to life than a pleasing face. He's far from ugly, his wealth is close to legendary and he's accepted everywhere. All the mamas want him for their daughters, which must drive them to tears, because he's never thrown his cap at any of them. Won't even dance, if you'll believe that. Shows up everywhere, but won't put one foot on the dance floor. Famous for it. Probably because he thinks it adds some sort of mystery to his reputation, I suppose. He's simply…useless."

Then Nate frowned, his hands drawing up into fists. "Or he wants everyone to think he's harmless. Damme, Georgie, why did it take me so long to remember? Do you know who his uncle is?"

They'd reached Nate's curricle, and he handed Georgiana up onto the seat. "Nate, how would I know any such thing?"

"I'm sorry, Georgie," Nate said, quickly vaulting to his seat and taking the reins from his tiger. "Sir Willard Humphrey. Used to run the admiralty, during the war. And a staunch Tory, Georgie. And, although I know I've told you Brentwood is already as rich as Croesus, he's also in the way of being Sir Willard's only heir. Georgie? What was it your friend said? That Brentwood had shown up, just shown up, hoping for an audience with the queen?"

"Yes, that's what she said, to win a wager of some sort," Georgiana said, her heart sinking as she thought about how happy Amelia had looked, how her eyes had shone when she spoke of the earl. "I take it Aunt Rowena's fears have led you to think this way?"

Nate tooled his pair of bays past a dray wagon that had no business being on the street at this hour. "I'm being a hysterical old woman. Is that what you mean, Georgiana?"

"Georgie. You call me Georgie when you're…agitated. I'm becoming used to it. And, no, that's not what I mean. Not precisely. But I do think you're seeing bogeymen in the most innocent of associations. Amelia is not a silly, brainless chit. If she finds merit in the earl, then I'm sure it is there to be found."

"So I should just shut my flapping jaws and mind my own business?"

"I didn't say that, either, but yes, I think so. Right after we find out what he's really up to. Because this business of arriving unannounced to see Her Majesty in order to win a wager is simply too much of a clunker for either of us to swallow. After all, we're not looking at the fellow through besotted eyes, are we? But to kill the queen, as Aunt Rowena is worried may happen? No, I don't think he could do that, although we should find out what he might do, don't you think?"

Nate grinned at her, an unholy grin, and she adored him for it. "We're in league, then, you and I?"

"I suppose so, if you want to be, that is. I know you only had planned to placate your aunt."

"I didn't do that, Georgie. You did. And I returned the favor by showing my shining face in Half-Moon Street to dazzle your mother and stepfather all hollow. But we've already passed beyond that, you and I. Haven't we?"

Georgiana felt another pang of guilt intrude on her new happiness. "Amelia thinks so, at any rate. Oh, dear, she might be thinking her response to the earl's attentions is quite acceptable, seeing that you and I were also in those trees…and it would be all my fault."

"I don't understand. I'm a proud man, but I will admit that much, Georgie. I don't understand women. Actually, I believe that to be a whacking great part of their charm."

"What? Oh, do be quiet a moment, Nate, I beg you. I'm trying to think here."

Nate sniffed at the air. "Yes, that is the aroma of burning wood I smell. Think on, Georgie, as I drive on. We'll take the long way round to Half-Moon Street."

"Yes, do that," Georgiana said, biting at the seam of her glove as it covered her thumb. "Amelia said—what did she say? She said this was so wonderful, just the way she and I had dreamed of handsome princes and such at school. She was always a dreamer, Amelia was, although we were only girls then. And then I said…and then she said…and then she said that you said that you and I have been courting for some time, and so that it was all right."

She slapped the back of her hand against his arm. "I knew it was all your fault!"

"*Ow!* Now you sound like my mother, talking to my father. Only one question, Georgie. How is it all my fault? No, two questions. *What* is all my fault?"

Georgiana blinked, coming back to herself to realize that she was really being much too free with Nate. Why, they could have been friends of long standing, or even related to each other, considering the open and easy way she was with him. Brother and sister, possibly, except that she certainly didn't feel sisterly toward him, because when she wasn't sparring with him she was kissing him, or at least wanting to kiss him.

"Amelia has been abroad these past two years, and rather secluded prior to that," she said softly. "Her only associations have been with what I'm sure my mother would call the very fast set that ran with the queen, here and overseas. Amelia has no real notion of how to go on, not with real London gentlemen."

"And the country bumpkin does?" Nate asked, nearly earning himself another backhanded wallop.

"I at least have had my mother screeching in my ear, and Amelia was only at school for one term, while I had to suffer through three. I do know how to…how to go on. But Amelia? The king wouldn't go after the queen a second time, if he didn't have a mountain of proof that she has been…indiscreet. That's what Mr. Bateman said, and I have read the newspapers. Poor Amelia. She doesn't know what's up or down, what's accepted and what is…is…"

"Over the line? Beyond the pale? Yes, I think I understand. What I don't understand is how any of this came to be my fault, blast it, although I'm sure you're going to tell me."

Georgiana sighed. "Oh, I'm being silly, I suppose. But you told Amelia yesterday that you and I have been courting for some time, and I do believe she's looking at us and seeing what we were doing…back there, in the Park…and has decided that if I can, she can."

"Anyone can, Georgie. Many do."

"But it isn't proper, so stop grinning like an ape."

"Now I'm doubly damned. Amazing feat, you know—corrupting two young ladies in the space of one jaunt around the Park. And, now that I think of it, I got to kiss neither of them."

"Now you're angry," Georgina said. "I'm sorry, Nate. But you do see that you and I are different, don't you? We've been very honest with each other, and I don't think you think that the earl is being very honest with Amelia. Do you?"

"You know, Georgie, I'm beginning to forget how this conversation began, but I think it had something to do with how strange it sounded to hear that the earl just punted up the river for a wager, to see the queen. The rest, I'm afraid, is rather a blur."

"Poor Natey," Georgiana said teasingly, patting his arm. "All you have to remember is that you and I are going to stick as close as sticking plaster to the pair of them, to watch the earl very closely, to make sure he's not out to take advantage of Amelia's affections for some sordid reason."

AMELIA ALL BUT DANCED into the queen's bed chamber, still fairly well afloat after her drive in the park. Most especially after her interlude under the trees. And most definitely after Perry had walked her around to the side of the queen's residence, out of the way of prying eyes, to kiss her quite thoroughly once more before telling her how loath he was to leave her.

Catching herself up, she dropped into a graceful curtsy. "Your Majesty."

"Yes, yes, get up," Queen Caroline said, obviously in no mood for any formalities. "You're looking like the cat with canary feathers sticking out of her mouth. And starry-eyed, as well. You must tell me everything, trapped as I am here, with only old Lady Wakecliff dropping by to see if I'm dead yet. Was the Park splendid? Or did you forgo such tame nonsense and simply go off and bed the man?"

Amelia shot her gaze toward Rosetta, whose command of English was not perfect, but certainly good enough to have understood the queen's last statement, and the maid quickly took her leave.

"We chanced upon my friend Miss Penrose and her beau, Sir Nathaniel, while we were going about in the Promenade, ma'am, and they are of course delighted to have been invited to your dinner party."

The queen snorted. "Put me in my place, didn't you,

Amelia? The old woman is to know nothing. All right, we shall discuss the dinner party. Summon that butler person and the housekeeper. I feel a great need to order someone about, since you're so loaded down with Hanover cheekiness."

"Yes, ma'am," Amelia said, her earlier happiness defused, now that she was back in the queen's residence and the gravity of the woman's situation, and her near incarceration here in Hammersmith, came home to her once more. She rang the bellpull twice, her signal that the upper servants were needed.

She would not think about Her Majesty's reference to her "Hanover cheekiness," for she had convinced herself that there was no deeper meaning to the queen's words than that Amelia sometimes grated on her nerves, being too straitlaced for the woman's taste. It had nothing to do with being a Hanover, being of the queen's own blood.

A few minutes later there was a timid scratching at the door, and Amelia called out that the butler and Mrs. Fitzhugh should enter.

Pitiful.

Mrs. Fitzhugh's curtsy was so awkward and so deep, and she only half rose out of it before moving forward in a sidling sort of way, so that she very much resembled a crab scuttling across the beach.

And this other one. Nestor, wasn't it? Amelia didn't know where Mrs. Fitzhugh had found the fellow, but she wished there were some way of putting him back there again.

"Your Majesty," Nestor intoned, his voice squeaking only a little. "An honor to serve you."

The queen looked at Amelia, one kohl-darkened eyebrow shooting upward. "What a shabby lot. We are reduced to this?"

"Temporarily, ma'am," Amelia said quietly, wishing that Her Majesty had chosen to be amused by their rather motley crew of servants, rather than disturbed by them. "You will soon be housed and served more suitably."

"Yes, yes, don't condescend, child. Ladies in waiting, an entire court to amuse me. Gaggles of women, clutches of admirers, I should have all of them again, if I wanted them again. When I am better, when I am not so ill. You—oh, stop bowing, you twit! All the silver is to be polished at once, as I assume we have some. Use that jacket, will you, it's all it's good for. Flowers. Gunter ices. And someone to saw on a violin. Find them. Get them. Do them!"

"At once, Your Majesty!"

Amelia hid a smile. Her Majesty did so enjoy giving orders. She then inclined her head toward the door, as Nestor did not seem to know that he had been dismissed. But the man just stood there, staring at the queen, his mouth open, as if he longed to say something.

"The queen has no further need of you, Nestor," Amelia said quietly, and at last the man bowed his way out of the chamber…leaving Mrs. Fitzhugh as the queen's sole remaining target.

"Look, Amelia, she's ready to swoon. You—woman. We wish three menus prepared for our choice and approval. See to it. Amelia? What's that smell? Peppermint? I loathe peppermint."

Mrs. Fitzhugh—mouth closed so firmly her lips were pursed—curtsied again, then backed toward the door, turning and running at the last moment, then belatedly closing the door behind her.

"Scared to death of me, both of them. Good, they should be. How I miss my own servants. Purely a waste of eyesight to see that butler fellow in the queen's livery. Nearly a crime. Now, Amelia, go after that pair of imbeciles and ride herd on them until everything is as it ought to be. My dependence is on you. And call Rosetta back in here. You've arranged passage?"

"Yes, ma'am," Amelia said, although she hadn't. "Rosetta and her brother leave at the end of the week, ma'am. They're the last of them."

"The sooner, the better," the queen said, lifting a wineglass to her mouth. "Ah, Amelia, soon I will not possess the strength to leave this house, sorry as it is, and put this horrid seclusion behind us. Now, come sit down beside me and tell me all about the Earl of Brentwood. What does he say about me?"

Amelia raised a hand toward the door, thinking of the queen's first command to her, and about how she would arrange passport for Rosetta and Gerado, then smiled at her queen, who, of course, must be obeyed. "His Lordship says you are quite the most magnificent creature he has ever met, ma'am. He is much taken with you," she said, arranging her skirts around her as she sat on the floor, beside the queen's chair. "Another conquest, ma'am."

"Yes, yes," Her Majesty said, patting at her blond wig. "It is only to be expected. I remember one much like him, years ago, right here in London. A true courtier, Amelia, who brought me the most lovely presents and wrote odes to my beauty. Oh! Did I ever tell you about Perceval? My, there was a man…."

PERRY QUIETLY stepped up behind the man, pressed the tip of his cane into the fellow's back and drawled silkily, "I may be wrong, but I think I'm to say now, your money or your life, sir."

The man stiffened, then lowered his head. "He told me you were a downy one. Damn it, Brentwood, you gave me a fright. You mind if I pick up my stomach? I think I've dropped it here in the gutter."

Perry chuckled and lowered the cane as young Harry Townsend slowly turned around, to peer at him through the darkness.

"One minute you were there, and the next you were gone, only to show up behind me. Not very sporting, old man. How in blazes did you do that?"

"I doubt that is information germane to the moment, Townsend. What in blazes are you doing, following me? Because your belly *should* be in the gutter. Your liver very nearly was, you know. Or do you believe I delight in having someone dog my steps as I walk home from my club?"

"I wouldn't, no," Harry said, the flash of his white teeth in the light from a nearby lamppost showing that the man had regained his composure. "I suppose there's no use in dissembling?"

"In lying to me? No, Townsend, there isn't. Now, who sent you to watch me?"

"A friend of mine, sir. I won't reveal his name."

"No, of course not. I don't see you as a paid assassin, Townsend. Or are you so badly dipped that you'll take any sort of employment?"

Harry Townsend lifted his chin a fraction. "If you wish to deliver insults, it is, of course, your prerogative, My Lord."

"So, I'm right, you have been paid. I would suggest you learn to stay away from the gaming tables, if you're ever to be your own man, Townsend. Now again, who sicced you on me?"

"Oh, all right. It's not as if I ever liked the fellow above half. Rolin. Jarrett Rolin. And I was only to watch you, and if you were to ask me why, I'd tell you I don't have the foggiest notion, because I don't. Rolin's a queer duck. But if I was to hazard a guess, it's probably because of how you and your friend Westham routed him so publicly not that long ago—we've all heard how you made a fool of him. My own mother dined out on the story for a month before she left for home, as she was lucky enough to have been at the ball. Good show, by the way. Rolin's always chasing the ladies and has ruined his share of them."

Perry gave a moment's thought to the events of the month past and knew that Jarrett Rolin, who had escaped to his rundown estates after the event, had probably had just enough time to see himself as the innocent, injured party…and Perry as the man who had socially destroyed him. His friend Morgan and his bride were safely away, honeymooning in the Lake District of all the mundane places, which left Perry here, as the only available target for Rolin's revenge.

How fatiguing.

"And where is Rolin now, if you please?"

"Damned if I know. Sorry. Probably rented himself some dingy rooms somewhere. He had to sell his town house, I heard, and my friend Dilly bought up his team for a song just last week, at Tatt's. Would have gone for the curricle, too, but it has green wheels, you know. Dilly says he clashes with green. Completely under the hatches now that everyone's called in their notes, Rolin is, and the creditors are nipping at his heels. You and the earl really did put a crimp in the man. I met up with him in a gaming hell in Nassau Street—you know the place?"

"I do. Go on, tempted as I am to hear more about Lord Dillwood's difficulties with the color green."

Harry shrugged. "Not much more to tell of it. We were playing whist, just the two of us—at his invitation, now that I think of it. He kept pouring the wine for me, now that I think of that, too. I was scribbling my vowels like a madman, and he ripped them up in front of me, saying he would much rather I did him a small favor."

"You were to follow me, yes, I believe I understand. But what would be the sense of that, Townsend, if you cannot report to him about my comings and goings?"

Harry's handsome but fairly vacant young face screwed up as he applied himself to the question. "Well, blow it, I don't know. Oh, wait. He said he'd find me. That's what he said—he'd find me. Not that I have much to tell him, except how you were catching some billing and cooing in the Park with that little brown-haired chit in service to the queen. Not quite up to your usual standards, is she, Brentwood? Not exactly a raving beauty or—"

Perry rubbed his knuckles as he looked down at young Harry, who was now sprawled on the cobbles, shaking his head to clear it.

"Sorry? Did you trip? It's those fancy red heels, I'll wager. Slippery going on these wet cobbles. And now, pay attention, please. You are to forget seeing me with the young lady in question, Townsend. Do you think you can do that?"

Harry put thumb and forefinger to either side of his jaw, which he then worked back and forth experimentally. "Oh, I'm sure I could do that, My Lord."

"Good fellow. I thought so. Here, allow me to assist you to your feet," Perry said, extending his arm, a fairly heavy purse of gold coins in his hand, coins that were quickly transferred to Townsend's pocket. "Are you all right? Ready to listen?"

"Think a tooth's loose, you know. Damn. I suppose so…that is, yes, yes, more than ready to listen."

"Good. You have been following me without incident, Townsend, and doing a very fine job of it, too, although you've never been so bored to flinders in your life. The earl visits his clubs and makes the rounds of the parties, all deadly dull stuff. The worst part is that the earl dismisses his coach whenever he stops at

White's, as he does last thing every evening, and walks himself home. Alone. Can you remember all of that, Townsend, or must I repeat myself?"

"No, no, that's fine. White's, every night last thing, stroll home alone. I've got it. Setting yourself up to nab him, aren't you, My Lord?"

"There's a good fellow. Good evening to you, Townsend. Wait for Rolin to find you, then run along home, and by home, may I suggest Lincolnshire? I believe that's where your worried parents wait for you," Perry said, and turned away, continuing on to the corner, where Clive Rambert stood, fairly dancing in place, waiting for him.

"Good thing yer came back in one piece, M'Lord, else the guv'nor would've had my head inna basket. What a night! Yer leadin' him, him followin' yer, me taggin' after the pair of yer. Coulda stuck a posie in yer hat and had us a parade."

"Yes, thank you, Clive," Perry said, smiling, but a smile that quickly faded. "We've got a slight problem, my friend, in the way of an enemy it appears I've recently acquired."

"Anythin' to do with the guv'nor and the queen, sir?"

"In a roundabout way, yes, if my uncle actually approached this man to do the job I wasn't doing. Even if he hadn't, I'm afraid this fellow would by nature target Miss Fredericks as the perfect way to wound me, as he's the sort of coward who looks always for the weakest target. If he were to know about her, that is."

"And will he, sir?" Clive asked, beginning to breathe

faster as he tried to keep up with Perry's brisk pace through the dark streets of Mayfair. "Know about Miss Fredericks, that is, sir."

Perry stopped, looked at Clive, looked through him.

Rolin wasn't ready to show himself yet, which explained young Townsend. So, no, he wouldn't know, if Perry avoided Amelia until he could locate the bastard and deal with him. But how long would that take? A few days? A week? More? London was a large city, with many places for a man like Jarrett Rolin to hide himself when he didn't wish to be seen.

Could he avoid Amelia? Did he want to avoid her? Could he walk away?

"Clive, I have a mission for you," he said as he began walking once more.

"I'm apposed to be workin' for the guv'nor, yer know, and just keeping an eye on yer."

"A question, Clive. You were walking behind our friend Townsend tonight, sneaking from doorway to doorway so as not to be seen, even while keeping a sharp eye on us both. Correct?"

Clive didn't answer.

"Oh, come, come, my friend. You know what I'm going to ask."

"No. Blast me, no, I didn't ken when yer took off and left that Townsend fella standin' there, tryin' to figure out where yer'd gone to. Yer're a sneaky one, no lie in that."

"So, Clive, it would follow that if I wished to avoid you, I would have relatively no problem doing so?"

Perry put a hand to his ear. "Pardon me? I'm sorry, friend, I don't believe I heard that."

"I said, damn me for a blind man, no, yer'd show me yer heels soon enough. I don't know how yer did it, M'Lord, but yer tweaked me good. One minute there, and then—poof! Yer wanna tell me just what yer did over there when Boney was runnin' about? Because yer're a slippery one, M'Lord, no gettin' around that one."

"You flatter me, Clive, thank you. Now, down to business."

"Not going ta tell me what yer did. Knew that, knew that when I asked," Clive said, shaking his head. "But I'm not a slow-top all through me, no I'm not. Yer want me in the queen's house, keeping a watch on Miss Fredericks while yer go huntin' this Rolin cove. Right?"

"I'm convinced Dovey would be pleased to welcome you aboard," Perry said as they reached his doorstep in Portman Square. "And now that you have brought me safely home, I bid you a fond good-night, Clive, unless you harbor some notion that your guardianship of me includes tucking me into bed—and, no, that was not a question. I trust you'll be installed in Hammersmith, bag and baggage, by noon tomorrow?"

Clive nodded his head and turned away, kicking a loose cobble out of his path as he went...and Perry waited a few moments before he turned in the opposite direction, heading for his uncle's residence. Time was moving toward three in the morning, but old men found their beds early; surely the man had slept long enough.

Ten minutes and a swift inspection of the drainpipe

at the rear of Sir Willard's house later, Perry was standing at his uncle's bedside, staring down at the man in mingled surprise and amusement.

"Fetching nightcap, Uncle," he said in a loud, clear voice. "But the bed warmer fills me with amazement and, quite frankly, awe. I can see that His Majesty's rumored physical failings are not yours."

Sir Willard's eyelids had popped open by Perry's third word, and by the last word, Sir Willard's companion, a rather buxomy creature of no more than twenty, had screeched once, then pulled the covers over her head.

"How in bloody hell did you get in here? Oh, never mind. You probably picked a lock, then murdered all my best staff. You know what a devil of a time it is, getting one's staff up to snuff."

"*Your* staff seems to be doing well enough," Perry said, hooking a large white work apron with his cane, and lifting it from the floor.

"Don't be snide." Sir Willard propped himself up on his elbows. "I do have a front door, you know. And a knocker."

Perry lowered his cane, allowing the apron to fall onto the bedcovers once more. "And what fun would that be? I tell you, Uncle, seeing you here? Why, my admiration knows no bounds. However, I think we can dispense with your…protégée."

While still glaring at his nephew, Sir Willard yanked the covers off his companion, at which time the buxomy young maid shrieked, tried to cover herself and then slid out of the bed, her bare bottom glowing briefly in the light of a small bedside candle before she scampered into the dressing room.

"Satisfied, Nevvie?"

"I'm sure one of us was," Perry said, gracefully settling himself on the bed. "Now, to be serious, because I tell you, Uncle, I am about to be deadly serious. When I didn't respond to your demands to present myself here—did you think about Jarrett Rolin, or did you summon Jarrett Rolin?"

Sir Willard struggled to push himself up against the pillows. "I don't see what—why?"

"You did summon him," Perry said, doing his best to keep his tone even, his expression unreadable. "And you showed him the same broadsheet you showed me?"

"Well, yes, I—"

Perry couldn't help himself. "Damn it, old man! Do you know what you've done?"

"Don't you take that tone with me, boy! What have I done?"

"Rolin knows what you're about, for one thing. He knows what I'm about, as well, seeing as how you told him. All that business about getting to the queen through Miss Fredericks. Seduce her if you have to—that is what you said to him, isn't it?"

Sir Willard pulled off his nightcap, tossed it onto the bed. "And what if it was? The bastard was born to seduce women. It's what he does, about the only thing he does."

"True, Uncle," Perry said, reining in his temper, at least for the moment. "And unless you've been living under a rock—a possibility I see more as your natural habitat with every passing day—you know that Westham and I recently routed him for attempting just that."

Sir Willard ignored the insult. "I heard. You publicly disgraced him, had him all but run out of Mayfair. How else did you think his name came so readily to mind? But I don't see how—wait a moment. He's still here, isn't he? And he's coming after you?"

"Ah, my felicitations. You've got a mind sharp as a tack, don't you, Uncle," Perry said, getting to his feet once more and beginning to pace the carpet. "He'd like nothing better than some revenge against me, and against Morgan, except that he's not here. But I am, Uncle. I am here, and Rolin now has double the reason to hate me, because not only have I socially destroyed the bastard, but I've taken away his chance for a fat purse from you and your Tory friends by pushing him out of the way in this asinine exercise you've set me on. Or do you believe the man so brick stupid he hasn't already figured that out?"

He stopped pacing to glare at his uncle. "I'll have to deal with him now, you know. I was done with that part of my life."

"Deal with…you don't mean… Good God, Perry, you're going to kill him?"

"Think, Uncle, for once in your life, of something, of someone other than your miserable Tory cause. I volunteered to play snitch for you because I knew that otherwise you'd use Rolin, and that could not be allowed. But you'd already contacted him, which I did *not* know. Now Rolin knows about Amelia, knows I've been sent to court her. He knows what I'm supposedly doing for you. How better for him to revenge himself on me—and you, uncle—than to target her? And make me look guilty into the bargain, I'm sure. Because this time, Uncle, the man will settle for nothing less than blood."

"Is…is that what you'd do?"

"With limited resources, no friends and a mind twisted with the need for revenge, you mean? No, Uncle, I should hope I would not, not even then. But Rolin? It would be his first thought. I'd say he could go to Brougham, warn him that you Tories were after the queen, but Brougham is no fool and already knows that. Besides, Brougham wouldn't hand over a purse for the information, and Rolin, seeing no profit for himself, could not care less about politics. It's me he wants, and Amelia would have to seem the perfect weapon. Handed to him by you."

Sir Willard chewed on this for a few moments, then shook his head. "No, sorry, I don't see it. He'd come after you—Lord knows he's got reason enough. He wouldn't go after Miss Fredericks unless she was…hold up a moment! I don't believe it! You called her Amelia, didn't you? That's a little free and easy. You're smitten with the girl? God's eyeteeth, Nevvie, are you out of your mind? She's not for you. She's one of Caroline's little orphan tramps—no family, no background of any note. Ain't even a stunner, from what I've heard, and she has to be corrupted, chasing here and there with the queen. Birds of a feather, fouled together and all of that. I'm innocent, in any case."

"Are you quite finished?" Perry asked, beginning to wonder why he'd bothered to come here at all, and most definitely why he still held his uncle and sole surviving relative in any affection.

Yanking back the covers, exposing his bone-white, beefy legs and one still-bandaged foot to the night air and Perry's disgusted gaze, Sir Willard slid his bulk to the floor, tugging down his nightshirt, which had exposed even more of the man's unlovely anatomy. "Perry, you have to think, boy. You've got the line to consider, your father's good name. Bed her, certainly, she's bound to have been bedded before, but don't go all arsy-varsy over the chit. That's not why I sent you there, damn it!"

"I'll show myself out," Perry said quietly.

"No! I'm sorry, son, if I sicced Rolin on you. I didn't mean for that to happen. Kill him, it makes no nevermind to me, or anyone else, come to think of it. And the girl? Hell's bells, Nevvie, it's just a shock. You? Never thought you'd be bit. Do you really think Rolin is dangerous?"

"Not for long, Uncle, damn you. Not for long." Perry tapped his curly brimmed beaver back down on his head and turned to the open window.

"Just so it doesn't lead back here, Nevvie," Sir Willard said quickly. "Just so it doesn't lead anyone back to Liverpool. God, boy, the door. Use the bloody—oh, hell's bells, I don't know why I bother…"

"SUCH A FUSS AND BOTHER, Clivey," Maryann Fitzhugh said, fluttering from place to place in her small sitting room, looking at the menu she'd left on the table, flitting back to read once more the menu she'd rescued from the waste bin, smoothed out again and was now reconsidering.

Clive sat at his ease in the window seat, a weak, watery sun at his back, watching his flustered beloved. "Yer said Her Majesty wanted three, Dovey. She won't get them if you keep ballin' them up and tossin' them in the scrap. How about parsnips? I'm partial to them. Parsnips, Dovey. Go on now. Write that down."

Mrs. Fitzhugh rolled her eyes. "Queens don't eat parsnips, Clivey. They nosh down on quail eggs and pigeon tongues. Nasty stuff. The nastier the better. Oh, laws, Clivey, I'll be out of here on my ear, you just count on it, and he won't like that. And don't you just sit there. I thought you were come here to help me. Oh, look at me, I'm all at sixes and sevens."

"Sorry, Dovey. Too busy admirin' that pretty flush yer gets in yer cheeks when yer're all aflutter. Shame it always turns into a bumpy rash. Who's this *he* yer're talkin' about?"

Mrs. Fitzhugh yelped and slapped her hands to her cheeks just as there was a knock on the sitting room door and Miss Fredericks entered a moment later.

"Good morning," she said, smiling at Clive and the housekeeper. "Mrs. Fitzhugh, I do hope you don't mind, but I've taken the liberty of making up three different menus for you, as I am more conversant with Her Majesty's favorites."

"Cheeky, that," Clive said, getting to his feet. "Beggin' yer pardon, miss, but it's not like Mrs. Fitzhugh, here, hasn't been runnin' houses for some of the snoot-iest gentry in all of London. She has. Don't need no help scribblin' down pigeon tongues, that she don't."

Mrs. Fitzhugh silenced Clive with a glare that could possibly have cooked those pigeon tongues, and turned to Miss Fredericks. "I suppose I could just give them a look? Seeing as how you went to all that trouble and all."

Miss Fredericks handed over the pages, looked again at Clive, and said, "Is the earl here, then?"

"No, miss," Clive said, shaking his head. "Me and Maryann—we're old friends. We're visitin'."

"Oh," Miss Fredericks said, frowning slightly. "Isn't that…isn't that nice. Well, sorry to have interrupted you. Good day."

Once the door was closed, Mrs. Fitzhugh turned to Clive once more and began smacking him with the menus. "Out of my mind, that's what I was, telling the man you were a good one. Cheeky, is it? Sassing Mis-tress Fredericks! Get out, Clivey. Just you get out!"

Clive, who had been holding up his crossed arms to protect himself, at last grabbed at the menus as he stood up, to look at his beloved. "Yer told who I was a good man, Dovey?"

Mrs. Fitzhugh's eyes went wide and she tried to step back, only to have Clive take hold of both her wrists. "Clivey. Clivey, let go, you're hurting me."

But Clive Rambert, in love or nay, happy to be reu-nited with his Dovey or not, was first and foremost a Bow Street Runner. And nobody's fool. "That's how I got here? That's how I got picked? Yer told Sir Willard about me. Didn't yer, Maryann? And that's how yer got here, ain't it?"

"Who?" She lowered her eyelids, hiding her eyes. "I…don't…"

"Yer knew I was still aboveground. Yer knew, Maryann. Yer knew where I was and yer knew what I was doin'. Didn't yer?" He gave her a small shake. "Didn't yer!"

"I…I might have…mayhap have seen someone I thought was you…maybe…"

"And the other day? All that big hoo-ha over seein' me again? What were yer doin' while I was gone, Maryann? Trottin' the boards? That was some playactin', makin' me think yer were shocked all hollow to see me. Why, Maryann? Tell me why!"

"Please, Clivey, let go of my arms. You're hurting me."

"Too bad. Yer broke my heart, yer did. Twice! Tell me about Sir Willard. Tell me how yer got here." He turned her about, gave her a push so that she landed in the window seat. "And no more lies, Maryann. I'll have no more lies from yer."

She drew her arms and legs close to her in a protective manner and mumbled, "I told you he wouldn't swallow it, Mrs. Fitzhugh."

And then, as Clive stood there, fascinated, she began having a conversation. With herself.

"Quiet, Maryann, let me think."

"I'll not be quiet, Mrs. Fitzhugh! We could still be sewing up costumes at Covent Garden instead of worrying ourselves silly about pigeon tongues, if it weren't for *your* flapping tongue. Listening to Sir Willard pillow talk to that chippy opera dancer, and tapping him on the shoulder when he was leaving, to tell him you knew the perfect man for the job. If Sir Willard would do something for you. And now look. What a disaster!"

"Yes, I did it. I can think, Maryann, which is more than *you* could ever do. Sitting all night with one smoky candle, sewing fine seams for all those tarts and tramps. You could no more go to Clive and tell him that than to tell him you were once one of those round-heeled chippies, till your knees gave out. But I got you in here, where you could see him again, work your wiles. And now you tell me you didn't want to do it? Ha! Pull the other one, Maryann, it's got bells on!"

"But I shouldn't have listened to you, Mrs. Fitzhugh. I just wanted to see him so bad, that's all."

"You wanted, but I'm the one who figured out the how of it. Give him Clivey's name and get a place here, to help. Except you're such a whiny ninny."

Clive just stood there, eyes half-bugged out of his head, while this conversation washed over him. His memory clicked back over the years, to a much younger Maryann, who had tended to live much of her time in a dream world where she was not a poor blacksmith's daughter, but a fine lady clad in silks and satins, talking to her fine friends conjured up out of her imagination.

He'd sit and watch as she danced across the meadow for him, flowers in her hair. One of them gazelles, that was his Dovey. None too pretty, skinny as a stick, but her heart was always dancing. Dancing and dreaming. And then he'd taken her innocence, and then he'd left her to fend for herself, no virgin to get herself a husband, but only another soiled dove, wings too sooty to ever hope to fly (Clive also had his poetical side…).

It was his fault. It was all his fault.

"Ah, Dovey, what a mess we've made, the two of us," he said, gathering the thin, stiff-backed woman into his arms, where she sobbed and sobbed.

While Clive cogitated. He was here because Dovey had been hiding behind a door while Sir Willard spilled secrets while he was spilling his old-man seed. He was here because Dovey had known where he was but was too ashamed to seek him out. He was here because Dovey had struck a deal with Sir Willard, who had somehow gotten her out of the opera house and into the queen's residence, to spy on the woman.

He was here because Sir Willard did not put all his eggs in a single basket.

"It'll be all right, Dovey. I promise, it will be all right." He held his Dovey close and whispered to nobody in particular, "Crikey, what do I tell His Lordship? He's goin' to go spare."

"Who, Clivey?" Mrs. Fitzhugh asked, sniffling.

Clive grimaced. Was he really about to tell his Dovey that the two of them weren't the only ones sent by Sir Willard to snoop about the queen? No, he was not. Only a looby would spill secrets to a female. "Nothing, Dovey. Yer just cry, there's a good girl."

AMELIA PICKED UP the small stick the spaniel had brought back to her and tossed it once more, laughing as the floppy-eared animal went on the chase once more.

"Yours?"

She turned about sharply, startled, to see the Earl of Brentwood standing there, leaning on his ever-present cane, his handsome, smiling face caught by the early-afternoon sun. He was so beautiful, from his clothing, all in the first stare, to his truly marvelous green eyes. And that mouth? Shame on her, she'd dreamed about that mouth.

"My Lord—Perry," she said, wanting to kick herself for stammering. What was the matter with her? She'd chatted with heads of state, princes and kings, for goodness sake. But one look at this man and her tongue went all thick and her body went…oh, dear, *soft and gooey* seemed like such embarrassing words. "You startled me."

"I seem to have that effect on some people, yes, but surely not you, Amelia," he said, motioning for the spaniel to come to him. The dog, a female, obeyed at once, neatly dropping the stick at his feet. "A fine animal. She has a name?"

"Lucretia Borgia," Amelia said, watching as the dog went racing after the stick once more. "But I call her Lucy."

"So she's yours," Perry said, holding out his crooked arm, so that she would take it, and they walked after Lucy. "Do you mind that I've shown up unannounced and unsummoned yet again? Before you answer, may I simply say that I could not stay away?"

Amelia lowered her head, hoping the brim of her bonnet hid her delighted expression. "The queen will be so pleased."

"I did not come here to see the queen, Amelia." Perry picked up the retrieved stick yet again and this time, tossed it a rather prodigious distance, nearly into the decorative stand of trees and shrubbery that was woefully overgrown.

Lucy retrieved the stick yet again, but when Perry lofted it into the trees, the dog looked that way, yipped her disapproval and headed for the terrace.

"You've worn her out, poor old thing," Amelia said, not surprised that Perry didn't immediately steer her toward the terrace, as well, but only continued on, until they were standing beneath the shade of a convenient oak. Most definitely out of sight of any of the windows that overlooked the gardens and river.

"I have a confession to make. The same one, I'm afraid, as before. I'm a bad man, Amelia," Perry said, turning her toward him, placing his hands on her shoulders. His gaze concentrated on her mouth. "A bad, bad man. Some would even say dangerous."

"I am becoming more and more aware of that, yes," she said, throwing caution to the winds, and not at all sad to see it go. "Are you going to kiss me again?"

"I should ask first, shouldn't I?" His smile turned her knees boneless. "Very well. Miss Fredericks, would you be thoroughly opposed to the notion that I should like to kiss you? I would begin, I believe, with your delightful mouth."

"Begin?"

Now his smile made her breath catch in her throat. Yes, she had met princes, heads of state. But never before in her life had she been so…so *taken* with any man. Never before had she thought beyond a silly flirtation, beyond a few stolen kisses in a dark garden. There was more, so much more, to her reaction to this man. She wasn't a naive schoolgirl. She'd been curious before, but never curious enough to act on that curiosity, never interested enough, moved enough. Until now.

"Yes, sweet Amelia, begin. Forget the Park. A first embrace is more experiment than decision. Impromptu, unplanned, and with no thought save the moment. And often clumsy, ashamed as I am to admit to that failing."

He used the tip of one finger to lightly trace her bottom lip, so that her mouth opened on an involuntary sigh. "This kiss, Amelia, if you allow it, begins everything. And, even if I am risking all to admit this to you, for the first time in my rather checkered life, I do not already see the ending. Nor do I want to."

There was nothing she could say to that, so she said nothing, but simply closed her eyes and waited for the pressure of his mouth against hers.

He touched his lips to hers, lightly, then withdrew, advanced again, still lightly, tenderly. Again. And then again.

Just as she was about to reach up and grab him by the shoulders, impatient with all this gentleness, he was kissing her cheeks, her brow, her closed eyelids.

Breathing became a voluntary exercise, one she chose to ignore as his breath began to tickle at her left ear, as his teeth lightly nipped at her sensitive lobe…as his tongue explored her ear as if he were mapping an uncharted area, investigating, discovering. The tingle that began at her ear skittered all the way down to her toes.

She had to work to remember how to swallow, but her mouth had gone dry, anyway, her throat thick. She slid her arms around his waist to anchor herself, as she knew she was in danger of floating away, of losing all touch with anything so mundane as the ground beneath her feet.

Now his lips blazed a trail down the side of her neck, and she tipped her head to the side, granting him complete access.

He did not touch her, other than to keep his hands lightly against her upper arms. He did not threaten her as he gently breached her every defense, silently struck down every inhibition and raised his flag of capture as she gladly surrendered any remaining vestiges of maidenly common sense.

"Beautiful," he whispered, somehow now cupping her face in his warm hands, looking down into her face as her eyelids fluttered open, so that she was amazed with what her eyes now saw. He was looking at her as if she was something rare, even precious.

"I…I'm not beautiful," she heard herself say, and wondered why she suddenly no longer so firmly believed what her mirror had told her plainly all of her days. "I'm not. You're beautiful."

His small, lopsided smile teased at the not unbecoming scar on his cheek. "No, pet, I'm merely pretty. Pretty is a curse as well as a blessing. But you are beautiful. True. Loyal and loving, against all odds. Steadfast. You become more beautiful each time I look at you."

The queen. He meant the queen, of course. It was true that most everyone had abandoned Her Majesty in her disgrace, but staying did not mean that she was some sort of saint. The queen had been good to her. Others might take and take and take, but someone had to give back. That the someone was her, Amelia had never questioned.

"Please, I'm doing nothing out of the ordinary, Perry. In a way, the queen is the only mother I have ever known. She's certainly the only home I've ever known."

Perry smiled again, shaking his head. "And you haven't been approached by Liverpool's minions, offered vast sums of money to bring damaging testimony against Her Majesty? You stay in the background, Amelia, but you are closest to her, have been with her longer than anyone else, know more than anyone else. I'm not saying you would build yourself up by helping to destroy her, but surely someone has offered you the opportunity."

Amelia stepped away from him, turned her back. "There have been contacts, yes. In Germany, in Italy. And here, since our arrival, while we were still staying with the Lord Mayor of London." She turned back to him. "But I would never…"

"I know, you would never betray her. Although, from our brief meeting I can tell that Her Majesty could prove a trial to love at times. Royalty excels at being unlovable and demanding, I'm afraid. I cannot begin to tell you how proud I am of your integrity, Amelia. The world is not precisely overburdened with that particular quality."

He traced her cheek with the back of his hand. "It shines from you, you know. That honesty, that integrity. That loyalty. Your face is alight with it, and I find that I have never seen any face half so beautiful in my life. I'm...humbled by you."

Amelia blinked back tears. "I'm not...I'm not a paragon, Perry."

And then she told him. She told him about her silly dreams and hopes as a child, dreams and hopes that had lasted into adulthood, even as the rational part of her dismissed them. How she had examined prints of Princess Charlotte, even snippets of the princess's handwriting, in the hope of finding some resemblance. Yes, they had all dreamed, all the orphans the queen had at times shuffled in and out of her life, but when Amelia was the only one that stayed, with even William gone now, the silly hopes and dreams had stupidly lingered.

"The queen's bastard child," Perry said, once she had finished. "Not William Austin, but you. Considering the circumstances, Amelia, it's easily understandable that you might dream such a dream."

"Perhaps. But that's all it was, you know. It is not possible that...well, you know. Even the king, all those who want her kept from her crown, have only approached me about things such as Her Majesty's sleeping arrangements on our travels, tawdry questions on tawdry subjects. Even they have never thought that I could be...that I could be..."

"That you could be the one person, the one sure person, who could possibly destroy her," Perry said, pulling her close once more. "Ah, pet, you've got a lot on your plate, don't you?"

She rubbed her cheek against the fine, smooth cloth of his jacket. "This should not concern you. I'm sorry."

He stroked her back, and she felt safe somehow. "I'll tell you what I'll do, pet. Clive and Mrs. Fitzhugh seem to have some prior association. What do you say you move him in here? Just to be someone else you might… rely upon."

Amelia looked up at him. "I saw them together this morning," she said, smiling weakly. "What an odd pair, don't you think?"

"True love knows best, I would suppose. But seriously, Amelia, you can put your trust in Clive, to vet whoever comes knocking on the queen's door, for one, and he could have a note to me at any time if you need me."

"Thank you, Perry. That's very kind. You said I was beautiful, and I know I'm not. But when I say I trust you most wholeheartedly, I hope you know I mean it."

"I DON'T TRUST HIM."

"Yes, I do believe I remember hearing you say that the last three times you said it. Please, Nate, sit down." Georgiana Penrose pushed her spectacles higher on the bridge of her nose, not because they were slipping but because old habits don't die quite so easily.

Nate obeyed with pleasing alacrity, then took Geor-

giana's hands in his. "Georgie. I don't believe you understand the gravity of this."

She pulled her hands free. "Oh? You mean I don't understand that my very dearest friend in the entire world
could be, even now, the victim of a scurrilous, unprin-
cipled rascal intent on using her to gain damaging information against the queen for his uncle, this Sir
Willard person? That men of the Earl of Brentwood's
social rank do not chase after insignificant creatures
such as a disgraced queen's companion? That the fact
that the earl showed his face at the queen's residence
without so much as a hint of an invitation, and telling a
story so ridiculous as to be absurd, could only mean that
he was lying through his teeth to that very dear, gullible friend? That I'm not frantic with worry for that
friend, who, I'm afraid, has already half convinced herself that she is tumbling into love with the man, who she
thinks it's just fine to kiss because she saw us kissing
each other? Is that what I don't understand, Nate?"

Nate pulled a face and scratched at a spot behind his
left ear. "All right. You do understand. But, much as I believe I'm right—what if I'm wrong? I don't run with the
earl's set, but I know he's well liked, well respected. I
made some discreet inquiries last night, at my clubs—"

"How discreet?"

He considered this question for a moment. "I waited
until those I questioned had been drinking deeply and
were fairly well oiled, so they wouldn't wonder at why
I was asking. But that's not the point, Georgie. Some
people think he's a fribble, a rich fribble. But there were

one or two others, the older ones, who motioned me to move closer so that they could whisper to me, who said he was a dangerous man. I came away thinking that he did serve in the war but yet not in the war. Something very secretive, something very deadly. And not deadly for him, only for those he came in contact with."

"An assassin?" Georgiana was definitely impressed. "Mr. Bateman has a book in his library on assassins. They blend in with the enemy, then dispose of powerful political and military people, disrupt chains of command, I think it said. It's not a very honorable thing to do, as war is supposed to have rules, so that even while we garner the benefits, some might frown on the earl for his tactics, say he wasn't being honorable. But I must say it makes more sense to this country girl to cut off the chicken at the head."

Sir Nathaniel leaned forward and gave her a smacking kiss on the mouth. "You're such a Trojan, Georgie."

"I suppose that's a compliment? Or are you next going to ask me to throw horseshoes with you, like the rest of your chums?"

"Widgeon," he said, but with affection. "I know you're a female, you know. Quite the prettiest female I've ever seen. But I won't say I'm disappointed that you're also a rousing great friend. Slap up to the mark, Georgie."

Georgiana knew Lord Byron would have perhaps phrased such praise differently, but she doubted that an ode to the twinkle in her eyes would have had half the effect of Nate's sweet, honest words. "We do...rub along tolerably well, don't we?"

He took her hands in his, looked at her with an intensity that curled her toes (a new experience for Georgiana). "I feel as if I have known you forever. How long has it been?"

"Forever," she said, feeling a blush steal into her cheeks. "Now stop this. My mother could walk in at any moment."

"Better Mr. Bateman," Sir Nathaniel said staunchly. "I believe he and I will soon have something to discuss."

"Oh, Nate," Georgiana said, throwing herself into his arms. "You're such a widgeon, too."

"Here, here, you'll muss my neck cloth, and it took my man a devil of a time to get it right. But if that means you like me, I shouldn't take umbrage, I suppose," Sir Nathaniel said, his handsome young face splitting in a grin as he held her tight.

Georgiana gave him a fierce squeeze in return, then sat herself back, attempting to compose herself. "What do we do, Nate? I know you said you don't travel in his set, that the earl is older and doesn't run about like you and your friends, still being silly and frisky. How do you get close enough to him to watch him, to be certain we're right? Because we must be certain the earl is up to no good before we say anything. It is one thing for me to break Amelia's heart, but it would be the worst of all possible things to break it for no reason."

"SHE TRUSTS ME!" Perry all but shouted as he threw his wineglass at the fireplace. "Damn it all to hell, Clive, she trusts me!"

"Wimmen. Can't count on a one of them to have a lick of sense, sir."

Perry halted his pacing in his private study and turned, one eyebrow climbing his forehead, to look at his assistant. "Do I detect a hint of trouble in your particular paradise as well, Clive?"

Clive took hold of the chair arms and pushed himself up from the slouching position he had dropped into when they'd first closeted themselves in His Lordship's study. "Yer're a sharp one, M'Lord. Saw straight through me. Sir Willard was right. Yer are the downy one."

"Oh, cut line, Clive. You moped all the way back here from Hammersmith. What happened with Mrs. Fitzhugh? She take a second look and toss you out on your ear?"

"Ha! Not after all the trouble she took gettin' me there, no sir."

Perry pinched the bridge of his nose between thumb and forefinger. "That was as murky as ink. Explain, if you please."

"I was hopin' not to, tell yer the truth, but I suppose there's nothin' else for it. Dovey—Mrs. Fitzhugh, that is—she ain't a housekeeper. Not trained up that way, yer know. She was one of them dancers at Covent Garden for a bit, then stayed on once she was past it, sewin' up costumes and the like. Sews a fine seam, sir. Just fine."

"Fascinating. Now you're going to tell me how she got from Covent Garden to Hammersmith, correct?"

"I suppose so." Clive scratched a spot behind his ear. "Seems Sir Willard's got himself a chippy there. At Covent Garden."

Perry sniffed. "Must be something in the man's diet. Either that, or I can only hope such a long-running libido runs in the family. Go on."

"I'm goin', I'm goin'. Embarrasin', that's what this is. I should have known, yer know? Sir Willard dribbled pillow secrets to his chippy, and Dovey was listenin'. She'd already seen me, knew I was a Runner, and told Sir Willard about me, makin' him promise to set her up in Hammersmith so she could pretend to see me. Pretend, yer see, because she already did see, but was too shamed to come up to me, seein' as how she'd been tipped on her back a time or two when she was a dancer, if you take my meanin'. Sir Willard, there's a downy one. He got himself two sets of eyes and ears with one blow. And yers, o'course."

Perry walked to the drinks table, picked up another wineglass and filled it halfway. "So your Dovey is also reporting to my uncle, who didn't bother to inform me of his coup. What has she told him thus far? You did ask, didn't you?"

"I did, sir, yes. So far, sir, she told him that she doesn't know just what Miss Fredericks does there, except that she's always at Her Majesty's beck and call, and seems to know how to give orders. Oh, and that tin case thing that the queen takes with her everywhere she goes? It's a big one, and it's in a box room just off the queen's dressing room. Big chest, traveling chest, sir. And locked up tight."

BERNARD NESTOR looked at the tin chest, his fingertips tingling. All of him was tingling, actually, as he had to keep fighting the feeling that if he turned about, the entire household would be standing there, having caught him out.

Not that he wasn't snooping about for the queen's own good. He had lofty reasons for doing what he was about to do. Certainly everyone would understand that.

He ran his fingers over the elaborate white painting on top of the large chest: Her Royal Highness the Princess of Wales, To Be Always With Her.

The queen kept her secrets in this chest. Brougham's spies had told him that, and what Brougham knew, Bernard knew. Such a conclusion only made sense even if he hadn't been told, seeing as how it was so important to her. If he was to find the proof for his theory of the true origins of Miss Amelia Fredericks, that proof had to be here, just waiting for him to free it from the shadows.

Bernard dropped to his knees to examine the lock. Formidable. It would take more than a pilfered hairpin to shift this one. If only he could simply take a hammer to it, but he could only do that if he could find a similar lock and exchange one for the other.

Still, that would leave the queen with a key that no longer worked.

Was that his problem? He didn't think so, as once the queen understood the power he would help her wield, one broken lock would mean nothing.

Cupping the heavy lock in one hand, Bernard returned to his favorite dream, the one where he stood up in the gallery of Parliament, waving evidence that Miss Amelia Fredericks was the rightful, legal heir to the throne, shouting, "Ah-*HA!* I've done it! The king and queen have another royal heir, and this one is a *Whig!*"

It was a lovely dream, one that went on to seeing himself as the queen's closest aide and confidant, seeing him as the new princess's guide and mentor as he explained the sensible alternative of tossing the Tories out of government and installing the Whigs once again. The king, already held in distaste by most of the populace, would see his subjects turn their backs on him entirely, to more fully embrace Queen Caroline, and toss roses at the new Princess of Wales, Princess Amelia.

So many dreams, so many plans.

"And the key to them all is the key that opens this chest," he whispered dramatically as he, with much reluctance, released the lock and got to his feet once more. He looked around the box room, spied a dingy candelabra and snatched it up as if it had been the object of his visit.

"Good afternoon, Nestor."

Bernard closed his eyes, his stomach turning almost far enough to reach embarrassing disaster, and slowly turned to see the royal princess—Miss Fredericks, he must remember to address her as Miss Fredericks—standing before him, her hand still on the latch of the now-open door.

"Miss," Bernard said, holding up the candelabra. "I was polishing silver, as per the queen's request, and Mrs. Fitzhugh told me about this piece. We should want them all, shouldn't we?"

"Yes, of course. Carry on, Nestor," Miss Fredericks said. "Oh, unless you have a moment to assist me?"

"Certainly, Miss Fredericks."

"Thank you." She went down on her knees in front of the tin case.

And then, as Bernard watched, amazed, Miss Fredericks took a large key out of her pocket and opened the traveling chest. He went up on tiptoe, attempting to peer over her head and catch a glimpse of the contents, and was hard-pressed to contain his disappointment when she rose once more, holding yet another locked chest. This one was small and wooden, no more than half a foot high and a foot long.

"If you'll hold this for a moment?"

Oh, God. His heart began to pound in his ears. He was holding it. The chest. Not the large tin traveling case, but a smaller chest. The sort that would be used to hide one's most precious documents.

Amelia locked the traveling trunk and got to her feet, holding out her hands so that he would return the small chest.

It stuck to his fingers. Could he dare to turn, run, escape this house? What would happen if he did? What if he was wrong, and nothing of importance was in this box? He would have destroyed his last chance, for nothing.

"I would be pleased to carry it for you, miss," he said, choking out the words.

"Thank you, but no. I'll take it to the queen, then return it. I've something to locate in my own trunk, so you needn't linger, Nestor. But perhaps you might have someone brew you a cup of tea and have yourself a short rest before you return to the silver? You're looking rather pale."

"Thank you, miss." Bernard all but whimpered as Miss Fredericks turned her back on him.

But all was not lost. He was now certain he knew where all his answers resided. He would find a lock that was a twin to the lock on the larger chest, break the old lock, take the small chest, replace the broken lock with its twin, and…ah, and then! Then he would be Sir Bernard Nestor. Bernard Nestor, Earl of something-or-other. No! Duke. That was it! He'd be a duke!

Forgetting the candelabra he'd put on a shelf in order to hold the smaller chest for Miss Fredericks, Bernard wandered out of the box room, down the hallway, his eyes clouded with his heady dreams.

"I BROUGHT YOU SOMETHING, Your Majesty," Amelia said, dropping into a deep curtsy before placing the chest on the bottom of the chaise where the queen was lounging, a tin of boiled sweets close at hand.

The book she had gone to the box room to retrieve was already safe in her own chamber, silly as it was for her to want to look at it again, cry again as she read of the funeral procession of Princess Charlotte and her stillborn son.

"My box? I didn't ask for my box."

"Yes, ma'am, I know. But I had a thought, if you don't mind. I thought that perhaps we should think of another place to keep it?"

"I always keep it in my personal traveling trunk. You know that, girl."

"Yes, ma'am." Amelia took a breath, let it out slowly,

seeing again the strange, unhealthy glitter in Nestor's eyes as he'd stared at the chest she'd given him to hold for her. "But it is possible that we are not the only ones aware that you do so."

The queen sat up straight, her nose all but quivering. "Who? Tell me immediately, Amelia. What did you observe?"

"The king would go to all lengths to discredit you, ma'am, we've agreed on that. Our new staff? We don't really know them, do we? It just seems...well, it seems prudent to keep your most precious belongings where they would not be easily discovered."

"It was that Fitzhugh drab, wasn't it? Sneaky eyes, smelling to high heaven of peppermints. Curtsies like a hog caught in a bog. Turn her off, girl. Turn her off today!"

"And replace her with whom, ma'am? Turn off our new butler and get what in return? No, ma'am, I beg you to reconsider. I think we must simply be diligent in protecting Your Majesty's privacy."

"Answer my question, girl. Who was it? What did you see?"

Amelia knew she'd get nowhere until she told the queen everything. "I went to the box room to fetch a book I'd placed in one of my traveling trunks, ma'am, and I saw Nestor, our new butler, ma'am, kneeling in front of your traveling trunk, touching the lock. He has no idea I observed him."

"My bloody damn husband sicced him on me! Spies! I'm surrounded by spies, traitors, back stabbers! I can't keep on, Amelia," she said, her bottom lip beginning to tremble as she fell back against the cushions. "I have no protectors. No ladies in waiting, no courtiers. Gone, all gone, now that I'm no use to them. Only you remain, Amelia. I am aught but a weak, sick, tired woman. Utterly friendless, defenseless. Is this how one treats a queen? At least the French queen died swiftly, with one chop to her neck. He kills me by inches, Amelia. The man won't be happy until I'm in my grave. Or does he build a guillotine at the Tower? Tell me. Tell me!"

Amelia fetched her queen a restorative glass of wine, which the woman drank down in one long gulp. "Ma'am, I will not ask you if there is something…something perhaps dangerous to you inside this chest. That is not for me to know. But if there is, perhaps the best thing for Your Majesty to do would be to remove it from these premises?"

"Ha! And do what? Tie it up in a weighted sack and sink it in the Thames? Burn it? No! I cannot have my treasures destroyed, even if they end by destroying me. They're all I have, all that's left to me. Ah, sweet Lord, I am so oppressed…"

"Oh, ma'am, please, you must be strong. The king can only destroy you if you let him. You are Caroline of Brunswick, Queen of England, ma'am. You must never forget that."

The queen, who had been burying her face in the lifted skirt of her gown, lowered the material and looked shrewdly at Amelia. "Sometimes, girl, you are more of me than I am. You have a plan, don't you?"

"Yes, ma'am. I told Nestor I would be replacing the

chest in your traveling trunk, so he will only look for it there. But the Earl of Brentwood, ma'am? I'm confident that, if I were only to ask him, he would take the chest to his own residence and keep it safe for you. After all, ma'am, no one can find what isn't here."

Her Majesty whimpered, held out her arms until Amelia picked up the box and laid it on the woman's lap. The queen reverently stroked the inlaid lid. "My memories. My memories are all here, safe in here. No, Amelia. I cannot let them go. Don't ask me to let them go. There has to be another way."

Amelia thought for a moment. Entrusting the chest to Perry had seemed such a good answer, such a logical answer. But there was her own book, her own hiding place. "I suppose I could keep the chest in my chamber? No one would think to look for it there. There is a cabinet beside my bed. It has a lock."

The queen hugged the chest to her. "And you could bring it to me here? Bring it to me whenever I ask. Yes, yes, do it, Amelia. Keep the chest safe. Keep me safe." She lowered her eyelids for a moment, then looked up, straight into Amelia's eyes. "Keep us all safe."

ESTHER PIDGEON poked her head around the corner of the hallway, checking to make sure it was safe for her to proceed.

Not that she should be terribly worried; she was housed in an asylum of imbeciles.

The consumptive-looking butler she, as a lesser servant, was forced to address as Mr. Nestor.

Mrs. Fitzhugh, a woman of low breeding who did not know a ladle from a demitasse spoon and who spent most of her time locked up in her private sitting room with that Clive Rambert person, a wholly unsuitable creature. They probably copulated, and a more unpalatable mental image she could not contemplate.

Then there were the Italians, with all their gibbering and hand waving. Not that Esther paid much attention to foreigners, who couldn't have a full brain among them. Everyone knew that about foreigners.

The dozens of lesser staff? Truly, never had there been a more apt description for a staff.

No. There was no one here to fear.

Why, she might even feel an urge to linger, to enjoy herself awhile, as feeling superior was such a cheering emotion, except that her brother would soon wonder where she had taken herself off to—whenever he took time to notice she wasn't at the dinner table, whenever he bothered to read the note she'd penned before she left, whenever he cudgeled his brain and realized that their aunt Mary, whom Esther said she'd gone to visit in Kent, had died five years ago.

She had to act when she had the opportunity, linger only long enough afterward so that no suspicion fell upon her, and then hie herself home, to await Florizel as he drove up in his magnificent gilded carriage, to whisk her away to his palace, the last obstacle to their union gone.

The kitchens had been bustling in preparation of the dinner party, so that Esther could not chance being seen

there, among so many people, so had wisely chosen to
offer to fetch the tea tray up to Her Majesty's chambers
herself. Everyone had been most grateful to her, and
much too busy to see that she had not taken the tray up
directly, but had stopped for a moment, hidden in a corner of the hallway, to fuss with the contents of the tray.

But now everything was back in its place, more than
back in its place, and Esther moved on, head held high,
her ears ringing with the sweet words her dearest Florizel would whisper into her ear once he'd learned how
she'd saved him. Mentally she began penning the note
she would send to him, informing him of her genius.

"CHILDREN! THANK GOODNESS you got my note! Come,
come. Georgiana, sit with me," Aunt Rowena said, patting
the cushion next to her. "No, no, Nathaniel, you are not to
remain standing there, glowering down at me. Sit! Sit!"

Nate looked at Georgiana, who was fighting a smile,
and grudgingly sat himself down on the edge of a facing sofa. "Aunt, I am a dutiful nephew, I really am. But
I had expected to arrive here to see you broken and
bloody, at the least. Didn't we, Georgie?"

Georgiana freed her smile. "No, that would be you,
Nate. I thought Aunt Rowena's note was perfectly understandable. She has uncovered new information, and
this information needs our immediate attention. There
was nothing in it about being broken and bloody. Was
there, Aunt Rowena?"

The old woman glared disapprovingly at her nephew.
"There most certainly was not. Although, now that you

mention it, I suppose I could be in danger, seeing as how I'm the one who's been given the damning information."

"Oh, good grief," Nate said, pulling out a pair of dice he then began rolling through his fingers. He'd paid five pounds to a sharp to teach him the trick. "Another dream, Aunt?"

Aunt Rowena laid one bony hand on Georgiana's forearm and leaned toward Nate. "So much more than a dream, Natey. The cards. The cards told me all."

Nate looked at the table between them and saw the Tarot cards and, before he could catch himself, muttered, "Oh, bugger it."

"Nate!" Georgiana warned, then giggled.

What a brick she was, his Georgie.

"A thousand apologies, Aunt Rowena," he said, knowing he was coloring to the roots of his hair. "Tell us about the cards."

"No."

"What? What do you mean, no? Dash it all, Auntie, we all but broke our necks rushing over here, so don't you go cutting up all stiff at me now."

Aunt Rowena sat back and folded her arms over her slender breast. "You are not approaching this with the seriousness it deserves, Natey. I won't be made a fool of."

"Too late for that," Nate mumbled, wisely this time only loud enough for himself to hear. "I'm sorry, Aunt. Please, Georgie and I only want to help. But we can't do that if you don't tell us what's going to happen, now, can we?"

"He's right, Aunt Rowena," Georgiana told the woman. "We really do want to help."

The old woman looked from one to the other, then said, "Oh, very well. Someone is going to attempt to assassinate Her Royal Majesty."

Nate couldn't help himself. He knew better, he really did, but he had to ask. "When?"

"Oh? Suddenly you have this deeper interest? Very well, Natey. The when of it is immaterial, for it has already happened. But she escaped without harm."

"Figures. Can't say she's right or wrong, can we, if the queen escaped."

"Another perished for her," Aunt Rowena said quietly. "It was all here, in the cards. But there will be another attempt. I feel sure of it."

Nate looked to Georgiana, whose cheeks had gone pale. "Georgie?"

"She said…she said…"

"I know." He got to his feet, holding out a hand to Georgiana. "Aunt Rowena, if you will excuse us? I believe Georgiana would like to visit her friend Miss Fredericks, who is in residence with the queen."

"Unless she's dead," Aunt Rowena said, picking up the Tarot cards and holding them out to Georgiana. "Shall we look here?"

"Thank you, Aunt Rowena, but no," Nate said, bending to kiss his aunt's cheek. "We really must be off."

He practically had to run to keep up with Georgiana as she hurried from the house out to his curricle, and they set off on the ride to Hammersmith.

"You do know it's only Aunt Rowena, don't you?" he asked once they were away from the worst crush of traffic. "Dotty Aunt Rowena? Rooms to let in her attic and all of that?"

"I know, I know. But if you're right about the Earl of Brentwood being out to help the Tories destroy the queen, and since your aunt Rowena was right about the queen being in danger, as having the Earl of Brentwood turning Amelia's head to get to the queen certainly could be construed as danger, since you say he's such a secretive and dangerous man, and you think you are right about that, although I'm hoping you're not because Amelia seems quite taken with the earl, then if one thing is true, the next thing could also be true."

She turned on the seat, her eyes wide. "Couldn't it?"

Nate blinked. "Um…could you say all of that again? No, no, wait, don't, as my eyes are already crossing and somebody has to tool this team. We'll just go visit Miss Fredericks. That seems safest. Although we'll be hours early for dinner, you know. We're neither of us dressed for it, either. Queens probably get really starchy about that sort of thing."

"Oh, for goodness sake, Nate, just hurry."

Perry found Amelia in the gardens, exactly as she said she would be. He could barely remember tooling his bays out of Mayfair, or tossing the reins to his tiger when he at last reached Hammersmith.

"Amelia!" he called out, running to her as she sat on a stone bench overlooking the water, dropping to one knee without a thought to his new buckskins. "What is it? Are you all right? You're not hurt? No one's tried to hurt you?"

As he spoke, he ran his hands down her arms, as if to check for injuries. "I came as fast as I could when I read your note. What happened? I have to tell you, I could only decipher every third word you wrote. God, I don't think I've ever been so frightened in my life."

She looked at him as if only just noticing his presence. "Oh, Perry, I'm sorry. I didn't mean to upset you. I'm…I'm fine."

He moved to sit beside her, take her hands in his. "No, pet, you're not. That would be obvious to a blind man. You've been crying. Is it the queen?" As he asked the question he hoped that she wouldn't know that he could not care a whit about the queen. His entire concern, his complete fear, had all been for Amelia. If he hadn't realized how important she'd become to him before her note had arrived, he damn well knew it now. It was unsettling. It was shocking. It was wonderful. "Amelia, please, be brave. Talk to me. Is it the queen?"

She bit her lips together, shook her head.

He longed to kiss away the dried traces of tears on her cheeks. "Sweetings, tell me what's wrong."

And still she wouldn't look at him. "It…it's Lucy. She's dead."

Perry sat back in sudden shock. He had been half expecting to hear that Jarrett Rolin had made his appearance and done something that could only end in Perry seeking him out and killing him. He'd then begun to think that the queen had finally fallen victim to the ill health she proclaimed at every opportunity. But Lucy?

"Your dog? What happened? She seemed fine earlier. Was there some accident? She ran into the road?"

Amelia shook her head. "Oh, look at me, I'm crying again. You must think I'm silly. Lucy was just a dog."

"She was your dog, Amelia," he said, drawing her into his arms as fresh sobs racked her body, and holding her while she wept.

Once the worst of her tears had subsided, he handed her a handkerchief, which she accepted, blowing her nose and wiping at her eyes. "Thank you. I brought Lucy here with me from Italy, you know. Poor old thing. If I had left her there…"

He pressed the tip of his index finger against her lips. "You can't think that way, pet. Lucy would have been devastated to have been left behind. Now, tell me what happened."

Amelia took a steadying breath and nodded. "We were having our tea, Her Majesty and I. It's really more of a formality, I suppose, as the queen is happiest with her candies and a glass of port at this time of day."

"I think I just lost my appetite. But go on, I'm sorry to have interrupted."

She attempted a smile. "Her Majesty has a very varied taste. I drink tea and eat the occasional cake, although the offerings since we arrived here in Hammersmith have not been such that I am very tempted, I'm afraid. Indeed, we seem to send more back to the kitchens than either of us eats. It's rather embarrassing, actually." She closed her eyes. "So, as I was not at all hungry, I…I fed one of the cakes to Lucy."

Perry felt his jaw tighten, his every muscle tense. "And she died?"

Amelia nodded her head fiercely. "She gulped it down all in one bite and was begging for another when suddenly she…oh, Perry, her eyes went all wide, and she yelped. And then she just lay down. Fell down."

"Christ on a crutch," Perry said. "I know they want her disgraced, but to do this? No. No, that makes no sense."

"What are you talking about, Perry? Are you thinking the king ordered Her Majesty poisoned? Because I thought so myself at first, as I dashed off my note to you. But then, when I'd had a moment to think, I realized that the populace would feel sure they could lay the death at the king's door. There'd be riots."

"Riots would be the least of his problems. No, the king couldn't have ordered it. And Liverpool is convinced this ridiculous trial will serve his purposes. But I agree, believing the death deliberate would be a reasonable first thought. Amelia, are you certain Lucy wasn't already sick? By the look of her muzzle, she was far beyond a puppy. No, don't bother to answer. We both saw her at play, and she was fine. Where is the body?"

"I don't know. I wrapped her in a sheet and had Gerado take her away. Her Majesty was very upset, you understand. I'm afraid I had to let Rosetta mix her some laudanum. There will be no dinner party."

"Hang the dinner party."

"Oh, but she was so looking forward to it."

"I'm sure something can be arranged. Amelia, we have other problems."

She leaned her head against his shoulder. "I know. It's just easier for me to worry about Her Majesty's happiness than it is for me to think someone may have just tried to kill her. And she's bound to think of it, sooner or later, and then there will be no containing her fear."

"Amelia! Amelia, are you all right?"

Perry and Amelia turned on the bench to see Miss Georgiana Penrose and Sir Nathaniel running hand in hand across the scythed lawn.

"My goodness. How could they know about Lucy?" Amelia asked.

"I imagine a footman told them," Perry said, as it seemed a logical answer. And would have been, if Sir Nathaniel wasn't looking at him as if he expected to see a dagger in his hand, ready to plunge it into Amelia's back. What maggot had the young looby gotten into his head?

"Miss Fredericks, My Lord," Sir Nathaniel said, all but skidding to a halt in front of the bench as Perry stood to make his own bow. "How delightful to see you again, My Lord. May I have a word?"

"You may have any number of them, my good man, if they'll explain your agitated appearance," Perry said coolly. "Miss Penrose, if you would be so kind as to keep Miss Fredericks company, I believe Sir Nathaniel and I will take a stroll along the hillside."

"Goodness, Georgiana, you look so fierce. Is something wrong?" Amelia asked Georgiana as her friend sat down beside her, rather militantly, as if she'd just been told to stand guard and would lay down her life in the effort if necessary. "I don't understand…"

PERRY WALKED ALONG in silence, at last realizing that in his haste to shed himself of Portman Square to get to Amelia he'd totally forgotten one of his affectations, his cane. The woman had completely undone him, and he couldn't help but smile at his own unraveling. How very extraordinary to care so much for another person.

"Her dog is dead. One of the servants told us when we arrived. Murdered, the man said, when he wasn't spouting off in his own language," Sir Nathaniel said once they'd passed out of easy earshot of the ladies. "You want to tell me about that, My Lord?"

Perry stopped, turned, looked at his companion. "I know that's what you asked, boy, but something in your tone tells me you'd rather be asking if I was ready to make a clean breast of things, and admit to having poisoned Lucy."

Sir Nathaniel frowned. "Lucy? E-gods, man, is there no limit to your dirty dealings? You killed one of the maids, too? I thought it was just the dog. No wonder that Italian was wailing like that."

Perry fought down the urge to rub at his forehead, even as he silently asked himself, *Do I really have time for this intense young fool?* "The dog, Sir Nathaniel. The dog's name was Lucy."

"Oh." Sir Nathaniel looked abashed, but only for a moment. "And you poisoned her?"

"Yes, of course," Perry said, continuing on along the hillside. "I thought I'd begin small, with the dog, and then work my way up to the queen. It's patently obvious."

"Well, no need to cut up stiff about it," Sir Nathaniel said. "It's not like Georgie and I haven't figured out you're here on orders from Sir Willard. Your uncle, you know. He used to be head of the Admiralty and I know that because I worked there during the war, doing my bit. Staunch Tory, your uncle, and you his only heir."

Now Perry halted again, and looked back to where Amelia and Miss Penrose had their heads close together in conversation. "Damn you, you idiot! Is that what Miss Penrose is saying to Amelia? That I'm some sort of Tory spy, out to discredit the queen?"

Sir Nathaniel backed up two paces. Stronger men, when faced with Perry's icy ire, would have already been halfway back to their curricles, plans for a restoring trip to the country half-formed in their minds. "You…your uncle didn't send you here to spy on the queen?"

Perry hesitated, only a moment, but that moment was long enough. Long enough for Sir Nathaniel to notice the hesitation.

"May I call you Nate?" Perry asked, caught between wanting to rush to Amelia and drag her away from Miss Penrose and knowing that the time had come for some honest speech with Sir Nathaniel before bad went to worse. If he tried to approach Amelia right now, the young fool would probably tackle him. "My friends call me Perry."

Nate's forehead went rather red. "I'm certain that I am honored, My Lord. We don't exactly rub elbows in the same set. You being older and all."

"True. I've given up tipping the Charlies and jumping my horse over dinner tables these past years, to become a boring old stickler. But I do remember my grass time, as I'm not quite that ancient."

"Oh, stap me, I keep putting my foot in it, don't I? But you haven't answered me, My Lord—Perry. Georgie and I—Miss Penrose, that is—we'd already figured out you're Sir Willard's kin, and I for one didn't swallow that clunker of you showing up here to win a wager. I'd do that. My friends would do that. But you wouldn't do that. Miss Fredericks told Georgie all about it, you understand. So, even though I was only jostling Aunt Rowena along, saying I'd find a way to protect the queen, all at once it began to look as if she was right, after all. But I still didn't believe that business with the bird or the cards, except that Georgie got all frazzled and looked as if she was about to have a come-apart, and we rushed here, and the dog was dead, and you were here and—well, it's all of a piece."

Perry chanced another look over his shoulder. Amelia and her friend still had their heads together. "I'm sure it is, to you. Who, pray tell, is Aunt Rowena?"

"My aunt on my mother's side," Nate said, and the blush was back. "She got it into her head that the queen is in danger. She gets a lot of things into her head, but this time m'mother asked me to go see the queen and then tell my aunt that everything was fine and I'd protect Her Majesty. Imagine that! Me, protecting a queen. But Aunt Rowena swallowed all that gammon whole, and then I met Georgie and we're rubbing along well enough that now I'm here all the time and Aunt Rowena is over the moon."

"Your aunt and the queen are acquainted?"

"I can't say for certain on that. But she likes her, thinks she's being cruelly used. Even m'father says so, and he's a dashed Tory. Except that my sire so forgot himself that he said some would think it would be easier all round if someone just killed the queen, and Aunt Rowena heard him and pitched several fits until I agreed to help. So when we started thinking—Georgie and me—about you and Sir Willard, Aunt Rowena's notions seemed almost sane. And when she said she saw death here today? Well, Georgie all but grabbed me by the neck and dragged me here to check on Miss Fredericks. Clear now?"

"If there are fuzzy areas, I believe I am content to allow them to remain undisturbed. And remember, the dog may have been poisoned or may have simply died. We cannot be certain. We can only be vigilant. Now tell me, Nate, is Miss Penrose informing Miss Fredericks now of my familial connection to the Tory cause?"

Nate peeked over his shoulder. "I suppose so. She might be. Georgie was all hot to tell her not to trust you. But if you're not in league with Sir Willard and his cronies, that's all right, isn't it?"

"It had better be, Nate, or you and I are going to experience the shortest friendship in history."

"Hooboy," Nate said, sighing. "Is it true you kill people?"

Perry smiled, but the smile didn't quite reach his

eyes. He was too busy deciding how much of Nate was silly youth and how much of him was possible ally. "No matter why I came to be on the scene, Nate, and no matter how I managed to get myself here, my intentions lie completely in seeing to Miss Fredericks's welfare and, because of her, the queen's welfare."

"Georgie will be in alt to hear that, seeing as how she thinks it's my fault you got to kiss her."

Perry blinked. It wasn't often he allowed himself to show any sort of reaction, no matter what the news, but this young buck had a definite talent to say the damnedest things. "I assure you, my man, I have only made Miss Penrose's acquaintance the once."

"Oh, no, not her. Not my Georgie. Miss Fredericks. You kiss her, don't you? Oh! No, no, I never said that. Really. Never said that."

"Yes, that seems best. Let us return, if you're willing, to the queen's dilemma, shall we? Her Majesty must be protected at all costs, I do believe we agree on that?"

Nate nodded furiously.

"Ah, wonderful, we've cried allies, then? It becomes more likely that someone is out to dispose of the queen before the Bill of Pains and Penalties is initiated. And that, my new friend, while a formidable problem and a definite disaster if it were to happen, is only the half of it. Have you ever heard of Jarrett Rolin?"

Sir Nathaniel blew out his cheeks. "Rolin? There's a nasty piece of work. Wouldn't want him within a continent of m'sisters."

"Ah, good, we agree. And here is the problem, Nate.

Jarrett Rolin, for reasons of his own, is out to destroy me. This is, of course, my problem. But if you know anything about Rolin, you know he is a cowardly bastard who would much rather attack me without confronting me directly."

"He ruins women," Nate said, nodding his head. "My friend Freddie told me about his cousin. Damn shame. Had to marry her off to the assistant vicar before she popped."

"Yes, thank you. So you understand. Now, Nate, let's carry this further, shall we? If you were Jarrett Rolin and you wanted me destroyed, how would you do it?"

"From a distance, that's sure as check, if half of what I've heard about you is true. But that's not what you mean, is it?" Nate seemed to think about this for a few moments, then whirled about to look at Amelia. "Do you really think…?"

"With very good reason, yes, I do think exactly that. There is more to the story, complications and coincidences that muddy the water even while making it more dangerous, and I would ask that you and I meet at White's late this evening where I will tell you all about Sir Willard, Jarrett Rolin and why you're going to convince Miss Penrose that she is entirely wrong in her conclusions and Miss Fredericks is entirely right in placing all of her trust in me. Can you do that?"

The younger man screwed up his face. "She's sharp as a tack, you know. She'll want to know my reasons."

"Which you may not give her. She's bound to run straight to Miss Fredericks to warn her about Rolin. I don't want Amelia to worry more than necessary."

"Uh-oh. You may not have to worry about that, Perry," Nate said, pointing toward the ladies.

Perry looked in that direction just in time to see Amelia, her skirts lifted above her ankles, racing pell-mell toward the queen's residence, while Miss Penrose looked at him, chin raised in defiance, glaring at him as if to challenge him to dare, just dare, to chase after her friend.

"Damn it all to hell," Perry said, watching Amelia go, one hand pressed to her mouth, probably to stifle her sobs. "Bloody damn it all to hell!"

"Aren't you going to run after her? I think females expect you to run after them."

Perry shook his head. "No. It's probably better this way. Safer. Nate, it would please me if you'd remember our appointment tonight. As long as you're going to be here, mucking things up, you might as well at least know what's going on. You do seem to have a nose for adventure."

"Is that what this is? Right now, Perry, my new friend, I'd say it sounds much more dangerous than a simple adventure. Going to take me some time to get over that, you know…that Aunt Rowena could be right."

Shall We Dance?

Here we go round the mulberry bush,
the mulberry bush, the mulberry bush.
Here we go round the mulberry bush,
so early in the morning.

—Anonymous

AMELIA LIFTED HER SKIRTS and raced up the stairs to the queen's chambers, following the hysterical shrieks, her heart pounding with fear.

She raced down the hallway, scrambling in the pocket of her gown for the key to the queen's chambers. "Clive, thank God you're here. What happened?"

Clive Rambert, Bow Street Runner, lovestruck spy and so many other things he had begun to lose count, shrugged his shoulders, attempting to look as innocent as possible. "I dunno, Miss Fredericks. I was walkin' past on my nightly rounds, just like I've been doin' every night, and she started screechin' like that. Sorry, her majesties don't screech, do they? Exceptin' this one is, sure as check. Screechin'."

Amelia attempted to insert the key in the lock, but her hand trembled so badly that she at last stepped back and handed the key to Clive. The queen had insisted upon remaining in her chambers ever since Lucy's death two weeks ago, and only Amelia and Rosetta, who had not been returned to Italy, possessed keys. Queen Caroline barely slept, she barely ate, and she drank almost constantly.

"Here we go," Clive said, turning the key in the lock, then depressing the latch and pushing open the door…all the better to hear Queen Caroline's screams.

Bless Clive! No matter that he had come to be here because of that perfidious Earl of Brentwood; he was here, and in a household of women (for who would count Nestor?), a man like Clive Rambert could only be seen as a godsend. What would she have done without him these past dozen or more long, fairly horrible days?

"Your Majesty?" Amelia called out, taking up a small branch of candles from a hallway table and holding them above her head as she entered the vast chamber. "It's me, Amelia."

"Amelia! It's gone! My chest! My treasures! Gone, all gone! I sent Rosetta to fetch it—and it's gone!"

Amelia nearly sagged to her knees in relief. "Oh, ma'am, don't you remember? You entrusted the chest to me."

Amelia located her queen lying on her bed, still fully clothed, her heavily made-up face a ruin thanks to her near-constant tears. The smell of spirits more than hung in the air; a person could almost chew it. Her Majesty was of the opinion that strong spirits destroyed poisons in the stomach, and seemed to have a glass at her side day and night.

The queen pushed herself up straight in the bed. "You? Why would I give it to you? You're nothing but another damned one of *them.* Lying, cheating, selfish, killing monsters!" She grabbed at her barely covered bosom. "And who is that? No men! I'll allow no men.

Men destroy! They're good for nothing save putting babies in our bellies. I've no more need of that, gel, let me tell you. No more need. Get him out!"

Amelia looked beseechingly at Clive, who was already tugging at his nonexistent forelock and bowing himself out of the chamber. She dropped into a curtsy, equally prepared to leave, as it was clear Her Majesty was beyond coherence at the moment. "I will fetch the chest, ma'am."

"No! No, sweet girl, don't go. Don't leave me. I'm moldering here, dying here. I am so, so sore afraid." Her wine-sour breath caught on a sob. "So alone and unloved."

Amelia could no more ignore such a statement than she could ever entertain the thought of leaving her queen. "You are loved, ma'am. Greatly loved. If you were only to leave your bed, allow the draperies opened so that you could step onto your balcony, see your subjects as, daily, they take to their boats, praying for just a glimpse of their queen. You must be strong, ma'am, summon up all of your courage. Soon you'll be traveling to Westminster, ma'am. We must prepare. Mr. Brougham told me so himself today, when he visited. He's quite concerned."

The queen reached for her ever-present wineglass and lifted it in a mock salute. "Hah, so I've got Henry wetting himself, do I? Good. It's listening to him that landed me in this terrible prison. Don't take the allowance, Majesty. Exile? You don't want exile, Majesty. You must come back, claim your throne. And for what? I was happy, Amelia. We were all so happy. Now I'm here, and alone, and dogs are dying…"

"We can't be sure Lucy was poisoned, ma'am. We've already discussed this, remember? She was rather old, and the voyage from Italy could have proved too arduous for her."

"You tell your fairy tales to yourself, gel. I know what I know. Did Henry tell you? Liverpool has another witness lined up to tell lies about me." She waved the empty wineglass in front of her, signaling for Rosetta, who had slipped back into the chamber and been sitting in a corner, knitting, to refill it. "Carson. Callow. No, Carstairs. That's it, Carstairs."

"But…but Carstairs only served as butler since we arrived in England. He knows nothing," Amelia said, then amended as the wily Rosetta coughed in warning, "not that there is anything to know. All the charges are without merit, ma'am."

"Don't mollycoddle me, Amelia, I know what's truth and what's not. Rosetta will be next, and that brother of hers."

"Gerado," Amelia supplied, knowing that both servants should have been sent back to Italy, even over Her Majesty's protests after Lucy died that she could not bear another new servant in her presence. "I'm sure neither would say a word against you. Tell Her Majesty, Rosetta."

Rosetta shrugged. *"Cu'e orbu, bordu e taci campa cent'anni 'n paci."*

"English!" the queen shouted. "Nothing but English here."

"She said, ma'am, that he who is deaf, dumb and blind will live a hundred years in peace," Amelia explained.

The queen's red-rimmed eyes filled with fresh tears. "My Pergami often said that."

Rosetta crossed to the bed and looked down at the queen, her expression one of mingled affection and exasperation. "I say nothing, Majesty." Then, as she walked past Amelia on her way out of the room, she paused and made a rather rude gesture with one hand and added, "Makes for me to take bites of all her food? You English, worse than the Medici."

"Yes, thank you, Rosetta," Amelia said, stifling what would only be a long-suffering sigh. "I will sit with Her Majesty. Perhaps you have something you wish to do?"

"Chi non fa, non falla," Rosetta said cheekily, and walked, loose-hipped, toward the dressing room.

He who does nothing, makes no mistakes.

Amelia sighed, wondering if that was true. She had done nothing for the nearly two weeks since Lucy had died. Nothing but sulk, and weep into her pillow, and call herself every kind of gullible fool, and wait for the man who never dared to come back to Hammersmith. Or had never wished to return. No! She didn't have time for that now, time to think of Perry, who had betrayed her, used her. She approached the queen.

"Are you quite sure, ma'am, that you don't want me to bring you your chest? It would only take a moment."

"A moment to live, a moment to die. Amelia, you're right. I must put a stop to this. I cannot live in fear. Henry wants me out and about, being seen. If I am to die, let me die standing on my feet, as a true daughter of my father." She held out her hands to Amelia, who quickly assisted the queen to her feet. "We were going to have a party. A dinner party. With that handsome earl of yours and your friends. We must do that. We must show the world that we are alive and innocent."

She winked at Amelia. "Well, you can be innocent. I'm afraid I'm well past that. Saturday night, Amelia. Violins, Gunther ices. I so long for one of Gunther's ices. See to it."

Amelia fought back the urge to grab at the wineglass the queen had abandoned and drink it all down. "I'm afraid that the Earl of Brentwood no longer visits, ma'am, although Miss Penrose and Sir Nathaniel are here often, to bear me company."

The queen turned on Amelia, her eyes glittering. "What did you do, gel, chase him away? I want him here, I command him to be here. He's much too pretty not to be here. See to it."

"But, ma'am…"

"I said, see to it. Am I to be disobeyed, like some powerless old woman? I give you everything, Amelia. I protect you. I have all but given my life for you. If I want that pretty fellow here to fawn over me, he will be here. Do you understand?"

"So now you're sure he's here? I don't understand why. You're certain? Seems like we've been chasing him forever, and never in the right places."

Perry put a finger to his lips, warning Nate to silence, then nodded.

Jarrett Rolin was here, staying at this tumbledown

inn near London Dock. Not at this moment, no, as Perry had come up here alone at first, to knock, before returning to gather up Nate, who had been showing off for the bribed landlord, dazzling him with some trick with a pair of dice.

It had taken nearly a fortnight of looking, many a greased palm and misdirection, but Perry was certain that this time he had at last found the man's lodgings. He might have been successful earlier with Clive's help, but Clive had remained in Hammersmith, keeping a careful eye on Amelia and the queen. Not that Rolin would go after Amelia now, now that Perry was no longer seen courting her.

That was the only benefit to be derived by her steadfast refusal to meet with him, to even read the many notes he'd had Clive deliver to her.

Did she really think he would give up, go away? But this estrangement was for the best; Amelia would remain safe and Perry would eliminate Rolin. That was how he'd survived in Spain and France all those years; knowing which problem posed the most danger and solving that one first, then moving on to the next. It seemed cold, even to him, to place Amelia second on the list, knowing the hurt he'd caused her, but better she should hate him than to have Rolin free to do his mischief.

After that, his dearest Amelia was in for the shock of her life.

Perry took hold of Nate's arm and urged the younger man to step behind him as he led the way down the narrow, greasy hallway to the door marked Number Twelve.

"Locked, I'm sure. Well, that's it, then," Nate said, clearly anxious to be away. "Unless you want me to break it down. I'm not against the idea, you know."

Perry rolled his eyes. "Would you mind keeping that mouth of yours shut, just for the moment?"

"Sorry," Nate said. "It's just that I've never done anything like this before. It's rather fun, even if this place stinks to heaven of blue ruin and vomit. An adventure, you understand."

"I cannot tell you how delighted I am for you, and your nose," Perry drawled, then looked up and down the hall before dropping to one knee to examine the lock. He reached into a small pocket sewn into the inside of his waistcoat, extracted a slim bit of metal, inserted it in the lock…and a moment later, opened the door to Rolin's small suite of rooms.

"Oh, I say, that was neat and tidy," Nate said, following Perry inside. "Is that what you did in the war?"

"Close the door, Nate," Perry said, crossing to the draperies and pulling them back, admitting weak rays of dusty sunlight that did nothing to enhance the shabby furnishings. "How low you have fallen, Mr. Rolin, and how gratified I am to see it."

"Bit of a mess, clothing everywhere. Doesn't even have a man to serve him, just as you said. Forced to drape one's own neck cloth, shave one's own face, strip off one's own boots. Neat trick that, if you can do it. Blister me, is that a boot jack nailed to the floor? It is. Would you look at those boots over there? Ruined the leather, just ruined it, and those are Hobbs's finest, you can tell. A gentleman can't fall much farther than a boot jack."

Perry, who had been carefully sorting through the few papers he'd located in a locked drawer, turned to look at his companion. "If you're quite done having your sensibilities shocked, perhaps you could have a look around the other room? Don't disturb anything. We don't want Rolin to know we were here."

"That's understandable. I wouldn't want to know anyone was here if I lived here. Mortifying, you know. What am I looking for, if you don't mind."

"Weapons, for the start of it. Vials of poison, although I highly doubt Rolin is behind that. He has no reason to want the queen dead."

"No," Nate said, rather cheerily, Perry noticed. "Just you. He wants you dead. I suppose I might, too, if you'd ruined my life."

"Rolin destroyed his own life. I merely nudged him over the precipice he'd been teetering on for years. Now go."

Perry had always worked alone. He'd rather work alone. The addition of Clive was much in the vein of the occasional assistant he'd incorporated into his more complex assignments, and he'd much rather the clever Runner was with him now. And yet, Sir Nathaniel had proven himself to be willing and most definitely eager.

Perry used the tip of his cane to poke at rumpled piles of clothing Rolin had not bothered to place in the small clothes press, and avoided looking too long at the insects crawling over scraps of stale and almost petrified food-stuffs that cluttered a small table.

Had Rolin moved on, leaving all of this behind in his haste to be gone? Had he gotten wind of Perry's pursuit, sensed that his enemy was getting closer?

"Nate?" Perry called out, realizing that stealth and silence meant nothing now, since in this section of London, nobody listened, nobody cared. "Do you see any baggage in there?"

The younger man poked his head out of the room. "I thought you said I should be quiet. No, I didn't see any. Just a bed in here, with sheets probably crawling with bugs. You think he's taken a flit?"

"It's possible, yes, even probable. And he left in a hurry. I've had to be less than discreet a time or two in my inquiries. It's not as if I can buy silence with a few coins. And as twisting the necks of those I spoke with is frowned upon, it can't be helped if I speak to someone and that someone drinks up the coins, then brags to his friends about the gentry cove who plied him with silver while he asked questions about some other gentry cove."

Nate had narrowed in on a few words of that explanation. "Twisting necks, you say? Killing, you mean?" He ran a finger under his neck cloth. "That's fairly dreadful, you know."

Perry looked at his hands for a moment, once again seeing them as they once had been, as his most effective weapons. How did one explain war to someone who has never experienced it? Life and death to one who has never been in fear for his own? He retrieved a crumpled sheet of paper from the floor. "Yes, indeed, my friend. Much more civilized to repeatedly hack someone with a sword or shatter his head with a ball from your rifle. Or blow him to bits with a cannonball. I see your point. Now, what have we here?"

"Something he didn't want anymore?" Nate suggested.

"Or something he felt he no longer needed," Perry said, frowning over the list of names. "Even something left for me to find, something to alarm me, to send me chasing off in entirely the wrong direction."

"All that on one small scrap of paper? What has he written?"

Perry held on to his temper with a control difficult to maintain. "Our friend Rolin hasn't been idle. He's compiled a list of names. Very inventive of him."

"Really? Am I on it?" Nate asked, peering over Perry's shoulder. "Not that I'm the sort to hide behind a woman's skirts, but I don't think my Georgie would like that above half."

Perry handed Nate the list, as he'd seen it enough. Perry's name was there, along with Nate's and Georgiana's and Amelia's. And Sir Willard's. And, most damning of all, was the line that read *Earl and Countess of Westham.* With a thick line drawn through the names.

Morgan and his Emma. The newlyweds, off somewhere touring the Lake District. Two people very much not on their guard; definitely not expecting to encounter a Jarrett Rolin intent on revenge.

The line Rolin had drawn through the names could be interpreted as a mission already satisfactorily concluded.

The bastard. Rolin wanted him panicked, wanted him reckless with grief. Wanted him sloppy. Definitely did not want him thinking.

A slight, not in the least amused, smile raised one side of his mouth. The man was to be disappointed, as Perry had already sent not one but two Runners searching for Morgan, and had just last night been informed that his friend and his bride were safely ensconced at Westham.

But Perry wanted this over. He'd set himself up every night, walking home from his club alone. And yet Rolin had refused to approach him. Perhaps because he now knew that Perry was aware of his presence, perhaps because this list was no more than a search for alternative, weaker targets. Morgan and Emma were crossed off as possibilities because Rolin couldn't locate them, and the others were listed because Perry appeared to have some affection for each of them.

"You're being dashed quiet," Nate said, and it was only then that Perry realized they were back on the street. "I've been thinking, too. He's not just after you and Amelia now, is he?"

"He's not after anyone right now, Nate. He's running, and scheming impossible schemes. He won't come back here. I already have a Runner watching his estate, in the event he rabbits there. However, bent as he seems to be on exacting his revenge, he's probably more dangerous now than ever. I'm sorry to have involved you and Miss Penrose."

"Oh, Georgie isn't going to go all female on us. Really, she's as pluck to the backbone as ever you could hope. We'll be fine. How about Sir Willard?"

They stepped around the corner and climbed inside Perry's town coach, as the alleyway had been too narrow for it, and because the only way to be even marginally safe from nuisance attacks in this area of the metropolis was to arrive in the most imposing way possible, along with a coachman, tiger and three armed outriders. Ah, civilization.

"I doubt Rolin was serious about that, Nate. After all, a dead Sir Willard makes for a wealthier Perry Shepherd. Not exactly what Rolin would wish. Still, I would be remiss if I didn't warn the man, wouldn't I?"

Nate looked at Perry as he sat across from him on the velvet squabs. "You're looking more jolly than I would have supposed. You're going to enjoy telling him, aren't you?"

"Ah, Nate, my friend. Such a short acquaintance, and already you know me so well."

"I don't know you at all," Nate said, then sighed theatrically. "And the more I'm with you, the more I know that."

AMELIA SAT OVER THE NOTE that, thus far, contained only the words, "My Dear Earl of Brentwood, your presence is required at the queen's residence at eight of the clock this Saturday evening for a dinner party hosted by Her Majesty."

She didn't know what else to say. How to say it. How should she sign the note? Should she sign it at all? What would he think when he saw it? Was it too cold, too abrupt, too much of a command?

"Oh, this is silly," she said, sanding the page and then folding it. One of the footmen would deliver the thing, Saturday would come, Perry would arrive punctiliously, she'd speak to him—punctiliously—and she'd never see him again.

She should have known. This wasn't the first time someone had attempted to use her to get to the queen.

She should have known. She certainly was no match for him; not in lineage, certainly not in looks. He was beautiful; she was not.

But his flattery had weakened her, his truly outstanding good looks had dazzled her, and his kisses had all but destroyed her.

Not, not destroyed her. Awakened her.

It had been the truth about his perfidy, his lies, his hidden agenda that had destroyed her.

Georgiana had told her to forget him, to not be embarrassed that she had believed all his lies. After all, he'd only seen the queen the once, and no secrets had been told, no damning evidence uncovered that Perry could take to his uncle, which his uncle could take to Lord Liverpool.

And now, after all her warnings, Georgiana was actually defending the man to her, telling her she should allow him to apologize, to explain.

How could she do that? After all she had told him? After all she had allowed him?

It was at night, alone in her bed, that Amelia shivered, remembering how quick she had been to trust him, how she had even suggested to Her Majesty that he could become a safe repository for the queen's most cherished memories and secrets.

Georgiana and Nate still visited Hammersmith every day, attempted to amuse her, coddle her, and just seeing her friend and her beloved together tore something inside Amelia. She was happy for her friend, not jealous, not really.

But was it so terrible to wish for a happiness of her own? A life of her own? A love of her own?

And still they told her that Perry had never planned to find a way to further damage the queen. They'd admitted that he had first come here on orders from his uncle to do just that, but now they were sure he had never really seriously planned to do anything more than meet with Amelia in order to make his uncle happy.

"And that other thing, Georgie. Remember, he already knew about Jar—" Nate had said to Georgiana, but she had quickly dug an elbow in his ribs, and he'd said no more.

Amelia trusted Georgiana, and had grown to like Nate very much, but she was not ready to see Perry again. Not yet. Even if he crawled here on his knees, apologizing for his lies. She did, after all, have her pride.

She'd told him her silly dreams. She'd welcomed his kisses, his caresses. She'd been about to give herself to him, body and soul, without a word of love, without a promise of anything more.

If he hadn't completely lied to her, he hadn't been completely truthful, either.

"Notes. He sends me notes. If he truly cared, he'd have beaten down doors to get to me. He'd have come here, demanding to see me. Oh, how I dread this dinner party."

She picked up the note and went in search of a footman to deliver the dratted invitation to Portman Square.

CLIVE RAMBERT KISSED his Dovey, immediately noticing that she was not quite kissing him back. "Here now, love, still worrying your head about menus? I thought that was all settled the first time."

Maryann pushed him away. "It's not that, Clivey. Mrs. Pidgeon has taken over everything, and I'm that grateful to her, seeing as how I don't know if I'm on my head or my heels thanks to that Mr. Nestor."

"Nestor? That stick? Don't tell me he tried a nip at yer bottom, Dovey, because that fish won't swim. Not that yer're not a prime 'un and he'd be lookin' high to look at yer, so don't go cuttin' up all stiff like that. He just don't seem the sort. Never had me a butler, Dovey, but if I did, it wouldn't be him. Does he ever do anythin'?"

Maryann picked up the sheet she had been darning and sat herself down in the rocking chair Clive had fetched her from somewhere in the attics. She was always happier, these days, with a needle in her hand. "He polishes a lot of silver, Clivey. Over and over again. And he counts things. Counts the sheets, counts the plates, counts the carrots in the larder. Always walking around with that tablet of his, always poking in corners. And telling me to mind my own business or else I can just take myself off."

Clive nodded. "He is always pokin' somewhere, isn't he? Yer don't do that, butlerin'? I thought that's what he was supposed to do."

"I don't know, Clivey, except that Esther—that Mrs. Pidgeon—says she thinks he has a cast or something in one of his eyes, and that means he can't be trusted." She motioned for Clive to sit down beside her. "She said she thinks it's Mr. Nestor what poisoned that dog."

"Really? Strange, that. I didn't think anyone for sure ever said the dog was poisoned. Did yer tell her that?"

Maryann deftly wove the thread in and out, across the half-repaired hole. "I don't know, Clivey. I may have. You and me talked about it some, remember? Why?"

"Why? Because if yer did, then that's all right. But if yer didn't, if nobody did, then yer tell me how Esther Pidgeon came to think the dog was poisoned? Old dog, right? Coulda dropped over anytime."

He got up, began to pace. "I've got too much, Dovey. Watchin' the queen, watchin' Miss Fredericks. Checkin' all the locks on all the doors. Watchin' that Nestor, because yer don't like him, and starin' down that Italian when he looks at me all crooked. Never thought much about the Pidgeon. Crikey, chasing down housebreakers beats this all hollow for easy."

"Poor Clivey. How can I help you?"

He grinned. "Well now, Dovey, I've got this itch…"

"Not now, Clivey. Goodness, the sun's still out. And I haven't got a thing to say to Sir Willard, and he'll be expecting me to tell him something. What did I say in my note last week, Clivey?"

Resigned to not having his itch scratched until after evening prayers, Clive thought a moment, then said, "I think what yer said was that the queen won't leave her rooms and the dog died. Oh, and yer told him I'm bein' a great help to yer, sniffin' out anythin' that will help the king."

"Yes, I remember now. Well, the queen's still locked up, the dog's still dead, and you're still here. What do I tell him this week?"

"I don't expect yer have to tell him anythin', Dovey. His Lordship's taking care of all that."

SIR WILLARD GLARED at his nephew. "Oh no, that won't work with me, Perry. You just want some of your own back, which I find to be juvenile in the extreme. Rolin? After me? Nonsense."

Perry braced his hands on the arms of the chair and made to rise. "In that case, Uncle, I'll bid you good day. So sorry to have troubled you."

"Sit down, damn you," Sir Willard ordered. "You come sneaking through windows, you do your best to make a fool of me, then you disappear for nearly a fort-night, just to come strolling in here, grinning like some village idiot, delighted to tell me Jarrett Rolin wrote my name on some list and left it in a hovel along with half his wardrobe. I imagine that means you haven't found him yet?"

"Obviously," Perry said, unsurprised that his uncle would take little time zeroing in on his nephew's failings. "What I have managed, what you and I have managed between us, is to involve three entirely innocent people in Rolin's quest for revenge. I'm not proud of that. Are you?"

"Ah, back to this Amelia Fredericks person. I'm told you haven't been back to Hammersmith. Did she chase you away?"

"Clive has reported to you. Of course. But those three people, Uncle? Two of them are Sir Nathaniel Rankin and Miss Georgiana Penrose. They put their heads together, remembered I am, for my sins, your only relation and concluded that you'd sent me to woo Miss Fredericks in order to worm my way into the queen's presence, into her secrets. Naturally, as Miss Fredericks is their friend, they immediately apprised her of this conclusion, and I have been rather effectively banished."

Sir Willard steepled his fingers, his forearms resting on his ample belly. "Pardon me a moment, Nevvie, while I relish this moment. The grand Perry, lowered by a mere female. The mind boggles, and the heart, mine at least, rejoices. I'm even beginning to like the gel."

"From what I am hearing, Uncle, you like most anything in petticoats, and preferably out of them. We will not discuss Miss Fredericks."

"Amelia. When you were clomping around my bed-chamber, all in your altitudes, you called her Amelia. You know, I thought you were being the better man, possibly even noble, staying away from her in order to distract Rolin from possibly using her to revenge himself on you. But now? Now, Nevvie, I think I'm looking at a lovestruck idiot who doesn't have the faintest notion how to get back in his beloved's good graces."

He leaned forward in his chair. "Go to her, boy. Grovel if you have to. I don't think I could stand to watch as you slip into some sad decline."

"I doubt that is your concern. You only want what you sent me there for in the first place—information that would help you and your cronies destroy the queen."

Sir Willard waved one hand dismissively. "Oh, that. Liverpool says he has plenty now. A pair of those Italians she dragged here, brother and sister. A purse apiece, and they'll be brought in front of the Lords the first week of the investigation, and there will be no need for more testimony. In fact, once the queen is apprised of these new witnesses against her, she'll agree to all of our terms."

Perry kept his expression blank. "How fortunate for you."

"And you're wondering why I'm telling you, aren't you? You won't betray us, Perry. You can't. You agreed, as a gentleman, to do as I asked, and you cannot in good conscience reveal anything you know."

Perry got to his feet. "That must be some Tory code I've never heard, Uncle. I certainly don't ascribe to it, not when your target is a sick, frightened, defenseless woman. Although you shouldn't flatter yourself too much, as I know you only told me about these witnesses so that I'll be the one to tell the queen the game is lost, checkmate. I wouldn't count on that, either, Uncle."

"Perry! Don't be a fool, boy. The sooner this is over,

the sooner you can talk this Amelia of yours round to whatever in blazes it is you want from her. Once you're rid of Rolin, of course. I apologize for that, son, I really do. I knew he was wild, but not that he's totally lost his senses. Do take of that, will you?"

"At this point, Uncle, I'd much rather give him a loaded pistol and a map to your study. Good day."

And with that, Perry quit his uncle's residence, a bad taste in his mouth, little satisfaction in his heart and an almost unbearable desire to race to Hammersmith…and arrived home to find Amelia's note summoning him to exactly where he wanted to be.

"I DON'T WANT HIM HERE, Georgiana, so stop looking at me as if I'm counting the minutes, eager to leap into his arms or some such ridiculousness."

"No, of course not, Amelia," Georgiana said, doing her best not to smile as she watched her friend pace her bed chamber as the clock neared eight. "Is that a new gown?"

Amelia stopped her pacing and looked down at the cream silk confection that had been a present from the queen while they were in Italy. The style was French, the silk imported from China, and it was, she knew, quite the most flattering thing she owned. Especially when worn, as she was wearing it now, with the emerald choker and earrings the queen had given her on her sixteenth birthday. "No, of course not. Did you really think I would go to that sort of fuss and bother for a small dinner party?"

"Only if the Earl of Brentwood was to be among the

guests," Georgiana said, no longer able to withhold her smile. "Oh, cut line, Amelia, you know you can't wait to see him again. He sends you notes every day, Nate told me. And Nate told you that even if his uncle did send him here, once he was here His Lordship took one look at you and decided that his uncle could just go hang, he would have nothing further to do with the scheme. You'll have to forgive him sometime."

Amelia subsided into a chair, for two reasons. One, her slippers, dyed to match her gown, had never been comfortable. And two, the closer the clock hands moved to eight, the weaker her knees became. "Georgiana, he lied. It doesn't matter that he's sorry. When I think that I was going to entrust him with—no, no, I can't forgive him. He had no right to come here."

Georgiana pursed her lips, had a silent conversation with herself, then sighed. "All right, Amelia, you're making me do this. I mean, it's not my fault and Nate can't be angry, and since he wasn't supposed to tell me in the first place, I see no reason why I can't tell you in the second place, because it's not as if I need to know, it's that you *should* know."

Amelia took out a small linen square edged with fine lace and began picking at it with her fingers, a nervous habit she really should try to overcome. "Georgiana, would you mind terribly if I told you I haven't understood a word you just said?"

Georgiana pushed at the nosepiece of her spectacles, another young lady with a habit to break. "No, not particularly, because I know I ramble sometimes. Do you remember Miss Stanley? She taught deportment. She said she despaired of my ever learning when to keep my tongue from running on wheels. She said—"

"Georgiana? You're doing it again. I think you want to tell me what it is that Nate told you that he shouldn't have told you but that I should know. Oh, dear, now I'm doing it."

Georgiana giggled. "Yes, you are. It's as if we're back in school, isn't it, except that this is very real. Nate's been dragged into every alley and byway in London with the earl. He ate a meat pie he bought from a hawker and was sick for two days, poor lamb."

Amelia remained silent, because if she commented she knew she'd have to hear much more about Nate's illness, and she really didn't think that was germane to whatever it was Georgiana wasn't supposed to know and wasn't supposed to tell her.

"Oh, dear," Georgiana said, "I'm usually not this obtuse, really. Being around Nate seems to have addled my brains. Especially now that he's talked to Mr. Bateman and we're going to be officially engaged. Do you really think the queen was serious when she said Mr. Bateman could have the party here? Mama's so in alt she's unbearable, and it makes me nervous, having her dote on me, but I am getting a lovely new gown out of the thing, so that's all right."

"Georgiana, please. It's almost eight."

"And you want me to get on with it. I don't blame you. So," she said, taking a deep breath and then letting it sort of *whoosh* back out, "even though Sir Willard—

the uncle, remember—asked His Lordship to come here
and sniff around for dirt on Her Majesty, and His Lordship wanted nothing to do with such a tawdry business,
he found he had to because if he didn't, his uncle was
going to commission someone else to do it, anyway, and
His Lordship doesn't like this other person above half."

Amelia ran all of this back through her mind a second time, remembering that Nate had been about to say
something about "another reason" one day, but Georgiana had stopped him. "Who?"

"I don't know him, but his name is Jarrett Rolin, and
Nate says he's a rum touch, a very bad man. Sir Willard
was going to send him here to pretend to court you
while he dug dirt on Her Majesty, because he wanted His
Lordship to, but His Lordship kept ignoring his notes
and only found out about the plan at the same time he
found out that Rolin would take his place if he didn't do
it, so His Lordship knew he had to do the job or else this
Rolin fellow would come here and ruin you. He's an
honorable man, His Lordship. He didn't even know you
then, and he was already hot to protect you from ruin."

"I don't *ruin* all that easily," Amelia said, stiffening.
"But there's more, isn't there?"

So Georgiana, falling back on the notion that one may
as well be hanged for a sheep as a lamb, told Amelia
everything she knew about Jarrett Rolin, the Earl of Westham, and Perry Shepherd, including the fact that His
Lordship and Nate had been hunting the man down in all
sorts of low places (ergo the bad meat pie incident). "Nate
says His Lordship is going to kill him when he finds him."

Amelia looked down at her handkerchief to see that the lace was all in tatters. "Kill him?"

"Nate says His Lordship did some terrible and secret things during the war, and when Nate finally dared to ask what His Lordship would do once he found this Rolin fellow, His Lordship wouldn't answer him. He only said that he would *remove* the problem."

"Because he thinks that *I* could be in danger? Because this Rolin person hates Perry and his friends and wants to harm them, too? Well, why didn't he simply tell me?"

Georgiana shrugged. "I imagine he thought that a female shouldn't know such things. Nate thought that, until I assured him that females are much more dangerous when they know they should know something and someone isn't telling them. So, are you going to forgive him?"

"Georgiana," Amelia said with as much patience as she could muster. "I am here to serve and to protect Her Majesty. If Perry had never come here, I wouldn't be in danger, now, would I? After all, I'm not such a looby as to not have seen through anybody you describe as so patently a rogue as this Rolin person."

"You didn't see through His Lordship," Georgiana pointed out, then wished she hadn't. "And Nate says Rolin is quite the dasher with the ladies, so you might not have seen through him, either."

"In other words, Georgiana, I'm a silly, stupid woman who should not be trusted in male company?"

"No, I didn't mean that. You were right to like His Lordship, because Nate says he's top drawer—and I really must stop using all this cant, but it makes such sense when Nate uses it. And you are fond of His Lordship, Amelia, you know you are. Otherwise, you wouldn't be so angry with him."

"THINK SHE'LL TALK TO YER, sir?" Clive asked as, in the role of footman, he was the one who opened the door in answer to Perry's rap on the knocker. "She's that mad, yer know. Tried to weasel out of the festivities, but the queen told her she didn't want to hear about bellyaches or megrims and she'd best be ready to show herself once yer showed yerself. How do yer think I look in this here livery? Dovey says I look like a May game."

By this time, Perry had stripped off his gloves and removed his hat, which he was tempted to place on Clive's head, except that Clive's head was already covered by a rather pathetic powdered wig.

"You look just fine, Clive. Where is the Italian?"

"Oh, him. He went off a while ago, grumblin' in that queer tongue of his, sayin' as how Her Majesty wants him to carry her train when she pokes her head inta the drawing room. Big doin's, sir. Food enough for the First Foot, and yer could drink yerself under a table a dozen times before yer made a dent in the wine we got ready to serve. Oh, and I peeked in a fancy box Miss Fredericks took from that there trunk we're supposed to be searchin', and she showed me the diamonds she took from it. Big as goose eggs, sir, I swear it. Good thing the queen's got a nice, strong peasant neck."

"I couldn't be sure, Clive," Perry said casually, "but

in some quarters, I do believe you could be considered to have just committed treason. We are always very careful not to notice that our English royalty is heavily steeped in good, solid German stock."

Clive placed Perry's belongings on a large round table that also held a prodigiously ambitious arrangement of flowers, and all but skipped after him down the hallway. "Is it true, sir, that the first George couldn't even talk the language when he got here? And that all he ate was sauerkraut?"

"Another time, Clive. Am I the first to arrive?"

"No, sir. Miss Penrose is already here, locked upstairs with Miss Fredericks, and Sir Nathaniel is doin' m'rounds for me, checkin' to see if that Rolin fellow is hidin' himself in the bushes. A good sort, Sir Nathaniel, but enjoyin' himself a mite too much, if you take m'meanin'."

"I agree, Clive. But, as he was on to us, anyway, I find it better to have him with us, rather than enjoying himself too much on his own. You agree?"

Clive shook his head, which set off a shower of white powder onto his velvet-clad shoulders. "Too many of us, sir, is what I'm thinkin.' You, me, the boy, Dovey. And that Nestor."

"Nestor?"

"The butler, sir. Always pokin' his nose somewheres or the other. And if he's a butler, I don't know where he's been butlerin', because he ain't got a inklin' what butlerin's about, or so says Mrs. Pidgeon."

Perry helped himself to a glass of wine, immediately

appreciating its fine bouquet. Clive was right; the wine, at least, would be excellent. There had to be tradesmen in London who were optimistic enough about the queen's chances in Parliament that they'd extended her credit.

"And who, pray tell, is Mrs. Pidgeon? I thought your Dovey was the housekeeper."

"Oh, she is, she is, but Mrs. Pidgeon used to serve the queen before she done her flit, and she came back and asked Dovey to let her join the staff. Ridin' herd on half a hundred servants, just here in the house? Dovey would be all about if not for Mrs. Pidgeon."

"So you don't think my uncle sent her?"

"Mrs. Pidgeon? No, sir. Just Nestor. There's a passel of us, sir. Not that Nestor lets on, so I don't lets on that I know. If I did, Sir Willard'd probably just send another one. Not a trustin' sort, your uncle. But I'm watchin' this Nestor close as an inkleweaver, so don't yer go worrin' yer head about that."

"I have the greatest confidence in you, Clive. Even if you do look like a tripped-out monkey in that rigout," Perry said, saluting his co-conspirator with his wine-glass. "Ah, and here comes another compatriot in arms. Nate, good evening to you. Been out beating the bushes, have you?"

Nate closed the French doors and headed straight for the drinks table. "Thirsty work, that, poking about the posies. Good evening to you, Perry. I am happy to report that there is no sign of Jarrett Rolin hunkered down behind any of the bushes. I'm beginning to think he's taken a flit. Probably scared all hollow that you'll skewer him. I know I would be, if I was him."

Perry looked to Clive, who shrugged. "My congratulations, Clive," he said. "I thought certainly you wouldn't have been able to contain yourself."

"Yer said not ta tell, sir, so I didn't blab."

"Blab what?" Nate asked, spreading his coattails and seating himself in one of the satin, blue-on-blue-striped chairs. "Oh, I say, Clive, that's not sporting. Keeping secrets from me. And I thought we were rubbing along so well. I'm crushed, Clive, crushed."

"Ah, now, sir," Clive began, but Perry waved him away and the man escaped to the foyer once more.

"Word has come to me that Rolin has surfaced in Wimbledon, of all places. It would seem he has an aged aunt there who has taken him in. As the Runners I hired have returned from Westham, I've sent them to watching the aunt's house."

"Until we get there, right?" Nate said, looking eager, as only a young man can. "When do we leave?"

"We don't. Rolin will be back once he's talked his aunt out of a few hundred pounds, and the Runners will follow him. Unless you think I should simply travel to Wimbledon and skewer him out of hand?"

"Well…" Nate said, looking at the carpet.

"Think, my friend. I can't simply attack someone who has not attacked me. He's angry, yes, but a list of names is just that, a list of names. Having me followed? Again, I came to no harm. Rolin may simply be testing himself, deciding whether the risk is worth the revenge.

No, unless he moves, makes some overt act, I in good conscience can do nothing."

Nate's cheeks were red. "So what was all that running about in aid of, I ask you? Oh, wait, don't tell me. You were being very public about it, now that I think on it. Coaches and outriders, giving everyone your name as you dropped purses while asking for Rolin by name? Dragging me along with you, because I'm really not as good at this sneaking about as I think I am, so all I did was cause even more attention? You were just trying to scare him off, weren't you? Oh, that's just shabby, that is." He dropped his chin to his chest. "I feel so...*used.*"

Perry laughed. He really did like this young hothead. "Relax, Nate, he'll be back. If he'd run home to his estate, I'd say I'd succeeded in making him see sweet reason. But he only ran as far as Wimbledon. He'll be back. Really, he has no other choice. That's my only regret, you know, that I've left him no other choice. He can't show his face in Society again, not after last month's debacle. His debts have been called, he's lost his few friends, his town house, equipages and horseflesh have been sold—and I hear his estate has been posted for sale. He has nothing left save the hope of some revenge."

"He could just take what funds he can salvage from his estate and flee the country," Nate suggested.

"And leave me here, to crow over Society? No, that's not the sort of thing that would sit well with Jarrett Rolin."

"Well, Nate, as you say, if that don't beat the Dutch," Georgiana said, striding into the drawing room ahead of Amelia. "I'm supposed to keep secrets, and then the two of you go all but shouting the man's name. It's a good thing I already told Amelia, or—*oops*."

Nate rushed to Georgiana's side, but Perry ignored them both as he turned to look at Amelia. To stare at Amelia.

Her cheeks were rather pale, but those deep brown eyes were eloquent with more emotions than she could possibly attempt to hide. Her chin was held high, and her gloved hands were drawn up into tight fists.

She looked wonderful. Fierce. Proud. Angry. Apprehensive. Young and a little frightened, yet determined to brave it out. Mostly, she looked so achingly vulnerable.

And if he told her any of that, he'd probably be ducking a thrown vase a moment later.

"Amelia," he said, bowing over her proffered hand, still drawn up into a fist, although that was another thing he wasn't brave enough to point out. "I have been counting the moments."

"While I, My Lord, have been counting the lies. If you'll excuse me," Amelia said, withdrawing her hand even as she brushed past him, to smile a warm greeting to Nate. "I cannot tell you how cheered Her Majesty has been ever since she decided to host the party for your engagement, Nate. The anticipation has done wonders for her."

Perry stood and watched as Amelia took her seat and Nate raced to fetch her a glass of sherry, not surprised to realize that, much as he liked the boy, he could cheerfully have wrung his neck if it weren't for the fact that he knew Nate's heart rested with his Georgie.

Amelia had chosen a chair that kept her back to him, but it wasn't as if he was rooted to this spot, so he walked over to rest his hands on the back of the chair, leaned down and whispered in her ear, "I would have worn sackcloth and ashes but I didn't think the queen would approve. Please, pet, if you refuse to read my notes—and a few of them bordered on the brilliant—then at least give me a chance to speak with you in private."

She kept her head steady, looking straight ahead of her. "I know all about your uncle, Perry. And this Jarrett Rolin person. And I'm sure you've convinced yourself that, between the two of them, everything you did was totally justified."

"I am, it was," Perry said, feeling hopeful…and realizing that never before in his life had he even come within a mile of the sort of abject groveling he was prepared to do now.

"And I forgive you. For that. But you made a fool of me, Perry, and I let you. That is not so easily forgiven."

"No, I imagine it's not," he said, moving away from her just as Clive *harrumphed* in the doorway and announced, "Her Royal Majesty, Caroline Amelia Elizabeth, Queen Consort of England!"

Everyone who hadn't been standing, stood, and they all bowed or dropped into deep curtsies as Caroline Amelia advanced into the room. Her cheeks were rouged, her eyes blacked with kohl. Her hair was a mass of ebony ringlets crowned by a wreath of palest-pink rosebuds. Her gown…Perry had to remember to lock his jaw; otherwise it would have fallen open.

He'd heard about this sort of gown from some gossipy matron who'd seen Her Majesty on the continent, and then had read a snippet of a letter written by Lady Bessborough that Sir Willard had somehow gotten his paws on in one of his dubious ways.

Was this the same outrageous rigout the queen had worn for a fancy dress ball in Genoa? Could there possibly be two?

Lady Bessborough, Perry remembered, had written that she'd been appalled, sorry and ashamed, and could not bear to listen to the whispers and the snickers that had accompanied the then Princess of Wales as she danced at the ball.

A gown of some white stuff, fashioned to resemble a child's frock except that the shoulders, back and front all dipped dangerously low, cut to expose Her Highness's flesh to the middle of her stomach.

As Perry did his best not to look at Caroline's fat, flabby, pale, exposed skin, he could only think that Lady Bessborough had been kind in her description.

Seeing the queen, in the flesh, as it were, lent credence to other stories Perry had heard over the years. Of the parties, the outlandish pantomimes where Her Highness performed for her servants; even the supposedly shell-shaped phaeton, pulled by two piebald horses, that she'd ridden in beside that Pergami fellow in Genoa, Her Highness rigged out in a huge pink feathered hat and a gown that stopped just at her knees. Not to mention the driver, purported to be a child clad only in flesh-colored tights, playing the role of operatic cherub.

When Perry saw the Italian footman, dutifully holding Her Majesty's train, he nearly sighed in relief to see the man dressed in the queen's livery.

"Your Majesty," Amelia said, once Caroline had bidden her rise from her curtsy. "It is so good to see you escaping your chambers, and with the glow of health surrounding you."

Gad! How did the girl keep a straight face, spouting such nonsense? How did Amelia stand it…or did she simply accept what she saw as nothing out of the ordinary?

No, that was impossible. She'd been in society. Granted, foreign society, but she'd been in the company of English subjects traveling abroad; she had to know that the queen was outrageous, more than outrageous.

As the queen inclined her head to him, Perry approached, bowed over the woman's hand, which she turned at the last moment, obviously expecting him to kiss her palm. For his sins, he did just that, careful not to notice that the woman's nails were none too clean.

He stepped back when he was dismissed and watched as Nate and Georgiana paid homage to the bizarre queen. He could not suppress a sigh of relief when the chinless, knee-knocking little man, who could be no one save this Nestor fellow Clive had spoken of, entered the room to announce that dinner was ready to be served at the queen's pleasure.

AMELIA DIDN'T KNOW whether to be relieved, proud or nastily amused as Her Majesty made it a point to flirt most outrageously with Perry throughout the dozen courses served in the large, horribly stuffy dining chamber. Her Majesty then kept him close by her side once they'd all returned to the drawing room. The queen did not allow gentlemen guests to be on their own for port and cigars; not when she wished them with her.

Perry had kept her amused with light banter, silly gossip and more than one joke he'd leaned close to whisper into Her Majesty's ear, causing that woman to laugh so heartily that twice she'd snorted wine up her nose and dissolved into fits of coughing.

"My friend Perry seems to have made himself a conquest," Nate said as Georgiana, Amelia and he sat on a pair of couches, the queen and Perry moving about the large drawing room, arm in arm, admiring the art on the walls, and cabinets filled with jade figures and other collections. "You wouldn't be jealous, would you, Amelia?"

"Nate, stop it," Georgiana said, looking at Amelia with such sympathy in her eyes that Amelia had to suppress a frustrated scream. "We all know Perry is simply being polite. Isn't that right, Amelia?"

"I'm pleased to see Her Majesty in such good spirits," she said, noncommittally. "And I'm quite sure I wouldn't mind whatever Perry would do. I…I could not care less what he would do."

"Oh, that's putting it on too thick and rare," Nate said,

settling back against the cushions, resting one ankle on his knee.

"Nate!"

"No, no, Georgiana, don't scold him. I admit it, Perry is being quite charming."

"Oh, that's him all right," Nate agreed. "Charms the ladies all hollow, that's what I've heard. All that money, all those smashing good looks. And the oddest thing. Runs from marriage, but that's not it, lots of us do."

"Nate…"

"Sorry, Georgie. *Some* of us run from the parson's mousetrap. Not me, oh no, not me. Can't wait, and that's no lie. In any event, Perry over there? I heard he don't dance. Props up the pillars at all the balls, is polite to a turn with the ladies—but he don't dance. I'd ask him why, but he's not the sort you ask, even if you might think about it."

Amelia chanced a look at Perry when the queen giggled, sounding happy as a young girl. "I'm sure I shouldn't wonder why he does it—or doesn't do it. Not dancing, that is. It makes him stand out, I should imagine, makes him seem more…more unattainable. Just the sort of thing he'd do. After all, he's really nothing more than a fribble. He's said so himself. Just as he's told me he's a bad, bad man."

Perry and the queen turned, and Amelia quickly lowered her gaze to her hands, ashamed to realize that those hands were trembling. "I think he frightens me."

Georgiana leaned forward to whisper, "Oh, don't, Amelia."

Amelia blinked at the tears stinging her eyes. "I can't help it. I don't know who he is. I don't know what he wants from me."

Nate had also leaned forward beside Georgiana, and reached across the low table to pat Amelia's hand. "He wants to keep you safe, Amelia. I mean, I know I wouldn't want to be Jarrett Rolin right now, not for anything."

"That has little to do with me. The way Georgiana explained the thing, I would only be a tool for Mr. Rolin, to hurt Perry."

"Yes, that's exactly it," Nate said, grinning in triumph. "And would Perry care a snap if he wasn't all arsy-varsy over you?"

Amelia bit her bottom lip as she chanced another look in Perry's direction. He was looking at her, his expression unguarded, and Amelia felt herself melting beneath the heat of his gaze.

He excused himself from Her Majesty, who seemed to be wilting from the exertion of the evening, and motioned for Nate to attend her as he returned his gaze to Amelia. He inclined his head toward the French doors.

As if in a trance, Amelia got to her feet and went to him, stood very still as he lifted her shawl from the chair back where she'd draped it earlier, placed it over her shoulders and escorted her out into the dark gardens.

"I shouldn't leave Her Majesty. She might need me," Amelia said as Perry turned to close the French doors behind them.

He turned once more, held out his arm, and she slipped hers through his elbow. "Nate will dance attendance on her. He's had plenty of practice, I understand, dancing attendance on old ladies."

"His aunt Rowena," Amelia said, nodding. "Yes, I've heard all about her from Georgiana. Although I doubt Her Majesty would thank you for terming her an old lady. Where…where are we going?"

"After my bungling? I should think that would be up to you, Amelia. I know I should like us to take up where we left off when my stupidity was revealed."

"I understand what you did and why you did it. Georgiana explained all of that to me," Amelia said as they walked along the terrace in the light of a full moon. "What I don't understand is why you couldn't be honest with me."

"Ah, the same question I've asked myself a dozen times or more. I don't know, Amelia. I suppose I thought, foolishly, that as I wasn't going to dance to my uncle's bidding in any case, there was no reason to tell you."

"And Jarrett Rolin?"

She watched as Perry's lips drew into a tight line. "Miss Penrose has told you everything, hasn't she? Yes, pet, and Jarrett Rolin. I didn't want you frightened. It was bad enough I had exposed you to danger."

"Georgiana says you're going to kill him."

"Really? That has to have come from Nate. I'm afraid he sees me as a rather dangerous fellow."

"Which you are," Amelia said, stopping in front of a stone bench and sitting down. "Sir Willard and his Tory friends wouldn't have sent a fribble to spy on the queen, now, would they? And I doubt very highly that fribbles make dangerous enemies like Mr. Rolin."

Perry looked at her for a long moment, then sat down beside her. "No wonder the queen keeps you close, Amelia. One day, I promise you, I'll tell you anything and everything you may want to know about me. But for now, can I ask only one thing? Will you trust me?"

She avoided his gaze, because even here, in near darkness, the heat from those cool, green eyes could only confuse her. "I did. I told the queen we could trust you. I...I almost handed you exactly what your uncle and Lord Liverpool would have paid a king's ransom to see. I told the queen you'd keep her secrets safe."

"Ah, pet," Perry said, slipping an arm around her shoulders, pulling her close against his side. "You must have been devastated when you heard what Nate thought was the truth. I can't even ask you to forgive me for that. And, sorry as I am to say it, we're far from done with intrigue."

Amelia remained where she was, because she'd longed to be in his arms again, even when she'd hated him, hated herself for wanting those arms around her again. "Surely there can't be more."

He tipped up her chin with his hand. "We're talking about mine uncle, pet. Surely there can. The thing of it is, I don't know if he's all but dared me to warn you so that the queen agrees to forgo the crown without the bother of a trial, or if he's told me because he's finally been sickened enough by all of this and wants a stop put to it. A complex man, mine uncle."

Amelia smiled. "And his nephew is as uncomplicated as a spring rain."

"Point taken," Perry said, helping her to her feet. "We can't be gone long or else Her Majesty will miss me."

"You enjoy that, don't you? That you've become important to her."

"She's important to you, Amelia. And, God help her, she's such an incredibly pathetic and sad creature. How could anyone not wish to protect her?"

"Thank you," Amelia said, wiping a tear from her cheek. "I know that was hardly flattering of you to say, but she is pathetic. Frightened. And very sorely used, by everyone. She has been, since the first time she stepped on shore to be bride to the most selfish, hateful creature ever spawned. I've a book, you know, one that was written to mark the death of Princess Charlotte. If only half of what I've read in it is true, your new king should be flogged."

Perry squeezed her hand. "I can't order him flogged, pet, but I can help put another spoke in his wheel, which is why I'm going to tell you what Sir Willard told me, and to hell with his motives for doing so. The Italians, Amelia. They've been paid to give testimony against Her Majesty."

Amelia nodded. "Yes, I know. More than thirty of them, Mr. Brougham says, all brought here from Italy to testify. But he isn't worried."

"No, not those witnesses, pet. Two others. Two others who are still in Her Majesty's employ. Brother and sister, I believe."

Amelia clapped both hands to her mouth, her eyes going wide. Rosetta and Gerado? Gerado, who hadn't the brains of a flea. But Rosetta! Rosetta, who saw everything, heard everything. *Knew* everything.

"But...but they've been with the queen since the beginning, ever since Pergami— Oh, no!"

"Amelia. Listen to me," Perry said, guiding her back into the shadows. "I've made arrangements. Clive and I will get them away from here tonight. I've got men who will take them straight to Dover, and wait with them until they're aboard ship. Tonight, pet. We have to do this tonight."

"This will be the end of her," Amelia said quietly. "She won't let anyone near her after this. As it is, she's ordered her chamber doors locked and hides inside like a frightened child. How will I tell her? How can I possibly introduce new servants into the household?"

"How about Clive's Mrs. Fitzhugh? I know she's not all that suitable, but Clive trusts her, and she'd never do anything to upset him."

"Mrs. Fitzhugh? Oh, dear, the peppermints. No, not Mrs. Fitzhugh. Perhaps Mrs. Pidgeon? She used to serve the queen, years ago. Yes, that should work. Oh, Perry," Amelia said, collapsing into his arms once more. "When will this be over?"

He stroked her back, pressed a kiss against her hair. "Soon, pet. I promise you. Soon."

"It was all to have been settled long ago, you know. I've seen the letter he had directed written to her, in the book I told you about. But the king lied then and still persecutes her. He won't rest until she's dead."

"And you won't leave her."

"No, I won't leave her."

"Not even to find your own happiness?"

Amelia walked to the French doors, waited for him to open them. "You already know the answer to that, Perry."

"Yes, for my sins, I do."

ONCE THE SMALL PARTY was over, and it ended the moment the queen got deep enough into her cups to begin weeping for her "dear, lost Charlotte," Nate and Georgiana took their leave, and Perry took up Clive and went off to the servants' quarters while Amelia herself undressed the queen and put her into bed.

In order to keep herself from thinking about what was happening with Gerado and Rosetta, she then retired to her own chamber, unlocked the cabinet beside her bed and retrieved the book on Princess Charlotte she'd promised herself she would not read again.

Turning the pages, she located the copy of the letter, supposedly from husband to wife, written over twenty years earlier:

Madam,

As Lord Cholmondeley informs me, that you wish I would define in writing the terms upon which we are to live, I shall endeavour to explain myself upon that head with as much clearness, and with as much propriety, as the nature of the subject will admit. Our inclinations are not in our power, nor should either of us be held answerable to the other, because nature has not made us suitable to each other…that even in the event of any accident happening to my daughter…I shall not infringe the terms of the restriction, by proposing at any period a connection of a more particular nature. I shall now finally close this disagreeable correspondence, trusting that, as we have completely explained ourselves to each other, the rest of our lives be passed in uninterrupted tranquillity.

How cold. How heartless. Even if the heir should die, he would not, not even for the sake of England, deign to return to his wife's bed.

And uninterrupted tranquillity? So much for the word of a future king, as he'd made his wife's existence a hell, keeping her from her daughter, twice petitioning Parliament for a divorce.

Paying servants to testify against her…

Amelia closed the book and knelt on the floor, to put it back in its hiding place. And saw the queen's chest of treasures. Was the original of that outrageous communication locked inside? Would Her Majesty keep anything so terrible?

Curiosity was a mortal failing Amelia hadn't escaped, and she'd often wished a peek inside that locked chest, hoping to see her own name. Until tonight. The queen had enough people poking about in her life, digging at her secrets.

Amelia closed and locked the cabinet, not willing for the chest and the book cataloging two sad, destroyed lives to be stored together. She placed the book on the bedside table and climbed into bed, snuffing the candles before she lay back in the darkness, too exhausted to think, even to weep.

PERRY WATCHED as a cursing, weeping Rosetta was pushed, hands tied, into the traveling coach by the men he'd commissioned to take the woman and her brother to Dover, then rubbed at his chin, for the fiery servant had attacked him with some expertise, actually landing a solid punch before Clive, less inclined to be gentle with females, dragged her off him.

"Planted you a wisty facer, didn't she, M'Lord?" Clive said as they watched the coach disappear into the darkness. "What was it she kept screechin' at yer?"

Perry smiled, then winced at the soreness in his jaw. "The dear woman was explaining her perfidy, Clive. Without the references as to the sexual proclivities of my mother, I should say it comes down to *Meglio fringuello in man che tordo in frasca.*"

"Oh, well, that explains it, don't it?" Clive said in obvious disgust.

"She said, my friend, better a finch in hand than a thrush on a branch. You would be more familiar, I think, saying that a bird in the hand is worth two in the bush. It would seem the woman had decided to take the purse offered her, rather than put her hopes in the queen's ability to survive a trial."

"Can't say as I blame her," Clive said as they returned to the door leading to the kitchen. "Was there something else yer needed from me tonight, M'Lord?"

"Just that you turn your head, Clive, once you've told me which is Miss Fredericks's chamber and pointed out the servant stairs."

"Oh. Like that, is it?" Clive's grin disappeared as quickly as it had appeared. "I didn't say anythin', M'Lord. Not a word. Third door down on the left, M'Lord, and the stairs are right over here. Not a word."

Perry considered explaining to Clive that he was only going to Amelia's rooms in order to tell her that the servants were on their way to Dover, but he knew the man wouldn't swallow such a crammer. Nobody would. So he merely nodded to Clive, climbed the narrow back stairs and turned down the hallway... only to quickly plaster himself to the wall, because Nestor was out and about, and looking damned suspicious.

He waited until the man had, after looking furtively up and down the hallway, disappeared behind a door at the very end of the hall.

Perry followed after him.

He dropped to his knees and peered through the large keyhole, to see the butler also on his knees. As Perry doubted either of them were about to offer up their evening prayers, he watched a little longer, at which time the butler removed a small hammer from his pocket and took the impressive lock of a large, tin traveling case into his other hand. He raised the hammer...and Perry stood up, opened the door, slipped inside, closing that door behind him.

"The queen's going traveling, Nestor? Is the lock

broken, or is that what you're here to accomplish?" he asked silkily, and the hammer, unused, dropped to the floor.

Nestor looked behind him, saw Perry and turned in one motion, arms outstretched as if he planned to tackle the earl. This effort failed, and a moment later Nestor's back was pressed against the row of shelving, his feet dangling a good foot above the floor, the forearm pressed against his windpipe making it painful to breathe.

"Who sent you?" Perry whispered, his face mere inches from Nestor's. And when the butler didn't answer fast enough, Perry lifted him a little higher, slammed him against the shelves once more. "Who?"

"No…nobody, My Lord. Nobody sent me. I…I can't breathe."

"No, you *won't* breathe, Nestor. Possibly not ever again. There's a difference between can't and won't, and that difference lies with me."

Nestor's eyes were popping out of his head and his forehead was turning blue. Even this didn't satisfy Perry, who was of a mind to exterminate the little bastard the way he would step on a bug.

"If I put you down, will you tell the truth?"

Nestor tried to nod his head, even as he clawed his hands at Perry's forearm, but nothing he did had any effect. *"Mmmmuff!"*

"I'll take that as a yes," Perry said, releasing the man, who crumpled to the floor, coughing and spitting. "Now. Who sent you? And I warn you, I usually don't ask twice, and I never ask a third time."

Nestor continued to choke, even as he held up one hand, as if begging His Lordship's indulgence while he coughed his guts out through his nose. "It…it's me. My…my idea. Come to…come to help the queen…"

That stopped Perry. He knew the place was crawling with Sir Willard's hirelings, all of them out to help discredit the queen. That someone would have come here to help Her Majesty had never entered his head. Well, there was Nate, but that had more to do with Aunt Rowena than any sort of protective instinct toward the queen.

Perry reached down and picked up the butler by the collar of his ill-fitting livery. "Quiet now," he warned tightly. "Let's the two of us nip downstairs to Mrs. Fitzhugh's parlor, shall we? You look like a man who could use a restorative glass."

Nestor nodded furiously, and Perry, after checking the hallway to make sure they could move along it undisturbed, pushed Nestor ahead of him, toward the stairs…sparing only a moment to slip the hammer in his pocket…and take a long look at the queen's infamous tin traveling trunk.

HE'D BEEN SO CLOSE. His hand had been on the lock, the hammer raised, poised to come down…to unlock the queen's secrets.

Now Bernard Nestor was cowering in a chair as Clive Rambert held a pistol over him, Mrs. Fitzhugh peeked at him from underneath her nightcap, and as His Lordship smiled at him with all the good humor of a tiger about to rip out his throat.

"Nestor here has taken it upon himself to save the queen, Clive, which, somehow, has led him to attempt to break into Her Majesty's traveling trunk," His Lordship said amicably. "Isn't that right, Nestor?"

"*That* trunk, M'Lord?" Clive asked. "So Dovey was right? You said there was somethin' shifty about him, didn't you, love?"

Bernard attempted to look earnest, definitely not shifty, and not simply so frightened he was sure he'd soon soil himself, and with Mrs. Fitzhugh watching. "It isn't what you think! Nobody sent me. You can murder me, you Tory dogs, but I labor in the service of my rightful queen!"

"Oh, good grief," His Lordship said, sinking into a chair and propping his elbows on the table. "Now I'm a Tory dog."

"You…you're not? But Sir Willard…"

"Ah, yes, Sir Willard. I can see how you might come to that conclusion. However, you'd be wrong. So, you're working with Brougham and the Whigs?"

Bernard rolled his eyes. "I should say not! Fools, the pack of them. I worked under Mr. Brougham and his brother for five long years, and they've bollixed everything, at every turn. No, My Lord, I'm here to *save* the queen, not simply to help myself."

"Believe that, My Lord," Mrs. Fitzhugh said, shifting a peppermint from one side of her mouth to the other, "and you'd believe anything. No chin, you know. Can't trust a man with no chin."

"I'll take that under advisement, Mrs. Fitzhugh,

thank you," His Lordship said, then motioned for Bernard to continue.

Which he did with alacrity, explaining all the reasons behind his belief that Amelia Fredericks was, in truth, the legal heir to the throne of England, and how he was certain the proof was in a small chest kept locked inside the queen's traveling trunk. Wooden thing, with fancy carving all over it. And another lock.

"Sitting right on the top. The princess took it out and had me hold it for her," Nestor concluded, holding out his hands. "I had it. Right in my hands." He dropped his hands to the tabletop. "And then she took it back."

"Well, damn me for a tinker," Clive said, once Bernard was through. "Miss Fredericks a royal princess? M'Lord? M'Lord, where are yer goin'?"

"Never mind that, Clive. Nestor? If you're right…" His Lordship closed his mouth, shook his head. "It would appear Nestor is on our side, at least in theory. Fill him in, Clive. All of it."

"Yes, sir," Clive said, but he said it to His Lordship's back, because he was already gone, loping toward the servant stairs. "Looks like a man just been punched in the belly, don't he, Dovey? Here now, Nestor, drink up, and welcome aboard."

PERRY STOOD in the box room, staring at the tin-clad trunk. Glaring at it. This had to be it, the trunk his uncle had told him about, the one the Tories hoped held all the damning evidence they'd need to discredit the queen. As if they knew they hadn't gotten enough with their suspicious stains and urinals.

"Damn," he whispered. "Damn, damn and blast."

Then he dropped to his knees, pulled a thin sliver of metal from his waistcoat pocket and set to work.

The lock yielded easily enough, but Perry hesitated, knowing that, yet again, he was going behind Amelia's back, digging his nose into the queen's, and Amelia's, business. And without being asked.

But he had to know. Holding his breath, Perry pushed back the lid to reveal an interior occupied by satins and furs and velvet boxes he assumed contained the queen's jewels. But no wooden box, intricately carved.

Amelia had taken it, that's what Nestor had told him. But had she returned it? Was it, even now, in the queen's chambers?

No, wait! Amelia told him just tonight that she had been about to trust him with the queen's secrets, until Nate had warned her away. Had she actually been about to give him the chest, ask him to keep it safe?

"God's teeth, no wonder she wouldn't answer my notes."

Perry lowered the lid, replaced the lock, feeling guilty yet again. That should be enough for him. He had no good reason to look further. None at all.

"Amelia? A royal heir?" He rubbed at his forehead as he muttered to himself. "Christ, what am I thinking? Nestor's a zealot, and probably half-mad into the bargain. Thank God Brougham turned him off before he could voice his insane theories to him, or else Amelia would be dragged through the investigation along with the queen. I—"

He shut his mouth, at last realizing he was babbling to himself like some village idiot.

Amelia. His Amelia. He needed to see her, now. He needed to speak with her, now.

He needed to hold her. Now.

AMELIA STIRRED SLIGHTLY in her sleep, then lifted a hand to rub at the faint tickling on her cheek. Her eyelids opened wide when, instead of her cheek, she felt fingers under hers. Fingers that slid around her hand, squeezed ever so slightly.

"Amelia? Don't cry out, pet. It's me. Perry."

Perry? She must be dreaming. She'd fallen asleep dreaming of him. But no, this hand was real. Warm.

She felt his weight join her on the bed, and turned to see him perched there, still dressed in his evening clothes. She shook off his grasp and quickly pressed herself up against the headboard, pulling the covers up to her chin. "Perry? What's wrong? The queen? Is it the queen?"

"No, not the queen," he said, employing the tinderbox to light the bedside candles. "And her servants are well on their way to Dover."

Amelia swallowed with some difficulty, unaccustomed to having a man in her chambers. The queen had often entertained from her bed, but that was the queen. And this was Perry.

"Then I don't understand," she said, pushing her

hands through her hair, which she'd been too tired to plait herself, now that they were a household totally without a single lady's maid in residence.

"No, I suppose you don't," Perry said, his smile soft and rather sad. "I shouldn't be here."

That was true enough, but if Amelia agreed with him, he might leave. "If it's important…?" she said, her words trailing off as she felt the blood rushing into her cheeks.

His hand came up to trace the line of her cheek. "I've missed you terribly, you know. When you were hating me."

"I never hated you," Amelia said, stifling a sigh as his palm cupped her cheek, trailed down to her neck, his thumb lightly rubbing at the skin just behind her ear. "I could never hate you."

He shifted his position on the edge of the bed, so that he was sitting almost facing her, leaning toward her, his steady gaze on her mouth.

Amelia closed her eyes, waited for his kiss.

"Do you trust me, Amelia?" he asked, his breath warm and wine-sweet on her face. He touched his lips to hers, only briefly. "Please. Do you trust me?"

"I do," she said thickly. "You know I do."

"God, how I've dreamed of this," she heard him say, and then his mouth was on hers again and, together, they were sliding down on the pillows, until she was lying on her back once more, and he was leaning over her. Kissing her. Kissing her…kissing her.

Amelia raised her arms, clasping them around his neck,

and Perry shifted yet again, moving entirely onto the bed, pulling back the bedcovers. He stretched at his full length beside her, his arms sliding around her, pulling her up and over so that she lay halfway across his body.

His hands now cupped her cheeks, framing her face as he turned her this way and that, nibbling at her lower lip, sucking it inside his own mouth. With teeth and tongue he conquered her every inhibition, and she felt her body going liquid as she lay against him.

She could feel the hardness of his body through the fine white lawn of her simple night rail, and when he moved beneath her she couldn't help but be aware of his arousal. She felt a tightening between her legs, utterly foreign to her experience. A yearning…

He shifted his attention to her throat, to the bare inch of skin visible above the buttons of her night rail, his hands joining his mouth as he worked each small button free, as she found, to her amazement, that she had braced her hands against the pillows on either side of his head. In order to lift herself. In order to grant him access to those last few buttons. So many buttons.

"Beautiful," she heard him say as if to himself as he pushed the now-gaping night rail off her shoulders. "My beautiful Amelia."

The material of her night rail binding tight against her upper arms, Amelia could only keep her head raised as the cool night air mingled with Perry's warm breath against her bare skin.

Her eyelids closed tight, she flinched only slightly as his hot, moist mouth captured her nipple, flicked at it for a few mind-shattering moments with his tongue, before he turned his attention to her other breast, replacing his mouth with the softly pinching thumb and finger of his hand.

Sensations alien yet welcome rushed through her as her heart pounded in her ears, as the burning tightness between her legs grew into an ache that had her softly moaning Perry's name with each ragged breath.

She didn't want to move, not so much as an inch, even as her arms began to tremble, as her passion made her limbs weak, and she moaned in protest when Perry put his hands on her waist and gently pushed her onto her back.

"No," she said, eyes tightly closed.

Perry's hand, lightly rubbing at her belly, went still. "You're right, pet. I shouldn't."

"No!" she said, opening her eyelids wide in sudden panic. "I didn't mean no. I meant *no*. Please don't leave me."

"Never," he said just as he kissed her again, as he slid his hand up to cup her breast once more. "But we both know I should, me more than you."

"I know," Amelia told him. "But which is the greater evil, Perry? I know what I'm doing, please believe that. And I don't want you to go. Please, must you always make me ask?"

Perry's chuckle was low and genuinely amused. "I told you, pet, I'm a bad, bad man. But you, darling Amelia. You are my sweet redemption."

"Oh, Perry," Amelia said, her fears flying from her,

her inhibitions taking wing along with them. "Show me what happens next."

"It would be my pleasure," he said, and his mouth, when it touched hers once more, was curved in a smile.

His mouth never leaving hers, he managed to free her arms from her night rail, and she didn't care if this showed an expertise he must have gained from long practice. He kissed her throat, her breasts, her belly, all the time easing her night rail down and over her hips, pushing it past her most private secrets, to her knees and beyond.

And then he was rising above her, looking down at her nakedness in the soft light of the candles, his eyes aglow with a hunger that had an answering ache growing inside her.

On his knees on the bed, he slipped out of his evening coat, tossing it to the floor, to be followed by his waistcoat, neck cloth and shirt, leaving him in nothing but the long knit pantaloons that looped over the soles of his evening shoes.

She swallowed down hard once more when his hands went to the buttons of his pantaloons, and she was secretly pleased when he opened the buttons but did not remove the pantaloons, rather lowering himself beside her once more, so that the bare skin of his muscled chest brushed against her softness.

"I wouldn't frighten you, pet," he said, gently coaxing her back to her former passion as he once again lavished his attention on her breasts, one hand lightly circling the sensitive skin of her belly, stroking the rise of her hip.

"I'm…I'm not that frightened," she admitted, throwing any remaining caution to the wind and giving in to the impulse to stroke his hair, to kiss his bare shoulder, even to nip at his skin with her teeth.

And the hunger, the ache, grew inside her as he left her again, if only for a few moments.

Amelia was only mildly shocked when she felt his bare leg against hers, the soft hairs prickling her skin as he rubbed his leg over hers, insinuated it between her knees.

She held on to him with both hands now, running the tip of her tongue along the base of his neck, loving the salty taste of him, bereft when he shifted his body, until he had claimed her nipple once more.

Her eyelids tightly shut, she concentrated on the sensations racing through her, so that she was acutely aware when his hand moved again, moved lower, when his fingers slipped between her legs.

This shouldn't happen. Surely this shouldn't please her. And yet it did; it pleased her very much. His fingers, gently touching her, learning her, deftly spreading her, then stroking the most intimate parts of her.

Amelia's knees seemed to draw up of their own accord, her heels digging into the soft mattress as Perry's touch became even more intimate, his forays including an unexpected penetration that had her lifting her hips in anticipation of more, more…

He shifted again, raising himself up slightly to look into her now widely open eyes. "I don't want to hurt you, sweetings."

"I know," she said, her chest rising and falling rapidly, both with passion and a new fear. She'd heard the stories; she wasn't completely unawares. But no one, surely no one ever had felt the way she did now. "I don't care."

"I do," Perry whispered, bracing himself on one elbow as he watched his hand move between her legs.

The heat he was generating was so nearly overpowering, and yet when she looked at him, at the expression on his handsome face, she forgot the heat, and tears stung her eyes. He was worried for her. He cared more for her than he did for himself. That was evident in the look on his face.

She couldn't help it. She allowed her knees to drop open, silently telling him that whatever he did, whatever he had to do, he did with her permission.

She felt his thumb circling her in a way that brought a fresh flood of heat, a tighter, keener concentration of feeling that seemed to build upon itself as he increased the pressure. He moved his thumb faster, faster, so that she barely noticed when he slipped a second finger inside her…and when he suddenly plunged deeper her cry was more of shock than pain, quickly forgotten as his thumb circled, as his fingers continued to possess her.

"No more pain, Amelia," he whispered, turning to look at her, his eyes eloquent with concern…and a heat that mimicked her own. "Only pleasure. Feel it, Amelia. Let me give you pleasure."

She fell back against the pillows, giving in completely to what he did, the way his fingers moved on her, the way her own hips began to move in rhythm with that touch.

"Oh…" she said as something seemed to flower inside her, as an even greater heat washed over her, as she was vaguely aware that Perry was moving over her, his hand leaving her and a new pressure taking its place.

His breath was hot against her ear, the weight of his body welcome against her burning skin. She felt his hands on her thighs as he urged her to lift her legs, wrap them around him, as she had wrapped her arms around him, as she raked her nails over his tight, rippling muscles…as he filled her.

"Not like this, Amelia. I swear it, never before like this. Now, Amelia," he said, his voice rasping against her ear. "Together, Amelia. Together…"

She held on as he thrust deeply inside her, moving faster and faster as she desperately tried to match his rhythm…as suddenly she could, she did…and when he cried out it was only a moment after she had done so.…

PERRY WATCHED the gray light of dawn slipping into the chamber and silently cursed the end of night.

Amelia had already retreated across the wide mattress in her sleep, curling in on herself as if in anticipation of the reaction she would have if she woke to find him still there.

She'd clung to him last night after they'd made love, but she hadn't wanted to talk to him, which he had considered fortunate, because he hadn't the slightest idea what either of them could say.

He shouldn't have done it; shouldn't have come

to her, shouldn't have kissed her, shouldn't have… shouldn't have…

He reached over and touched her hair, stroked an errant lock away from her face.

Amelia Fredericks, orphan.

Amelia Fredericks, future Queen of England.

Amelia Fredericks…his now and forever, or his never again. His curse was low and directed entirely at his stupidity, his arrogance, his unforgivable behavior.

He had never before realized the degree to which fear could destroy his honor as a gentleman.

How love could devastate.

With a last look at Amelia, he carefully turned back the covers and slipped from the bed, intent on dressing himself and being gone from the chamber before she awakened and he saw the shock in her eyes…that shared knowledge that what they'd done, no matter how achingly important at the time, had been accomplished only through the loss of her innocence.

And he couldn't even go to the queen, ask for Amelia's hand and make everything all right, not until he knew Amelia's true heritage. Because, rather than be happy for Amelia, the queen might be horrified to learn that the heir had been compromised.

Perry clenched his hands into fists. Weren't things complicated enough, without him barging in here, frantic with love, to make everything even worse?

He was dressed in mere minutes, his shirt and waistcoat only partially buttoned, his neck cloth loosely hung around his neck, and was about to pick up his evening

SHALL WE DANCE?

coat—the one with the sleeve partially ripped at the shoulder thanks to the tight tailoring of the cloth and his haste in shedding it—when he noticed the book on the bedside table.

Memoirs of Her Late Royal Highness Charlotte Augusta.

He picked up the book, opening it to the illustration of the princess, seeing what Amelia had seen. There was little physical resemblance between them.

He paged further. The memoir had been published here in Paternoster Row, in 1818, a hastily assembled collection including facsimiles of Charlotte's handwriting and specimens of her compositions, poetry and music.

Walking toward the windows and the growing light filtering through a gap in the draperies, Perry paged further, looked at a sample of music signed with the princess's own hand.

There were scraps of ribbon tucked between several of the pages, most certainly put there by Amelia.

Pulled in by his own curiosity, he sat down on a delicate slipper chair and began to page and read, page and read.

Concerning the marriage between the Prince of Wales and Princess Caroline of Brunswick:

> Rare is the example of connubial happiness resulting from the matrimonial alliances of royalty.

A communication from His Royal Highness to the wife he'd banished:

…even in the event of any accident happening to my daughter…I shall not infringe on the terms of the restriction, by proposing at any period a connexion of a more particular nature.

And more:

In November of the year 1802, the Princess Charlotte being then nearly seven years old, the Princess of Wales, under circumstances of the most eccentric and extraordinary kind, adopted a child of very obscure parents, of the name of Austin, and he was suckled and brought up under her own immediate eye.

Perry read with horrified fascination the lengthy letter Caroline had written to her husband, a copy of which she'd had delivered to the newspapers so that all of England could read of her distress, begging permission to see her own daughter, a permission, he read further, that was denied.

His attention was caught by a description of the manner in which Caroline at last left England:

Her female domestics were taken onboard from Worthing. The princess had one conspicuous article among her baggage, being a large tin case, on which was painted in white letters: Her Royal

Highness the Princess of Wales, To Be Always
With Her.

No wonder his uncle knew about the case; it would
appear the entire world knew. No wonder the entire world
was now curious about the secrets that case might hold.

But Perry's heart, that part of him he'd never before
paid any particular attention to, was most touched as he
read lines purported to have been spoken to Princess
Charlotte by the Prince of Saxe-Coburg on the day of
their marriage:

> I hail the happy day, with joyful, thankful mind,
> that makes thee mine—my lovely princess. Ever
> will I love thee—honor thee—give to thee the
> best affections of my heart…

"Beautiful, isn't it? And then he lost her and his
child," Amelia said from behind him, and Perry turned
in some shock, to see her standing there, dressed once
more in her night rail, her soft auburn hair a tangle
around her face and shoulders. He looked at her, but she
refused to meet his gaze.

Perhaps it was better that he was still here, that she
understand that he hadn't just taken, that he *wanted* to
be here. With her.

She held out her hands and he put the book in them.

She turned the pages, lifted the last bit of ribbon
and read:

"On the arrival of Mr. Dykes, the messenger, at the residence of the Princess of Wales, Her Royal Highness was just risen; and the dreadful intelligence was no sooner conveyed to her than she fainted three times, and for some days afterward seemed scarcely conscious of surrounding objects. Her health from that period has been visibly impaired."

Perry shook his head. "Her daughter, her grandson. I can't imagine her grief."

"I can," Amelia said, her voice hard, "because I was there. Do you know she asked to be present when the princess was brought to childbed, that she'd asked to be allowed back to England the moment she learned that the princess was pregnant? That the princess begged to have her mother with her? But her request was not granted. Her Majesty is convinced things would have gone very differently if she had been allowed to be with her own child. I hate him, Perry. I know I shouldn't say that, but I really, really loathe our new king."

Perry got to his feet, took the book from her hands, then drew her into his arms. "I'm so sorry, Amelia. I don't know how I have never realized the depth of the king's meanness. Can't we persuade the queen to leave England before the trial? There's nothing for her here."

Amelia rubbed her cheek against his shirt. "Only her hatred for her royal husband. That's here, Perry. She wants one victory over him, just one, that he has to see the crown placed on her head at the coronation, that he has to acknowledge her as his queen consort. Is that so terrible?"

"It is if that hoped-for revenge kills her, if it destroys those around her," Perry said, leading Amelia over to the bed. He shouldn't say anything; this wasn't the time. But then, when would the time be right? "I saw that you marked the page telling of the queen's adoption of William Austin."

Amelia smiled at him, a sad smile that tore at his heart. "Yes, William. The two of us, silly dreamers. I told you about that. But he's gone now, always taking himself off somewhere, while I…while I…"

"While you stay. Because you love her, because she has no one else to love her."

A single tear slid down Amelia's cheek, and she tried to smile. "Never forget my silly dream, Perry. My silly, childish dream. To me, the queen has always taken the place of my mother."

"Yes," Perry said, retrieving his evening coat and tossing it onto the bed. He had to say the words. "Amelia, what if it's true?"

"What if what is true? Oh! Don't be silly. It was William everyone thought was…I mean, there was that Delicate Investigation or whatever it was called, trying to prove that William is proof of the queen's adultery. No one has ever thought to question *my* birth…I mean, that would be…"

"Damning evidence, yes," Perry said, then said the rest, "unless it could be proved that you were not the product of the queen's adultery."

"That I was not—I don't understand."

Perry raked his fingers through his hair. "I don't, either. But…but if it could be proved, if information could be found…"

Amelia's gaze immediately went to the bedside table, to the locked cabinet that made up its base. Perry, at least a part of him, wished he were not quite so observant. "No," she said, returning her gaze to him. "No, that's impossible. Ludicrous. It was a child's dream, Perry, but even a child's fanciful dream didn't include a royal father."

But Perry continued to push. "The queen lived in seclusion in Blackheath for years after she was banished. He could have visited her there. He had only the one heir, and we know he's fathered at least two royal bastard sons. Perhaps his father wanted another royal heir, in the chance something happened to Princess Charlotte. A male heir. The late king held the purse strings, remember. He could have demanded his son do his royal duty."

"Sons. Kings always want sons."

"Yes, but would Caroline carry another heir, just to have it taken from her as Princess Charlotte had been? Or would she hide it, keep the child her own secret, especially once the king, her father-in-law, her only protector, had gone mad yet again?"

She pressed her hands to her ears. "Stop it! Stop it! I don't want to listen to this! I can't listen to this!"

He placed his hands over hers, drew them down to her lap. "And I don't want to say it, sweetings. But don't we need to know? If it can be proved, then Caroline is undisputed queen, and you are the Princess of Wales.

The entire succession changes. The Tories will lose their power, the Whigs will take it. *Everything* would change."

Her expression went frighteningly blank for a moment, then hardened. "And when did you begin to wonder about all of this, Perry? Please, tell me. Before or after you sneaked in here and seduced me? Before you made a fool of me, allowed me to make a fool of myself? Did your uncle send you here to ruin me, just in case I might be the heir? Has that been the point all along?"

"Amelia, no! Last night wasn't supposed to happen."

She slid past him, off the bed, and dragged on her dressing gown. "Oh, I should say not! It was one thing to romance the plain little orphan girl to learn the queen's secrets. But to take her to bed, simply on the off chance she might be the queen's brat—bastard or otherwise? How very lowering for you, My Lord, and how base, how conniving, to think that bedding me would somehow give you power. Whigs, Tories. The queen's right. Bastards, all of you! Get out, Perry. Just get out."

Perry picked up his evening coat, then slammed it to the floor. "Stop it! Curse me, Amelia, because I deserve it. But don't belittle yourself. I've wanted to make love with you almost since the moment I first saw you, and if that damns me to hell, then I'll go. Gladly. I admitted that my uncle sent me here, but you have to know that after that first stupid lie, I've never lied to you again. I would never lie to you again."

Amelia dropped her chin to her chest, then looked up at him through wet, spiky eyelashes. "Go, Perry. Please."

"I can't, Amelia. The idea of you being the heir was not mine, and if one person has thought it, more can be thinking it. Friends of the queen, and her enemies. Hell and damnation, Amelia, that miserable tin case is even mentioned in that damn book over there! It's like some perverse treasure hunt, and it won't stop until the treasure—all the queen's secrets—are found. We have to know, one way or the other. *You* have to know."

"And you think that the answers are all in the queen's private papers? But your uncle is with the Tories. He wouldn't want it proved that I'm…that I could be…"

Perry sighed, shrugged. "I don't know what my uncle wants, pet. I do know he sent me here. He said he wanted me to find evidence *against* the queen, but I'm learning to never believe my uncle completely. I'm convinced now that he didn't direct me to you simply because he thought you convenient. He has his own questions about your birth, I'm sure of it. And there are others, one who has already found his way into the queen's household."

"Who?"

"Nestor. I found him in the box room with a hammer last night, ready to break open the queen's traveling trunk. He's convinced evidence exists that would prove you the heir. He's Henry Brougham's man, Amelia. He says he's not, but he does admit he's worked under the man for the past five years."

Amelia drew her dressing gown around her more tightly. "I saw him, too, the other day. It's why I brought the case to the queen, hoping she'd allow me to give it to you, for safekeeping." She lifted her hands, laced her fingers together tightly. "I don't know whom to trust."

Perry sat down beside her once more. This was why he'd had to tell her, even if telling her damned him forever in her eyes. She had to realize that she could be in danger. "And I can't blame you, pet. If you're the queen's daughter, her true daughter, some will want it proved, and some will want you…removed."

She looked up at him, her eyes flat and cold. "And if I'm Sir Sydney Smith's daughter, or Perceval's, or any of the others who visited the queen in Blackheath? Then the queen is destroyed, once and forever. Forgive me, Perry, but I can't seem to forget why you came here in the first place."

Perry slipped his arms around her shoulders, but she held herself stiff in his embrace. "I didn't come to your rooms last night to seduce you, Amelia, or to steal the queen's secrets. I came because I couldn't stay away."

She nodded, stiffly. "Yes, of course. I must be fascinating, in my own rather unique way," she said, turning her head away from him. "But now that your curiosity is satisfied, now that you know I am only a woman, you may leave me. Leave me alone."

"I can't, Amelia. You have to understand, now, that you could be in danger."

She shrugged his arms away and slid her bare feet to the floor, putting half the distance of the large chamber between them. "Oh, yes, I'm in danger. Again. From this Rolin person who is your enemy, not mine. From your uncle and Lord Liverpool. From Nestor, of all people. All of them, *using* me. But none so badly as you used me last night, Perry."

She drew herself up, looking more queenly than ever Caroline had been able to do, and said, "I asked you to leave, My Lord. I shall handle my life now, not you, not anyone else."

Perry knew defeat when it stared him in the face. "At least let Clive stay. And Nestor, although I don't know what good that zealot will be."

She nodded, biting her bottom lip between her teeth. Perry picked up his evening coat once more and left the chamber, for he had somewhere to go.

"YOU KNOW, NEVVIE, you keep barging in here and one day I'm going to be shocked into an apoplexy, and it will be on your head," Sir Willard said, pulling off his nightcap. The same young maid who'd been warming his bed the first time Perry had "visited" him in his chamber grabbed the nightcap and held it against her ample breasts as she ran for the dressing room.

Perry just stood there, staring at his uncle.

"And look at you. Been out all night, haven't you? Dressed in the dark, too. Hair all which way, and that's a morning beard or I miss my guess." Sir Willard pointed at Perry's jacket. "That's ruined, you know. God, son, you're a disgrace to the name."

"Oh, I doubt that, Willie. I think you bear off the palm

with that one," Perry said, locating a decanter on a table in the corner and pouring himself three fingers of Burgundy. He downed the liquid, then returned to the bed to glare at his uncle. "How long were you going to wait before you told me?"

Sir Willard didn't bother to dissemble. "I warned you to stay away from her until this was over."

"Oh yes, that you did, in your own inimitable way. I remember. Now tell me what you've got."

"Get me a glass of Burgundy," Sir Willard said, pulling up the covers. "It's not too early, as the sun isn't quite up yet. You didn't do anything stupid, did you, Nevvie? I'm not sure, but I think you could be shot if you've just come from doing what I think you've been doing, and if she is…she is…well, I won't say it."

"No," Perry said, all but throwing the requested wineglass at his uncle, "but I will. If she's really the Princess of Wales. Damn you, Willie, how many intrigues are you running?"

"Liverpool doesn't know," Sir Willard said, then took a sip from his glass. "I'm not harebrained, Nevvie. Caroline detests the man and with good reason, as he often served as Prinney's conduit, delivering his nasty notes to her. A real stickler, Liverpool, and unwilling to see what's in front of his face, in front of all our faces. Our new king? What a complete waste! I doubt he'll live out the year if he doesn't stop insisting his leeches bleed him every time he hiccups. We could be on the brink of revolt if he dies, and a squalling infant is all we're left with. No, Nevvie, I may be Tory to the bone, but I'm

England to the marrow. Rather the Whigs to settle the populace for now, until clearer heads can take power once more."

"Meaning you, of course," Perry said, a sour taste in his mouth. "How were you going to manage that?"

"Through your pretty face, of course. A plain girl like that? I never thought for a moment that you'd fail to gain her affection. But damn it, boy, I never thought you stupid enough to ruin her. If word were to get out—if you've put a bastard in her belly—"

"She's not the king's daughter. She can't be."

Sir Willard, who had been getting dangerously red in the face, shut his mouth, looked at his nephew. "You're sure? You've found proof of her birth? Found something in that damn tin box, did you? Well, good. Bring what you found to me, I'll burn it. We're not done yet, Nevvie."

"I am," Perry said, so disgusted he didn't know if he could remain in his uncle's presence another moment without disgracing himself completely by hitting an old man. "She told me to go away. I left Clive there, because you've put her in danger, you stupid bastard, but I've been banned from the household."

"With the proof?"

Perry threw his wineglass at the fireplace. "No, blast it, without the proof. If there is proof. God's teeth! Amelia won't speak to me, the queen's household is crawling with intrigue, you're sitting here like some overfed spider weaving webs—and I've still got Jarrett Rolin to deal with, damn you."

"He hasn't shown himself? It's been weeks," Sir Willard said. "Maybe he's given up, gone home."

"Would you?" Perry asked, staring at his uncle.

"Probably not. I've taken the time to learn more of what you and your friend Westham did to him. You were both very naughty, you know. It will be years before he can show his face in Society again, if ever. You're a very mean man, Nevvie, for all you act the fribble. Have you set out traps for him?"

"I haven't come here to discuss Jarrett Rolin. What made you think Amelia may be the heir? And don't lie to me, Uncle, because I'm not in the mood for lies."

Sir Willard snapped his mouth shut tight and returned Perry's stare. Then shrugged. "Oh, very well. Liverpool put it to me to find the most damning piece of evidence against the queen that I could. Ordered me, damn him."

"His mistake," Perry said, summoning a weak smile. "Go on."

"I'm going, I'm going. I hired a few men to ferret out what I could, which was very little that wasn't already known." He drained his wineglass. "And then I realized that if anyone knew anything damning about Caroline it would be Henry Brougham, her advocate, although he's as power mad as Liverpool in his own way. I spent several mornings in my town coach, sitting outside Brougham's residence, until I noticed one particular fellow who scurried there early every morning and did not leave again until late at night. So I set a man to watching him for another week, and was informed that the minion often carried papers with him when he left—and didn't always bring them back the next morning."

Perry was fairly certain he could follow the tale from there, but allowed his uncle to finish.

"Had one of my men make a visit to this fellow's rooms one afternoon when I was sure he'd be gone. He brought back some interesting notes that I read, then had returned to the rooms. Quite an astonishing theory the man was pursuing. Quite astonishing."

"Yes, I've met the man. Bernard Nestor, correct?"

Sir Willard's face turned red once more. "Damn you, Perry, how do you know that?"

"You don't know, Uncle?" Perry asked, at last smiling in real amusement. "Bernard Nestor is currently serving, not well, I'll admit, as butler to Her Majesty. Oh, and Clive and Mrs. Fitzhugh have resigned from your employ and are now working for me. I suppose all you have left is Mrs. Pidgeon."

"Who?" Sir Willard asked, frowning.

"Yes, yes, of course. You don't know her. I've had the Italian servants sent home, as you wanted—everything is falling into place so neatly, isn't it, Uncle? You couldn't chance their testimony, not until and unless you knew Amelia is the heir. I don't know how many more servants you've insinuated into the queen's household, probably a dozen, but Mrs. Pidgeon is most assuredly yours, so don't bother to deny it again. She doesn't have the vocabulary of a servant. Now, tell me why you're still snooping and peeking and not acting. Does all your dependence lie on the hopeful contents of the queen's tin box?"

"I told you. Yes, damn it, it does. And why I thought to trust you with my last hope is a mystery that will probably haunt me to my grave."

Perry approached the bed. "There is more than one way to approach the question of Amelia's parentage, Uncle."

Sir Willard pushed himself up against the pillows. "What do you have in mind?"

Perry had debated with himself all the way from Hammersmith, but he knew that the easiest way for him to proceed was to feel out his uncle—although he was already fairly thoroughly convinced of his uncle's loyalty, which was to himself—and then keep him as close, as involved and as possibly damned as possible.

"There's birth, Uncle, and there's conception," Perry said quietly.

"Con-conception? My God, of course!"

"We need a historian, Uncle. Someone who has spent his life cataloging every bit of minutia about our illustrious new king. What he eats, what he wears, where he goes, his every engagement. His every move, most especially in the early months of 1801. Is there such a man?"

Sir Willard levered himself out of bed as Perry turned his back, the better not to see the man's bare bottom as his nightshirt bunched around his belly. "I can think of two," he said, striding to his desk in front of the windows. "One is dead, but the other? The other retired some years ago, to Bath. Royal archivist, or some such thing."

He selected a bit of stationery and picked up a small

knife, using it to sharpen the pen he then dipped into the inkwell. "Give me that date again. When was the gel breeched?"

"William Austin was adopted by the queen in November of 1802, at about six months of age. Amelia was born in December of the previous year. If the queen adopted Austin when the rumors began, in order to divert attention from another orphan infant already in her care, the two births too close together to have been to the same mother? It's a brilliant plan, if that's what happened."

"Yes, yes, the date. What dates shall I ask him to report on, Perry?"

Perry counted backward in his head. "Late February? March? The queen resided in Blackheath at that time, so that Princess Charlotte could visit with her once a week. It's entirely possible her father went along a time or two, on orders from his father. We should probably also attempt to determine if Prinney's allowance was raised at that same time. When do you think you'll have an answer?"

"If old Symons hasn't stuck his spoon in the wall, you mean? A fortnight, I suppose." Sir Willard put down the pen, sanded the sheet. "What will you do in the meantime, Nevvie?"

Perry pulled at a loose thread in the rip in his sleeve. "Put Sir Nathaniel out as guard dog along with Clive at the queen's residence, and go hunting. What else have you left me, Uncle?"

"Good," Sir Willard said, oblivious to Perry's anger as he folded the sheet and began heating a wax stick, to seal it. "You can always charm her again if she's not the king's heir, or prepare yourself to flee to the continent, if she is, and your foolishness bears fruit. Now go on, go hunting, while I pretend not to know what that means."

"I STILL DON'T SEE why we don't go back to where we knew he was, now that we know he's not in Wimbledon anymore," Nate said, doing his best to imitate Perry's long, easy stride as the two of them headed toward yet another watering hole his father had warned him never to frequent—which helped to make this afternoon's excursion doubly enjoyable. "Oh, not that he probably went back there to get those boots. I wouldn't, would you? But we're coming up empty this way, and I've got to take myself off to Hammersmith in an hour, to drag the ladies around the Park."

Perry stopped in his tracks in front of a coffee house he'd already told Nate he hadn't frequented since his first years in London. "The queen, as well? The queen's going to drive in the Promenade?"

Nate was grateful to be able to catch his breath. They'd been running about London for ten days, as long as Perry had been banished from Hammersmith, and Nate wasn't sure if His Lordship was running toward Jarrett Rolin, or away from himself (a thought Nate congratulated himself as being very deep indeed for a man of his tender years).

Still, he could only consider it a bleeding shame that the Runners who'd been watching Rolin in Wimbledon had lost him on the way back to London. Then again, was it any better to be talking about Amelia, when it always seemed to make the scar on Perry's cheek go all white and cold?

"Yes, Her Majesty is going. It was her idea, actually, after Henry Brougham put it to her," Nate said. "And she's taking up Georgie and Amelia, and even Mrs. Bateman. That's Georgie's mama. Going to be a crush, even in that fancy landau that Brougham arranged, since the queen wanted nothing to do with a closed carriage. Old as dirt, but the tits in the traces are fine enough, four good-looking blacks. Still, a squeeze. Why? Don't you think Amelia should be in the Park?"

"No, I imagine she'll be fine. After all, you'll be there, guarding her. Jarrett Rolin is the sort that avoids crowds when he's up to his schemes."

"A coward at the heart of it, I remember. And Clive will be riding up on the bench with the driver," Nate added, hoping that piece of information might remove the frown from Perry's face. The fellow had been deep in the doldrums long enough. Too bad Perry couldn't find Rolin and shoot him or something; a little murder would probably do the man a world of good. "Aren't we going in there?"

Perry turned about and headed back the way they had come, signaling with his cane for his coachman. "We've been hunting mare's nests, Nate, but I wanted to keep busy. The last thing I wanted was for Amelia to go out in public until Rolin was taken from the field, but if there's no other way, I suppose I should take advantage of the opportunity."

"But you already said Rolin wouldn't do anything right there, in the Park, with everyone to see. Would he?"

"I doubt it, no. But as I've given him every opportunity to confront me, I can only conclude that he'd still much rather attack through Amelia. Or Georgiana. Or even you. That's who he's watching, even if we have yet to catch him at it. Perhaps today will be our lucky day. Now, come along. I want the queen's equipage to be in the Park no later than five."

"If I spy you out behind a tree, I suppose I shouldn't wave and point you out to Georgie?"

Perry grinned, and Nate swung the gold-tipped cane he'd taken to carrying, feeling that he had accomplished something very good.

AMELIA HAD OFFERED UP three very creditable excuses to the queen, who had pooh-poohed each and every one of them, so that now they were stuffed like sausages in the ancient landau and heading into the crush of traffic all aimed toward the Park.

And if Mrs. Bateman didn't stop all but standing up in the landau to cry "Yoo-hoo!" and wave to everyone, Amelia might just give her a push and tip her out onto the street.

Poor Georgiana. How could such a sweet, wonderful girl be the product of such a crass, social-climbing mama? Her husband's Tory leanings be damned. The gossips be damned. From the moment Mrs. Bateman had heard of the queen's kind offer to host a small engagement party for her daughter and Nate, Mrs. Bateman had spent her days making a complete cake of herself.

Her Majesty called Mrs. Bateman one of her ladies-in-waiting, and Mrs. Bateman had taken that to mean she should show up in Hammersmith every morning, to giggle and fuss and be happily milked of all the gossip she could divulge. All to the queen's complete delight.

If Amelia hadn't been so involved with her own unhappiness, perhaps she might have done something to depress Mrs. Bateman's pretensions, but she'd been willing enough to have been left to her own devices while Her Majesty was entertained.

And now, at Mrs. Bateman's pleadings, and with Henry Brougham's enthusiastic agreement, they were all on their way to the Promenade, only a day before the Bill of Pains and Penalties would first be presented to the House of Lords.

Amelia, who had been relegated to the facing seat, with Nate wedged in between Georgiana and herself, used her parasol to shade her features as she watched the queen. Her ensemble today, thank the Lord, was nothing out of the ordinary, although her rouged cheeks, painted lips and wildly curled blond wig were all, well, unfortunate choices.

Mrs. Bateman held a lace-edged parasol over the queen's head, and constantly asked after Her Majesty's well-being; was Her Majesty too warm, possibly chilled, did the sun bother Her Majesty's eyes, would she care for anything, anything at all?

"Yes, dear woman," the queen said at last as she

winked at Amelia. "You would have the blessing of a grateful queen if you could but sit very still and sew your mouth firmly shut."

Beside Amelia, Nate tried to smother a snort, and Amelia bit her bottom lip, turning her head to look out over the Park, as they had just entered and had come to a stop behind a long line of other equipages.

And she saw Perry.

She coughed into her gloved hand, hoping her heart, which had taken a sudden leap in her chest, then seemed to stop, would begin to beat once more. Only then did she chance another quick glance in his direction. But he was gone.

Had he seen her? How could he help but have seen her, stuck on display as she was in this ridiculous old landau, and in the company of the Queen of England.

Everyone saw them. The whole world and his wife, as Clive had said as he warned her to stay in the landau, not wander off if someone should ask her to walk with them.

As if anyone would. She knew no one. Most especially Perry Shepherd, Earl of Brentwood.

"Causing no end of attention," Nate whispered to her out of the corner of his mouth. "Look at them, Amelia. Goggling like a bunch of loobies. Good thing I told m'mother not to give it away to my aunt Rowena about this or—oh, no." He covered his eyes with one hand. "Could you tip that parasol over my head, Amelia?" He lifted his hand a fraction. "No, never mind. Here they come."

"Oh, Nate, look," Georgiana said, proving to Amelia that she wasn't the only female in England who didn't understand men, "there's your mama and Aunt Rowena. My goodness, I had no idea your aunt could move that fast."

Amelia leaned forward in her seat, placing a hand on Her Majesty's knee. "Ma'am? Would you allow Sir Nathaniel's mother and aunt a moment? They'd be so grateful."

Her Majesty, who had been quite busy lifting her chins and pretending not to notice that the entire world was staring at her, inclined her head regally. "Her Majesty is always eager to meet her subjects."

Amelia, with great effort, did not roll her eyes at Her Majesty's formal speech that was so unlike the image she had projected in the years they'd traveled the continent—unless she encountered English travelers, at which time she either ignored them, shocked them or insisted they come sit beside her and tell her all the gossip.

"You are too kind, Your Majesty," Georgiana said, waving to Aunt Rowena.

With the landau still trapped in traffic, most of Society had front-row seats as the two ladies made their curtsies to the queen, Aunt Rowena dipping so deeply that Amelia wondered if, once bent in half, the poor old woman would remain there forever.

"Yes, yes, rise. Get up, get up," Her Majesty said, then deigned to speak a few words to the women before dismissing them, because now that *they'd* been allowed to approach, *everyone* seemed to be climbing down from their curricles and phaetons, their horses, or simply hieing themselves across the grass, all of them eager to pay homage to their queen.

They came from all sides, surrounding the landau. Behind her, Clive was muttering to himself, obviously upset by this sudden crush of humanity, and with no escape possible.

"Perhaps, Your Majesty, if I may be so bold," Mrs. Bateman said, "you might wish to join your subjects, who long to see you?"

"Here now," Clive said, although Amelia doubted anyone else heard him, "somebody dub that loose screw's mummer before the queen takes it in her head ter—yer there! Shut that bloody door!"

"Clive, *shhh*," Amelia warned quietly. "That's Mr. Brougham. He wouldn't do anything to harm the queen."

"Shall we all get out, do you think?" Georgiana asked, leaning across Nate, whose eyes had gone rather wide. "Nate? What's wrong?"

"Nothing, sweetings," he said, swallowing hard. "I'm just wondering who should help carry my remains to the family mausoleum, once Perry gets through using my guts for garters. Amelia? Stay here, please?"

"Amelia? Your arm?" the queen said, and with only a quick whisper to Nate that she was very well able to take care of herself, Amelia folded her parasol and hastened to assist Her Majesty, who already was being helped to the ground by Henry Brougham.

Somehow, someone had procured a striped satin

chair, probably from one of the houses bordering the Park, and Her Majesty was ushered to it by Brougham, Mrs. Bateman positioning herself behind it, to hold the parasol over the queen's head.

While some of the crush, cast in the role of either curious onlookers or disgusted Tories, remained at the outer fringes of the crowd, even more were lining themselves up as if the queen's drawing room had somehow been convened in the Park.

One by one or two by two, they advanced. They bowed. They curtsied. They mumbled greetings and apologies, and more than a few were motioned forward by the queen, allowed to kiss her hand.

The woman was in her glory. The sun shone down as if in approval; the air smelled sweet with the perfume from several score of fashionable creatures. Flowers were produced, masses of them, a glass of lemonade offered, and the queen's laughter, deep and full as most men's, rang out over and over again.

The chair, the flowers. Clearly Henry Brougham was not one to miss his opportunities.

Amelia felt tears burning in her eyes, happy tears, and turned away, nearly overcome by this belated show of affection, even allegiance, to the queen. She reached for her reticule to pull out a handkerchief, only to realize it did not hang from her arm, but had been left behind in the landau. As Nate was busy protecting Georgiana from the crush of people, she didn't bother saying anything before excusing herself as she gently pushed her way through the crush, back toward the landau.

"Hello there, Miss Fredericks," a rather tall, definitely handsome man drawled, stepping in front of her to block her way. He didn't remove his curly brimmed beaver, which was placed rather forward on his head, casting his eyes into shadow. "I would ask a boon, dear lady," he continued as Amelia backed up a pace, only to feel herself bumping into a large body that didn't budge an inch as its owner grumbled, "Here now, wait your turn."

Amelia wasn't stupid. Perhaps she hadn't been precisely wise to leave Nate and Georgiana, but she was only going a short distance, no more than fifteen yards, to where Clive stood on the seat of the landau, watching over everyone.

And yet here she was, boxed in on all sides, and if she were to scream, call out, nobody would even listen. Or, if they did react, it would only be to tell her to be quiet.

Where was Perry? He'd run off the moment she'd seen him. Was he still close by? He certainly wasn't close enough!

She could faint. No, that wouldn't work. Pretty women could faint and be rescued in a heartbeat. Plain women could be trampled.

"If you'd be so kind as to let me pass?" Amelia said, sure she was looking at Jarrett Rolin, even though he'd never been described to her.

"In a moment. To repeat, I would ask a boon, dear lady," he said, his voice as smooth as silk, and quite unhurried.

Amelia nodded, refusing to speak.

"Ah, I believe my name and reputation must have preceded me, Miss Fredericks. How…predictable of my friend Brentwood. And how convenient that the boon I ask is that you relay a message to him. Are you listening, Miss Fredericks?"

Now she looked up at him, anger replacing common sense. "I'll thank you not to condescend to me, sir."

"Ah, some spirit. Perhaps that's the attraction, what brought you first to His Lordship's attention. Although I know different. Do you?"

She did, but she wasn't going to admit that to this odious man. "Is that the message?"

"Hardly. And I thoroughly hate myself for this, but I really don't care if he's tumbled you, as that was never my plan. Quickly now, as I'm sure he's nearby. The message is this, Miss Fredericks. Nobody is safe. Tell him. *Nobody is safe.*"

The sudden chill that skipped down Amelia's spine had her closing her eyes as she fought a shiver, and when she opened them, Rolin was gone and Perry was in front of her. "Oh! Did…did you see him?"

"Where's Clive? Bloody hell, is this his idea of keeping an eye on you?" Perry took hold of her arm and pulled her toward the landau. "Did I see—*Rolin?* Damn it, Amelia, he was here?"

She could only nod as Perry opened the low door to the landau and all but heaved her onto the velvet squabs. It was as if they'd never been apart; as if they were still so free and easy with each other that they could speak to each other without the slight formality, with no hesitation or uneasiness caused by their night of—no, she would not think of that night. Not now. "Yes, he talked to me. You mean, you didn't see him?"

Perry remained outside the landau, his entire body alert, his gaze searching everywhere. "I was lucky to find you in this mad scene. Bless the woman's heart, she does know how to take her revenge. The king's going to be gnashing his teeth when he hears of it. Did he talk to you? Did he…did he touch you?"

"No, he didn't touch me. He wanted me to give you a message," Amelia told him, longing to touch him, longing for him to touch her. Couldn't he sense that? Was she so unimportant, now that he might soon have Rolin within his sights? "He said to tell you that nobody is safe. He was terribly smug about it, too. Perry, I—"

"That son of a bitch! Clive!"

"Right here, M'Lord! I'm that sorry I—"

"Never mind that now," Perry said, cutting off the man's apology. "Amelia…" he hesitated, clearly not ready to say anything that might end in keeping him where he so clearly did not want to be. "Amelia, please tell me you understand."

"I do understand, Perry," she told him as he reached into the landau, took her hand in his. "I understand that you must do what you must do about Jarrett Rolin. I had no idea things sat so seriously between you."

"And us?" Perry looked up at Clive, who was leaning back over the driver's plank seat, grinning. "Go away," he said tightly, and Amelia felt the springs give as both the driver and Clive quickly jumped to the ground.

"I really don't think we have anything else to say to each other, Perry," she said quietly. "I believe we both have concluded that we made a mistake, each for our own reasons."

He squeezed her hand. "You know that's not true. My God, Amelia, when you stepped down after the queen, when I lost sight of you in this mess of humanity?" He shook his head. "You really have no idea how important you are to me?"

She had been about to give in, give up, toss her stupid pride over her shoulder and tell him how much she'd missed him. Until he said those last words to her. "Important to you? Yes, I have a very good idea of how important I am to you. And why."

"Amelia, no. That's not what I meant. The blazes with England, with the succession, with all of it."

"I want to believe you, you know I do. But that's impossible, Perry, and you know that as well as I. The queen goes in front of the House of Lords tomorrow. It's too late to change that, to stop what begins tomorrow. It's too late for anything now. Or do you think this crush of false admirers will change anything? I most certainly do not. Her Majesty and Mr. Brougham are only deluding themselves to think otherwise. You can't help, Perry, even if your motives are entirely pure, and I very much doubt that."

"I don't give up easily, Amelia," he told her, his gaze so intense she had to look away.

"Oh," she said, squeezing Perry's hand. "There he is. Rolin. Here, step up here and you'll be able to see him. He's taken off his hat and he's waving to me."

Perry had vaulted into the landau before she'd finished speaking, following the direction of Amelia's pointed finger. "Where? I don't—"

And then he was gone, having vaulted over the side of the landau, sprinting across the grass expanse even as Jarrett Rolin, with a jaunty wave that ended in a salute, gracefully swung himself into the saddle and urged his horse into a fast trot out of the Park, into the crowded streets of Mayfair, as if daring Perry to follow him.

PERRY HAD DRESSED in subdued colors, from his oldest buckskins to a brown hacking jacket his valet had twice attempted to discard, his neck cloth a simple black grosgrain ribbon ineptly tied around the collar of his unstarched shirt.

He didn't bother to avoid a large, muddy puddle as he walked into yet another inn yard as the rain that had begun hours earlier sent more moisture dripping from the wide brim of the shapeless hat loaned to him by one of his footmen. His drab greatcoat was wet through to his shoulders.

He'd been on the move since dinnertime, and it was now past three in the morning. He'd spent that time greasing palms in every posting house and inn he knew of that rented saddle horses, for he already had made it his business to know that Jarrett Rolin no longer owned any horseflesh of his own, or had any friends from which to borrow a nag.

The White House in Fetter Lane was a target of last resort, as it was too large, too well-known, too heavily frequented by those wishing to ride in one of the more than two dozen coaches that left here every day, even though the buildings were fast falling into disrepair.

Then again, Jarrett Rolin had always been one to take foolish chances, and that audacious wave this afternoon could have been an invitation for Perry to find him. But why?

Even in the middle of the night, the stables were bustling, and Perry had to wait until a team of coach horses was led into the yard before he could corner a young hostler and cross his palm with a coin.

"A bay gelding," he said when the boy eyed him suspiciously. "About fifteen hands, no more, the tail cropped. Do you know it?"

"Oi suppose Oi could, guv'nor," the boy said, swiping at his runny nose. "Yer wants it?"

Perry did not react outwardly, although inside, his weary body discovered fresh energy. "Not the horse, boy. The man who rode him today."

The boy's gaze slid toward the inn, then shifted back to Perry. "Cove might be 'ere. Mayhap Oi glimmed 'im a time or two."

Another coin found its way from man to boy.

"Rum touch, that 'un," the boy said, biting on the coin, because this one was gold. "See'd a sticker on 'im whenest 'e wuz climbin' inta the saddle. Wanna knows where?"

"I know where he keeps it, thank you," Perry said. "It's his location that I lack." When the boy frowned, he added quietly, "Have you any idea how quickly those coins can be back in my purse, boy?"

"Fetched 'im m'sister when 'e asked, but Oi won't do that agin. Betts won't walk straight fer a week, if yer get m'meanin'. Top o'the stairs, last door down." When Perry turned to head for the inn, the boy called after him, "The sticker, mate! Keep yer glimmers out fer that!"

Perry pulled open the door to the inn, staring down a very large man who had tried to push through the doorway ahead of him before he thought better of it. Hat pulled down, shoulders hunched, he affected a slight limp as he entered the tap room and stood with his back against the wall, searching the dimness.

He hadn't had to bother. No one even looked at him, to be able to remember later that a tall man with a limp had been here just before they discovered Rolin's body. Nothing here but a few drunken youths with more dash than brains, a scattering of whores taking shelter from the rain, a few travelers asleep on the settle near the fire, their bits of baggage in their laps. A lone barman was half asleep behind his table.

Backing out of the tap room, Perry counted to five, made sure he wasn't observed and then quickly mounted the stairs to the top floor.

He listened at the door to the last room on the hall and heard the muffled groans that came from the other side.

"Bitch! I said *all* of it!"

Jarrett Rolin's voice.

The sound of a slap. Another moan, this one louder, and definitely female.

Perry shrugged out of his greatcoat, then carefully tried the latch, which opened with only a small *click*. A single fat, smoking candle revealed Rolin's outline as he stood in front of the uncovered window, his pantaloons down around his ankles, a woman kneeling in front of him, his hands roughly gripping her head.

"Now there's a sight to make me wish I'd forgone dinner this evening," Perry drawled, and the woman, Rolin's hands no longer holding her head, fell back against the floor, then quickly got to her feet. She spat in Rolin's direction, then brushed past Perry, a torrent of curses tumbling from her bloody mouth.

"Brentwood. A rare flower of young womanhood that, don't you think? You're early, old fellow. I hadn't expected you before the morning. Obviously. Shame you spoke, you could have watched, learned something," Rolin said, the epitome of calm in his near nakedness.

"You've always been such an inspiration, Rolin," Perry said. "If one had aspirations for the gutter. Now, you will oblige me by getting dressed."

"I would not think of obliging you in anything, Brentwood, unless you wished me to assist you on your way to hell. However, with that door open, I am feeling the draft."

"How droll. But, anything to oblige," Perry said, kicking the door closed behind him, then tossing his greatcoat onto a rude dresser beside it.

Rolin was being too calm—obviously the bastard had a plan. Very well, he'd play along. He'd played many a game himself, in France, in Spain; very deadly games. This could prove diverting.

Perry kept his hands visible, his pose only vaguely

threatening. "You say you were expecting me? You know, Rolin, I believe I am suddenly faced with a dilemma. Having found you, I no longer have any idea what I should do with you. Would the application of sweet reason work to convince you that the continent or America would make for much more comfortable surroundings for a man of your…unfortunate circumstances?"

Rolin was buttoned into his pantaloons once more, and turned to lift his jacket from the back of a chair. "That's not an appealing plan, actually. I have another, better idea in mind, which is why I became bored with skulking about and showed myself, hoping you'd find me so that we could have a small talk. How did you find me, by the way? You saw the rented excuse for horseflesh, correct?"

Perry took two steps to his left, away from the flickering light of the candle, moving slowly, keeping his body lightly balanced on the balls of his feet. "No, I saw you. Then I simply followed the smell. So, you won't leave the country? What do you want?"

Rolin folded his coat over one arm. "Afraid of me, Brentwood?" He held up one hand, holding thumb and forefinger an inch apart. "I was this close this afternoon. This close." He allowed his arm to drop to his side.

"Any closer to her, Rolin, and we wouldn't be having this conversation. You'd already be dead."

"Good, I was right! Acceptable enough, but no raving beauty, is she? There is, however, I will admit, something about the woman, a certain purity, a rather commendable courage. She would have made an interesting conquest. That was naughty of you, to warn her away from me. And then it occurred to me. How much is this woman worth to the esteemed and quite wealthy Earl of Brentwood? It's why I decided we two needed to talk. You're right, Brentwood, I suppose Paris could hold some appeal. But, alas, not in my current embarrassed circumstances."

Perry watched Rolin's hands without really looking at them. "And I suppose, as I am largely responsible for that embarrassment, you've concluded that I should fill your pockets and wave you off at Dover, believing you'd stay where you were put? I wish that were possible, Rolin, I truly do. But I can't trust you, can I?"

Rolin smiled, clearly believing he held the upper hand. "Now, now, don't be hasty, we're still negotiating. An allowance was more in line with my conclusions. Revenge gains me nothing save your sorrow. I think I'd rather see you grovel than grieve. It's more profitable. Put simply, I agree to stay away as long as the allowance arrives promptly every quarter. And, with that allowance, it wouldn't profit me to see you dead, now would it? And you can't kill me, you know, not now. I don't think Miss Fredericks would approve. Lord knows I wouldn't. Besides, I'm weary of our dance, aren't you?"

Perry had mentally cataloged every piece of furniture in the small room, knew its position, had calculated that it would take but two strides to reach the candle, throw the room into darkness. "War was easier," he said, carefully coloring his voice with defeat. "God, we English are entirely too civilized."

"Yes, we are, aren't we? Some of us. Some of us less so. The allowance, Brentwood. May I suggest three hundred pounds a quarter? I have, as you know, rather expensive tastes."

Perry pretended to consider this for a moment, then gave a single, slight shake of his head. "As long as we're negotiating, I think I'd rather beat you into a jelly and then sell you to a ship bound to some very distant port. Do you think you have the makings of a common seaman, Rolin?"

Rolin smiled. "I could still come back. You'd never be able to stop looking over your shoulder. No, I've considered everything and made my choice. Much better the allowance, old fellow. My word as a gentleman."

Perry cursed under his breath. His first instinct had been the right one, even if Amelia would never understand, could very possibly move even farther from him if she learned he had blood on his hands. And God knew he was sick of killing.

But sometimes there was no other choice.

Perry decided to push. "Gentlemen, are we? Then what do you say we adjourn to someplace more suited, and settle this like gentlemen?"

"A duel? Now you're simply being silly. What purpose would that serve? The loser would be dead, and the winner would have to flee the country. Either way, your Miss Fredericks would be unhappy. Give over, Brentwood. There's nothing you can do but pay the allowance. It's why I've never bothered to fall in love. Females complicate everything."

Perry knew he could pretend to play the game, pay Rolin to leave the country, then have him taken care of at some later date. But if he knew this, so did Rolin, unless his greed had outstripped his intelligence. It might, but Perry doubted anyone could be that stupid.

"All right. The allowance it is," he said, relaxing his body, as if no longer considering himself to be threatened in any way. "Come back to Portman Square with me, and we'll work out the particulars."

"Certainly," Rolin said, shaking out his coat, brushing at it with one hand. "Lead the way, Brentwood. I just want this over."

"I couldn't agree more." Perry smiled as he retrieved his greatcoat from the dresser. How much better that his decision had been made for him. He very deliberately turned his back on Jarrett Rolin....

FOR A SOCIETY that for the most part had turned its back on Caroline of Brunswick decades earlier, the ladies and gentlemen of the *ton* had raced back to Mayfair in droves, in hopes of catching a glimpse of the disgraced queen on her way to Westminster.

Perhaps their queen had gained appeal thanks to the general dissatisfaction with her husband, the new king.

Their appetites possibly wheted by Brougham's tactical maneuver of putting Her Majesty on display in the Promenade the day before, lords and ladies unabashedly lined the streets along with shopkeepers and hawkers and crossing sweepers as the queen's gilt-and-crested coach proceeded toward Westminster.

Mr. Brougham had certainly outdone himself by demanding all the trappings accorded royalty, Amelia thought as she sat in the rear-facing seat and watched Her Majesty smile and wave to the cheering throng.

The coach, flamboyant in both color and size, was drawn by no less than six matching bays, and a gaggle of soldiers wearing the queen's uniforms rode on fine horses along each side of the carriage, ostensibly to hold back the cheering crowd that threw flowers as the queen passed by.

Pageantry and chamber pots. Amelia didn't know whether to laugh or cry...or be incredibly angry.

She didn't bother searching the crowd for some sight of Perry, because Nate had come to Hammersmith early that morning to tell her that he'd received a note in the earl's own hand relating to the necessity of his absence from London for at least a day.

She'd pressed Nate until he'd shown her the note. There was no mention of Jarrett Rolin, but only the request that Nate inform Amelia that he was well. She'd spent the night nearly mad with worry, and he hadn't even bothered to write to her directly?

"Amelia! Is it too much to give your queen your attention?" Her Majesty demanded, bringing Amelia back to the moment.

"No, ma'am. Forgive me. I was...I was so caught up in marveling at this truly wonderful tribute to Your Majesty. With each cheer, each corner we turn to be met by yet another street lined with those who love you, my heart grows lighter. You will triumph, ma'am. You have already triumphed."

"Yes, yes, let us all go swimming in the butter boat," the queen said with a dismissive wave of her hand. "Placate the old woman, while praying she doesn't find yet another way to disgrace herself. Only answer me, Amelia. Are you quite sure this is the correct ensemble? I feel impossibly dowdy."

Amelia looked at the nearly black gown with its insert of lace at the bosom that extended halfway up the queen's neck, then at the pure white turban covering most of Her Majesty's dyed black hair, hung over with a long sweep of black silk—the entire effect being nearly nunlike. True, the queen did look every day of her age, but at least she looked respectable, and very much in mourning for the late king.

The past fortnight had put some sparkle back in the woman's eyes, as well. As the date for the trial approached—the Tories could call it what they wished; to Amelia it was still a trial—many of the queen's acquaintances had arrived in London and had begun making their way to Hammersmith.

Lord Guilford, Lady Charlotte Lindsay, Lord Glenbervie, Sir William Gill, all respected by their peers, had visited and had promised to testify on the queen's behalf.

With them they'd brought gossip, much juicier than Mrs. Bateman could know, much of it in a very derogatory vein about the King of England and his longtime "companion," Lady Conyngham.

Her Majesty had laughed until tears ran down her face when they had recited for her one of the rude but popular verses being heard everywhere about the ever-more-rotund king and his pudgy companion, and demanded they repeat it again and again:

> 'Tis pleasant at seasons to see how they sit,
> First cracking their nuts, and then cracking their wit:
> Then quaffing their claret—then mingling their lips,
> Or tickling the fat about each other's hips.

Amelia lifted a gloved hand to her mouth, remembering the verse, and then the carriage halted and it was time for the circus to begin.

"Amelia? Child? I don't feel well," the queen said, putting out a hand to her. "What if Brougham is wrong? What if they know? Could they know? They *can't* know."

"*Shh,* ma'am. There is nothing for them to know."

The queen lifted her chin. "Yes, you are of course correct. There is nothing for them to know. Some things are mine, Amelia. England has taken enough from me, I will not allow more."

CLIVE FOLLOWED AFTER Nestor as the butler made his evening rounds.

"I told you, I'm not going to take the chest, even if I knew where it is, and I don't," Nestor said, rounding on Clive as, working together, they checked the locks on the windows.

"Dovey says yer need more chin before she can trust yer. I'm not such a looby, but I still don't trust yer. Yer're too keen on provin' yerself right."

"I *am* right," Nestor protested hotly. "Even His

Lordship thinks I might be right. A better day is dawning, Rambert, a better day for all of England. You'll see. The king is hated. Loathed, Rambert. When we can tell everyone that Princess Amelia is the true heir, the queen will lose her last detractor, and it will be her churlish husband who is banished to a…to a *place* like this."

"Yer wants ter shut yer flappin' mouth?" Clive asked, grabbing Nestor by the elbow and pushing him into a window alcove. "Not the sort of thing the whole world and his wife need ta know, right?"

Nestor pulled at the lapels of his satin coat, adjusted the wig on his head. "There's no need to become physical, Rambert. It's nearly midnight and the queen and Princess Amelia have been safely closeted together for hours. Poor dears, having to spend the day listening to that idiot Sir Robert Gifford—tedious man, but often brilliant—prosing on about the many witnesses he will call to bring testimony against the queen. The princess must be having some difficulty settling Her Majesty."

"Miss Fredericks said Her Majesty was top o' the trees today," Clive said, with some pride, because he, who had previously been as political as a cobblestone, had come to feel sorry for the queen.

"She can only sit and listen, or take herself off to the retiring room they were forced to grant her. She can't lift a finger to defend herself. It's so unfair!"

"True," Clive said, backing out of the alcove. "And it'd be a sorry thing if yer were the only one she had watchin' her back. But yer ain't. Come on now,

Dovey's got tea and scones waitin' on me. Ah!" He inclined his head to Esther Pidgeon. "Yer needin' somethin', missus?"

Esther only shook her head and continued on down the hallway.

Clive waited until Mrs. Pidgeon had reached the servant stairs before he shot out his arm, backhanding Nestor in the belly. "Heard yer, she did, yer whackin' great fool. Princess Amelia, is it? I oughta lop off yer tongue."

Nestor rubbed at his stomach. "So what if she did? His Lordship's sure she's here on orders from Sir Willard, and he's with us now, correct?'

"He don't know that fer sure. We none o'us knows that fer sure. Slippery piece of work, Sir Willie. Now what do we do? We have ta tell His Lordship, yer know."

Nestor pulled at his collar, easing it away as he swallowed with some difficulty. "Must we? I mean, couldn't we just watch her? After all, there's two of us, and only one of her."

Clive considered this. "Poor man has enough on his plate, don't he? What with him bein' all arsy-varsy over Miss Fredericks, and the rest."

"Exactly! Poor man has to know she's lost to him once it's out she's the princess," Nestor said, motioning for Clive to precede him down the hallway, toward the servant stairs. "I should think we'd be doing him a very great favor, not telling him."

"All sorts of new servants cloggin' up the place," Clive said, as if to help convince himself. "Dozens and dozens of them. No knowin' who's who anymore, is there? And we can't be sure she heard us. And she's only a female. Can't go worryin' about females."

Nestor pulled out his handkerchief and wiped his suddenly damp brow. "You're a very smart man, Clive Rambert."

"Yeah, I know that," Clive said. But he'd really like to talk to Dovey about this, except that Dovey relied on Mrs. Pidgeon more than a little bit. "So we watch the bird, the two o'us, and we don't tell nobody. Agreed?"

Nestor replaced the handkerchief. "Agreed. We've checked everything, Rambert—Clive. I wouldn't mind one of those scones, you know. Nobody will be breaking in here tonight."

PERRY QUIETLY CLOSED and locked the window in Amelia's dressing room and took a moment to collect himself. Only then did he enter the bed chamber, to find that a low fire burned in the grate and a few candles were lit but Amelia was not in residence.

Very well, he'd wait. Not happily, but he would wait.

He had spent a long night and an even longer day dealing with Jarrett Rolin, his passage through the countryside made less noticeable or noteworthy, yet much more time consuming, as he was slowed considerably by the demonstrations that seemed to be going on in every small hamlet and byway. Parades, speeches, bonfires, all in support of the queen.

It was amazing, really. None of these loyal subjects had ever even seen the queen, and knew little or nothing about her—except that she wasn't the king. And that seemed to be all they needed to know.

Perry had stopped at his uncle's upon his return to London, to learn that the archivist Sir Willard had contacted was indeed alive, and a full accounting of the king's activities in the early months of 1801 would be sent shortly.

"How shortly?" Perry had asked.

"Such haste, Nevvie," Sir Willard had responded. "Don't you want to hear what happened today? It was quite the show. I do believe there is nothing half so humorous as government attempting to be solemn, most especially as it concerns the two-edged sword of infidelity. As if a man-jack of them has ever kept to their marital vows. Why, while we waited for the queen to arrive, I amused myself touting up the bastards produced by just the first three rows of my peers. I quit when I got to twenty. And I don't think I can count high enough to include all their various mistresses. And yet there we were, asked to condemn someone for being just like us. Of course, at the bottom of it, she is female. Lot of cheek, a female thinking she can act like a man."

"They've already gotten into the particulars? I thought there'd be a lot of posing and puffing, at least for the first few days."

"Oh, they puffed and posed. Gifford spoke first, dropping hints like a proudly strutting youth who'd just bedded his first woman and wanted the entire world to know. I have to say the queen's solicitor general— Thomas Denman, you know him?—was rather eloquent in the few words he was allowed before we adjourned for the day. The queen was there, you know. My God, she's aged badly, nearly as badly as the king himself. The pair of them look as if they've been ridden hard, then put away wet. I spent an hour in front of the mirror this evening, looking for evidence of dissolution in my own face."

"Fascinating as all this is, Uncle, and I'm convinced you think it is, could you answer my question? The information?"

"A few days, a few days. You do know that you could very possibly have all your questions answered if you'd only unbend your scruples far enough to pry open one small wooden chest. But enough of that. Are you in need of funds, Nevvie? I don't think I've ever seen you looking quite so shabby and down at the heel. And that greatcoat is atrocious. What are those stains?"

Perry hadn't answered, but had left his uncle to return to Portman Square, where he allowed his valet to cluck over him for a bit before heading to Hammersmith.

And now here he was, and he kept hearing his uncle's words: *All your questions answered if you'd only...*

No. He couldn't do it.

He walked around the large, canopied bed, to stare at the bedside table. The book was gone. Good.

But the locked cabinet that made up the base of the table was still there.

His palms itched. His conscience burned.

And his need to know won out.

The cabinet hung open in seconds, and he was holding the intricately carved wooden chest closer to the candles, visually examining the lock.

With a glance toward the closed door to the hallway, he did the unthinkable, the unpardonable.

He opened the chest.

Bits of dried flowers. A thin curl of white ribbon, like that found on a christening gown. Fingernail clippings, obviously those of a small child, wrapped in folded brown paper. A gold locket that, when opened, revealed a miniature that was undoubtedly the reportedly heavily mustachioed Pergami. Another folded brown paper, the words written on it labeling its contents as soil from the Holy Land. A brooch fashioned of two distinct shades of braided human hair.

And more. Womanly things, personal memories, emotional trinkets.

Perry felt dirty, personally dirty, to have invaded the queen's privacy.

It was only when he saw the wax-sealed, folded sheets of vellum at the very bottom of the shallow chest that his fingers began to tremble. There was writing on the top folded sheet: "For Amelia."

He wanted to rip open the seal. Every instinct he had told him the answers, all the answers, would be revealed to him if he just read what the queen had written.

And then he realized something. He no longer wanted those answers.

He closed the chest and replaced it in the cabinet, calling himself every kind of fool…but then what is a man in love if not a fool?

"STUPID FOOLS!"

"Yes, ma'am," Amelia said, as if by rote, for the queen had been alternately weeping and crowing over the day's events for the past three uncomfortable hours. At the moment she was crowing again, and deep in her cups, for she had been drinking all the night long as she sat against the plumped-up pillows of her bed.

It had taken a full hour for Amelia to convince the queen to allow her impressive covey of newly acquired maids to undress her and then get her into that bed.

"They whisper of a green bag of evidence? How long has my husband been spying on me, I ask you, to have collected so much of what he calls evidence of my guilt? Ha! Evidence of his own perfidy, that's what it is. Amelia, more wine!"

Amelia sighed, considered suggesting that the queen try to sleep now, preserve her energies for the first day of testimony against her tomorrow, but then did the woman's bidding, because otherwise she would risk an explosion that she was too weary to face. Only once, in her concern for Her Majesty, had Amelia ever watered the woman's wine, and that was not a trick she'd try again.

The queen took the wineglass, then reached out with her other hand, gripping Amelia's wrist with the strength of a vise. "Don't worry, they'll never know. When I'm gone they'll still not know. I've waited too long in any case."

"Ma'am?" Amelia said, doing her best not to wince, because the queen's grip did not loosen, but intensified.

"If I might suggest that you allow me to summon your maids once more and—"

Amelia lost her footing as the queen pulled at her, and she half fell onto the bed before she could right herself and sit down properly.

Her Majesty leaned close, her wine-sour breath mere inches from Amelia's face. "You must be made to understand. I wanted to hurt him. I had every right to hurt him. *All* of them. To take, take, take, and then dare to come to me to demand more? He *knows,* Amelia. He has to have known, all these years. It has driven him to destroy me, what he knows and cannot prove."

Her Majesty pulled Amelia into a fierce embrace. "Too late. I've left it too late, my revenge turning on me when my dearest Charlotte died. He has to destroy me now, because he knows we both left it too late."

"Ma'am, please calm yourself," Amelia said, gently disengaging herself, and genuinely worried now, because the queen looked positively ill.

"No! You *protect* yourself, Amelia." The queen seemed to lose all her strength, and lay back against the pillows, closing her eyes. "Sweet child, I don't die fast enough. Protect yourself…"

PERRY SAT in one of the wing chairs, staring at the cabinet door. If he knew the truth, would that truth protect Amelia or damn her? And what of the queen?

Bernard Nestor felt he'd found the truth, even if he couldn't prove it. Uncle Willard was hot on the hunt. How many others were there?

And when had he become such a man of scruples that he refused to satisfy his own curiosity?

"I can't protect her, no matter if she's royal, bastard or what the world believes her to be," he muttered to himself, shaking his head.

How he wanted her to be no more than Amelia Fredericks, orphaned infant taken into the queen's household, or even the bastard child of a misbehaving queen. Those were not insurmountable problems to a man of his social standing. He could protect her. As his countess no one would dare point at her, use her.

But if Prinney had bedded his wife again, on orders from the king, and Amelia had been the result? If Caroline, having already been robbed of her daughter Charlotte, had been careful to confuse Amelia's parentage in order to keep that daughter safe and with her and out of the clutches of the monarchy?

If that could be proved, Amelia was lost to him forever…and quite possibly in mortal danger.

ESTHER PIDGEON SAT in her small attic room, sipping from the wine bottle she'd hidden beneath her apron as she'd made her way to the top of the house. As usual, she'd detoured down the long hallway that ran past the queen's chambers, daily building her courage for that ultimate moment when she would destroy, once and for all, the albatross that hung so heavily about her Florizel's neck.

She'd nearly been caught out with the bottle, but that Clive Rambert and that ridiculous Mr. Nestor had been too busy talking to each other to notice her as she'd stopped, readjusted her apron.

And heard Bernard Nestor refer to Miss Fredericks as Princess Amelia!

They were wrong, of course. They had to be wrong. Princess Charlotte had been the sole royal issue, and to debase that dear girl's memory by flaunting anyone as *ordinary* as Amelia Fredericks as the new Princess of Wales? It was sacrilege! Florizel would be devastated to hear such dreadful news, to know that his hated wife had formed the mind of a child of his. No, no, it was not to be borne. He couldn't want her, not a woman grown, and so wholly corrupted by her obscene, fornicating mother.

Not that it was true.

Esther frowned at the bottle, seeing it nearly empty, and reached under her bed for the decanter of brandy she'd filched from the drawing room yesterday morning.

But if it was true?

"Like mother like daughter," Esther said, pulling the crystal stopper out of the decanter, punching at the air twice, as if marking some invisible playing board. "Dead One and Dead Two."

IT WAS AFTER TWO when Amelia was finally free to return to her own chambers, so weary she knew she would not call for her maid but merely strip to her shift and fall onto the bed to sleep like the dead until morning. And then, suddenly, she was very much awake.

"Perry?"

He quickly got to his feet as Amelia walked toward him across the dimly lit chamber.

He held out his arms to her, but she stopped short, shook her head. "You shouldn't be here, and I shouldn't be pleased to see you." Her gaze shifted to the bedside table, then back to him. "Did you find what you came for, Perry?"

"Honesty in the midst of intrigue could be dangerous," Perry said quietly, "but I'm done with intrigue, done with secrets. So, Amelia, if you're asking if I opened the queen's chest of treasures, yes, I looked. An old woman's sentimental trifles, Amelia, and no more, except a letter addressed to you."

Amelia kept her expression neutral, but not without effort. "And you read it?"

He shook his head. "It's not mine to read. The queen's secrets are not mine to know. I've been crashing about for weeks, Amelia, being about as cow handed and selfish—yes, selfish—as a man can be. But I realized you'd never forgive me if I didn't give up the hunt. Besides, I've already found *my* treasure. I found you, Amelia."

She put a hand to her mouth as a small sob escaped her. "Always so smooth, Perry, always so glib and so convincing. I don't know when to believe you."

"I deserved that," he said, and she was grateful he didn't try to reach for her again, because she was close to throwing herself into his arms, willing to forgive him anything, as long as he held her, as long as his lies pleased her. Lord knew the truth had not been kind to her tonight.

She lifted her chin, trying for defiance. "Yes, you did deserve that, Perry. And I suppose I deserve the truth. Did you kill Jarrett Rolin? No more lies, Perry. Please."

"The man chose suicide. Unfortunately, he also chose me as the instrument of that suicide."

Amelia walked over to one of the pair of wing chairs, sat down before her weakened knees could collapse. "I said the truth, Perry."

He sat down in the facing chair. "It is the truth, Amelia. In the end it was Rolin's decision to die. I'm not happy about that. I found him because he wanted me to find him. He'd seen you and decided to end the game he was playing, not by destroying anyone I cared for, but by offering to go away, to never return to England if I agreed to set up an allowance for him."

"But…but that would just mean that he'd line his pockets. It doesn't mean that you could trust him to keep his word."

Perry smiled, and Amelia felt a pleasing warmth spread through her. "Many wouldn't see that. I adore you, pet. Yes, I couldn't trust him to keep his word, and Rolin had to know I couldn't take that chance, not with you. Still, he deluded himself that I wouldn't realize that in time for me to turn my back on him. It's me he's wanted all along. I'll admit that surprised me, knowing the man, but I think he went rather mad with the anger he felt when I destroyed him in front of half of Mayfair. He actually thought he could kill me."

"If your back was turned, as you said," Amelia threaded her fingers together in her lap. How clearly she was thinking! She felt this *calm* that had settled over her as the queen had bidden her move closer once more, Her Majesty's eyes tightly closed as she whispered truths into Amelia's ear. "Am I correct in deducing that you obliged him by deliberately turning your back?"

Perry's smile was rather embarrassed. "I believe I can be very glad you're not my enemy, Amelia. You see through me as if I was a pane of glass. Yes, I turned my back on him, and on the knife I knew he always carried in a special sleeve fitted into all his coats."

"And yet you're here, and he's—?"

"Enjoying his eternal rest in the Rolin family mausoleum, duly prayed over by the local vicar. I was the only mourner present. The vicar is writing his condolences to Rolin's aunt in Wimbledon, informing her of her nephew's unfortunate curricle accident. Although I doubt she'll grieve overlong, as I discovered several pieces of rather fine jewelry in Rolin's belongings, and those are also being returned to the lady."

Amelia's mind was whirling. "But he came at you with his knife, correct? How did you explain his wounds to the vicar?"

Perry got up from the chair, leaving the revealing light of the fire. "He had no wounds, Amelia. It was an accident with the curricle, remember? He was thrown clear but, unfortunately, the fall snapped his neck."

"But—"

She jumped slightly in her chair when Perry turned to her, his jaw tight, his eyes glittering dangerously. "Enough, Amelia, it's finished. You know what I had to do, and I've done it. I'm not proud of what I've done, but it was necessary. The man made his choices. We all make our choices, and then have to live with them."

Amelia's first thought was of the queen, and that woman's choices. She bit her lips together, nodded. She'd seen Jarrett Rolin, and had immediately sensed that the man was capable of any villainy. There may have been some other way of rendering him harmless, if he had been another man. This man had chosen his own fate, and the pity of it was that Perry was left to be the instrument.

"You're right, Perry," she said at last. "You defended yourself, you defended all of us. I think I'm very cold-hearted, because I can understand that you had no choice."

She stood up, held out her hands to him. "But if you ever frighten me like that again—"

"Never," he said, taking her hands in his, raising them, in turn, to his lips. "I wish there had been some other way, but there wasn't. We both knew it. Amelia, I—oh, damn." He was looking at his hand, and so she looked, too, and saw the blood that had trickled out beneath his shirt cuff.

"Perry! Why didn't you say anything? Come here, come over here, sit down!"

"It's nothing. I...misjudged slightly when Rolin first came at me. I'd intended to throw my greatcoat at him but he moved faster than I had imagined."

"Yes, yes, not now. Let me help you with your coat."

Amelia winced when Perry winced, the two of them

easing him out of his jacket, and she saw the spreading red stain on the sleeve of his shirt. "Didn't you have someone bandage this?" she asked as she ripped at his neck cloth and began unbuttoning his waistcoat and shirt, with not a thought to the proprieties.

Perry sat back in the wing chair, his smile amused and maddening. "I fear you have the advantage over me, madam," he said teasingly, then laughed when she smacked him on the shoulder and ordered him out of his shirt.

"Happy now?" he asked, once he was bare to the waist and the bandage his valet had applied earlier was exposed, completely saturated now. "Look like a stuck pig, don't I? I suppose I can't fob you off by telling you it's only a scratch?"

But Amelia was gone, racing to her dressing table, to pour water into the ewer. She dipped a small towel in the water, grabbed several other dry towels, and hurried back to Perry, kneeling in front of the chair.

"Oh, good, you've unwrapped it," she said, doing her best not to show her alarm at the at-least-five-inch-long gash on his forearm. "You need that sewn, you know."

"So my man told me," Perry said as Amelia spread one towel under his forearm, then cleansed away the blood on his skin. The wound was oozing, not all that badly, but definitely enough for blood to have worked its way through the bandage on his ride to Hammersmith.

"I'll fetch Mrs. Fitzhugh and Clive. He's told me she's a wonder with a needle."

"Ah, pet, do you really think that necessary? We could simply wrap it again, couldn't we?"

Amelia removed the wet towel and pressed a dry one against the wound, and Perry gave out a small yelp. "Why, you baby. You're afraid of Mrs. Fitzhugh's needle?"

"I most certain am not afraid of—no, no more lies. I most certainly am. I'm terrified, scared spitless of Mrs. Fitzhugh's needle. And I must tell you, I had no idea you were such a staunch little soldier. Most females would be fainting by now."

"Most females haven't ridden into Jerusalem on a donkey, My Lord," she said archly. "I've seen quite a lot of the world, and more than one injury. Now you sit here, while I fetch help. I don't want to use the bellpull, not knowing who would answer it at this time of night."

"It's late," Sir Nathaniel said, leaning over to kiss Georgiana Penrose on her still-rather-flushed cheek. "I have to take you home now, you know. Not saying I want to, but there's no sense putting it off."

Georgiana turned onto her side, mattress springs creaking, and stroked the back of her hand down his face. "I know. But I feel so decadent, Nate, and it's a lovely inn. Must we leave already?"

"We shouldn't be here at all. Your mother would have my liver on a spit if she knew, no matter that we'll soon be spliced," Nate said, reaching toward the bottom of the bed to retrieve his trousers.

"Yes, you're a bad, bad man, seducing your very own fiancée this way, night after night. For shame, Nate.

Oh, and would you see if you can find my shift? I last remember seeing it as it went flying across the room."

"Wanton," Nate said, giving her a playful tap on the buttocks before he climbed from the bed. "And I think it was you seducing me tonight, stap me if I don't."

"How very ungentlemanly of you, Nate. Where are my spectacles? Oh, drat. Do you have any idea how maddening it is to have to search for one's spectacles when one can't see to search? Oh, thank you," Georgiana said, taking the spectacles from Nate and putting them on. "Ah, much better. Nate! Look at your back! Did I do that?"

Nate attempted to look at his own back, a fruitless exercise at best. "Probably. Unless it was someone else sneaked in here, grabbing at me and moaning, 'Nate! Nate! Oh, *yes!*'"

He laughed, ducking when Georgiana launched a pillow at him, then dove onto the bed once more.

"I thought you said we should leave," Georgiana said when he pushed her down onto the mattress.

"Just what I don't want, puss. A wife who listens to everything I say. Especially when I've been known to say some dashed stupid things."

"Such as?" Georgiana asked, reaching for the buttons of his trousers.

"Such as before Perry went haring off after Rolin…telling him, certainly, Perry, I'll meet you just outside the Hammersmith house two days hence at ten in the bloody morning." Nate grinned as Georgiana rubbed herself against him. "Can you imagine? Why, I should already be home in bed."

"Morning will come when it comes, Nate. And besides, you're already in bed," Georgiana reminded him.

"I DON'T WANT to hear it," Amelia warned Perry as he grumbled that it was time he was up and gone. Mrs. Fitzhugh had insisted he lie on Amelia's bed while she sewed up his wound—men being so apt to faint at the sight of a simple embroidery needle—and Amelia was determined that he would stay there, at least until he regained some of his color.

"Amelia, be sensible. If anyone were to find me here—"

"They'd have to explain to me what they were doing in my bedchamber," Amelia finished for him. Goodness, but she was being forceful—and she very much liked the feeling. "No one will see you, Perry. Just rest for another hour, and then you can leave."

She sat down on the edge of the mattress. "Did it hurt?"

Perry grinned at her. "Oh, nothing of the sort, dear lady. Why I don't offer myself up to a daily slicing and sewing, I shall never know. Of course it hurt. It hurts."

Amelia bit her bottom lip in her effort not to smile. "I think perhaps Clive fed you a little too much brandy," she said, smoothing back his hair from his forehead.

He looked so dear, so vulnerable, so very much in need of a woman's soothing touch. And yet, not twenty-four hours earlier, he had killed a man with his own hands; snapped the man's neck, wrapped the body in a rug, sneaked it out of London, seen it interred and come here to see her. All with that gaping gash in his arm.

Wasn't that sweet? Oh, no, of course not. The business with Rolin could never be called *sweet*. And yet he had come to her, come racing to her, his thoughts all of her...

"What are you thinking?" Perry asked her, taking her hand in his. "You're smiling, yet you look rather sad. Is it still Rolin? I swear to you, Amelia, if there had been another way, if he had only—"

"I know," she said, squeezing his hand. "Sometimes choices must be made, difficult choices. Choices that affect others as well as ourselves. In our turn, we can only do what we believe best."

Perry pushed himself higher against the pillows. "Why don't I think we're only discussing what happened to Rolin? What is it, Amelia? What happened today?"

She fussed with the covers, pulling them halfway up his chest. "Nothing. Well, nothing I care to discuss right now. Her Majesty...she was in a mood to reminisce tonight, that's all. The trial has brought back all sorts of memories for her."

"About her marriage? About her daughter?"

Amelia nodded. "Yes, all of that. Nothing important."

Perry lifted her chin, sat up fully so that she was very much aware of his strength, his power over her; not physical, but emotional power. "What happened, Amelia? What did she say to you? Did she—Christ, of course she did. I saw your face when you first came in here. You looked as if someone had taken a hammer to you. What did she tell you?"

"It's not my secret, Perry."

"Not your—the hell it isn't! As far as I know, half of London may think it's your secret. Amelia…sweetheart…whatever it is, we can find a way to live with it. I promise you we can."

But Amelia had found time to think as she had changed into her night rail and dressing gown while Mrs. Fitzhugh and Clive had been working over Perry. Yes, it might be her secret as well as the queen's. But Her Majesty hadn't meant to tell her; the wine and her overwrought emotions had prompted her, not any very good reason to finally speak.

Perry had told her there was a letter addressed to her, hidden in the queen's private chest. Someday that letter would be hers, and even if she already knew what was written in it, she would not, could not, divulge its contents sooner. Not even to Perry.

It was sobering to believe, horrible to know, but there did exist some things that were bigger than the wants or needs of two people in love.

"You love me," Amelia heard herself saying, and although she was surprised at the words coming out of her own mouth, she didn't regret them. "Don't you, Perry?"

He raised one eyebrow as he grinned at her. "I do, but I think I should have been the one to mention that fact. And you're changing the subject quite clumsily, not that I can find it in me to mind. Do you love me?"

"I could never love anyone else. I seem to be overwhelmingly attracted to pretty rogues masquerading as fribbles. You've spoiled me terribly for anyone less."

"But you're not going to tell me what the queen said to you tonight."

"No, I'm not. Do you hate me now?"

"Come here," he said, shifting on the wide bed to allow her room to lie down beside him. "Careful now, I'm an injured fribble."

She settled her head in the crook of his shoulder. "You should be resting."

"You say that as you lie here, pressed against me?" He moved his uninjured arm until his hand lightly rested on her breast. "I've been wounded, Amelia, I'm not dead."

Amelia lifted his hand and put it back on his own chest. "No, you're not. What you are is incorrigible. And I'm going to go sleep in my dressing room."

She didn't even get a chance to move before Perry had turned, pinning her to the mattress. "Did I ever tell you that I am unreasonably proud of being incorrigible? I believe, in point of fact, that I have a certain natural flair for incorrigible. Why, if you were to apply to mine uncle, to any number of people, I'm sure they would be more than happy to tell you that Perry Shepherd is far and away the most incorr—"

Amelia clamped her mouth to his, cutting short his silliness, because she thought that was a good idea.

It was her last truly rational thought for quite some time, as she'd much rather concentrate her wholly irrational thoughts on the feel of Perry's lips against hers, the welcome exploration his tongue began of her mouth, the way he allowed her to push him onto his back so that she could slide her leg across his thigh.

She broke their kiss and moved lower, exploring his bare chest, her lips following the trail her curious fingers had blazed.

There was no rhyme or reason to her exploration, not even a great passion; only that he was here, he was alive rather than lying dead somewhere at Jarrett Rolin's hand.

She touched him because she could. She kissed him because she could. She loved him because when she'd thought about a world without him she could not see herself in that world, either.

His injury had frightened her, shown her how very close she'd come to losing him, and if she'd had a shred of pride left in her she did not even notice its departure.

She loved this man. Her whole world had turned upside down today, filled her with confusion, but of this much she would always be sure. She loved this man.

He was here because he wanted to be here, because he loved her. He'd said he loved her. No matter who she was or who she wasn't, he loved her.

With a boldness new to her, she nuzzled the soft blond hair on Perry's chest, then followed its narrowing path down to the buttons on his pantaloons.

A moment's hesitation, no more, and her steady fingers pushed open the buttons one by one, even as she felt Perry's hand on her head, lightly stroking her hair.

Breathing hurt, actually hurt, as she slid her hand inside the opening and closed that hand around him. Her eyes closed, she felt a rush of anticipation as his body responded to her touch. Skin soft and smooth as silk, and yet firm and unyielding.

She moved her hand, exploring again, all sensation, thrilling to his obvious pleasure. She wanted to see. To know. She wanted to—

"God's teeth, Amelia, I still could die tonight, if you don't stop that," Perry said, covering her hand with his own.

She looked up at him, confused, and saw his smile. "Was I...am I...*oh.* I'm so sorry...I had no...I didn't mean to..."

"I do love you," Perry said as, holding up his injured arm to keep it out of the way, he drew her to him once more, kissing her face, her hair. "You have no idea of the power you hold over me, do you?"

"No...but I shouldn't have...I mean, you're wounded, and..."

"Yes I am. And, being wounded, I do believe I should be allowed certain...certain *indulgences*...um, to be *indulged.*"

As he spoke he was employing his good hand to slowly raise her night rail, up and over her hips. Then he lifted his own hips and Amelia, caution still thrown to the winds, aided him in pushing down his pantaloons, and she at last got a glimpse of what she had begun to explore.

She bit her lip and looked up into his face. "Tell me," she said, her heart pounding, tendrils of desire licking at her heated skin. "I don't know what to—"

But that was a lie, because she did know what to do. She didn't know how she knew, but as she levered herself to her knees and straddled him, Perry's smile told her that his thoughts mirrored hers.

He moved so that he could slip one hand beneath her, and she lifted herself slightly. When she settled again, it was to be filled with him, and instinct guided her once more as she leaned into him and began to move, her night rail covering her so very modestly as she gave in to a passion that had little to do with modesty.

The world was Perry. There was nothing else she wanted, nothing else that could possibly mean more than the look in his eyes as he reached for her, as he cried out her name.

"HUZZA! HUZZA! Long live the queen!"

"You know, Amelia," Her Majesty said as the royal carriage once more made its way through the crowded streets, "I would enjoy this adulation more if my head hurt less. And you look no better than I feel. What happened last night? I really don't remember."

Amelia summoned a weak smile. What had happened? *Everything.* "Nothing, ma'am. We spoke of yesterday's events, and then you fell asleep. But it was a trying day, ma'am, and very forgettable."

She felt the queen's sharp gaze on her and made a great business of looking out the window of the coach. "We're nearly there, ma'am."

"Yes, yes," Her Majesty said with one last, long look at Amelia before she turned her attention to the two titled ladies who rode with them, insisting that they and several others attend the theater with her that evening, once the day's testimony was behind them.

Amelia sighed silently. Brougham had put the

thought of parading herself about London to the queen, and she had grabbed at it with both hands. Anything, anything at all she could do to discommode her husband.

Didn't the woman understand that everyone was using her to their own ends? That they were pointing fingers at her, laughing at her, dining out on tales of whatever she said to them, whatever she did in their presence?

Perhaps she did know; surely she knew. Knew and didn't care. She was behaving with a reckless disregard for herself, for her health, her reputation, her future, that was truly frightening. That, or Her Majesty actually believed victory lay in that future, which was impossible. Simply impossible.

And there was nothing Amelia could say to dissuade the queen. She could only wish it all over, finished.

She only wished to be with Perry, even as she knew that the queen would never allow it, never allow her to leave her household.

"Amelia! Woolgathering again? What think you of this? A ball! We shall put on a ball!"

Amelia blinked, then glared at the two titled ladies who flanked the queen on the facing seat, their smiles nearly predatory. "Oh, ma'am, I don't—"

Her Majesty threw up her black lace-mitted hands to silence her. "Not a ball! Not precisely a ball. In mourning, remember? But a dancing party, Amelia."

"We have, may I remind Your Majesty, already planned a small, informal party to announce Miss Penrose's betrothal to Sir Nathaniel."

"Yes, yes, a piddling thing. Now we will make it *bigger,* Amelia. My dear ladies here will draw up the invitations yet today. It is imperative I do not show myself cowed by these baseless accusations. It is imperative that I triumph over them!"

"Yes, ma'am. It will be seen to, all of it, as Your Majesty wishes." Amelia smiled weakly, wishing for herself nothing more than to reach across the coach and choke both of the smiling ladies-in-waiting, looking entirely too self-satisfied.

PERRY LAY on his back, Amelia tucked into his side, and smiled up at the hangings over her bed in some satisfaction. Every night, after the household had retired, he had come to Amelia, been welcomed by Amelia.

His was not a perfect life right now, but it did come amazingly close. "I'm going straight to hell, pet, and I know it, but I wouldn't give up one moment being with you for any hope of eternity."

Then, when she giggled, he looked down at her smiling face. "What? Laying it on too thick and rare, as our friend Nate would say?"

"I think so, yes," Amelia told him, sitting up and pulling the covers modestly over her breasts. "Not that I'm saying you should stop. However, there is something I'd like to discuss, if you think you can be serious for a moment."

He leaned over and kissed her bare shoulder. "Ah, here it comes. Throw a little attention the chit's way and she's wanting nothing more than to talk linens and china patterns. Very well, but I think you'll find the Brentwood closets already fairly well stuffed with them."

"You assume a lot, My Lord," Amelia said. "You know, I should not feel light and carefree in the midst of all this, but you do seem to have that effect on me. Shame on both of us. However, that said, sir, I do not recollect having heard a proposal of marriage, nor have I accepted one."

"No, you damn well didn't, but that hasn't kept us from making a possible start on my heir, has it? Are you still worried, Amelia? About the contents of that box."

She shook her head. "No. Well, yes. But I worry for the queen, not for me. It is true, if we were to marry, quickly, and I were to produce that heir you've mentioned, also quickly, then I don't think anyone will ever—" She bit her lip to keep back the words.

Perry sat up, turned to lay his hands on her shoulders. "Ever force you onto the throne? Ever parade you as definitive proof of the queen's adultery so many years ago? Will ever do *what*, Amelia?"

She leaned her head against his chest. "I want to tell you, I really do. But the queen confided in me in her panic, and after drinking entirely too much wine. We've never spoken of it again, Perry, and it has been a week. I don't think she even remembers that she told me. I think she wants me to know only after she's gone. Ours hasn't been the most...*normal* association."

Amelia lifted her head, tears in her eyes and said, "She told me...she told me that she doesn't die soon enough. That's so incredibly sad."

"And yet I see no sign of any sadness in the woman," Perry said, leaving the bed to pour them each a glass of wine. "The theater, the Park, the dinners? She seems to grow stronger every day, and you seem to grow more afraid, sadder. Do you have any idea how impotent I feel in all of this? How much I hate sneaking about like some lovesick youth, never to wake with you by my side?"

"Oh, Perry, I'm sorry."

"No, don't be sorry. Let me speak to her, Amelia. Let me assure her that you're safe with me if she would only give her approval that we marry. I can have a Special License within a day or two, and we can—oh, never mind. You won't leave her until this is over, will you?"

"I *can't* leave her, Perry. That doesn't mean I condone what she's doing now. But, please, I want to talk to you about this absurd dancing party. Mrs. Bateman is delighted, but even Georgiana wishes there wasn't going to be such a fuss." Amelia cocked her head as she looked at Perry. "Nate tells me you don't dance. Is that true? Don't you know how?"

"Yes, that's it, I don't know how," Perry said, pulling a face at her. "It's one of my great regrets. Of course I know how. I simply don't, that's all."

"Because it lends you some sort of cachet? Makes you seem more mysterious and unattainable to the ladies?"

Perry collapsed against the pillows once more. "Poodle Byng and his dogs. Brummell and his neck cloths. Byron and his famous sulks. Sherwood refusing to dance. It seemed a harmless enough prank to tweak Society when I began it…" he muttered, frowning.

"Yes, many things do. You and Her Majesty might wish to someday have a small talk about the folly of decisions that could, in time, prove difficult. But, please, go on. Is that really why you don't dance? In order to titillate the ladies?"

"Consider me as being thoroughly abashed and ashamed," he said, then grinned at her. "I warned you, pet, from the beginning. I was, until meeting you and realizing the total folly of my existence, a wretched, shallow and entirely worthless individual."

"And incorrigible," she told him. "You forgot incorrigible. Will you dance with me?"

"We'd turn the whole social world on its head if I do, pet, much as that makes me immodest by saying so. And, yes, I would be delighted to dance with you. I'll dance with you now, if you wish."

"Oh, don't be silly. You would not."

Perry leaned in against her neck and whispered, "There are many ways to dance, sweet Amelia…"

"AND THEN, after Nate sings, the queen has said we shall dance," Georgiana told her mother as the two walked through the large, now empty room in the mansion in Hammersmith. "We've been practicing the waltz, but poor Nate is dreading taking the floor when it's just the two of us."

Mrs. Bateman, still wearing the rather dazed expression that had been her only expression for weeks now, simply nodded, then wandered off when Mrs. Pidgeon stood in the doorway, her hands folded in front of her, and politely *harrumphed* her presence.

"Yes, Mrs. Pidgeon?" Georgiana asked, approaching the woman, whose curtsy was less than that of a menial, not that Georgiana could know that, as she'd rarely been curtsied to in the past. "I'm sure Miss Fredericks and the queen will be returning from the city in an hour or so. Is there something you need?"

"No, miss. But I was wondering…exactly where will the queen be seated during the entertainments?"

"Oh! You know, I don't really know. I'd ask Miss Fredericks, but they've all been so busy, what with the trial. What do you suggest?"

"Well, miss, I should think we might arrange suitable seating over there, in front of the draperies that so cleverly hide the door leading to the serving area. For Her Majesty and Miss Fredericks and the most important guests, such as your mother, Miss Penrose. That way the servants can, er, nip in and out without being seen, then first serve anything to Her Majesty that she may desire."

Georgiana looked at the two-story-high wall of rose-colored velvet draperies, already knowing that there was about ten feet of space behind them, as well as several doors. She imagined a row of chairs in front of the draperies and thought it a rather dull arrangement. But then, as long as she was free to move about with Nate, did it really matter? "I suppose that would be most convenient. Thank you, Mrs. Pidgeon."

The woman curtsied again. "Oh, no, Miss, thank *you*."

"I WILL THANK YOU not to read any more of that to me, Nevvie. I was there, you know," Sir Willard said as Perry paced the carpet of his private study, reading aloud the events of the previous day's testimony at Westminster. Sir Willard rarely visited, but he had shown up unannounced only a few minutes earlier.

"Oh, but Uncle, surely we can not hear too often about the damning evidence. I particularly liked the way it was pointed out by one of your fellow shocked and horrified Tories that the supposed wine receptacle found in Her Majesty's coach—with particular mention to the dried bits crusted to its inside bottom—has an opening of the exact same dimensions as the man's own private receptacle in *his* traveling coach. Thus, of course, proving that Pergami used the one put in evidence as a urine receptacle, and in sight of the queen."

"It was an embarrassing few minutes, yes, as you well know," Sir Willard agreed, sipping his port.

"Not half as embarrassing as conjuring up images of you all racing to your coaches in order to measure openings on traveling chamber pots. And all the time, there sits the queen, her feet perched on the footstool so graciously provided to her while this gravid, portentous evidence is submitted. I tell you, Uncle, the mind boggles."

"Yes, and the stomach turns in revolt. Why do you think I'm not there today? I had to plead illness to be excused, but I could not abide more of this nonsense about stains on bedclothes and reports that a carriage door was opened only to discover the queen with her hand down Pergami's smallclothes."

"And his hand on a nefarious mission of its own. Yes, I had all of that yesterday, while I was in attendance, which is why I, too, cried illness today so that I didn't have to hear more. It would appear half of the House of Lords has all come down with the same mysterious ailment."

"Who wouldn't be sick, being forced to listen to such nonsense?"

"But we've heard from over thirty Italian servants now, and they've all been discredited. Brougham and the queen's solicitor haven't even mounted their defense yet, and it's obvious the king has lost. How does it look, Uncle, seeing you, such a staunch Tory, leave just as the king's ship begins to sink?"

"Yes, yes, now I'm a rat, deserting the royal sinking ship while proceedings adjourn later today for a few weeks to allow Brougham time to mount a defense. Not that he has to bother. I hear you, Perry. Now, do you want to know why I'm here, or are you so glued to that newspaper that I shall simply take myself off again?"

Perry threw down the newspaper. "In truth, Uncle, I'm delaying the inevitable, coward that I am. May I assume you've heard from the archivist?"

"You may. And I've burned his letter to me and have been thanking God all morning that the fellow is creeping into his eighties and cannot remain aboveground for long. Surely not long enough to wonder overmuch at the reason behind my questions."

Perry sat down, said nothing.

"Prinney—he was Prinney then, remember—did on three separate occasions visit the then Princess Caroline in Blackheath during the second and third month of the year in question."

"I see," Perry said, his rather numb mouth having difficulty forming just those two words.

"Yes, I think we both see. It's possible, Nevvie. But provable? I really don't see how, not if either of them denies it. Even if either of them declares Miss Fredericks to be the rightful heir, that declaration would be impossible to prove unless they both agreed, and Lord knows those two couldn't agree on anything, not even if their very lives depended on that agreement. No, I'm out of it, Nevvie. I never should have been in it, save that Liverpool kept pushing me to find something, and that idiot Nestor fellow had me running about, chasing his pipe dream. My true regret is having involved you, although as usual, you seem to have landed on your feet."

"So you don't think anything will come of it, one way or the other?" Perry asked, trying not to be too optimistic even as he hoped his uncle was right. "Even if Amelia could be the rightful heir."

"I could be the King of Spain if my mother had played my father false, what of it?" Sir Willard said, leaning heavily on his cane. "Take the girl and run with her, Nevvie, if that's what you want. Get her away before someone lacking my recently discovered scruples thinks to take a second look at her."

"And you, Uncle?"

"I told you, I cried off from the circus due to my delicate health. About damn time this gout served me. I'll be leaving for my estate from here, to rethink my life."

"At your age, Uncle?"

Sir Willard put his hand on Perry's shoulder. "If not now, Nevvie, when? This is going to end badly, you know, with neither the king nor his unwanted queen wholly satisfied. What is transpiring here is ugly and vicious, and this is only the beginning. The man won't be crowned until next June, remember. I want no part of anything else that takes place from now until then."

"GEORGIE, I CAN'T. I thought I could, when you first told me, but I can't. I won't. I— Did the queen really say she liked my voice? Don't tease, Georgie, that wouldn't be nice."

Georgiana squeezed Nate's hand. "I'm deadly serious, silly. Amelia tells me that the queen was quite impressed when you sang for her in the garden last week. Not that you knew you were singing for her."

"I was singing for you, only because you dared me, and only because no one else was there. I *thought* no one else was there," Nate said, pouting. "That will teach me to show off, most especially here."

"But you were wonderful," Georgiana told him, leading him into the now completely decorated ballroom, to be greeted by the smell of all the flowers placed around its perimeter. Nate immediately began to sneeze, loudly and repeatedly. "Oh, you poor dear. It's the flowers, isn't it?"

Nate pulled out a large white linen square and blew his nose. "No, I'm sick, most probably dying. I can't sing tonight, Georgie. Deuced sorry, and all of that, but I just can't."

"Oh, very well. I can see you're going to make my life a horror, pouting and twisting me around your little finger. Now tell me again how beautiful I look in my new gown. I adore when you lie to me."

"YES, MAJESTY, all is in readiness for this evening," Esther Pidgeon said, rising from her curtsy to answer the queen's question. "All that awaits is Your Royal Highness's approval."

The queen signaled for Nestor to assist her to her feet, and chairs all around the long table were scraped back as everyone else hastened to rise.

Georgiana's parents, struck nearly dumb throughout the entire dinner due to their awe of Her Majesty, stood huddled together, Mrs. Bateman alternately gaping and giggling.

Nate and Georgiana, lost in each other as usual, wandered off in quite the opposite direction, leaving Perry to watch as Amelia hastened to her queen's side, surreptitiously flicking at the crumbs that littered Her Majesty's broad expanse of bare bosom above the most outlandish gown it had ever been Perry's misfortune to see.

"I suppose no one could dissuade her from wearing that?" Henry Brougham said as he stood beside Perry. "I'd heard of it, of course. She wore it several times in

Italy. Nothing quite so off-putting, is there, Brentwood, than the sight of an old woman's knees."

Perry, long past any surprise at his sympathy for the queen, answered through clenched teeth. "It was, as I recall, your idea to strut the poor creature about like some prize hen. I believe you have a lot to answer for in this entire debacle."

"And what do you know of politics, sir? I should keep to my tailor and my horseflesh, were I you." Brougham drew himself up smartly, turned and, along with his brother, followed after the queen.

Perry winked at Clive, who was making himself as obvious as possible in trying to remain unnoticed. "You see, Clive? Nobody takes me in the least seriously. It's a curse of my extraordinary good taste and, I say with all modesty, my exemplary good looks."

"A curse for them, most like, what don't take the time to get ta know yer for the slippery piece o'goods yer are," Clive said, winking.

"Thank you, Clive, I'll take that as a compliment."

"Take it any which way you like, sir. There's somethin' I think I should be tellin' yer, sir. Not that we wanted to bother yer overmuch, seein' as how yer've been busy sniffin' around—that is, courtin' Miss Fredericks and watchin' the queen and all."

Amelia had lingered in the dining room, allowing the queen's attendants—Lord, but they seemed to increase in number every day—to escort her to the ballroom. She turned and smiled at Perry. "Yes, yes, tomorrow, Clive. Now, if you'll excuse me?"

"Yes, sir," Clive said, shaking his head. "Not like yer was goin' to listen with more'n half an ear anyways."

Perry smiled at Amelia as he offered her his arm and they began the walk to the ballroom. "I've missed you these past two hours. When we're married, pet, we will not sit at opposite ends of the table."

Amelia's smile was faintly wicked, and he silently marveled at how beautiful she was to him. Had he ever thought her ordinary?

"Really, My Lord? And where will we sit?"

Perry pretended to consider the question. "I believe, if you don't mind, you shall sit on my lap and I will feed you grapes."

"Grapes, of course. Peeled grapes. And soup, dearest. How will you manage that?"

"I won't. We'll foreswear soup and live on grapes. Peeled, of course."

Amelia laughed. "Oh, thank you. I think I need some silliness. It's good to have these first weeks of testimony behind us, although being seated beside Henry Brougham is a constant reminder that when the Lords reconvene, everything will turn nasty again."

"Yes, I was sorry to see where he was seated. Has he no other dinner conversation?"

"None. And the more I listen to him, the more I know that he cares not a snap for the queen but only his own ambition. He was particularly put out to see Her Majesty's gown this evening, and demanded that I take charge and see that she makes less the cake of herself. As I said, or even if I haven't, the man wears on me.

Now where has Nate dragged Georgiana off to again? We're supposed to be inspecting the arrangements and pointing out where everyone should sit as the queen receives her guests."

"I should imagine they're in the gardens, billing and cooing. I can only envy them."

"And me," Amelia said with such seriousness that Perry threw back his head and laughed, which immediately brought him to the queen's attention.

"Ah, Brentwood," she said, holding out her hand. "Come amuse me while everyone dances about, sorting earls from viscounts and the ladies from the mere misses. If the pecking order is not correct we will be bombarded with such weeping and gnashing of teeth that we won't hear the music. I would dance, you know. You have my permission to lead me into the second set, as the duke over there will cut up stiff otherwise."

Perry bowed. "An honor I do not deserve, Your Majesty."

She motioned for him to move closer. "And yet I'm told by my ladies that you don't dance. But you couldn't say no to your queen, could you? Oh, don't scowl. I have so little real power, allow me to wield it where I might."

"With your permission, ma'am, I should ask that you allow me to waltz with Miss Fredericks."

"Amelia? So that's the way the wind blows, does it? I thought there was something about the girl these past weeks. But no. It is their queen who will be on the tongues of all of Mayfair tomorrow, not you. I refuse. You may not dance with anyone save me. You are to be my coup. And, may I remind you, Amelia is *mine*. I decide for her."

"As you say, ma'am," Perry said, bowing once more, and then the queen waved him away as she took up her thronelike chair at the very center of the line of chairs positioned in front of the velvet draperies.

"You look angry," Amelia said, having returned from speaking with Mrs. Fitzhugh, who appeared ready to faint at any moment. "What did the queen say to you?"

Perry took Amelia by the elbow and walked her to the far end of the ballroom. "She commanded me to open the second set with her, and forbade me to dance with you. She reminded me that you are hers and that she decides for you. And she can damn well go to the devil!"

"Shhh!" Amelia warned him. "I don't mind. Really. It's enough that you wanted to dance with me."

"No, pet, it's not. The queen was warning me off. Blast it, Amelia, we have to settle this. We have to confront her. Or are you willing to spend the rest of your life dancing to her tune?"

Amelia blinked furiously, her eyes bright with tears. "Don't do this, Perry, please don't do this. Once the trial is over, once Her Majesty is crowned along with the king…"

"That's not going to happen, Amelia. He'll never allow it. She'll be the queen in name, but that's all. She'll end her days here in Hammersmith, unless she takes it into her head to go traveling once more. And you'll go with her? Is that what you're telling me? And all for a secret you refuse to share with me—me, the man you swear you love?"

"I do love you. I want to tell you. But it's not—"

"Don't say it again, Amelia. Don't tell me it's not your secret, because it damn well is."

He looked at her for long moments, shocked at his own vehemence, amazed that he could love her so much and still she wouldn't trust him.

"All right, Perry," she said at last. "I'll tell you. I'll tell you everything and anything you want to know. If you need that in order to really love me, then I'll tell you."

"Christ," he said, stabbing his hands through his hair without a care for his appearance. "No, that's not it. Is that what you think? That hearing the truth would have me running from you? Amelia, *nothing* could make me leave you. Nothing. If you don't believe that, we *have* nothing."

She bit her bottom lip, a nervous habit he'd come to adore.

"Don't tell me. I don't want to know. I don't *have* to know. If you leave England, I'll follow you. If you stand with the queen until the bitter end, I'll stand beside you. I mean it, Amelia. Don't tell me."

"Until the queen is gone," Amelia said, and he wiped a tear from her cheek with his finger. "Then I would very much like to tell you. I'm near to bursting as it is. Oh, Perry, I love you so much."

He needed to hold her. He looked across the room, saw that Mrs. Pidgeon was taking charge of the queen and her court with all the strength of purpose of a sheep dog herding its flock. "We've still got a few minutes. Let's step outside."

"IF YOU WERE but to step this way, My Lord, and take your seat?" Esther Pidgeon said, longing to grab the doddering old man by his hair and drag him to where she wanted to put him. "Yes, yes, thank you, Your Grace, and your lady wife, as well, please?"

How she detested this lot of aged, overfed and treasonous creatures who had dared defy her Florizel to pay court on that ridiculous harlot of a queen.

But all that would end tonight, and in plain sight of these ragtag witnesses, so that her Florizel would be held blameless in the tragedy.

Esther spared a moment to look up at the huge chandelier that hung directly above the queen's chair, then to the velvet-covered chain that ran across the ceiling to be tied to the wall behind the draperies.

The chandelier was raised and lowered with that chain, for cleaning, to fit it with candles, or simply to light them for an evening such as this. Then it was raised up once more, the chain carefully secured. And abandoned, with no one close by to see when the chain snapped.

Such a terrible accident!

The harlot queen would die. Others would die or be badly injured, but that was the price they'd pay for turning their backs on Florizel. And Amelia Fredericks would die, if not tonight, then tomorrow, perhaps as a victim of her own grief. Yes, that would do nicely.

Barely able to contain her glee in anticipation of seeing her brilliant plan unfold, Mrs. Pidgeon went on the hunt for another group of the queen's most favored guests, herding them into their seats before the doors opened and those already lined up on the stairs, stuffed together like cattle, were allowed in to make their bows and curtsies to the doomed queen.

"How IS THIS, Nate?" Georgiana asked, dropping into yet another curtsy, this time holding on to the left side of the skirt of her new gown, rather than the right. "Better?"

"It would be, I suppose, if you weren't looking ready to topple. Here now, I've got it. You keep your one hand on my arm, get that gown out of the way with the other, and try it again. There you go, Georgie! Now remember, I'll be bowing at the same time, so hang on. It wouldn't do to have you sliding off my arm."

Georgiana let go of her skirt and wiped her gloved hands one against the other. "Is it too late for Gretna Green, Nate? I mean, if this is only the beginning, by the time we're married I'll be worn to a frazzle. I'd much rather we just ran away."

"Oh yes, that would put you in tight with m'mother, I must say. Right before *your* mother takes off my head. Even Aunt Rowena is talking flowers and guest lists, instead of harping on how she saw the queen, toes cocked up, in her tea leaves. Not that we haven't already seen her knees."

Georgiana tried to cover her giggle with her hand.

"What do you think of Her Majesty's gown, Nate? Do you think it will become all the rage?"

"Not for my wife, it won't! Some things is private, Georgie. Not that I'm the sort that cuts up stiff at anything new, but I'll have no truck with the world ogling my wife. Those knees are *mine*."

"Oh, Nate, you say the sweetest things sometimes," Georgiana told him, going up on tiptoe to kiss his cheek. "Look, here come Amelia and Perry. Yoo-hoo! Over here! Come hide with us!"

"I think it's too late for that, love, now that you've screeched out where we are. See? Now here comes Clive, and he's got that Nestor fellow with him."

"AND I SAY we don't tell him." Bernard Nestor was all but skipping to keep up with Clive as they crossed the terrace. "And tonight of all nights? Why tonight?"

"Because I don't like her, that's why. My poor Dovey, pushed all behind the door while that one struts about, puttin' herself in charge. Dovey's that sick about it."

"That's still no reason to tell His Lordship she could have heard us talking. Besides, Mrs. Fitzhugh is a total failure at housekeeping for a queen. I had to tell her three times that a duke is higher than an earl. Everybody knows that."

"Only those what care," Clive said, continuing on his way across the terrace. "I just have a bad feelin', keepin' things from His Lordship. We got ta tell him about the bird."

Clive halted, his face going red, when he realized

he'd been looking at Nestor and not paying attention to the fact that he'd all but walked into Sir Nathaniel…which Nestor might have told him, but the idiot man was so busy bowing to Miss Fredericks as if she was royalty that Clive could have walked straight through Sir Nathaniel without a word from him.

"What did he say, Nate?" Georgiana asked. "Did he say *bird?* He did, he said *bird.*"

"Is there something wrong, Georgiana?"

Clive rolled his eyes. Now Miss Fredericks was asking questions and looking queer at him, while Nestor was still bowing and scraping like a looby best hauled off to Bedlam. "It's nothin', miss. I was just wantin' a word or three with His Lordship, beggin' yer pardon."

Perry, who had been amusing himself playing with a curl on Amelia's nape, looked up in some impatience, for he had managed to get Amelia to the terrace, but no farther. "Nestor, stop bowing, please. What is it, Clive?"

Clive shifted his eyes toward Nate and Georgiana, then to Amelia and last to Perry. "It's…if we could just maybe walk a ways, sir?"

"No," Georgiana said quickly. "I think you should say whatever it is right here. You said something about a bird? Nate, don't you remember? Aunt Rowena saw a bird."

"Pity she can't see the bats in her own belfry," Nate said, looking at Perry as if for help. "It's nothing. Just my batty old aunt. Ha! Batty. Belfry. That was rather good, Georgie, don't you think?"

"Hush, Nate," Georgiana said, looking at him lov-

ingly. "Perry? Aunt Rowena told us she saw a bird
bringing death to the queen. Now, I know that's just
silly, but now that—what's your name? Oh, thank you.
Now that Clive here is talking about birds, I really think
we should, well, listen to him."

Clive was digging the toe of his new evening shoe
into a space between the flagstones. "Thank you, miss."

Perry looked at Amelia. "Why do I feel I've lost total
control of all of these people?"

"Possibly because you have," Amelia said, smiling.
"Go on, Clive, tell Miss Penrose about the bird. Is it a
large bird? Perhaps an albatross?"

"No, miss, whatever that is. Not a bird at all. Just
Mrs. Pidgeon."

Sir Nathaniel slapped a hand to his forehead. "Of
course! Bird. Pidgeon. Pidgeon's a bird. Well, if that
don't beat the Dutch. There, are we done now?"

Behind Clive, Nestor began to moan.

"Clive, if you might elaborate?" Perry prompted.

"Huh?"

"Tell us more, Clive, please," Amelia said kindly.

"Tell *her?* I don't think so, Clive," Nestor said, at last
finding his voice.

"Nestor," Perry said, "do you know that, inside my
head, I have already counted to two? Remembering that
I have made it a point never to count to three? Clive, tell
me what you feel I need to know."

Clive's eyes went wide as he looked at Perry. "We
was checkin' on the place last thing at night, just like
yer always said ta do. So we're walkin' and we're

talkin', and him over there was goin' on about you-know-who, sir, and callin' her you-know-what, sir, like he does, much as I kept tellin' him ta shut his potato trap and stop sayin' such, and when I turned myself about, there was the bird."

Perry's lips tightened. "Oh, do go on, knowing that I'm riveted to your every word."

"Well, sir, Bernard here said as how she probably didn't hear him, and I said as how yer should know—I did, sir, I did say just that!—and he says oh must we, all twitterin' and scared and so I says as how His Lordship has fair enough on his plate anyhows, and then we figured that we're two and she's only the one and we could keep an eye on her right and tight."

"Clive, please..." Nestor said, stepping half behind the smaller man.

"No, no, we tell it all now. And then, M'Lord, Dovey was cryin' that terrible because the bird wouldn't let her have anythin' to do with this here party here tonight and that fair broke m'heart, and then she said who did she think she is lordin' over her because it was Dovey what took her in, and I started thinkin' that if Dovey only met up with the bird here then maybe the bird isn't His Lordship's bird and maybe we should be watchin' her even more and tellin' yer about her, seein' as how if His Lordship didn't send her like he did us then maybe somebody sent her and—" Clive stopped, drew in a long breath. "Dovey isn't likin' her anymore, sir, and that's a fact."

"Well, that was clear as mud," Nate said, which earned him a jab in the ribs from his betrothed.

"All right, thank you, Clive. Nestor. I'll take this under advisement. However, from the way Mrs. Pidgeon is glaring at us from the doorway, I do believe it time we took up our places inside. Nestor, back to your duties, but keep yourself handy. Clive, you come with us, immediately after you straighten that neck cloth."

"Perry?" Amelia asked as they made their way back inside and walked in the direction of the four remaining empty chairs. "Surely you don't think Nate's aunt Rowena's vision means anything?"

"No, pet, I don't. But I am kicking myself for dismissing Mrs. Pidgeon as yet another of my uncle's additions to Her Majesty's household. He denied it, but he'd deny having a nose if it stood to profit his motives, so I allowed myself to disregard the woman."

"And now?"

"Now, my dear, we will take up our places like good little subjects the queen desires on display, and we will watch Mrs. Pidgeon like hawks, keeping to the bird analogy, if you don't mind the obvious."

"Do you really think the queen could be in danger? Tonight?"

"The trial has been adjourned, Amelia, and before my uncle took to his heels, he told me there are only nine votes to reconvene. I don't wish to raise your hopes, but I can't see a vote going against the queen. I still say she'll never be crowned, the king won't allow it, but she may have already won this round. That alone could have made someone very unhappy."

"But Mrs. Pidgeon? She certainly doesn't appear threatening in any way."

"No, but she was part of the household when Lucy was poisoned."

"We don't know that Lucy was—oh, all right, she was poisoned. I don't want to believe that, but I do."

Amelia curtsied to the queen as Perry bowed, and then he escorted her to her seat to the queen's far left as he, in his turn, took up his chair two to the right of Her Majesty, Georgiana and Nate sitting together, just to his right.

The doors opened, Nestor performing that office with a flair only slightly marred when he nearly tripped over his own feet, and the evening began....

THERE IS NOTHING quite so formal and downright tedious as an evening that included royalty, unless Queen Caroline acted as hostess.

She laughed and joked and winked her way through nearly an hour of bowing and scraping by her many guests, drawing some of them closer to whisper into an ear, or even to slap a wrist with her fan, punishing the person for being absent too long.

And then there were the performances. An Italian singer—not a prudent choice, as the queen insisted upon joining in on the choruses in her own rather good Italian, reminding everyone present of the absent Pergami.

The singer was followed by a harpist who seemed to play on for hours, and Perry had to bite his lip when he heard Georgiana whisper, "Nate, you wake up this instant."

And all the time, Perry watched Mrs. Pidgeon, who stood at the end of the velvet drapery, hands neatly folded in front of her, quietly giving orders to the many servants who were offering refreshments to the assembled guests.

From the opposite end of the drapery, Clive watched the woman as well, while Nestor, who was quite possibly as subtle as a red brick through a window, made it a point to annoy Her Majesty every few minutes by coming up behind her to ask if there was anything, anything at all, Her Majesty might require.

In fact, the only people acting even the least odd were Clive and Nestor, and Georgiana, who seemed to think it her duty to tell him, twice, that Aunt Rowena was quite serious about a bird meaning the death of the queen.

Ridiculous. And if not ridiculous, why would anyone make an attempt on the queen's life in the midst of a crowded ballroom?

And where better, Perry's mind had answered him, and he continued to watch Mrs. Pidgeon.

At last the harp was carried off by two of the footmen, and the violinists began sawing on their instruments, alerting everyone that the dancing was at last to begin.

The queen began things, not by having the elderly duke lead her out onto the floor, but by taking herself out there alone, then spinning in a circle, her outrageously short skirts flying out to expose all of her knees, her arms raised as she cried out, "Come! Come! Enjoy yourselves! Your queen demands it!"

There was some murmuring from the astonished

guests, but then they rushed onto the dance floor *en masse,* as a queen's invitation was always also a royal command.

Perry stood, watching Georgiana and Nate join the set forming closest to them, and made his way toward Amelia.

"She just stands there, Perry," Amelia said when he sat down beside her in the chair vacated by one of the ladies. "And the longer she stands there, the more I wonder if Nate's Aunt Rowena is right. Isn't that silly?"

"Perhaps. Perhaps not. But can we take that chance?"

"No, I suppose not. Oh, dear, she's twirling again. I begged her not to, but she told me if people are going to talk about her anyway, she might as well give them something to say. As if they didn't find enough to say after that night on Lake Como, when she danced for the servants."

"Coward that I am, I think I'm dreading leading off the second set with her."

"Oh, don't worry, Perry. I should have told you, but there wasn't time. She rarely dances a second set, not if she dances all of the first one, and it would appear she plans to do just that. We're fortunate if she gets through this one before she's so exhausted she has to be helped back to her chair. Her Majesty's expectations always outstrip her strength. I imagine she only teased you that way because Georgiana had told us that you are known never to dance. She couldn't resist playing with you."

"She also forbade me to dance with you, remember?"

"I remember." Amelia began tugging at the fingers of

her gloves. "That was…mean. No, I don't want you to think Her Majesty is ever…" Her voiced trailed off as she looked up at him. "Her Majesty can be complicated."

"Yes, I know. Treating you as her beloved daughter one minute, then deliberately hurting you the next." He hesitated a moment, then added, "Almost as if she feels very close to you and at the same time she resents you. Perhaps you remind her of someone she dislikes very much."

"Perhaps," Amelia said, once more tugging at the fingers of her gloves. "I'm sorry we won't be able to dance. I'm sure you would have enjoyed shocking everyone."

"Amelia, everyone in this hot, overcrowded room can go straight to the devil for all I care. But I would very much like to waltz with you. Of course, at the same time, I would very much like to still have my head on my shoulders tomorrow morning," Perry said, grinning. "We could adjourn to the terrace, where no one can see us."

"I suppose we could," Amelia said, then frowned. "Oh, Her Majesty is leaving the floor. Excuse me, Perry."

"Naturally," he said, getting to his feet and then watching as Amelia all but ran to the queen's side, assisting her into her chair. Amelia had spent her entire life at this woman's beck and call, and there was something unnatural about the interaction between them. Something that made Perry almost believe that, in the queen, he had found a rival for Amelia's affections.

Love could certainly twist a man, to the point he looked for bogeymen where none existed.

Speaking of which...he turned his attention once more to Mrs. Pidgeon, who had spent the evening so firmly rooted to one spot that he wouldn't be surprised to see flowers growing out of her head.

But she wasn't there.

"Yer Lordship?"

"Clive," Perry said, not turning around. "Good man. Did you see where she went?"

"Behind these here curtains, sir," Clive said. "Could be nothin', but—"

Perry looked past Clive, to where the queen sat fanning herself while Amelia offered her a glass of wine.

The wine? Where had it come from?

No, not the wine. That would be too risky.

Perry looked around the room, no longer hearing the din of the music, the noise of a hundred conversations.

The doors to the terrace were all open, but that meant nothing.

Then he looked up. A half dozen chandeliers hung from the high ceiling, each of them ablaze with dozens of candles. White velvet sleeves covered the chains that held them in place, each running along the ceiling and down the far wall, to where the chains were secured.

One chain. Two. Three. Four. Five.

Six?

Perry looked at the sixth chandelier, and at the velvet-covered chain that, unlike the other five, disappeared behind the heavy draperies.

He looked at Amelia, still fussing over the queen. He looked up once more.

"Bloody hell!" he exclaimed, running for the end of the long wall of drapery, Clive close behind him.

He skidded around the corner of the drapery, nearly colliding with a footman carrying a silver tray freshly loaded down with refreshments, to see Mrs. Pidgeon standing just beside the hook holding the chain to the sixth chandelier.

She glared at him, then curtsied. "Is there something His Lordship requires?"

"I'm not sure, Mrs. Pidgeon," he said, advancing toward her. "Is there anything I should know?"

"No, sir," she answered, and Clive growled.

"In that case, if you wouldn't mind stepping aside for a moment?"

"Stepping aside, sir?"

"You grow redundant, madam," Perry said, and Clive, at a nod from him, took hold of Mrs. Pidgeon's arm none too gently and pulled her away from the wall.

Perry stepped closer, his hands clasped behind him as he examined the length of chain and velvet to a height he believed Mrs. Pidgeon capable of reaching without climbing on a chair, which would bring entirely too much attention to her.

Only a few inches from the large silver hook, he saw the slit in the velvet and pushed back the edges of the slit to reveal the chain. One link was cut almost clear through.

He took hold of Mrs. Pidgeon's arm. "Clive, move

Amelia and the queen out from under that chandelier. *Now.* Pull them both away by their hair if you have to. That damn thing could fall at any moment."

"Oh, no! How horrible! My Lord, what good luck that you should have—"

"That will be quite enough, Mrs. Pidgeon," Perry said, pushing her against the wall. "Wasn't that leaving much to chance? The noise, the vibration, they could have sent the chandelier crashing while the queen was dancing, and nowhere near it."

"I don't know what you're—"

"That's why you were standing there, isn't it, Mrs. Pidgeon. To stay away from personal harm, of course, but also so that you could watch. But it didn't fall. How disappointing for you. And yet how fortunate, when Miss Fredericks at last came within range. You did hope for the two of them, didn't you? For both the queen and Miss Fredericks?"

"Perry? Her Majesty is most upset at Clive and— what's going on?"

He didn't turn around at the sound of Amelia's voice, but only said, "Clive, now fetch Sir Nathaniel, if you please."

"Already here, Perry. Clive, Nestor and me."

"Good. And the queen? Is she safe?"

"Well, um…"

"The queen," Her Majesty said, "is quite safe, thank you. She was quite safe in her chair, until she was all but *lifted* from it and dragged back here. There is, of course, an explanation?"

Now Perry did turn, stepping slightly away from Mrs. Pidgeon, unfortunately, just as another servant, carrying yet another tray of wineglasses, pushed open the door from the preparation rooms.

The door came between Mrs. Pidgeon and himself.

The servant sprawled facefirst on the floor.

The heavy silver tray, now sans its servings of wine, was in the hands of Mrs. Esther Pidgeon as she let out a rather demented scream and ran straight for the queen.

Nestor yelled out, *"No!"* and stepped in front of Her Majesty, arms out at his side, obviously prepared to die for her.

The silver tray connecting with the top of Nestor's head created an awful *bonk,* and the selfless would-be hero dropped like a stone just as Perry and Nate grabbed Mrs. Pidgeon.

And Her Majesty clapped her hands, saying, "What a show! Again! Do it again!"

THE QUEEN'S RESIDENCE at Hammersmith was, at three in the morning, at last grown quiet once more.

The chandelier had been secured without disaster, and the dancing and drinking and general carousing had wound down at last, with only a few stragglers left to attend the queen, who had adjourned to her chambers to entertain from her bed.

Aunt Rowena, clearly one of the heroes of the hour, had been given permission to sit in a chair especially placed beside that bed, where she sat in her funereal black, grinning fair to burst.

Nate and Georgiana had slipped away hours earlier with a wink to Perry, and Clive and his Dovey had retired to the housekeeper's quarters soon after.

Esther Pidgeon, babbling and weeping, had been retrieved by her brother, Lewis, who promised to have a severe talk with his sister before sending her north to their aunt (this one still aboveground, and a teetotaler to boot) in Edinburgh.

And Bernard Nestor, the hero of the hour, a rather large bandage around his well-rung head, had been taken up by Henry Brougham, who himself handed the hero into his coach, saying that he had badly misjudged the fellow and promising him a position of much more importance, and at twice the pay.

Bernard, nodding, and still with a prodigiously loud ringing in his ears, smiled vaguely as Perry closed the door to the coach and signaled for the driver to start his team.

"And now, madam," Perry said, turning to offer his arm to Amelia, "I believe we have some unfinished business, you and I."

"We do, Perry?" Amelia said as they made their way through the foyer all the way back to the ballroom, where the candles were burning low and the flowers, although still fragrant, had begun to wilt. "Why, they're still here."

Yes, the musicians were still in residence, just as Perry had paid them handsomely to be.

The moment Perry and Amelia entered the ballroom, they lifted their violins and began to play a waltz.

Perry turned and bowed to her. "Miss Fredericks, if you would be so kind."

"Really, Perry? You don't have to, you know." She smiled. "I mean, consider your reputation as the peer who will not dance."

He lifted her hand to his lips, his gaze on her, lovingly. "A pox on my reputation, madam. I shall set a new fashion dancing only with one's wife. Every waltz, my love, from now until I'm tottering so badly I can no longer take the floor."

"Really. But only the waltz? What if I were to fancy a Scottish Reel?"

Perry made a great business of sighing, rolling his eyes. "If I must."

"I can see you'll always be incorrigible. And the very crack of fashion, just as you pretend you wish to be."

He stepped closer. "It sometimes frightens me, how well you know me. Now, darling, shall we dance?"

Amelia looked to the musicians, and then back to Perry. *"Quando si è in ballo, bisogna ballare,"* she whispered quietly. Lifting her skirts by slipping her right hand into the delicate loop fashioned just for that purpose, she moved into his arms.

"When at a dance, one must dance," Perry said, moving her into the first turn. "My Italian, it would appear, is not so rusty as I thought."

"Hush," Amelia told him, moving closer to him than was the custom, or accepted in Polite Society—not that she cared a snap for Polite Society. Not when Perry held her, smiled at her, loved her.

As the musicians played, Perry and Amelia floated around the ballroom, the skirt of her gown held in her hand, the two of them dancing together effortlessly, Perry leading without really leading, Amelia following without hesitation.

"I adore you, you know," Perry said at last, his expression one of love and just a trace of sadness. "And I will wait for you, forever if I have to."

"Forever, Perry?"

"You doubt it?"

"No," she said, shaking her head. "Please, let's walk. I have something to tell you. While you were otherwise occupied I…the queen and I had a moment to talk."

Perry halted so quickly that Amelia nearly stumbled. "She's leaving? Her Majesty's leaving England? Damn it, Amelia! Where? When?"

Amelia raised a hand to his cheek. "Her Majesty goes nowhere, Perry. She won, you see, at least this battle. Mr. Brougham brought news here with him tonight. The king is all but convinced that to continue the trial, to force a vote, would only serve to embarrass him further. He won't pursue a divorce, so no one is going to be peeking in any more of the queen's closets, into her secrets. It's over, Perry, and it isn't over. There's still the matter of the coronation." Amelia sighed. "Mr. Brougham said that the king is adamant that he will not have the queen present at his coronation."

"And what does Her Majesty say?"

"I believe her exact words were 'We'll see about that!' She seems to have found new hope, although I can't understand why. Except that her allowance has been restored. In any event, Her Majesty chooses to stay, and fight."

"With you by her side." He covered her hand with his own. "And me by yours."

Amelia blinked back tears. Happy tears, sad tears. "No, Perry. I won't be with her, at her own request. Her own order, actually. She's asked that you present yourself to her tomorrow, at noon, to petition her for my hand."

"Are you serious? Amelia, she'd really allow you to—"

"She…she asked me to go. And she told me…she told me to grab at love with both hands and to never let it go. She told me that nothing else is important."

Perry didn't know where to turn, where to look. "Tomorrow is so far away. She might change her mind. I want to go to her, now."

"She won't change her mind, Perry. Remember, she's already told me everything, so I understand her motives. It…it suits her to have me gone from London, at least until after the coronation."

"And I won't question that motive," Perry said, taking Amelia into his arms. "I'll never ask you for answers. I have what I want. I have you. A man can sanely ask for no more."

"Your Lordship?"

Perry shot a quick look toward the musicians, one of whom had stood up. "Yes?"

"Begging your pardon, Your Lordship. But are you done?"

"Done?" Perry repeated, grinning at Amelia as he

pulled her toward the open doors to the terrace. "Go home, my good fellow—we're done here. And yet," he said more quietly to Amelia, "we've only begun."

Endings and Beginnings

What are little girls made of?
Sugar and spice, and everything nice;
That's what little girls are made of.

—Anonymous

AMELIA ELIZABETH SHEPHERD, Countess of Brentwood, sat alone in the simple marble gazebo only just completed and dedicated to the memory of Her Majesty, Queen Caroline, that her husband, Perry, had ordered built on the grounds of their estate, overlooking the ornamental pond.

The queen would have admired it very much, for there had been one very much like it at the Villa d'Este at Lake Como.

Amelia had come out here to sit, to remember.

But soon she would walk back to her home, the first real home she'd ever known; to her husband, to her child.

"Dearest? Someone's been asking for you."

Amelia turned away from her memories at the sound of Perry's voice, and smiled as he carefully made his way up the four steps to the gazebo, their infant daughter wrapped in a soft wool blanket and cradled in his arms.

Caroline Amelia, her blond head nestled into her father's neck, her thumb firmly stuck in her mouth, was very much asleep.

"Asking for me? Oh, I very much doubt that. You're

spoiling her terribly, you know, carrying her about like this."

"I know, but I can't seem to find it in me to put her down. You have a rival for my affections, I'm afraid."

Amelia patted the seat next to her, and Perry, moving slowly, as he held precious baggage, carefully sat down.

"You know, Georgiana told me that Nate told her that he thinks you've gone absolutely dotty over our daughter. But Georgiana also says that she's sure he'll be twice as dotty when their own child is born."

"Nate is already dotty, on all counts, clearly past redemption," Perry said, grinning at her. "And if we're speaking of dotty, I've just had a letter from Uncle Willie."

"He hates when you call him that."

"He loves when I call him that," Perry said, gently rubbing Caroline's back. "He preens."

"If you call his ears going all red preening," Amelia said, remembering Sir Willard's last visit, when Caroline was christened. The infant had been dressed in the hundred-year-old christening gown that had been passed down in the Shepherd family, with a slightly yellowed-with-age white satin ribbon pinned to one shoulder. "What does Uncle Willard have to say?"

"He's over the moon about another variety of orchid that just arrived from some island. Went on for two pages about it. Do you know how difficult it is for me to think of the man up to his elbows in dirt in his greenhouse?"

Amelia adjusted her shawl around her shoulders. "He's found something he loves, Perry. You should be happy for him."

Perry grinned at her. "Well, when you say that, I suppose I am. After all, the man's been in dirt to his elbows all his life."

"Yes, and he's very sorry for it. Look how he's been so kind to Clive, setting up him and his Dovey to run that taproom. That was very sweet of him."

"No, pet, that was very prudent of him. Clive and his Dovey know entirely too much. Buying them a taproom in Leeds was fairly brilliant. Now, come on, walk back to the house with us. It's a fine day but growing cool."

Amelia leaned her head against her husband's shoulder. "Don't fret, Perry, I'm not out here being maudlin. But I do wish I could have been there for her, at the end."

"That was impossible, with your pregnancy. She understood, pet. And she was delighted for us. Now give me a kiss and promise you won't be long."

Amelia smiled, kissed her husband and adjusted the blanket about their sleeping daughter before Perry headed back across the lawn.

Blinking back tears, she slipped the gold locket from her pocket, opened it and looked at the miniature portrait it contained. She could still hear what had proved to be the last words the queen had ever spoken to her: *You've found love, and that's what's important, my child. Nothing else. Remember. Nothing else.*

Amelia closed the locket, held it tight in her hand. "Thank you…Mama," she said.

Then Amelia left the gazebo, lifting her skirts above her ankles as she ran to catch up with her husband….

Author's Note

You'll have noticed that I left Amelia's parentage un-
mentioned, save for those last few cryptic words she
speaks in the gazebo. I did that on purpose, so that you,
dear reader, can draw your own conclusions. I know I've
drawn mine.

I have spent nearly a quarter century writing about
England during the Regency, sometimes casting Prinney as an object of fun, sometimes in charity with him,
for he was a complex man; I'd never realized quite how
complex.

But I have never written about Caroline. Why? Because, I'm sorry to say, most histories of the time barely
mention her.

When they do, the stories are so conflicting, so sub-
jective, so dependent on the personal views of those who
have written them, that it is difficult to know what is true
and what is fiction.

But then I stumbled upon an original copy of the
1818 book, *Memoirs of Her Late Royal Highness Princess Charlotte Augusta*.

And so a fiction writer plays the game of "what if," which is what I have done in *Shall We Dance?* There was, of course, no Amelia Elizabeth, not in any history, although she became very real in my mind as I wrote this story.

I can tell you that there definitely was a Princess Caroline of Brunswick. I can tell you that her marriage to the future king of England was not a happy one.

I can tell you that she was kept from her daughter, that she finally left England and did a very good job of making a spectacle of herself, that there was a Pergami, that there was a William Austin, that there was a green bag, and there most definitely was a Bill of Pains and Penalties, complete down to the weighty discussions of clothing stains and chamber pots.

And, lastly, there was a tin traveling case with the words "Her Royal Highness the Princess of Wales, To Be Always With Her" painted on top in white letters. It was the book that first drew my mind to Caroline, and the mention of that tin case that first began months of "what if?" before I created Amelia.

Caroline's story doesn't end with the dismissal of the Bill of Pains and Penalties. She went on, feeling triumphant, to keep inserting herself into Society all through the months leading up to the coronation of George IV, even going so far as to write to him to ask what he wished her to wear to the ceremony. Imagine the king's dismay when he received that letter!

But as the months passed, the fickle crowd that had

cheered her grew tired of her, and looked forward to the coronation, looked forward to getting on with the business of England. Caroline, whatever her reasons, had stayed too long at the fair.

The day of the coronation, Caroline was driven to the Abbey and made a great business of knocking on the doors, demanding admittance. She was turned away, the reason given that she had not been issued a ticket of entrance, and returned to her home in disgrace.

Poor Caroline.

Nineteen days later, on July 30, Caroline, queen only in name, was taken suddenly and mysteriously ill while attending a performance at Drury Lane Theater. "I know I am dying," she reportedly said to any who would listen. "They have killed me at last."

By August 7, at the age of fifty-three, she was dead, all her secrets dying with her. Official reasons for this death were varied; an intestinal blockage, "female troubles," whatever.

But who knows? Who knows?

Perhaps Caroline did, for she'd already let it be known she wished her remains returned to her native land, and had ordered these words engraved on her coffin: "Caroline of Brunswick, The Injured Queen of England."

King George IV, becoming ever more sober and sedate, lived on for another nine years. He never did remarry, so that upon his death, Victoria, daughter of his brother, the Duke of Kent, became queen, and reigned over a much more restrained, circumspect Empire into the next century.

As George Noel Gordon, Lord Byron, another Regency Era personage variously cast as villain or victim wrote:

"'Tis strange—but true; for truth is always strange; stranger than fiction."

* * * * *

researching the cure

The facts you need to know:

- **One woman in nine** in the United Kingdom will develop breast cancer during her lifetime.

- Each year **40,700** women are newly diagnosed with breast cancer and around **12,800** women will die from the disease. However, survival rates are improving, with on average 77 per cent of women still alive five years later.

- **Men can also suffer from breast cancer**, although currently they make up less than one per cent of all new cases of the disease.

Britain has one of the highest breast cancer death rates in the world. Breast Cancer Campaign wants to understand why and do something about it. Statistics cannot begin to describe the impact that breast cancer has on the lives of those women who are affected by it and on their families and friends.

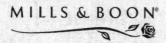

MILLS & BOON®

BCC/AD b

**During the month of October
Harlequin Mills & Boon will donate
10p from the sale of every
Modern Romance™ series book to
help Breast Cancer Campaign
in *researching the cure.***

Breast Cancer Campaign's scientific projects
look at improving diagnosis and treatment
of breast cancer, better understanding how
it develops and ultimately either curing the
disease or preventing it.

Do your part to help

Visit <ins>www.breastcancercampaign.org</ins>

And make a donation today.

researching the cure

Breast Cancer Campaign is a company limited by guarantee registered in England and Wales. Company No. 05074725. Charity registration No. 299758.